NO REGRETS, COYOTE

JOHN DUFRESNE

SERPENT'S TAIL

A complete catalogue record for this book can be obtained
from the British Library on request

The characters and events in this book are fictitious. Any similarity to real
persons, dead or alive, is coincidental and not intended by the author.

First published in the USA in 2013 by
WW Norton & Company, New York

First published in 2014 by Serpent's Tail,
an imprint of Profile Books Ltd
3A Exmouth House
Pine Street
London EC1R 0JH
www.serpentstail.com

ISBN 978 1 84668 975 8
eISBN 978 1 78283 029 0

Book design by Ellen Cipriano

Printed and bound in the UK by
CPI Group (UK) Ltd, Croydon CR0 4YY

10 9 8 7 6 5 4 3 2 1

NO REGRETS, COYOTE

1

My friend Bay Lettique, a sleight-of-hand man, does close-up magic. You can shuffle a deck of playing cards, spread them facedown on the table, and he'll pick them up in order, ace to king, by suit or by rank, your choice. He once asked me to think of a card—not to mention it, just to picture it—and he not only identified the card, he did it by asking me to open my wallet and pull out the five-dollar bill that had the rank and suit of the card written on Lincoln's shirt collar in red ink. Nine of diamonds. He can make a parakeet fly from his iPhone to your iPhone and from your iPhone to his shoulder. I've seen him slice a banana in half with a card he threw from ten feet away. At least I think I saw it. Bay says close-up works this way: I tell you I'm going to lie to you, and then I lie to you, and you believe it. Because you want to believe.

Bay used to run an illegal poker game out of a rented apartment at the Cypress Ocean Club here in Melancholy and would ask me from time to time to sit in on the game whenever he suspected someone was cheating. Could I tell him who it was? Which really meant could I corroborate his hunch. Usually I could, but too often the cheat was an off-duty Everglades Sheriff's Office deputy or an Eden Police Department officer, which meant Bay would have to call the sheriff and make a donation to the Police Benevolent Association in order to make the cop go away without Bay himself getting busted and shut down in the process.

Now that the Tequesta Tribe has opened the Silver Palace Casino, Bay spends most nights in their poker room separating tourists and senior citizens from their money. When I remind him that those old folks might be squandering their pensions, he says he, too, wishes they wouldn't be so reckless, but his job at the table is not to coddle them but to intimidate, infuriate, and devastate them. "I take their money or someone else does. There's no room for sympathy in poker." Bay is full of enthusiasms and contradictions. I worry about him. He says he can't not be sitting at the poker table. I tell him that's not healthy. It's not even about the money, he says. It's about what pumps the blood.

Last Christmas Eve, Bay and I sat at a sidewalk table at the Universe Café on Dixie Boulevard in Eden, drinking the last of several holiday martinis. Bay performed some magic for our waitress, Marlena. He did *Four Queens, Three Ways*; *Maltese Crosses*; *Ambitious Card*; and *Jack Under the Plate*. Marlena told us she was from Bucharest and was about to be evicted from her room at the Dixiewood Motel because she'd fallen behind on her weekly rent, fallen behind because she scalded herself in the restaurant's kitchen and had to go to the walk-in medical clinic on Main. The Universe covered the visit but not the Vicodin. She pulled up her sleeve to show us the angry red scar. Bay asked her if she was all set for pills. Truth was she could use a couple, she said. Bay lifted his napkin to reveal two pale yellow oval tablets. Percocets okay? he said. And then he wrote her a check for the past-due rent. Marlena kissed him and wept.

When she went back to get our bill, Bay suggested that Marlena would be in need of cheering up later on. We can't let her sit alone in a squalid motel room on Christmas Eve. This is America, for chrissakes! My cell phone played "Oye Como Va." The call was from my friend Detective Sergeant Carlos O'Brien of the Eden Police Department, requesting my immediate services. He had a situation in the Lakes. Five bodies, one weapon, one suspect, much blood. "I need you here, Coyote. Now." He gave me the address.

I checked my watch. Eleven-fifteen. "Ten minutes," I told him.

I'm not a police officer. That evening I'd be a volunteer forensic consultant. Carlos would get my pro bono counsel, and I'd get some excitement in my unruffled life and a chance, perhaps, to see that justice was done. Sometimes I work for lawyers who are trying to empanel the appropriate jury for their clients. Sometimes I sit in my office and help my own clients shape their lives into stories, so that the lives finally make some sense. A lack of narrative structure, as you know, will cause anxiety. And that's when I call myself a therapist. And that's what it says on my business card: *Wylie Melville, MSW, MFT, Family and Individual Therapy.* Carlos used me, however, because I could read minds, even if those minds weren't present. He said I *read minds*, but that's not it, really. I read faces and furniture. I can look at a person, at his expressions, his gestures, his clothing, his home, and his possessions, and tell you what he thinks, if not always what he's thinking. Carlos liked to call me an intuitionist. Bay said I'm cryptaesthetic. Dr. Cabrera at UM's Cognitive Thinking Lab told me I have robust mirror neurons. I just look, I stare, I gaze, and I pay attention to what I see. I'm able to find essence in particulars, Dr. Cabrera said.

Carlos told me that the neighbors heard what sounded like fireworks or like gunshots around seven o'clock that evening. *Pop!* And then *pop!-pop!-pop!* And then *pop!* All the neighbors came out to investigate, except the Hallidays, who lived . . . *had lived* here. Mr. Enzu Salazar from 723 across the street came over and rang the bell. And then he called 911. "We found this note on the kitchen table." Carlos handed me a typed letter, and I tried to remember what I'd been doing at seven.

> *To whom it may concern:*
>
> *To start off about this tragic story, my name is Chafin Halliday, my wife Krysia, my boys Brantley, 9, and Briely, 8, and my daughter, my precious angel, Brianna, 4. People have put obstacles in my way and no who they are. I am not insane. But this is no way to live like this. I have let my loved one's down. I have failed at fathership. I had to die I deserved it but to love them like I do and to live without them is to hard to bare which is why we are dead and why we are together on the other side. I could not leave my babies with strangers.*
>
> *Your's truly,*
>
> *Chafin R. Halliday*

My first thoughts were, Here is an arrogant and sentimental man who is either paranoid or under emotional siege, a man of simple and unexamined faith whose received values fit him like a comfortable old shirt, and here is his seemingly superfluous confession, but not his explanation or apology. He can't spell or punctuate and is curiously formal—the impersonal salutation and that affected middle initial—but not particularly insightful. Which concerned readers did he imagine he was addressing? And why on earth would he type and not write a murder-suicide note? Why no signature above the name? And that disingenuous closing that ineffectually insinuates sincerity—*truly*, indeed. This is a person who may have read about letters in a business English class, which he must have flunked, but who had never previously written one.

If you're going to bother to leave a note, and you're even going to type it up, if you're going to take the time, wouldn't you also take the opportunity to clarify the confounding events referred to? Instead, the writer of this note obscured rather than illuminated. He alluded to a story but omitted the first two acts. He called the killings a tragedy and not acts of senseless savagery and obscene cruelty. He muddied his motivation. He did not identify the alleged obstacles in his way or tell us who put them there. He did not explain why he thought he deserved to die or in just what way he had failed at fathership. And who uses the word *fathership* anyway? *Hood* not *ship*, right? *Fathership* sounds like the lead vessel in some intergalactic starfleet. Here's how you write a proper suicide note:

> *Dear A.*
>
> *As much as it hurts me to say this, I cannot join you on Saturday. When a guy doesn't know what to say to his girlfriend anymore, then she is not his girlfriend anymore. I am leaving you the engagement ring so that every time you look at it you can think about what you stole from me.*
>
> *T.*

T. was a client of mine. Twenty-one when she jumped off the Cypress Avenue Bridge and hit the foredeck of a passing Bimini yacht.

Carlos told me the CSI team would finish up shortly, and then I could poke around the house. The medical examiner had come and gone before even he had gotten here. The bodies were already at the morgue, which was fine with me. I asked Carlos what they'd found in the victims' pockets.

"The kids wore jammies; Mrs. Halliday was in a sweat suit without pockets. She did have a tissue crunched up in the sleeve of her sweatshirt. We found loose change and a wallet in Mr. Halliday's slacks. Eighty-four bucks, all the bills in order from ones to twenties and all facing the same way. A man after my own heart. But no ID."

"What pocket was the wallet in?"

"Good question." Carlos turned to the officer dismantling a camera tripod. "Sully, which pocket was the wallet in?"

"Back."

"Left or right?" I said.

"I don't know. Right, I guess."

I said, "You're right-handed."

"I am."

"No ID?"

"It was more a billfold than a wallet, really."

We were standing in the immaculate living room. Mexican tile floor, brown leather sofa, matching armchair and ottoman, a slate-topped coffee table on a sage-colored floral rug. On the coffee table a stone pitcher with a bouquet of red carnations and a chipped white enamel colander filled with artificial oranges. Over the sofa a framed print of a British sailing ship reaching port in a furious storm. No TV. No magazine rack. The room was a stage set. It was the first room you saw when you entered the house. So this was the Hallidays' presentation self, as it were. This was who they wanted you to believe they were. Ordered, neat, handsome, tasteful, and well off, comfortable but not ostentatious.

"Mrs. Halliday was shot in the back of the head by her husband as she was taking a batch of cookies out of the oven," Carlos said. He led me to the windowless kitchen, where we watched a technician, kneeling by the faint chalk outline of the victim, scrape what I hoped was charred cookie dough off the wall of the oven with a putty knife. She slid her evidence into a plastic bag. On a bulletin board, someone had tacked a reminder to call Pino.

"Then he walked to the den, where the kids were already opening their gifts. The TV was still blasting away in there when Officer Shanks arrived. The kids wouldn't have heard that first gunshot. And then Dad shot his children one, two, three. They were blindfolded. I guess he told them he had a surprise for them, and they played along."

"How were they blindfolded?"

"He tied linen napkins around their heads."

"Or someone did," I said.

"And then he ate the gun." Carlos put his finger in his mouth and cocked his thumb. "Put a bullet through his soft palate and into his brain. Blood all over his right hand, his arm, on his sleeves. Looks like murder-suicide."

"Where are the napkins?"

"At the lab. The door to the backyard was unlocked, but we went over the pool area with a fine-tooth comb—no footprints, no evidence anyone jumped the fence. The family was here alone."

"So why ask me what I think?"

"Because you have an open mind, and maybe we missed something. Maybe you can convince me otherwise. And like you say, we always want to know *why*."

"You don't think the killings could be drug-related?"

"If they were, the victims would have been tortured and decapitated, and their heads would have been lined up on the mantel like bowling trophies. They would have flayed Chafin's face and glued it to the lampshade."

Carlos showed me photos of the deceased on his iPhone. Mrs. Halliday sat on the floor, her back against a cabinet, and her head against the open oven door. A veil of blood from the exit wound obscured her features. She wore a green silicone Kermit the Frog oven mitt on her left hand. The killer must have eased her body off the oven door—with his foot, most likely. But why would he?

The children's blindfolds had been removed. Carlos said, "I've got pictures with the blindfolds on or off."

"These'll do."

The three children lay faceup, shoulder to shoulder, the younger boy's left arm out straight, a finger seeming to point to the Christmas tree. He died with what appeared to be a smile on his face and with his eyes half open. The girl looked to be lost in sleep. The spray of blood on the wall and carpet behind the older boy's head was extensive, like maybe he'd bolted up in alarm as he took the bullet. Each child had a small, raw hole in the middle of the forehead.

Chafin had been standing when the bullet tore through his skull and splattered blood and gray matter on the eggshell wall and on the popcorn ceiling. His body folded at the waist and dropped to his right. He landed face-first on the crèche. Blood spilled from his nose and mouth. Beside Chafin's head, three plaster magi proffered gifts, and shepherds knelt before the now-decradled infant.

The tech told us she was finished. There were a yellow saucepan and a blue teakettle on the gas range and a rack of cookies on the granite counter. Two or three missing. Would Dad have stopped to eat after the first fatal shot? Hungry cops? Four measuring spoons, each on its own hook, hung side by side on the wall like ascending musical notes. Black and white checkerboard tiles on the floor, white cabinets, stainless steel fridge. No children's drawings on the fridge door. Then I remembered: At seven o'clock, when these five lives suddenly ended, I'd been on the phone with my father, reminding him who I was and telling him I'd pick him up at eleven in the morning. Yes, tomorrow. Christmas dinner at Venise's. Your daughter.

Carlos said, "Halliday owned a restaurant on the Boardwalk that caters to our French-Canadian snowbirds. La Mélange. You heard of it?"

I had. "Poutine, Montreal smoked meat, guédille."

"They should call the place Heart Attack and have nurses waiting tables."

The tech snapped her suitcase shut and wished us a Merry Christmas as she left.

Carlos said, "With the economy like it is, restaurants are going under left and right. Must be stressful. We'll be checking on his finances, of course."

I said, "He wrote that note on a typewriter, it looks like."

"I'd say a Smith Corona portable, but it's not in the house."

"Are you wearing patchouli?"

"Who wears patchouli anymore?" Carlos told me he needed to talk to the press outside, and I should meet him out front when I finished.

I went through the junk drawer. What I thought was a book of matches turned out to be a clever little notepad from Chef Remy's. Twisties, pill splitter, birthday candles, a refrigerator lightbulb, assorted clasps, a meat thermometer, toothpicks, and packets of Lactaid chewables. I found the holiday Butterball turkey in the fridge and wondered what would happen to all this food. Someone must come and toss it all away. There were several plastic containers of take-away food from La Mélange. Multivitamins, Metamucil. There was a bowl of business cards on the counter by the Mixmaster. Truly Nolen, Maids to Order, Wok This Way, Style and Substance Salon, the Lawn Ranger. A new issue of *Saveur* ("French Bistro Cooking") on the granite counter along with a stack of utility bills. A crucifix over the door and a calendar from Phuong Nam Market with December 9 circled and *drs appt* written at the date.

There were two small steel desks in the boys' room, two wheeled backpacks beneath the desks, bunk beds, a globe, a dresser, and a neatly organized closet. On the wall by the door hung a wanted poster of the boys wearing cowboy hats and villainous scowls. A $500 reward was offered for the pair who were "caught serving God with their whole heart," although I assumed they were not sharing a heart. In Brianna's room a three-foot stuffed unicorn standing on a Disney toy box stared out the window. I found a Bible and a pair of spongy purple earplugs in the drawer of Mrs. Halliday's bedside table and a TV remote in Mr. Halliday's. I turned the TV on. truTV: "Not reality. Actuality." *Tru* as in *not quite true.* Chafin Halliday had a dark oak mission-style desk and matching chair in his office. On the desk, a banker's lamp and a leather cup with four sharpened pencils, points up. In the desk drawer, a ballpoint pen and a pad of sticky notes. The walls were bare, the wastebasket empty except for a to-do list: *Bank, PO, flash drive, those insoles, hot peanuts, hot peanuts, hot peanuts.* Was the absence of evidence, evidence of Halliday's absence in the home? Or was it meant to seem so?

I peeked into the den in time to see a uniformed officer pull up his sleeve and admire his two watches—one with a gold band, the other a black sports watch with what looked like a clipped price tag still attached. I saw a small, unwrapped, and empty gift box under the Christmas tree. I said, "Excuse me."

He turned. "Who are you?"

I told him.

"Seen anything interesting?"

"I have."

"I'll get out of your way."

The Christmas tree was strung with garlands of popcorn and cranberries and draped with tinsel. Some of the children's gifts were opened and sprayed with blood: a velvet-curtained puppet theater, a karaoke machine, snow skis, and video games (*Killzone 2, WrestleMania, Country Justice: Revenge of the Rednecks*). The Christmas stockings were hung on the mantel of the gas fireplace, lotto tickets sticking out the top of Mom's. A studio portrait of the family hung on the paneled wall. A mottled brown backdrop matched Dad's brown sport coat. Mom and the kids wear white sweaters, Dad a white turtleneck. He sits behind his wife, his visible arm at his side, his hand disappearing beneath the frame. Brantley stands behind Dad, his right hand clutching Dad's right shoulder, as if he were keeping Dad from floating away. Briely's left hand is tentatively placed on Mom's left shoulder. Mom's smile is bright and wide-eyed. Brianna's in Mom's lap and is the only person looking at what I expect is an assistant's smiling face and not at the palm of the photographer's raised hand.

I was aware of my antipathy toward Dad, but I didn't know where it was coming from. Maybe the autumnal tone of the portrait was depressing me. Then I realized Chafin Halliday reminded me of my cousin Archie Lambert, whom I have no taste for. Didn't make any sense that I should transfer my hostility for Archie to the late Mr. Halliday, of course. Archie was and remained a bully and a selfish lout who had never said a pleasant word to me in his life. One time when we were eight or nine, Archie stood on my head in a wading pool and would certainly have drowned me if my aunt Roxy hadn't pulled him off. Archie's a high school principal these days somewhere in Maryland.

I lifted the picture off its hook, carried it to the living room, and set it on the table. I sat and tried to imagine the family's life in this tidy and austere house. The boys are sitting beside each other at the table wearing their matching blue pajamas, eating quietly, and stealing the occasional glimpse at Mom and Dad. Mrs. Halliday dabs at her lips with a paper napkin and then wipes the egg yolk off the edge of her plate. Mr. Halliday chews his food vehemently, rolling his tongue along his gums, sucking his teeth, looking at no one. He grips a knife in one hand, a fork, tines down, in the other. The girl, in pink, kneels on her chair and sings to herself as she arranges her food on the plate so that the fried egg does not touch the ham or the buttered toast and is oblivious to the tension in the room that the rest of them feel. Something was said in the darkness the night before, something that an apology will not expunge. The phone rings. No one moves. The boys stare at their plates. The girl sings about a man who jumps off a roof with a cat in his arms and lands on his feet.

I thought about Halliday's vanishing right hand in the portrait, wondered why he had let it drop, what it might be up to and what he might have been up to in the life he lived outside this house. I suspected that family life mattered to him only to the extent that it represented a simulacrum of affable domesticity and the perception of order and decorum. He was regulated in his domestic life so that he could be violent and wild in his secret life. But what was that secret, and had it allowed this horror to visit the innocents at home?

Carlos and I stood in the sloping driveway in the Halliday front yard. Neighbors in robes and slippers gave on-camera interviews to newscasters. "You never think something like this can happen in your own neighborhood." "A nice, quiet family." "My boy Alex played with their kids." "We called them the Happy Hallidays." A hexagonal green and white sign by the lantana said the house was protected by Everglades Home Security. On the roof of the house, an inflatable Santa Claus sat in his sleigh and waved to us. Carlos said, "What do you think?"

I turned away from the flashing lights of the police cruisers. "I think Mr. Halliday lived his real life somewhere else."

"Do you think he did this?"

"I can't say, but let's suppose he didn't. What if someone wants us to think that he did?"

"Whoever that was did a convincing job."

"It's easier to comprehend insanity than malevolence, I suppose."

"It is if you're not a cop." Carlos took out a small pump bottle of Purell and squirted some in his hand and then in mine. "And maybe it is what it seems to be."

"But nothing ever is."

"Who would want to kill the children?"

"Maybe it was random."

"You're not making sense, Coyote. Do you think our Mr. Halliday *could* have done it?"

"Why would a man go through all of this gift-giving, all this holiday cheer, why would he buy lottery tickets, if he were planning to slaughter his family?"

"Maybe it wasn't planned."

Three people with filtered respirators, blue hazmat suits, and yellow chem-spill booties ducked under the police lines. Carlos said, "What the hell is this?" and yelled, "Sully, who called Mop 'n' Glow?" He held up his hand and asked the cleanup crew what they thought they were doing.

One of them said, "What we were told to do."

"Wait right here till I get the okay. What's the rush?" He asked Sully to check on the cleanup with Lieutenant Romano.

I said, "Find out who had the doctor's appointment on the ninth."

Carlos said, "Brianna's annual checkup."

"Who's Pino?"

"Working on that."

"The officer inside . . ."

"Which one?"

"The steroid case."

"I didn't hear that." He looked back at the house. "You mean Officer Shanks."

"Officer Shanks stole a watch."

"Are you sure?"

"He's wearing two."

"I'll talk to him." Carlos read a text message on his phone. "So what are your Christmas plans?"

"Going to Venise's."

"She taking her meds?"

"I hope so."

"Inez's not going to be happy about this. Another holiday ruined."

"If I could get a look at some home movies or a photo album or something, it might help. Didn't see any."

Officer Shanks called to Carlos to come inside. I said good night and shouldered my way through the crowd. A fiftyish reporter with preposterously red hair and cat's-eye glasses grabbed my arm, asked my name, and wrote it down. She handed me her business card: *Perdita Curry, True-Crime Novels.* Could it be? I thought. Factual and made-up at the same time? "I'd like to talk to you," she said.

"That makes one of us."

"I'll make it worth your while."

"So you aim to see that justice is done, Ms. Curry?"

"I could pretend to want that if it makes you happy, but, actually, I just know a good story when I smell one."

At home I switched on the floor lamp in the living room and listened to my voice mail while I poured myself a snifter of cognac. My sister, Venise, said she needed me to pick up a tube of buttermilk biscuits for the dinner tomorrow, and I wondered where I'd find a store open on Christmas morning. "Make that three tubes," she said. "And a can of Johnson's baby powder." Bay called to say that he and Marlena were drinking rum runners at Nitti's and feeding french fries to the catfish. My client Wayne Vanderhyde said he desperately needed to see me on the twenty-sixth, as early as possible. I called him back and said we'd have to make it Monday the twenty-eighth, but if he needed me before that, he could call. I sat in my reading chair and read through my script. *The canard is dry, the jambon stringy, the béarnaise is thin, the quiche is runny, the lapin gristled, the boeuf is "toeuf," the poisson I don't even want to talk about.* I was playing the waiter in the Eden Playhouse production of *Les Deux Gamines.* I said, *My dream is to be an electrician. But right now I'm stuck in my father's dream.* I used to sit here and rehearse with my cat on my lap, but Satchel died on Columbus Day of lymphoma. It may have been the saddest day of my life. Dr. Rafferty and I sat in Room 5 at the Eden Animal Hospital, crying and patting little Satchel, and I scratched his orange head and said we should get this over with. I watched her inject the solution and saw Satchel deflate when the barbiturate reached the bloodstream. I'd spent $5,000 on his hospital care and medications and would have spent $5,000 more. I still kept his empty cat bowl by the fridge and his photo on my desk. I was trying to decide if I should get another cat. But not a marmalade one. Pretty soon I'd be growing despondent, remembering Christmases past, so I poured myself another cognac. I put on some Mozart clarinet quintets. And, yes, I remembered Christmases past.

My mother, Birutė Paulauskaitė, was born in Lithuania. Her parents, her brother, Vytautas, and several friends from the local crafts school, along with seventy other political prisoners, were tortured and killed by the NKVD (the Soviet Secret Police) and the retreating Red Army in a forest near Telšiai in June 1941. She watched the massacre from the fortunate cover of juniper bushes twenty yards away in a stand of birches. And that is all she ever told us children about that day. She did tell us that the man who oversaw the slaughter, Nachman Dushanski, was alive and well and living in the USSR. When he fled to Israel after the fall of the Soviet

Union, an arrest warrant was issued, and Lithuania requested his extradition. It was denied. Israel refused to cooperate with the investigation. My mother could not understand how any decent human being, how any supposedly freedom-loving country, how the Jews of all people, could allow this monster to go unpunished. Dushanski escaped justice and died a free man in Tel Aviv in 2008, two years after my mother swallowed a lethal dose of Fentanyl.

Birutė loved my father, Myles, and often spoke with him in hushed tones behind the closed door of their bedroom. But she didn't talk much to her children. She spent Christmases alone in her room with her photographs while the rest of us tried to have a festive time in the living room. What I remembered best about Mom, besides her silence, was her ratty chenille bathrobe and her pink Dearfoam slippers. Whenever she thought I was lying, she'd tell me to stick out my tongue, said that if I was lying, it would be black. It was always black, even those times I was sure I was telling the truth. Then she'd wash my mouth out with Lifebuoy soap or spoon horseradish on my tongue and make me swallow. Cameron called her The Beast. Cameron, my identical twin, who looked exactly like me, people said, but was somehow more handsome, who always knew what I was thinking and could make me laugh at the drop of a hat, who was exuberant where I was languid, was brilliant where I was indistinct, who was quick-witted, resourceful, and blessed with talents, and who fell into a life of drug addiction, robbed my parents blind, and died in Room 201 at the Buccaneer's Inn here in Melancholy, beaten to death by his playmates with a studded mace and a stone war club when we were thirty-four.

I wasn't fooling myself: I wouldn't sleep through the night. But I set the alarm for seven-thirty just in case, lay down on the couch, closed my eyes, and I heard all this applause and looked up to find myself a contestant on a game show, *Two Lies and a Truth*, hosted by Perdita Curry. I was looking good—I'm always young in my dreams—in a stylish charcoal-gray suit I didn't remember ever owning. The three masked Halliday children were telling me three versions of what really happened in their home, and when I chose Child #1 as the truth teller, he took off his mask, and it was Cameron, and the joke was on me, and the audience laughed like crazy, and the phone rang, and it was Pino calling with vital information. I said, Pino who? He said, Noir. And I said, Are you trying to be funny? And he said to meet him at Mélange à Trois at noon, and I agreed and hung up, but then I remembered the family Christmas dinner, so I hurried to call him back, and I checked caller ID, but I got his Social Security number, and I scrolled down a file of other Social Security numbers, and I figured there had to be a button to push to reset the ID numbers to *Phone*, not *Social*, but if there was, I didn't know it. And then I woke up, and the cell phone was in my hand, and I thought I should call Carlos and tell him to meet Pino, but I saw by the clock it was 2:44, and I realized I'd dreamed the Pino call anyway. I checked the recent calls on my cell to be sure, and saw that I had a text message from my ex-wife, Georgia—her annual greet-and-gloat: "Merry Christmas from Barbados, Georgia, Tripp, and the kids."

2

The phone rang at six A.M. I let the machine pick up and tried to hold on to the dream I was having about being alone at a party where there's an Italian greyhound sitting in the middle of the room wearing an aluminum-foil costume. Bay said he wanted to be the first one to wish me a Merry Christmas, and then he and Marlena sang the first verse of "Blue Christmas," and then he told me that Marlena was making cozonac for breakfast. "Supposed to be better than sex," he said. He hung up, and I stared at the revolving ceiling fan and thought about this elderly man I'd seen at the airport a month ago. He was frail, ashen, and slumped in his wheelchair in the preboarding area at Gate C-9. His wife—she stood beside him reading a chunky paperback—had draped her handbag and several strapped carry-ons around his neck. I expected to see alarm or consternation, at least, on his face, resentment, maybe, for being treated like a packhorse. What I saw, however, was equanimity.

The phone rang. My father asked me where I was. "I've been waiting outside for forty-five minutes."

I said, "Dad, I told you eleven o'clock, not seven. I'll be there at nine. You have any tubes of biscuits over there?"

"You ever listen to yourself?"

Dr. Milton Hamburger had diagnosed Dad with Alzheimer's. Dad said he was merely closing up shop. At least he hadn't yet lost his ability to make a metaphor. And he did have his lucid moments. He was in and out of it, however, and he was hard to read. His expressions were often without nuance or blend. He could remember what he had for breakfast on June 15, 1944, in Guam (lemon gumdrop candy, two sugar cookies), but not that he just turned on the gas stove without lighting the pilot. Which was why I had to move him into an all-electric assisted-living facility, Almost Home at Sylvan Gardens.

Dad and I were at the Buy-N-Bye on Palm—the A-rab store, he called it—when Venise rang my cell and wanted to know where the hell we were. I stepped outside and stood beside the MIDLEAST FOOD sign in the window. I pointed out it was only ten and told her I'd managed to snag the last two cans of buttermilk biscuits in Everglades County and the baby powder. I thought she'd be pleased. She told me Oliver could inhale a can of biscuits by himself. Oliver Withstanley's her husband. I peeked in the window and saw Dad doing his last-minute Christmas shopping—lottery tickets and phone cards for everyone. I said, "Merry Christmas, Venise."

She said, "We need to get the food in the oven."

"No, we don't," I said. "I'm bringing a HoneyBaked ham. Slice and serve."

"You idiot! Ham is for Easter. Goose is for Christmas. Or turkey. Or duck."

"But we all love ham, Venise."

She screamed, "I will not eat cold meat on Christmas!"

A lanky old man on a squat, fenderless bicycle rode by. He wore a Santa hat and waved hello. I said, "I want you to make yourself a drink, Venise. Turn on some Christmas carols and relax. I'll be there in a jiffy, and I'll take care of everything."

When we arrived, Oliver was still in his gray flannel pajamas. He snatched the baby powder from the plastic sack, thanked me, and excused himself. Venise put the ham on a cookie sheet and slipped it into the oven. I explained that the heat would only dry the ham out. She told me I didn't know what the hell I was talking about. The first floor of Venise's house is a large open area, the kitchen separated from the dining area by a counter. The living room begins with the couch and carpet. The couch, the La-Z-Boy, and the upholstered armchair face a flat-screen TV set on a glass coffee table. Travertine-tile floor and rose-colored walls. Venise had covered the living room couch with clear, fitted vinyl, something she did whenever Dad visited. He'd had accidents in the past. I sat him down on the couch and turned off the TV.

Venise said, "Turn that back on. I was watching *Bad Santa*."

I said maybe we could put on some holiday music.

"I said turn it back on!"

I did. Dad took a nickel from his shirt pocket and scratched away at a losing lotto ticket. He dropped the ticket on the end table. "That one was yours," he said.

"Would you like a drink?"

"Gimme gadabber and a bing banger."

"How about a beer?"

"And a VO chaser."

"You got it."

Venise and Oliver lived in the house he grew up in. His bedroom had remained exactly as it was on the day he left home for college, which was not so much different than it had been when he was in elementary school. Twin bunk beds, framed photos of Hopalong Cassidy, Mary Hartline, and Albert Einstein on the wall, along with a dartboard and a paint-by-number portrait of a collie. His toys were all in their original boxes and stacked neatly on his bookcase. The same pine dresser and mirror, the same Roy Rogers alarm clock, and the same lamp with cattle brands on the shade. Oliver slept in his bedroom. Venise slept across the hall in Oliver's parents' old bedroom, which was okay with her because, she told me, Oliver's navel, his reproductive apparatus, and his armpits smelled all rank and yeasty (no, I told her, that didn't seem typical), and was okay with Oliver because Venise had sleep apnea, snored like an asthmatic horse, and suffered from night terrors. If she was startled awake by dreams, noise, or touch, she'd flail about and scream. I should tell you that Venise weighed three hundred and some pounds. She'd had her stomach stapled two years earlier, but seemed to eat as much as ever. I wasn't sure how that was even possible unless the staples had lost their purchase. Oliver ate plenty but managed to stay fairly slim, and that drove Venise wild.

The doorbell rang. Venise and Oliver had invited his cousin Patience Firestone to dinner as, I suspected, a possible romantic interest for me. Venise was unsettled by my living alone. She considered solitude egotistical and unnatural. Patience was petite and blue-eyed. Her straight black hair was cut in bangs and streaked with gray. She wore a white sleeveless blouse with the collar turned up, a turquoise skirt, black socks, and white running shoes. Her right arm was tattooed wrist to shoulder in an intricate Islamic geometric pattern of stars and diamonds. I took the casserole dish from her and set it on the table. We shook hands and introduced ourselves. Patience reminded me that we'd met at Venise and Oliver's wedding. She said, "You seemed very depressed, as I remember." She gave Venise a big hug and a bouquet of white roses. Patience said sure, she'd love a Bloody Mary, so I made us two. I introduced her to Dad, who said that at his assisted living facility there were lots of patients. He handed her a lotto ticket and a nickel. Another loser.

Oliver joined us. He had on orange and teal sweatpants, flip-flops, and his 2008 family reunion T-shirt, which featured a silk-screened photo of Oliver Hardy in bowler and tie, and beneath the photo I'M WITHSTANLEY. His walnut-brown hair was damp and slicked back. He smelled of talc and bay rum. He kissed Patience on the cheek. She sneezed. He made himself a White Russian and plopped down on his La-Z-Boy. The story of the Halliday tragedy came on the news. I noticed Perdita Curry standing behind the police department spokesman. Venise joined us, shook her head, and put her hand on Oliver's shoulder. She said, "What in God's name would drive a man to kill his own family?"

I said, "Maybe he didn't."

"They said he did. Weren't you listening?"

"On Christmas Eve." Oliver shook his head and *tsk*ed.

I said, "I was there, Venise. Last night."

Patience asked me why I was there. Oliver said he couldn't understand how a man could murder his children. Dad said he could think of several reasons. Patience said she'd read about this aquatic parasite that enters your brain through your ears while you're swimming and eats away at the gray matter until you become insane and essentially do the bidding of the parasite, and you become capable of horrific and inexplicable acts of violence.

Dad said, "Most of them are ungrateful."

Oliver said, "The wife was most likely having an affair, and he caught her at it. He snapped. End of story."

I wondered why the police spokesman suggested the murder-suicide scenario when it was forensically too early to make that determination, wasn't it? I knew he was probably correct, my concerns notwithstanding, but thought he might have been more circumspect.

Dad said, "You bring them into the world. You take them out."

Venise had fifteen kinds of mustard on the table. Creole, Dijon, English, Meaux, Bavarian, Chinese, honey, ballpark, horseradish, chili, Bahamian, wasabi, deli, Dusseldorf, and Sarepta. I carved the wizened ham and placed a slice on each plate. Oliver grated milk chocolate on his sweet potato casserole. Venise muted the TV but kept the remote by her salad plate. Dad reached for the biscuits and knocked over his red wine, and Patience hurried to sop it up. Venise said, "I'll have to toss out the tablecloth now." Then she had us lift our plates while she made a show of taking off the tablecloth and stuffing it into the trash. "Like I'm made of money," she said.

"Let it go, Venise," Oliver said.

Patience complimented Venise on the garlic mashed potatoes and the squash. Venise told us about her upcoming colonoscopy and her anxiety about the unpleasant gastrointestinal preparations. She said the medical procedure was Oliver's Christmas gift.

"The gift of good health," Oliver said.

Venise said, "I've always wanted one."

I said, "What did you get Oliver?"

She said, "What do you get the man who has everything?"

"Nothing," Dad said.

Patience said, "Well, that's sweet—the colonoscopy—if you think about it."

Oliver smiled. "What I really got her was a mobility scooter."

"That way I don't have to chance there not being one available at Publix," Venise said.

"Three wheels, electric, quiet as a whisper, straw basket up front," Oliver said. "It's the Celebrity edition."

"And I got him golf clubs," Venise said.

"You golf, Oliver?" I said.

"Not yet." He told us how much he was enjoying his retirement. "Best decision—" He looked at Venise. "Second best decision I ever made was going to work for the post office." Oliver quit high school because of his many intractable anxieties, but then managed to get himself a scholarship to MIT after he built a machine that could read Braille and scored an 800 on the math portion of the SATs. And then he quit MIT in his senior year after making a perfect score on the civil service exam. He went to work for the post office and, with his future now secure, began to relax. Oliver told us he spent a lot of time these days playing WorldWide Scrabble and shopping on eBay. He told us he'd just won an auction for a Tesla Shield, a pendant that emits a positive tachyon field. "Inside the pendant is a lost cubit caduceus coil." He raised his brow and nodded like we might be familiar with the coil and its amazing properties. He said it was all based on the principles of sacred geometry, zero-point energy, orgonomy, and harmonious frequencies of light.

I said, "What does it do?"

"Keeps you from aging, from getting sick, makes you stronger. Lots of things. You know how our DNA acts as an antenna for light energies, right?"

Patience and I cleared the table and tidied up while Venise and Oliver hooked up the karaoke machine and Dad wandered around the house opening doors. When I asked him what he was looking for he told me he forgot. I led him back to the couch and his drink. Patience loaded the dishwasher. She was of the scullery school that insists every bit of dinnerware should be scrubbed and rinsed before being put in the machine. Dad sang a halfhearted and halting rendition of "We Wish You a Merry Christmas" that included the lines, "Bring us some friggin' pudding / And a bottle of beer."

Patience told me she was attracted to men in wheelchairs, and she wasn't sure why, and did I think that was peculiar? I said, Just men in wheelchairs? She said, Lately. And I was reminded of my coincidental airport reverie from earlier that morning—the man encumbered with carry-ons—and how these synchronies seemed to happen a lot in my life. I'll dream about a guy I worked with thirty years ago, and then I'll read in the paper the next morning that the guy's father died. And in the father's obit I'll learn that the old colleague is married to a woman named Janet, and they live in Orlando. Or something about a person's appearance or behavior catches the corner of my eye. Her whimsical hat or a bounce in her walk. When that happens I've come to expect that I'll see that person later on that day, maybe in the express lane at Publix or in the car next to mine at a red light or Rollerblading on the Boardwalk. For about a month last year no matter where I drove in South Everglades I found myself at a stop sign or red light behind the same Ford Focus with the Florida tag: *FLA * PGH.* It was like I was following him.

I scraped leftovers into the sink and started the disposal. "When did you become aware of this attraction?"

"I think it all started when I re-saw James Stewart in *Rear Window* a couple of years ago. I sound crazy. I know it."

I said, "You're not crazy."

Venise belted out "O Holy Night."

Patience asked me if I could harmonize. I told her I knew what harmony meant and how it should sound, but had no idea how that sound was achieved. We sang anyway. We did "Good King Wenceslaus" and then we all exchanged gifts. I gave Dad a portable CD player and a box of CDs of old radio shows. Jack Benny, Fred Allen, Fibber McGee. I'd gotten Venise and Oliver a gift certificate to this Brazilian restaurant that they adore. Dad handed out his phone cards and then got this pinched and sour look on his face. When he eased himself up off the couch, it became evident that he had forgotten to wear his Depend. Fortunately, I had brought some along. Venise screamed and stormed off to her room. I took Dad to the bathroom and got him into the shower and his clothes into a plastic trash bag. I told him I was taking the soiled clothes to the car, and I reminded him to wash every square inch. I put a towel where he could reach it, said not to waste all of Venise's hot water.

I stuffed the soiled clothes in the trunk. Carlos called and said he wanted to meet for lunch on Monday. I told him I had a ten o'clock. He said he'd pick me up at eleven-thirty. I told him I'd meet him at Oppenheimer's. Oliver handed me a pair of polyester running pants the color of cheddar cheese and an olive-green velour something or other. I said, "What the hell is this?"

"A shrobe. It's got the cut of a shirt and the fabric of a robe. It's the latest in leisure wear."

When I got back to the bathroom, Dad was standing there in his diaper and sucking his thumb. I said, "Don't do that, Dad. Please don't. It's creepy."

He said, "Wah! Wah!" And he smiled.

I said, "Don't," and handed him the clothes. I got him dressed, and we said our goodbyes. Venise was in her room with a migraine. Patience gave Dad a kiss on his cheek. I told her I hadn't been depressed at Venise and Oliver's wedding. I'd been unhappy.

On the drive back, Dad said he felt humidified. He repeated the word and shook his head. "Not *humidified*."

"Humiliated?"

"Bingo!"

"Let's stop for a drink. It's early."

"Nothing'll be open on Christmas."

"The Wayside's open."

"I'm dressed like a rodeo clown."

"You'll fit right in."

We sat at a table by the unplugged jukebox and beneath a poster of LeBron James. The TV over the bar was muted. The Heat were playing the Knicks. I got myself a beer and Dad a VO and water. The bartender wore a pair of plushy antlers and a red clown nose that lit up when I left her a tip. I recognized the man and woman at the bar as the couple who sold the *Journal-Gazette* at the corner of Cypress and Main. They spend so much time standing in the sun that their tanned skins look like hides. A cigarette dangled from the woman's blistered lips. The Wayside ignores the state's no-smoking-in-public-buildings law. It also has a "Two Boswell" rule posted outside the entrance. Only two of the six Boswell brothers could be in the bar at the same time. Apparently, three is critical mass for the Boswells, and they inevitably begin pummeling each other and anyone else who tries to stop the brawl. I handed Dad his drink, and we toasted making it through another year.

Dad told me that lately Mom and Cameron had been visiting him at night, and sometimes he just wanted to sleep, but they refused to leave and kept gabbing about the stupidest things like the price of skirt steak at Winn-Dixie or about how Father Aucoin has been hitting the sauce pretty hard lately. He said, "I like it when Winston visits." Winston was our bulldog when I was growing up. "He curls at the foot of the bed and lets me scratch him behind the ears. And he farts all night long."

The bartender chatted with someone on her cell phone and nibbled at a bowl of beer nuts. I told Dad, "One and done," and walked to the bar to order our nightcap. I switched to cognac. Back at the table Dad said, "I was never able to make your mother happy."

"You tried."

"And she doesn't let me forget it."

I walked Dad to his suite and set his gifts on the table. "I'll take it from here," he said. I studied the family photo on his bookcase.

It was taken twenty-five or more years ago at a seafood festival on the beach. We were all there: Mom and Dad, Venise and Oliver, Cameron, some gaunt and gorgeous but haunted woman Cameron was dating, Georgia, and me. We were sitting at a long table, wearing plastic bibs and brandishing wooden mallets. Dad pretended to hit Mom with his. Mom wore large wraparound sunglasses over her eyeglasses and looked like she was ready to do some spot welding. She had a wide-brimmed straw bonnet and zinc oxide on her nose. The mallets were for smashing the shells of the all-you-can eat boiled crabs. Venise was slim. This was the day, I remember, when a massive earthquake struck somewhere in Central America. Georgia had her hair done in braids. I wondered if she still sucked her thumb and still fell asleep when she rode in a car.

Dad was crying at his table, tapping his knuckles on his forehead, sniffling. I asked what was wrong, and he looked at me and shook his head. I held his arm and told him it was okay. But what did I think was okay? "Tell me what's going on," I said. "What are you thinking?" He pushed me away.

I have this belief, or maybe it's a wish, that if you can just say everything that's on your mind, if you can express everything that's in your heart, if you can articulate your every thought and feeling somehow, you will be cured of your torment and relieved of your pain. You'll come back to life. I don't know that anyone's ever done that, of course, and I know that words are not available to some of us. And sometimes I know it takes too damn much effort to try to speak when all your systems have shut down, when death seems like your only hope, and you would welcome death if it came for you but you're too spent to chase after it.

Dad said, "I fell out of bed one night. And a week before that I fell out again."

3

My client Wayne Vanderhyde sat slumped on the middle cushion of the brown leather sofa in my office. He studied the framed Edward Hopper print on the wall opposite. *Automat, 1927.* "Not very subtle, are you?" he said.

"What do you see there, Wayne?"

"A woman surprised at how rancid her life has turned out to be."

"And what's she thinking, do you think?"

Wayne tapped his finger on his chin, sat forward, and told me I should never ever show my weapon to anyone unless I planned to use it.

"My weapon?"

"I don't mean your rapier wit or your eviscerating insight. I mean your pistol."

I told him I didn't carry a pistol. I didn't own one, and I had never fired one. He shook his head and advised me that that was information that no one should ever know. "Not anyone."

Wayne stocked groceries at the Publix on Cypress Avenue. He confessed to having no career ambition. He didn't want to move up in the store's pathetic hierarchy, as he put it, not even to assistant common-area manager. "What would be the point?"

"That depends on what you want in your life."

"What do *you* want?" he asked me.

"To be better than I am."

"That shouldn't be hard."

"And yet it is."

"All I want out of life is to be able to live like a normal person. That's why I'm here." He had said so at our first session three weeks earlier.

"Define a normal person for me," I said.

"You."

"How am I normal?"

He smiled, looked at the ceiling, and shook his head. "Diplomas," he said. "Desk lamp. Coffee table. Sofa. Matching socks."

"Guilty," I said.

"I'm dull. I don't enjoy people. I fly off the handle at the drop of a hat."

"How does that make you feel?"

"How the fuck do you think it makes me feel?"

I let him settle back on the couch and said, "So you want to be a therapist, is that it?"

He smiled, crossed his arms, and raised an eyebrow. He was wearing blue running shoes, jeans, and a blue V-neck scrub top. I asked him about the charm he wore on a silver chain around his neck—a pair of metallic eyes. He said the charm was a milagro meant to heal his eyes. He had macular degeneration, a genetic gift from his parents, who both had it. Not bad so far, he said, but a time bomb.

He told me he didn't believe in God except when he needed

someone to blame or someone to cure him. He wasted his time watching TV and surfing the Internet. Porn, mostly. That and he played an online game called *The Kingdom of Loathing*. "I can sit for hours and not shift my lazy ass. I have these weird fantasies."

"Weird how?"

"*That* I don't want to talk about."

"Would they be sexual fantasies?"

"In a manner of speaking."

I said, "You called me on Christmas Eve, Wayne. I think I detected alarm in your voice."

He nodded.

"What was going on?"

Wayne looked at me out of the corner of his eye. He pursed his lips, raised his left eyebrow. Could he trust me? he wondered. He said, "I opened the door to the master bedroom in an empty house—"

"An empty house?"

"On DeSoto Street. Nine hundred block."

"I don't understand."

"It's my new hobby. You told me I needed to get out of my house. So now I explore vacant homes."

"What do you do once you're inside?"

"Snoop around. People always leave things behind when they move. I take souvenirs. A grapefruit spoon, a child's drawing. And sometimes I leave things. I'll write an anonymous love letter and hide it in the back of a kitchen drawer for someone to find someday. Scribble sweet nothings and sign it, *Your secret admirer.*"

"And on Christmas Eve?"

"The Parkers lived in that particular house. I found their mail on the kitchen counter: electric bill, phone bill, *Car and Driver* magazine, circular from Bed Bath & Beyond. What do you suppose they mean by *Beyond*?"

"The Parkers?"

"Dave and Deb. I know they owned dogs. Big dogs. Two retractable leashes still on their hangers in the kitchen. Deep scratch marks on the back door, inside and out, about yea high." He held his flattened palm at eye-level. "The Parkers had grown so used to the dogs they probably couldn't separate the funk of dog odor from the ordinary smell of the house. But if you were to move in, you'd have to rip out the baseboards and the wall-to-wall and hose the place down with Lysol and bleach, and even then Klink and Schultz would still be with you, and their stench would remind you of the long-gone Parkers, living now in some FEMA trailer the government set up for evictees, and you'll wonder if they ever drive by the house and see you through the window and weep for the life they have lost."

"And the empty bedroom?" I said.

"It's night, of course, and I'm not foolish enough to open the door with my flashlight on and lose my invisibility. I ease the door open and see that the room is flooded with daylight, and that the light stops right at the doorway. That's the first surprise. Across the room, crouched in a corner, is an enormous male lion staring at me, snarling, ready to spring, and then he shakes his ass and pounces."

"This is a dream?"

"This is not a dream. I wrestle the lion for I don't know how long. I roll onto my side and get a look and see that he's a feline duplicate of me, and then at some point I pass out and wake up later drenched in blood and sweat and with my jeans and shirt torn to shreds."

When I pointed out that it was hardly conceivable that he or any person could vanquish an actual lion in real life, Wayne asked me how then would I account for the actual blood soaked into the real-life carpet. "This sort of thing has never happened to you?" he said.

• • •

I got to Oppenheimer's in downtown New River before Carlos did. The kid working the register was growing a Johnny Depp-ish goatee and wore these vintage silver eyeglasses with oval lenses. Maybe he was a Civil War reenactor. He'd have to pull his Dickies up over his *Family Guy* boxer shorts if he was going to carry it off. I grabbed a *Journal-Gazette* and ordered a coffee. Construction workers had uncovered what might be a Calusa Indian burial ground near the South River. Courts had put a hold on the development of a new mall till archaeologists had a chance to examine the artifacts. Meanwhile the Tequesta Tribe, jumping the gun, perhaps, said the site was sacred to native peoples, and they would protect it at all costs.

Page two: There were now thirty-six active, unsolved missing persons cases in Everglades County, including most recently an eighty-nine-year-old Alzheimer's victim, who had wandered away from his daughter's home in Ridgeland, and an eighteen-year-old female who lived alone, went out to the store, and never came back. Thirty-six people here one minute and gone the next.

A golf-ball retriever at Eden Golf Club was mauled by an alligator in the lake near the thirteenth hole. Two golfers went to his aid and beat off the alligator with their clubs, but not before the diver lost an arm. While the rescue was going on, the next foursome played through. Carlos walked in, went behind the counter, poured himself a coffee, and joined me. I folded my newspaper.

For a couple of weeks I'd had a squatter living in my yard. He'd set up camp in the shrubbery along the fence. I'd asked him nicely to leave. He said he had nowhere to go. I said, Try the homeless shelter. He said it was a dangerous place. I called the cops. No one came by. So I told Carlos. "I see this guy in the morning and at night, not every night, but most, especially since he's taken to leaving his sleeping bag and backpack behind the heliconias."

"He trusts you," Carlos said.

"I don't want him there."

"Is he hurting anyone?"

"No."

"What do you have against the guy?"

"It's my house." I told Carlos how today I had tried to ignore the guy. I walked straight to my car, and I heard, "What, you're not going to say hello?" He was sitting in his sleeping bag, leaning up against the fence, reading *Harper's*, which he probably stole out of my recycling bin. "Stuck up?" he said to me.

Carlos thought this was funny.

I said, "Would you put up with this?"

"No, but I wouldn't ask for help, either."

Carlos slid a gift-wrapped book across the table. "Merry Christmas from Inez."

She'd gotten me a copy of *An African in Greenland* by Tété-Michel Kpomassie. I opened to a random page and read to Carlos:

> *I was walking home alone and the night was still. Suddenly looking up, I saw long white streaks whirling in the wind above my head. It was like the radiance of some invisible hearth, from which dazzling light rays shot out, streamed into space, and spread to form a great deep-folded phosphorescent curtain which moved and shimmered, turning rapidly from white to yellow, from pink to red.*

I said, "Give Inez a hug for me." Inez and Carlos had been married for twenty years or so but separated about every two or three years, for six months to a year each time, and Carlos was worried that one of these days the separation would take. Inez and I had been in the same book club for a while. She once told me that literary theory was reading without imagination, and I've loved her ever since.

My father once told me that he wanted to see the northern lights before he died. He said he slept through them when he was a kid in Massachusetts. "When I got up in the morning, my old man told me what a spectacular show I had missed. I couldn't believe the dufus didn't wake me up."

Carlos said, "The Hallidays were each killed by a single gunshot fired from the same .22-caliber pistol, a Colt Woodsman, which we found in the den along with the bullet casings, beside the open hand of Chafin Halliday at the crime scene. Death was instantaneous in each case. There was no sign of struggle. There were no unusual footprints either inside or outside of the house. There was no damage to vegetation. No unexpected fingerprints were found. There was no sign of forced entry. The neighbors saw no one unfamiliar enter or leave the house."

"Why would Halliday own a gun?"

"The same reason everyone else does." Carlos opened his memo pad and looked at his notes. "Halliday purchased the pistol at the New River Knife and Gun Show"— he counted on his fingers—"seven years ago."

"I don't own a gun."

"A random search of cars in any South Florida mall parking lot will uncover handguns stashed in half of all the cars."

"Doesn't that worry you?"

"Very much."

"Handguns should be banned."

"I agree with you, but they are not, and we live in a complicated world. Your naïveté will not make it simpler."

Our waitress—Bluebelle, her name tag said—freshened our coffee. She had her blond dreadlocks tied back, one green eye, one brown eye. We'd need a few more minutes before we ordered, thanks. "Chili," she said, and winked her green eye. Outside on Magnolia Avenue, two rotund little men in blue shorts, white socks, sandals, and striped polo shirts walked down the street carrying plastic supermarket bags in one hand and holding white hankies over their balding heads with the other.

"No criminal history," Carlos said. "No evidence of any drug use. No enemies, none who would want to kill him anyway."

"Did you speak with Officer Shanks?"

"Taken care of."

"Was I right?"

"We found nothing funny on Halliday's computer."

"What computer?"

"The one in the trunk of his car."

"You didn't answer my question."

"No love notes to secretaries, no porn, no hidden confidential files. Mr. Halliday seems to have been a solid citizen."

Carlos ordered a ham, egg, and cheese breakfast sandwich, and I got the Chili Souper Bowl with atomic salsa. Two iced teas. Carlos said, "What's that Sherlock Holmes line you're always quoting?"

"'When you have eliminated the impossible, that which remains, however improbable, must be the truth.'"

"Chafin Halliday murdered his family and took his own life. The suicide note seals it."

Carlos told me that on the evening of the twenty-third Halliday worked late at his office in Melancholy, ordering food for the restaurant, and I said that sounded like a man planning a future. Halliday stopped by the home of a local state rep and dropped off a Christmas bottle of Johnnie Walker Blue. He got home at seven, made a long call to a friend in Rhode Island, and Carlos said that sounded like a man saying goodbye. Halliday left the house on the twenty-fourth at six-thirty in the morning as usual and stopped by the restaurant to leave Christmas bonus checks with his manager and then seemed to have spent a couple of hours at the Tropical Mall. He took the family to the movies at the IMAX in the afternoon. They got home around five-ish, and Mrs. Halliday preheated the oven to three-fifty.

"How do you know all this?"

"Receipts, witnesses, neighbors."

I asked about Mrs. Halliday.

"Born Krysia Plotczyk. A devout Catholic, soccer mom, vice president of the PTA. We're trying to reach her family in Gdańsk."

I said, "What was Halliday's motive?"

"I think he may have felt hopeless. He was in debt and had suffered some recent business setbacks. He used to own Gold Coast Cruise Lines."

"The gambling boats."

"He had a gold mine there for years, taking people out past the three-mile limit, plying them with booze, and then setting them loose on very tight slot machines and at the blackjack and poker tables. Halliday ran the largest unregulated gambling enterprise in the country."

"But then the Silver Palace opened up."

"Exactly. And the county voted to allow slots, video poker, and Texas Hold 'Em at the racetracks and jai alai. He started bleeding money. Couldn't pay his bills, laid off dozens of employees. The bank was threatening to repossess the boats. He had to sell, and sell fast."

"Who bought the business?"

"He wanted to sell to the Tequestas, but they weren't interested. The lobbyist for the tribe, however, was. He and a partner made an offer that Halliday thought was an insult."

"Who would want to buy a business with such bleak prospects?"

"These two guys had big plans to turn the boats into VIP floating nightclubs. *Nightclubs* being a euphemism for brothels. Halliday got no other offers, and he sold for less than he paid. He was still in debt and was likely going to lose the restaurant. And, who knows, maybe his family. And then what? Maybe he thought this was the only way out." Carlos shrugged. "Anglos," he said. "Who can tell how they think?"

"Your father's Irish."

"No one's perfect."

"So who were the buyers?"

"One's a little shady; the other's a pillar of the community."

Mr. Shady turned out to be a disbarred lawyer named Park McArthur, whose mother was murdered in a bungled robbery at her husband's jewelry store in Queens. Her husband, Park's stepdad, Artie Berman, put up a sizable reward, but Park, Artie's lawyer, "borrowed" the money and invested in a chain of adult bookstores in New Jersey. He got caught before he was able to return the cash, and he had to look for a new occupation and a new family. He moved to D.C. and opened an auto dealership, Park's Cars, and started advertising like mad on local TV and became a celebrity. He would dress up in a straitjacket offering "crazy prices" and "insane deals" until he was subdued by attendants or chased off camera by a man with a butterfly net.

Carlos said, "Around this time he met Jack Malacoda, his eventual partner. Malacoda's a prominent GOP fund-raiser and an influential K Street lobbyist. He's on the board of a dozen charitable foundations. Very powerful and connected guy who's got more money than God. He's fiercely religious and devoted to his family."

"There's two red flags right there."

"Cynic." Carlos is a little sensitive on the subject of religion. He's a fervent Catholic, a deacon at St. Jude's, and a daily communicant.

"A religious zealot opening a brothel?"

"It's smart business."

"Lobbying for gambling?"

"Gaming," Carlos said.

"Suspects?" I said.

"No motive. No opportunity. They've both been marlin fishing off Mexico since the twenty-first."

Bluebelle brought our lunch. We thanked her. I said, "Carlos, you're not putting ketchup on the eggs, are you?"

He finished squirting the ketchup, bit into the sandwich, and wiped his lips with a napkin. He stirred and stirred his tea with the straw and stared a hole into his sandwich.

I said, "Carlos, where did you just go?"

"I became a cop to put bad guys away." He brushed a fly off the rim of his glass. "Turns out there are a lot of very bad guys out there. How's Myles, by the way?"

"Dad's good. Thanks for asking. And by *good* I mean he's not worse."

Carlos told me he had to drive out to the Hills after lunch. A seniors-only condo had evicted tenants who didn't want to leave, a couple who had lived there for thirteen years.

"Why the eviction?"

"They took in their ten-year-old granddaughter after her parents were killed in a car wreck."

"Bastards!"

"It's the law, Coyote."

"What?"

"You and I might not like it, but those are the rules. You break the rules, you suffer the consequences."

"There's no room for compassion?"

"There is. This condo board, however, has opted for indifference."

"Where the justice?"

"Order is essential. Justice is a luxury."

"Are you serious?"

"You can't run a country or a business or a school or a family when there is disorder. Everything falls apart."

I said, "Maybe we've settled for order because it's easier to get than justice."

Carlos smiled. He told me not to turn around, and I suddenly had to stop myself from looking back.

He said, "What's behind you?"

"I don't know."

"You *should* know, Coyote. You should always know, because what's behind you may be gaining on you."

On the way home after work, I drove to the beach and toyed with the idea of dropping in at La Mélange to see if I could learn anything new about Chafin Halliday. I parked on Aviles Street alongside a black Camaro that had THE COSMOBIOLOGY OF I AND I painted on the back window. A redheaded vulture drifted in the wind over my head, leaned back, spread his wings, dipped his tail, and let the breeze carry him over the sea grapes to the beach, picking up speed as he went. He seemed so exhilarated. Three feral cats and I watched him sail, wishing we all could play like that.

Bay called on the cell as I walked along the Boardwalk. I told him some of what I'd learned from Carlos about the Gold Coast boats. He told me the games on the boats were rigged. In the six-deck blackjack dealing shoe, six aces were removed and six sixes were added. "A false shuffle here, a double deal there, and nobody's any the wiser."

I said that that sort of thing might make people angry.

"Not angry enough to kill five people," he said. "The folks that gamble on the boats take the bus from the Gulfstream condos. They pay their $29.50 and enjoy the cruise to nowhere. It's their social life. Real gamblers don't ride the boats. An hour and a half out to the three-mile limit, an hour and a half back. Three hours without gambling. Let's say you have to drive a half hour each way to the boats. Now you're talking eight hours of your time for four hours of action."

There were no seats inside La Mélange, so I sat at a small table outside. I ordered galvaude and unsweetened iced tea. I told the waiter that I was sorry about what had happened to his boss. He told me that the boss hadn't spent much time at the restaurant lately. Came and went. Last time he'd seen Halliday was the day he died, when he stopped by briefly around four to see the manager. But still it's so sad and so meaningless. You wouldn't think this could happen to a man who was so conscious of his security like Chafin was, paranoid almost. The guy at the next table was reading aloud to himself from a book. He must have been trying to learn Spanish. He said, "Hoy viene una noticia importante. Puede cambiar su vida." Or maybe he was reading his horoscope.

The waiter returned with my meal. He said, "Of course, none of us know what's going to happen with our jobs. Or if we'll be getting a paycheck on Friday. What a mess."

I asked him if the police had been by to speak with the staff, and he said they hadn't. I asked him if there was a typewriter in the restaurant's office. He said there was not. I got a text message from my friend Phoebe telling me she'd meet me at my house at eight. The man at the next table said, "Hace poco viento pero hace mucho sol."

When I parked the car in the driveway, I heard, "My name's Red, not that you cared enough to ask."

I walked over to Red's encampment. Now he had a hibachi and a bag of charcoal by his sleeping bag. I said, "Why are you here?"

"Red Soileau."

"Why my yard?"

"You seem like a pleasant fellow."

"Good night, Red."

"Good night . . ."

"Wylie."

"Wylie."

I saw the light flashing on my answering machine. I pushed the button. The male voice said, "Listen, shithead, keep your nose out of my business, or I'll shove a black sports watch up your ass."

I should tell you about Phoebe. We dated in high school, and I was crazy in love with her, and she with me, but I would never promise her the kind of long-term commitment she needed. Her dad was a bad memory, and her mom was a genial inebriate. Phoebe had no siblings. Some nights we'd walk through Whispering Pines Golf Course and lie on the greens and wait for the sprinklers to drench us. *How can I tell the future, Phoebe?* I would say. *Yes, I think I'll always love you, and I always want to be in love with you, but I can't know if I will be.* I was like a lawyer in love, negotiating a pathetic escape clause. We drifted apart. Eventually, I married Georgia Mears, and Phoebe married Gary Clarke, star quarterback for the South Everglades High Stevedores, and she became a nurse, and he became a cop and also became physically and emotionally abusive to her, and they divorced after years of turmoil, scandal, humiliation, and injury.

Phoebe and I became friends again, and then more than friends, when she was going through hell with Clarke. Georgia had already left me. First I was there for support, then support became comfort, and comfort became passion. And then passion was insufficient for Phoebe, and she married a Norwegian chiropractor, Dr. Kai Pedersen, and they lived a mile or so from me on Eden Lake. Those days we met when we could, and I cared about her more than I cared about anyone. She wanted me to move on with my life. There was little chance of her ever leaving Kai. He was a sweetheart, for starters, and at least for now he was here in the States as a permanent resident on a green card and had a year to wait before applying for naturalization. If they separated before then, it was back to Hammerfest for Kai. Lately she'd been telling me I needed to find a girlfriend I could build a future with. But I ignored her.

I answered the door and asked Phoebe if she'd met Red.

"The guy in the bushes? Not formally."

Phoebe brought me a Christmas present, a six-week-old satiny black kitten with golden eyes named Django. He weighed less than two pounds and looked like a bat. She said they told her at the Humane Society that he was the most playful kitten they'd ever seen. The sign over his cage read LOTS OF FUN!!! She handed me a bag of cat food, the Humane Society paperwork, and an appointment card for his checkup and booster shot at Eden Animal Hospital. We let Django out of his pet carrier, and he dashed off to explore the house. I poured Phoebe and me snifters of cognac. Phoebe took a little rubber squid out of her purse and tossed it to Django, who wrestled it into submission.

Phoebe and I sat on the couch. She told me about her holiday with Kai. They'd gone scuba diving in the Bahamas. Kai stepped on a sea urchin and got boinked on the head by a falling coconut. Django chased his tail, jumped straight up in the air. I told Phoebe about the Halliday killings. Django crawled headfirst into my shoe and fell asleep. Phoebe checked her watch and said she had to go. She said, "Take good care of my little guy."

I said, "Do you know a cop named Shanks?"

"He's an asshole. A friend of Gary's, naturally. Stay away from him."

When I got into bed, Django sat on the floor crying. I scooped him up and laid him on my chest. He sneezed. His nose was runny. He kneaded my T-shirt. As I drifted off to sleep, he climbed onto my head and chewed my hair. I listened to his congested breathing. I was happy to have a cat again. I dreamed I was in a bright, empty room that had no visible entry or exit. I heard gypsy music. I turned around and saw a snarling Wayne Vanderhyde with bloodied hands advancing toward me, and then I heard a scream, and I woke up.

4

I called the vet's and scheduled an appointment for Django. I told them how he'd come home from the shelter with a terrible cold. His nose is bubbling with mucus, and he has sneezing fits. He's all congested. The receptionist told me it's not unusual for them to pick up a virus at the Humane Society. Is he active? He's a dervish, I said. Is he eating well? Like a champ. I wiped Django's nose and his runny eyes with a damp washcloth. I fed him wet food that I'd warmed in the microwave. He danced around the dish, deliriously happy to be eating. I showed him the litter box. He seemed shamelessly disinterested. I got out a drawerful of Satchel's old toys and scattered them around the living room. I opened the front door and asked Red how he took his coffee. I poured a coffee-to-go for me and a coffee with cream and two sugars for Red. I told Django goodbye and turned on the radio to keep him company.

Red thanked me for the coffee and asked me if I was feeling all right.

I said I was. "Why?"

"I heard you scream last night."

"That was me?"

"Woke me out of a dead sleep."

"I had a bad dream."

"You have a heavy conscience?"

"Always."

Red sat on his rolled-up sleeping bag and tied the laces of his green sneakers. I asked him about his plans for the day. He told me first off he was going to the library to check his e-mail.

"It's Red123@homeless.net if you need me."

"You're right here."

"True."

I said, "You have a good day."

He said, "If you tell me where the garden shears are, I'll trim the bougainvillea for you."

"That's not necessary."

"It could use it."

I said, "Red, why don't you squat in one of those foreclosed houses around town."

"That's against the law."

"So is this!"

"What?"

"Trespassing."

"Most of the desirable foreclosures are already taken."

I shook my head.

"I'll see you tonight," he said.

"Don't wait up for me."

He winked. "Gotcha."

On the way to the office I drove down DeSoto Street and stopped at the house for sale on the nine hundred block. I wrote down the Realtor's name and phone number. I knew that the

SHORT SALE sticker was probably an indication that this stucco ranch was in foreclosure. The house lacked what they call curb appeal. The lawn needed tending, the shrubs pruning, and the hard water stains on the stucco could use a coat of paint. The house looked otherwise undisturbed and serene. I drove around the block and down the alley to take a look at the back. I peeked over the wood fence. The back windows were shuttered with aluminum hurricane panels. There was a shabby little swimming pool half filled with scummy water and a weight bench rusting in the sun. The screen door was torn like maybe it had been sliced with a knife.

When I arrived at the office, my client Cerise Beaudry was slumped on the floor in the hall, and she was beside herself. She could hardly speak for choking back tears. I helped her to her feet and unlocked the office door. I put my arm on her shoulders and led her inside to the sofa. "What's going on, Cerise?" I held her hand. "Talk to me, hon."

She sat there clutching the box of Kleenex on her lap and trembling.

"Take a slow, deep breath," I said. "We've got all the time in the world, Cerise."

She blew her nose and squeezed the tissue in her fist. She wiped her eyes, looked at the ceiling, and shook her head. She patted down her gray hair. She smoothed out the legs of her blue slacks and looked at me.

Cerise's thirty-one-year-old gay son, Ellery, had broken up with his steady boyfriend at a Thanksgiving dinner. Too much drama, he'd told Cerise. "Well, then last week," Cerise said, "Ellery got a call from the ex to come get all his shit out of the condo." When Ellery got there, the jilted ex let him in, pulled a gun out of his pants, pointed it at Ellery, who was scared speechless and must have thought he was a dead man. The lover then smiled and shot himself in the heart. Ellery called 911 and then tried to keep the man alive. "But you can't patch a shattered heart," Cerise said. "So then Ellery's covered in that asshole's blood. He rode in the ambulance and talked to the friend all the way to Everglades General. 'Stay with me,' he said. 'Hang in there.' The cretin died," Cerise said. Then the autopsy showed that the deceased was HIV-positive, so now Ellery was having his blood tested, but you couldn't be sure for three months. Cerise told me that Ellery was so devastated at what happened he couldn't sleep, and he was back on those goddamn prescriptions that took him so long in rehab to get off of, and he wouldn't talk to her, and he quit his job at the nightclub.

"I'm so sorry, Cerise."

She told me that the dead bastard's mother was now under observation because, it turned out, she'd already been suspected of being complicit in her son's seventeen previous suicide attempts and was being evaluated by doctors to see if she had that Munchausen-by-proxy thingy. "At the funeral, the crazy bitch threw herself on her son's casket and vowed to join him soon, and I hope to God she does."

Cerise cried into her hands. She put her head between her knees. "I'm overwhelmed," she said. "No matter what I do, life gets worse. My baby," she said, "my poor baby."

I said, "What do you need today, Cerise?"

Cerise, herself, is a suffering soul who told me at our first session years ago that her mother tried unsuccessfully to kill herself after she was raped by a priest. Cerise was nine at the time, and the priest had also fondled her. "She burned out her vagina."

"Excuse me?"

"With a glowing piece of wood she pulled from the fireplace."

"Why did she do that?"

"God told her to."

"But she lived?"

"Yes."

"She was lucky."

"You think so?"

Back then when Cerise first came to me, before the meds, she told me that the morning light through her bedroom window blinds cast shadows on her wall that instructed her how to conduct her day. She saw crosses everywhere she looked, including, one morning, in the middle of my forehead. I asked her what that meant. She said that I'd been sent to earth to save her. I said, Sent from where? From the Void Room, she said. By whom? The Doorman.

Cerise got by on her disability checks and by cleaning houses off the books. She cleaned my house one morning every other week in exchange for our sessions. She lived in a bedraggled single-wide at Trainer's Mobile Home Park on Melancholy Beach Boulevard. Either the roof was leaking, the AC window unit was kaput, or FPL had shut off her power. She had no car. I'd given her a bicycle, but it got stolen. She was on Clozapine for her schizophrenia. She got treated, if that's the right verb, at the psych clinic at Memorial, where they kept trying out new meds on her.

At that first session I asked her what she thought of God's asking her mother to mutilate herself. She told me when God talks, you don't question; you don't resist. She said, Yes, He spoke to her as well.

I said, "He's that powerful, then?"

She said, "I don't know if He's powerful, but knowing Him is a powerful experience."

"So why are you talking with me now and not with Him?"

"He stopped talking to me when I started on the meds."

"Do you miss Him?"

"Hell, no!" Cerise told me that Vladimir, her current live-in Russian boyfriend, didn't appreciate my calling him a parasite and a layaway.

"*Layabout*, Cerise. Parasite, layabout, and malingerer. And, well, you're not really supposed to tell him what I say to you."

"He will hurt you, Mr. Wylie."

"I don't think so. That would mean getting off the comfy chair."

"He can be a bad man."

"Does he hit you?"

"Not hard."

"Cerise, Cerise," I said. "We've talked about this pattern before. You let a man into your life, and the man takes advantage of your compassionate nature."

Cerise folded her hands and closed her eyes. "So be it."

I went home at lunch to check on Django. I'd built him a nest of flannel shirts on the couch, and there he was curled asleep with his arm around a plushy duck. Well, it's not really an arm, is it? I sat beside him and patted him awake. He crawled up my shirt and sat on my shoulder. He sneezed on my neck. I called Carlos and asked if he could get me into a foreclosed house.

"Why?"

I told Carlos Wayne's story.

He said, "The guy is nuts."

"I want to see what he saw in that house, smell what he smelled, hear what he heard, maybe figure out what triggered his fantasy."

"Call the Realtor."

"I need to be there alone."

"If your client broke in, like you say, and if the owners let the maintenance slide, then my guess is you can still get in the way your basket case did."

"I might get busted."

"You might."

I told him we should talk about the Halliday case. I told him I had rehearsal today. He said he'd meet me at the bar after his shift tomorrow.

Empathy is being able to imagine the link between you and the other. It's being able to blur the boundary between the two of you. I look at how a person moves his body and face, and I copy it, and I wait to see what thoughts and sentiments arise in my mind. Emotions don't lie, but you certainly can lie about them. You're angry, but you say, I'm not angry, but then, perhaps, just for a moment, you draw your eyebrows down and together, flash those vertical wrinkles on your forehead, press your lips together, and you feel that anger. Change your expression and you change your nervous system. If you move your hands in a tender way, you'll begin to experience tenderness. Learned that in acting class. Your natural-born liar understands that everyone is watching his transpicuous face, and he knows that an easy smile is the cleverest mask. You might ape his smile and think here is a contented man. Gestures, however, may belie the counterfeit smile. He brushes a nonexistent piece of lint from his slacks, drums his fingers, leans forward. Watch his feet. They turn toward what they like or desire and away from what they fear or suspect.

I was at the Eden Playhouse working on feeling T-Bone's exhilaration, his joy about life after death and the promise of eternal salvation. T-Bone's the character I play in the second play in our evening of one-acts, *The Sweeter the Meat*. He's a former alcoholic, junkie, outlaw biker, but now he's found Jesus. He's slain in the spirit and knows he is saved. Easy enough to slap on the brilliant smile, brighten the bountiful eyes. I stood on my toes like I couldn't hold the good news inside, like I was bursting with beatific energy. I started hopping, pounding my fists in the air. Hiroshi, our director, asked me to take it down a notch or several. "It's only life everlasting, Wylie; it's not a weekend with Cate Blanchett."

I drove to the Silver Palace to meet Bay for a drink. He was going to work in forty-five minutes, so he was drinking coffee. When he plays poker, Bay dresses like his idea of a tourist so that he'll stick out at a table full of surly hombres in shades and cowboy hats, so that he'll look all plump and ripe for the picking. That night he wore a red polo shirt, olive-green Bermuda shorts, blue socks with his slip-on sandals, a ball cap that read ARKANSAS THE NATURAL STATE, and a plaid fanny pack. His guileless getup was not going to fool the regulars, but it might fool a novice into thinking he's got a chance here to juice this orange. "Hope," Bay likes to say, "is the poker player's worst enemy."

We were sitting at the Center Bar in the middle of all the noise and frenzy. Bay lit a cigarette with his thumb and then blew out the flame. "Playing against the house is a loser's game. These slot jockeys think they're here to make money, but they're really here for the *chance* to make money. If they made money every time they came here, it'd be too much like work, and they'd quit."

"How's Marlena?"

"She wants me to take her to Disney World."

"Are you going to?"

"How could I say no?" Bay crushed out his cigarette, pulled another out of the air. "By the way, I asked around about the late Mr. Halliday."

"And?"

"Had a reputation for being tough. One time he bit the tip of a guy's nose off during a particularly difficult negotiation."

"Holy shit!"

"He paid for the guy's plastic surgery."

"How do you know this but the cops don't?"

"Who says they don't?"

"So do you think Halliday was clean?"

"Mr. Halliday ran a very lucrative cash business, Wylie. The gambling boats, I'm talking about. There aren't many of those around, and they tend to attract the attention of our Italian friends, if you know what I mean."

I knew what he meant. I was present at the final night of Bay's house game, the night these two sturdy, well-upholstered, pasta-fed gentlemen in thin black leather jackets walked in and told Bay to take a seat and told the rest of us to fold our cards and head down the street to the pub and buy ourselves thirty-minute cocktails. The gentlemen then told Bay they were interested in running the game. Bay said he wasn't looking for partners. When they didn't respond, when they didn't even blink, he said that maybe he could use some help, actually, and offered to cut them in for 20 percent. And then 40 percent. One gentleman smiled. The other did not. The smiler said, You don't understand. We are not here tonight to negotiate. Bay said, Now I understand, and then he handed over the keys to the place.

That happened not long after two African-American guys in baggy basketball uniforms and masks busted through the door with a steel battering ram and tried to rob the players. Easy pickings, they figured, until three guys opened fire, two of whom were cops, so there was no investigation to speak of, and the bodies were carried out to the Everglades and buried in the muck. So I was told. I was not present that evening.

A woman screamed. The red light above a video poker machine flashed, and electronic circus music played, the same dozen happy notes over and over. People gathered around the winner and her lucky machine. She took a photo of the screen display with her smartphone. An attendant asked her for her driver's license and

Social Security number. The winner bought herself an 18 Carat Gold Margarita and wiped away her tears.

I said, "You don't think Halliday got himself mixed up with the wrong people?"

Bay said, "Find out who catered the boats. Find out who picked up the trash."

I checked my watch.

Bay said, "You going to stay and watch me play?"

"I'm meeting Phoebe."

"I'll see you on New Year's Eve."

I met Phoebe at Kurosawa for the eleven o'clock seating. Kurosawa's our favorite restaurant, a little Japanese omakase place tucked into a Russian neighborhood in Sunny Isles. There are seventeen seats, two workers—Kevin the chef, and Wendy the waitress—and no menus. You eat what Kevin bought off the boat at Haulover Marina hours earlier or had flown in overnight from Tokyo. We sat at the bar so we could watch Kevin at work. "No more bad food" is Phoebe's motto. Life is short, she says, so meals should be long and ambrosial. We ordered our bento boxes and a bottle of soft, smooth organic sake. The night's fare featured carrot-egg tofu, eel tempura, simmered whiting and okra jelly with shiso, and simmered lotus root. We toasted the new year. We kissed in that European way—on both cheeks.

I said, "We have to stop meeting like this."

"Kai thinks you're gay. You knew that, right?"

"Why?"

"You're a bachelor." Phoebe put air quotes around the noun. "You act. You collect Fiestaware. Your house is cluttered with vintage bric-a-brac. You live with a cat. You read novels. You talk about movies in public."

"I have all the symptoms."

My cell phone vibrated. My father calling. "Hi, Dad. You're up late."

"Who is this?"

"It's Wylie."

"What do you want?"

"You called me."

"Why?"

"I don't know. Are you okay?"

"Stop playing games."

"Dad, I'm going to hang up. You go to bed."

"Who is this?"

"Good night, Dad. See you on Thursday."

I walked Phoebe to her car behind the Datcha dance club. She clicked her remote and the car's lights flashed. I opened the door, and she slid into the seat. "You need to find a woman who can reciprocate. You've done this before."

"I loved two women in my life, you and Georgia. The others were sweet but inconsequential romances."

"What about Molly Seagrove?"

I met Molly at Knew and Used, a secondhand bookshop in Eden where she worked. I had been surprised and delighted to find a copy of Edward Trelawny's recollections of the last days of Byron and Shelley, a book that I had previously owned, read, and lost three different times. I brought my prize to the register. Molly looked at it, smiled, and said she remained skeptical of Trelawny's claim to have snatched Shelley's undamaged heart from the funeral pyre. "But it makes for a good story," she said. "And that's what counts."

I asked her immediately if she wanted to go dancing. And I don't dance. She said yes and we found ourselves that night at the bandstand on the beach awkwardly bopping to fifties doo-wop played by Poochie and the Skylarks. We talked about books and movies and Molly passed my snarky but crucial *Forrest Gump/Black Swan* test: she disliked them both as much as I did. We went to her place on Cleveland Street. She led me through the darkened house to her bedroom.

When I picked her up that Saturday for an outing to Shark Valley, I met her mom, Désirée, and her two children. She hadn't mentioned any of them at the dance. Joey was seven, the girl, Carson, four. I took Molly and the kids to the beach the following Sunday, and, of course, the kids were jealous of the mother's attention to the interloper. Carson grew a bit more open to my presence after she and I took a stroll along the beach, carefully stepping around the stranded jellyfish. She looked up at me and said, "Would you like to hold my cute little hand?" And I did.

That evening I learned that Désirée and her boyfriend Snooky Scampini lived with Molly and the kids. Snooky was snaggletoothed and squinty-eyed. His dark hair was thinning; his lips were glossy. He was the only English-speaking dishwasher at the Mangrove Diner. He went to Mass every morning and twice on Sunday.

When I asked Molly about the kids' dad, she told me his name was Ezra Seagrove, and he was a calamitous drug addict whom the children loved to death. "He's not without his saccharine charms," she told me. Then she told me that she was still married to Ezra, and that led to an uncomfortable discussion and to tears and confusion and to my telling Molly that she needed to choose. And that was the last time I saw her. I said, "I can't do this." Knew and Used has since closed. The house on Cleveland Street was vacant for a year and a half before an Asian couple moved in. Snooky left his job at the diner. I still check the obits for Seagrove and Scampini. Molly once told me that her mom grew up in Atlanta and missed the place, and that's where I picture them now when I think of them.

5

The bar is called Leo's, but insiders call it the House of Blues. It's a cop bar in Eden owned by the Police Benevolent Association, the cops' union. It attracts male officers, county and cities, and the women who love them from all over South Everglades. It's always a little intimidating to walk in. Anyone who's not a cop is suspect. I'm barely tolerated, and that only because I know Carlos and have helped the Eden Police Department out with some cases, but I find it hard to relax in there. A lot of heavyset guys in Dockers with buzz cuts and brushy mustaches, wearing their polo shirts a size too small. Lots of aggressive posturing, cursing, trash-talking about the Dolphins, and arm wrestling.

The bar itself is pleasant enough, a kind of faux–Irish country pub. Stone floors, timbered ceilings, whitewashed walls. There's a pool table beyond the bar, a dozen high-tops in the center of the room, and a row of tables facing cushioned benches against the wall. That's where I spotted Carlos, his tie loosened, his reading glasses at the tip of his nose, studying a report and absently swirling a cocktail straw in his gin and tonic. At the back of the bar was a room that I'd never seen into. The door was always shut and, I'd guess, locked. Carlos called it the Debriefing Room, and when I'd asked him what went on in there, he said, Business. The door was guarded by a retired cop named Frankie the Golfer, who sat by the door in an upholstered bar chair that he leaned back against the wall. Over his head were memorial photographs of fallen officers. I slapped Carlos on the back and slid into my seat. I ordered a Ketel One martini, straight up, dry, with a twist, and a Bombay and tonic for Carlos.

Carlos said, "You still thinking about the Halliday case?"

"I don't think he did it."

"Why?"

"A hunch."

"A hunch?"

"Intuition. It's what you don't pay me for, remember?"

"Didn't I buy you lunch at Oppenheimer's?"

"I paid."

"Much appreciated. You're letting your imagination get carried away."

"That's what you want me to do."

"No, I want you around for your scrupulous observations."

"You haven't come across any photo albums or home videos or photo files on his computer?"

"Nothing."

"Doesn't that seem peculiar?"

"It does, but not everyone is sentimental. He had no pictures on his cell phone, either."

"The waiter at the restaurant told me Halliday was there at four the day he died. You said he'd been at the mall for a couple of hours and got home at five. How can he be in two places at the same time?"

"He can't. The waiter was mistaken about the time. We have credit card records from Banana Moon and Brookstone."

"Maybe his wife used the card." I got my dirty martini on the rocks with two olives speared on a plastic toothpick, served in a highball glass. Before I could say anything, Carlos held up his hand, thanked Gretchen, and then told me to let it go.

"How hard is it to remember a drink order?"

"Hey, there's no whining in a cop bar." Carlos held up a finger for me to wait, and he took a call on his cell. I saw Officer Shanks at the bar, chatting up a chiseled young brunette who'd obviously done some serious bodybuilding. Carlos ended his call.

I said, "I've been doing some research on Malacoda and McArthur."

"What did you find out?"

"Malacoda sets up these bogus think tanks and political action committees that undermine the values they claim to represent. The American Council for Environmental Preservation lobbies to ease pollution control."

"That's politics."

"His Concerned Citizens for a Healthy America is underwritten by Big Pharma."

"So he's not the Boy Scout I thought he was."

"McArthur's mother was killed by Vito 'The Busboy' Borzilleri and Remo 'Fungi' Lombardo. The Busboy's cousin Gaetano Borci was McArthur's partner in the auto dealership."

"So?"

"Seems fishy to me."

"Coyote, you don't know the rules of the game. Best you stay on the sidelines. Capisce?" Carlos excused himself. "Got to see a man about a horse."

On the muted TV above the bar came the subtitled notice of an Amber Alert for a missing fourteen-year-old girl who had been taken from her front yard in Eden Hills by two men wearing masks and driving a black SUV. I watched Officer Shanks admiring himself in the mirror over the back bar while he spoke with his bubbly young inamorata. Every time he saw himself he raised his chin slightly and turned to peek at his profile. The adoring glance in a mirror is, of course, something his fawning bodybuilder could appreciate. I thought he might blow himself a kiss. He liked what he saw in the mirror until he saw me watching him. Then he walked to my table, took a wide stance, put his hands on his hips, in a pose they call "command presence," I think, and said, "Your pal Carlos won't always be around to protect you."

I said, "From what?"

Shanks had a short, thick neck and a small, square noggin. His lips were thin, his chin cleft, his hair a few days gone from clean-shaven.

He said, "Watch your back, pussy!"

His eyes were tiny, almost translucent blue, unnerving and unblinking. These were the shuttered windows to his soul. He was determined that nothing be revealed there, but it was clear from his petulant gaze that nothing you could say would ever register with him, that, in fact, he held zero interest in anything you might say or think or feel. He was in the grip of a single thought, whatever that might be. This was a man who spoke, but never had a conversation.

He said, "I will not be disrespected. I'm the law, my friend."

Carlos said, "I'm glad to see you two boys have made up." Carlos smiled at Shanks and took his seat. Shanks made a gun with his thumb and fingers, pointed it at my face, and smiled. He went back to the bar.

I said, "Carlos, that dipshit just threatened me."

"Don't take it personally. He's one of our pit bulls."

"I want to report the threat."

"You just did."

"What'll happen?"

"I'll speak with him."

"You already have."

"Again." Carlos held up his hand and signaled for two more drinks. "This is a family matter. We'll take care of it."

"The guy's a psycho."

"Coyote, listen! A bad cop may not be respected, but he is protected."

"Why?"

"If he's tarnished, we're all tarnished. Now, I'm asking you as a friend to let this thing with Shanks go. I'll shorten his leash. I promise."

"You're supposed to protect us from guys like him."

"I know what my job is."

Gretchen brought our drinks.

I looked at mine. "What's this?"

"A mantini," Gretchen said. "Royal Crown and vermouth. It'll put hair on your chest."

Perdita Curry, of all people, took a seat at the bar, ordered a drink, and had a look around. She smiled at Carlos. I said, "You know her?"

"Badge bunny."

"A little long in the tooth for that, isn't she?"

"Wrote for the old *Journal-Gazette* until they caught her making up stories. Now she writes books."

"She told me. I met her outside the Hallidays.'"

"All her books have 'deadly' in the title. *Deadly Nightshade, Deadly Embrace, Silent But Deadly.* Inez has read a couple."

"Verdict?"

"Deadly prose."

Frankie the Golfer stood up. The door to the Debriefing Room opened, and a man, an attorney I recognized but couldn't name from local news broadcasts, walked out followed by two young assistants, I guessed, and a large balding gentleman wearing a blue guayabera and chewing an unlit cigar. The lawyer thanked the large man for his time, and they all shook hands. The lawyer and his assistants left the bar. The large man went back to the room and closed the door. Frankie the Golfer took his seat.

I said, "What was that all about?"

"Attorney Fine—"

"He's the lawyer on *Help Me, Howard!*" I just remembered him.

"The same. He's running for district court judge, and he's here to ask for the support of the union."

"The big guy?"

"Clete Meatyard. Head of the union. You don't become a judge, or anything else, in Everglades County without Meatyard's blessing. He's a thug, but he's our thug. The union's the most powerful political machine in the county."

"Why do you need a thug?"

"Because we deal with politicians and bureaucrats who have never had a gun held to their heads and have never had to worry if they'd make it home from work that day and if they'd ever see their wife and kids again, and those demagogues and number-crunchers want to tell us how to do our jobs. Sometimes you have to play hardball, and Clete Meatyard is our ace." Carlos took his straw out of his drink and placed it beside three others. He held up his glass. "Happy New Year, if I don't see you before that." We toasted the New Year and our friendship. Carlos said, "It takes a toll, Coyote. Dealing with depravity and cruelty all day long, day after day."

While I was at Leo's with Carlos, Wayne Vanderhyde, my contentious client—I would learn some days later, when his troubles, we might say, were over, when he sat down with Carlos and explained, or tried to explain, his confounding and appalling behavior—was just then at the Home Depot buying a Weber grill, a barbecue tool set, a gas-grill rotisserie, and a sixteen-inch Homelite electric chain saw. He drove home and assembled the grill in his backyard, cooled himself down in the outside shower, got dressed, peeked in at the girl in the bathtub, drove to a windowless strip club on Griffin Road called Taste O' Honey, sat down stage-side, and watched a woman named Sable dance to some Lynyrd Skynyrd number. Sable called herself a Holy Hottie. She had preternaturally blond hair, permanent eyebrows, and a tattoo of the crucified Christ on the small of her back. She danced for Jesus, she told anyone who asked. Wayne bought Sable a fourteen-dollar cola and himself a double shot of Jack Daniel's. Sable told Wayne that if Jesus were on earth today He'd be preaching right here at the Taste to the sorry likes of him and these other desperate and hollow men and to this flourish of strumpets on stage.

Wayne confessed to Sable that he was being tormented by dangerously wicked fantasies, and she prayed over him. He told her he had stopped taking his antidepressant medications. You don't need drugs, she said. He told her his new therapist was no goddamn help whatsoever. Sable told him all the help he needed was Jesus Christ. Accept Him into your heart tonight, Wayne. They went to the VIP room, and they fell to their knees, and they prayed for strength and forgiveness. Sable laid her hands on Wayne, and she began to weep and to speak in tongues. Wayne had a boner as stiff as an I-beam.

He stopped at Publix on his way home and bought an aluminum meat mallet, four bags of ice, a tank of propane, a meat thermometer, and six bottles of Bone Suckin' barbecue sauce. He ran into Dave Companion mopping up a spill in the dairy aisle. Dave said he was surprised to see Wayne at work on his day off. Wayne said,

"Why is that, Dave?" Dave shrugged and said he was just trying to make conversation. Dave would later tell a reporter that Wayne was a good worker—steady and reliable—but he was boring as dry toast and drab as dishwater. "He didn't interact with people. It just never occurred to him that that was something you did."

At the register, Myka Flores smiled and told Wayne she hoped she'd be getting an invitation to his barbecue. "What are you cooking, papito?"

"Pig."

When he got home, Wayne went online and updated his blog, which he called *In Private and in Publix.* He linked to a Borgesian website called *The Indiscernible Library*, which, it turns out, is a collection of books that have only appeared in other books. The books were unwritten, unpublished, unread, and they cannot, of course, be checked out. And then Wayne wrote that he had not written a number of books himself, and he listed three of them: *Until Nevermas*, *Boffo!*, and *Practical Gastromancy.*

6

I began my New Year's Eve festivities at three P.M. at a somewhat subdued party at Almost Home. I smuggled in some vodka in a Zephyrhills water bottle, picked up two plastic cups of ice from the snack table, and handed one to Dad. I poured. We toasted. "Another goddamn year," he said.

The staff had mounted large sheets of white paper on the cafeteria walls for writing down New Year's resolutions. As far as I could tell, only the aides had taken advantage, and their resolutions mostly had to do with diets and deprivation. There would be no more smoking of cigarettes, no third mojito, no Entenmann's, no Ben & Jerry's Chunky Monkey, no chicharrónes, no bacon double cheeseburgers, and no more Junior Torres, "who put me through hell and forced me to give up EVERYTHING I loved and EVERYONE I cared about."

Dad said the past was ahead of us. It's right there in front of our eyes. What we can't see is the future. It's always sneaking up behind us. He looked up at the bedsheet full of balloons tacked to the ceiling and said, "I won't remember this tomorrow, however." He asked me what year it was about to be, and I told him. He said when something is over, like his eighty-two years, then it all seems to have happened at once, in the blink of an eye. "That's a little hard to take," he said.

I told him we should start planning our annual vacation. Maybe we should go back to Arkansas, to Hot Springs. Go to the track, to the baths. Eat at Doe's. What do you think? His eyes were closed.

A man who looked like John Prine sat beside me, patted me on the knee, and thanked me for coming. He wore a navy blue cardigan over his white T-shirt. He called me David, said my mother, his sister Buttons, had told him I wasn't going to be able to make it this year. "Why would she tell me that?"

"It was a last-minute deal," I said. I told him things in Pennsylvania were just fine. Cold, of course. Yes, business was good. Couldn't be better.

He told me how much he had dreaded spending the holidays alone, and now he wouldn't have to. "It's not right to live so far from family." He told me about the prostate treatments and the trouble with his teeth. He said, "Look, I'm not going to keep you. Thank you, David. Your coming means the world to me." We stood. He wiped his tears and kissed my cheek. We hugged goodbye, a bit awkwardly, as relative strangers might, and he walked off down the hall. He waved once without turning around.

I went to the snack table to replenish my ice and saw an aide sitting by herself, crying. I said, "The holidays can be difficult." She nodded and wiped her eyes with a tissue. I sat at the table. She said, "I gave him everything. I did whatever he asked." I guessed that *him* was Junior Torres.

She said, "I even stuck around when he went to jail for stealing from the Dollar Store where he worked." She sat back, took a deep breath, and looked at me for the first time. She tucked a lank strand of brown hair behind her right ear. "We had a baby, and then he left me for this eighteen-year-old tramp. Bitch is still in high school." She cried.

I asked her if there was anything I could do. She said she wouldn't mind having some of my springwater. She smiled and told me her name was Gabriela. I got another cup of ice and poured. She told me all Junior cared about besides young pussy was his miserable paintball career even though he sucked at it. She said she kept on going back to him despite the beatings and the insults and the screaming in front of their daughter. But now she was moving on. She had no debt. She had her associate's degree and a good, secure job. She had her mother, who helped her with little Avalon. She had a future. She was going to soar, and Junior, that asshole, was going to crash and burn.

At ten seconds before five, more or less, the countdown to the new year began, and the balloons were released. I woke Dad, and we all sang "Auld Lang Syne." I walked him to his suite. He showered while I made us a pot of coffee. He came out to the table in the Ralph Lauren Chelsea plaid pajamas I'd bought him for his birthday. He took his fifteen evening pills. He told me about the New Year's Eve when he and Mom went to New York by train. "Before you kids were born." They ice-skated in Central Park; they went to Mass at St. Patrick's. "Your mother bought herself a silk kimono at Macy's." They stayed at the Taft Hotel near Times Square, ordered breakfast—Belgian waffles—from room service, ate the best steaks of their lives at the Taft Grill Room. "It was like we were in a movie, Wylie. Xavier Cougat and his orchestra onstage. We samba'd till two in the morning."

On the way to Bay's house, I stopped at Publix for cat food, cat treats, and cat toys. In the shopping-cart corral, a Venise-sized woman with a roll of fat sagging over her crotch stood in front of the scale that promised your exact weight. She told her hefty daughter that no, she would not step up on the scale; it only goes to three hundred. The daughter wore a T-shirt that read, IS IT HOT IN HERE OR IS IT ME? I figured I should get Red a little something to celebrate with. I'd noticed empty bottles of gas-station beer in my recycling bin. I saw Wayne Vanderhyde stocking soda in the beverage aisle. My first thought was to avoid him, but that seemed reprehensibly childish. I said hello and asked him what kind of beer he would recommend for my guest.

He said, "Beer's beer." He told me he drank Bud Light.

I said, "Happy New Year."

He said, "Back at you."

I told him I'd see him next week. I bought Red a six-pack of Dogfish Head IPA. I bought a Styrofoam cooler and a bag of ice. So now I'd stop at home before going to Bay's.

When I got home, Red was gone. I left the cooler of beer with a note and a New Year's greeting beside his recycled nylon camp chair. I gave Django a gourmet kitty treat, but he just batted it around the kitchen. We played with a rubber golf ball for a while until he decided that biting my finger was more fun. Reward the good; ignore the bad. That's what the cat books say.

I arrived at Bay's canal-side home around seven and let myself in. I saw a lot of unfamiliar men standing around the living room in casino souvenir ball caps and those wraparound sunglasses that some Italian designer had decided we should all wear for the next few years, the kind you can wear backward on your head when you're out at a fast-food restaurant with the kids. A couple of guys wore aloha shirts with pictures of Vegas landmarks and winning poker hands. More women than I would have guessed had plumped their lips and Botoxed their faces so that their conspicuously arched brows seemed similarly frozen in surprise. One slender and elegant gentleman in a white linen suit and black silk shirt stood facing the wall, stirring his drink and speaking earnestly to no one I could see and loudly enough so that I knew he had bought some doll named Yolanda a new silver Lexus. "That should clear up her psoriasis," he said. I assumed he had a Bluetooth attached to the ear on the dark side of his skull.

Bay handed me a glass of eggnog. We stood by the piano. He told me he had made $125,000 this year at the poker table, and many of the kind folks assembled here had made significant contributions to his income. They deserved a party. "I want to make two hundred thousand this year, but I'll have to play four instead of three nights a week to make it happen."

"That almost sounds like work."

"It's a hard way to make an easy living."

"What's the hard part?"

"Coping with the idea that you aren't doing anything worthwhile with your life, that you aren't making a difference, not making the world a better place." Bay pointed out a guy in a rumpled gray suit, sitting on the leather sofa absorbed with his PDA. "That's Open Mike," he said. "Mike Lynch." What Open Mike was doing, Bay told me, was checking on the NBA scores and on the latest lines on the college bowl games. "If the Suns don't cover the spread against the Celtics tonight, someone else will own Open Mike's Escalade in the morning." Bay told me that Open Mike had lost at least a hundred grand last year at the poker tables alone, money that should have gone to his son's medical treatment. His wife finally left him when she couldn't take his absence and heedlessness any longer. And through it all, the son's battle with leukemia, the separation, the divorce, he never, when he wasn't at work, missed a night in the chair.

"What's his job?"

"Firefighter. Works twenty-four-hour days, ten days a month. One on, two off. Plenty of downtime at the firehouse for him to play Internet poker. He told me he could have five games going at once and in six hours could get in five thousand hands. You can imagine how much he hates fires."

Bay told me that Marlena was working a New Year's party at the Universe. They'd hook up later at the Silver Palace, where he'd booked a luxury suite for the weekend. I told him about my wanting to get inside the Parkers' house on DeSoto Street. I wondered if his old partner could get me inside under the pretense of showing me the place. Bay had been my real estate attorney way back when. In fact, he found my house, loaned me the down, and did all the paperwork. It took me years to repay him. Bay told me that the ex-partner wasn't talking to him. "I got the bastard five hundred hits of Ecstasy, and he hasn't paid me, doesn't respond to e-mails, and won't answer his phone."

I was able to repay Bay the favor about a year after I bought the house when I became his therapist. After listening to him twice a week for six months, I was able to testify at a court hearing that Bay was under tremendous stress and was headed for an emotional collapse. So now he collected disability, not a lot, but enough to cover his monthly nut. And I lived with the knowledge that I was complicit in a fraud. Bay consoled me. "Corruption is our default mode," he said.

When Georgia left me, Bay sent over an escort friend of his named Cinnamon to keep me company. He'd already paid for her services, she told me. "He said to give you the whole girlfriend experience." Her driver, Franco, parked out front and read a James W. Hall novel while he waited. I told him he could sit on the porch. It would be more comfortable. He said he'd be fine. Cinnamon and I sat on the sofa. I apologized, told her I was constitutionally unable to proceed with our carnal commerce. "I think the nuns ruined me for this sort of thing." I made us drinks. A 7 and 7 for her, a vodka on the rocks for me. I asked her how she'd gotten into this business.

She said, "You don't approve?"

In fact, I didn't approve, but I didn't want to offend her, and she certainly didn't need my or anyone else's approval.

She told me she was working her way through med school at FIU. She'd graduate without any debt, which was more than most young doctors could say. "The job's boring, but it pays well."

"Boring?"

"After you've sucked a thousand dicks, they all begin to look alike. And the dicks they're attached to all begin to sound alike."

Bay told me later that Franco's wife was expecting, so he'd taken on the second job at the escort service. His day job at the dog track was shooting greyhounds in the back of the head for ten dollars a pop. I said, He does not. Bay said, Okay, he doesn't.

Bay said he'd find out on Monday if the Parkers' house was in foreclosure. When I told Bay about Carlos's idea of the importance of order, he said it's all just the illusion of order. "Everything is out of control, way beyond fixing. We've got about sixty years to right the ship before we reach the tipping point, and then all that's left is the endgame." On that note, I told him good night. I had one more stop to make.

At Venise's house the supermarket deli platters were spread out on the kitchen counter: Cubanitos, chicken tenders, peel-and-eat shrimp, and veggies with dip. I put the champagne I'd brought in the fridge, took the vodka out of the freezer, and made myself a martini. Venise, Oliver, and Patience were in the middle of a game of Monopoly. I refreshed their drinks. Oliver told me he'd bought twenty pounds of unrefined shea butter on eBay. Did I need any? I didn't. Treats blemishes and burns. No, thanks. Any old wounds? he said.

Patience went bankrupt when she checked into Venise's hotel on Indiana Avenue. She dropped her Scottie dog into the cardboard box, pushed away from the table, and told me I looked tense. She said, May I? and stood and massaged my shoulders, which suddenly felt like coiled steel.

She said, "Holy moley!" She politely punched at the muscle. "I could hit you with a sledgehammer and you wouldn't feel it. What's going on?"

"The usual."

"You need to get this mangle out of your body, Wylie. You'll get sick." She sat back down and took my hand in hers.

Venise said, "Patience can tell your fortune."

I said, "You're going to read my palm?"

Patience said, "You can learn a lot about a person by watching his hands."

"But you can't learn his future," I said.

Patience smiled. She turned my hand to the left and examined it, then to the right. She ran her fingers over mine. She looked at me and squinted. "You don't want anyone to know you, do you?"

Suddenly this parlor game was making me uncomfortable. I wanted my hand back.

Patience said she had a confession. She didn't read palms. "I just hold your hand, close my eyes."

I said, "What do you see?"

Patience closed her eyes. She said she saw a shimmering green sky and a field of snow, not snow, actually, but sand, and now the sky is mauve, and there seems to be a man flying toward her.

Venise whooped. She had vanquished Oliver.

At midnight we toasted the New Year and listened to the drunken neighbors firing off their pistols. Oliver said he was about to collapse, bade us good night, and shuffled off to bed. Patience said she'd wait for the shooting to stop before pedaling her bike home. We cleaned up the kitchen and wrapped the leftovers in foil. Venise said it looked like she wouldn't be starting her diet tomorrow.

7

I decided I'd get the year off to a flying start by making a list of everything I ought to do. Turned out I had eighty-eight items on my list, from *Colonoscopy* to *Organize the garage*. I drew empty boxes beside each task so that I could check them off as I went merrily along accomplishing the impossible. Django lay on his back and stared at me upside down. *More cat toys.* Lately I'd been getting these temporary floating zigzag question marks in my field of vision, which blinded me to whatever was behind them. That couldn't be good. So number two on the list was *Eye appointment.* Number three was *Solve the mystery of who killed the Hallidays.* Even though I wasn't sure it *was* a mystery. (I *was* sure, however, that the official version of events did not make sense. My response to their certainty would be patience. I trusted my intuition. I could afford to be wrong and had nothing to prove being right. I'd tell Carlos, You haven't solved the case. Yes, we have, he'd say. But I wouldn't take yes for an answer. I don't like the idea of a person or persons getting away with murder.) *Buy a camera* was on the list; *Reseat* *the toilet* and *Walk five miles a day.* This would be the year when I finally read Proust. Number seventeen: *Buy* In Search of Lost Time, *Modern Library set.* I pinned the list to the bulletin board over my desk and decided to do something not on the list—visit the foreclosed house on DeSoto Street.

I drove up the alley behind DeSoto Street and pulled into the gravel parking space behind the house. I grabbed my flashlight and hopped the fence. Something furry and freshly dead floated in the scum of the swimming pool. I reached through the tear in the screen and opened the patio door. The kitchen door was ajar. "Hello the house," I yelled and waited. Nothing. I walked inside and sneezed. I noticed a brown stain on the ceiling over the stove, like maybe an espresso pot had exploded years ago. I could tell from the scuff marks on the white tile floor where the kitchen table had been situated and the two chairs that sat opposite each other. I smelled the dogs, and sneezed again, but I didn't see the leashes on their pegs. I found a manila envelope stuffed with appliance warrantees on top of the fridge. I opened a drawer and found a note that read: *I see you everywhere I look. Your secret admirer.* And then in a different handwriting—printing, really: *Love what you've done with the house, You know who.* I put the note in my pocket. I walked to the master bedroom. I heard the squeal of brakes and I froze. The windows here in the front of the house were undraped and unshuttered. No cars out front. I relaxed, switched off my flashlight.

I stood where I imagined Wayne had stood, and I looked across the room to the corner where his lion had crouched. And then I saw what could have been a bloodstain or a wine stain in the shape of Africa in the center of the gray carpet. Had the stain provoked Wayne's fantasy? I wondered. And then I heard what sounded like a hoist and the clanging of chains. I listened. It was coming from out back. I tried the front door, but couldn't get the dead bolt to cooperate. I went to the kitchen, hoping no one would walk in and ask me what I was up to. I got out my cell phone and prepared to speed-dial Carlos. I peeked out the back door and saw my car hooked to the back of a wrecker. I ran out to the yard. Too late. The wrecker pulled away, towing my car behind it. I yelled and waved my arms over my head. The driver had to have heard me. I called Carlos. He told me where I could pick up the car. "Bring a hundred bucks cash with you," he said.

I cleared my throat and sat beside a blind man on the bus-stop bench. I wrote a reminder on my hand to check Wayne's signature against the note I'd found. The blind man quit his humming and asked me where I was going. He nodded and told me to transfer at Cypress to the #12 west, get off at Arborvitae, and walk through Maplewood Plaza to Oleander. He wiped his brow with a bandanna. I asked him if he had change for a dollar. No, he didn't. He had a bus pass—he tapped his shirt pocket—and had stopped carrying cash money altogether. "Been mugged six times."

"You've got a fork in your pocket."

"A knork." He took the flatware out of his pocket and ran his finger along the outer tines. "Sharp. Slice and spear with the same utensil. Take it with me everywhere."

I said, "I'm Wylie."

He said, "I'm Sly."

I said, "No way."

He punched a button on his watch, held it to his ear, and a woman's voice told him the time. He wiped the lenses of his sunglasses. His left eye was a pulpy red mass. I told him he seemed to be bleeding from his eye. He said it was a busted blood vessel. "The Cumadin makes it look worse."

"It looks really, really bad, Sly. I could take you to the emergency room."

He put his glasses back on. "Glad I don't have to look at it."

A blue Mini Cooper pulled up to the curb in front of us. A woman with a shaved head in the passenger seat took our photo with her iPhone. The Mini drove away.

Sly said, "I got twenty-twenty vision in my dreams. Can see the wives, my children, even the dead ones, my fourth-grade classroom, my dog Shep. And I can see myself. Yes, sir, I can see in my dreams all right. And I'm always a little sad to wake up in the dark."

When I got off the bus, I saw a postman in blue shorts and a pith helmet delivering mail to the apartments along Arborvitae Street. He was being shadowed by another postman with a clipboard. The shadow's iPod wires went from his ears down the back of his shirt. I had never heard the phrase "muscle milk" until two days earlier when I was in Shore's Diner sitting next to a thirty-something couple. She said to him, "You drink your muscle milk, and you smoke your cigarettes." They had my attention. Sounded like the beginning of a blues song. She folded a slice of limber bacon and laid it on her buttered toast. Then she folded the toast, dunked it in her coffee, and bit into it. He said, "Who taught you to eat like that?" She said, "No one has to teach you to eat or to pee." He said, "Someone taught you to squat so you wouldn't have urine running down your leg." Anyway, as I was walking past the golf store in the plaza, I looked down and saw a flattened carton with the words MUSCLE MILK. I don't think I would have noticed the carton if I hadn't heard the phrase recently and for the first time.

At the edge of the Home Depot parking lot, behind the tent where they had sold the Christmas trees, two uniformed police officers watched six guys transfer unmarked crates from one semi-trailer to another. One of the cops could have been the seemingly ubiquitous Shanks, but I had to walk closer to find out. And it was.

Shanks and Clarke. When the guys loading the truck saw me, they froze for just a second. I said, "What are you boys up to?" Shanks and Clarke both jerked and turned to see who the hell had gotten the jump on them. They looked spring-loaded. Shanks folded his arms across his chest and tilted his head back so he could look down at me. Clarke made sure I saw his hand resting on the butt of his service revolver. He said, "Get the fuck out of here, jerkwad."

"I'm just standing here."

"This is private property, and you are trespassing."

Shanks said, "It will not take much provocation for me to slap the cuffs on you, partner."

I stood there wishing I had a phone with a camera on it like the bald girl in the Mini, but knowing if I tried using it here, I would lose it in a hurry.

I asked Shanks, "What do you think happened at the Halliday house?"

Clarke got in my face. I could smell the chorizo on his breath. I took a step backward and said I was going.

"You have a nice walk," Shanks said.

"You have a nice watch," I said, indicating the black band on his wrist.

"Impoundment yard's just five blocks up on Oleander."

I missed the days when cops wore those visored service caps with the high crown and the shield right there up front. And they wore ties and black brogans and maybe a fitted jacket or a topcoat or a yellow raincoat. Now they're like storm troopers. The two squad cars passed me, followed by the loaded truck. Shanks gave me a toot and a wave when he drove by.

My car smelled like something had died in it. Then I saw the damp carcass—a possum, it looked like—on the floor behind the driver's seat. I walked back to the impoundment office and told the woman who'd given me my keys and taken my money what I had found. I said, "I want to complain."

She said, "Go right ahead."

"No," I said, "I want to file a written complaint."

She opened a drawer and slid a form to me under the glass partition. She said, "You're wasting your time." She pointed at the form with her pen. "It's in one eye and out the other."

So eyes were going to be a theme today, I thought.

She walked into a back room and returned with a green trash bag and a pair of stiff work gloves.

I drove with the windows down to Kmart and bought carpet shampoo and Febreze. I cleaned the mess as well as I could in the parking lot and then drove to Splash 'n' Lube and had them detail the car. A kid with gold teeth and a neck tattoo (bullet hole dripping blood) opened the back door and jumped away from the car. He waved his chamois in front of his face. He said, "You got a corpse in the trunk?"

Then I stopped at La Mélange to see if I might run into the elusive Pino. I walked inside. The place was empty. The waiter I'd met previously told me he was alone except for the cook, who was napping. He asked me if I wanted a coffee. I didn't, but thanked him. Join me, he said. On the house. He pulled out a chair, and I sat. He told me his name was Luis, and he went to the kitchen. I noticed a photo of Chafin Halliday on the wall. He wore a chef's hat and was carving a roast. The restaurant's name on his white jacket was backward, as if da Vinci had written it.

Luis returned with the coffees and we wished each other a Happy New Year. He asked me what I did for a living, and I told him.

He said, "Crazy people all day long?"

"Not crazy. In pain."

"My sister's crazy," he said. "She thinks her dog Charlie is the devil. She thinks Charlie is trying to control her thoughts."

I told Luis I'd once had a client who brought her dog to our sessions. Genghis, a bullmastiff, would sit alertly by her side and stare at me. Whenever I made a sudden move, he'd growl. If I leaned forward he'd stand. She told me Genghis was a wonderful judge of people; he'd saved her from more than one sorry relationship. I never actually had a client who brought her dog to the office, and I wasn't sure why I made up the story. Maybe to cheer Luis up. I gave Luis my card and asked him to give it to Pino. Tell him I'd like to talk to him.

Later at home I matched Wayne's signature to some of the handwriting on the note. I put the note in my cookie jar. I Googled *Eden family slain*, so I could see if there was anything new about the Hallidays. I helped Django up onto the desk. He stared at the computer screen and tried to catch the cursor. The first hit was, improbably enough, about another crime. On his way to a date with his estranged wife at a popular restaurant on the Intracoastal, Ivan Kouzmanoff stopped by his wife's house, shot his ten-year-old daughter, bound and gagged the fifteen-year-old babysitter, drove to the restaurant, kissed his wife on the cheek, ordered both of their meals, oak-grilled quail and marouli salads, finished the meal with a glass of ouzo, pulled out his pistol, shot his wife in the forehead, and turned the gun on himself. He did not leave a suicide note. Friends and family were stunned. I found out with a little more research that Mr. Kouzmanoff was an attorney who was working for the Tequesta Tribe on the South River burial ground case and that he was prominent in the county's Republican Party circles. He was a well-respected philanthropist—a wing of the McRaney-Lanuer Eye Institute was named for him—and served on the board of several Everglades County arts organizations, including the Eden Playhouse. So we were connected.

I got an e-mail from Phoebe letting me know that she had set up an account for me on thatsamore.com, that she was casting her baited line upon the waters, and that I'd gotten several nibbles already. She said she'd be screening the candidates and would get back to me. I e-mailed her and asked her to cease and desist.

She wrote: *This gal in Colahatchee said she's looking for a guy thirty-five to fifty-five who's a great kisser, won't hit on her mom, will take her to Bali, and goes commando. What do you think?*

I got ready for bed. Django watched me brush my teeth in the mirror. That's when it hit me—the photo of Halliday. I called Carlos and left a message on his cell. "Halliday was left-handed." The photograph had been flipped when it was developed.

8

Cameron was the happiest child I've ever known. He had a bright and constant smile and loved to laugh. He memorized books that he loved and would recite them at the drop of a hat. He was grateful for every meal and gift and said so. He was always thanking people for telling him something he didn't know or pointing out something he had failed to see. Life was a miracle, and Cameron was delighted to be a part of it.

Cameron went off to the state's Honors College—a barefoot-white-kids-with-dreadlocks kind of place—and I worked at Winn-Dixie and went to the local branch of the state U. I got my bachelor's in psychology, and Cameron dropped out of school two weeks before he would have graduated. He came back home, grew quiet, and wandered about the house in a state of blissful indifference. He spent more and more time alone in his room writing in his notebook, working on what he called his memoirs: *Cameron Lucida; Cameron Obscura.* He had, it seemed, become his own double, and now I was a shadow.

He told me he wanted to live on the edge, and so he invited death. Most of those invitations came in the form of prescription meds. He said, Only when you have death in your heart can you know how precious life is. I said, Don't you mean *love* in your heart? He had no ambition, no curiosity, no courage, no friends, no future. He coveted oblivion and chose to live his life in the languid pursuit of the beautiful lie, the pleasurable pulse of euphoria. He didn't work, but did spend what must have been forty hours a week searching through the house for hidden cash or items he could pawn.

The last time I saw Cameron alive, he was in a familiar position, sitting cross-legged on the sidewalk in front of Publix, insensible, a book opened on his knee, a lit cigarette in his fingers, his head slumped, his eyes shut, blacked out and heedless. I kicked the cigarette out of his hand, and he didn't move. I picked up the book: *The Monstrosity of Christ: Paradox or Dialectic?* I shook him awake. He didn't know who I was, so I told him. He said, Buy me a coffee, bro.

After Cameron's murder, I went to his room, #210, at the Buccaneer's Inn with Carlos, who told me the weapons, the drugs, the ball python, the kittens, and the boxes of fried chicken and biscuits had been removed, but everything else was pretty much as it had been on the night of the murder a week earlier. The blood-spattered carpet was covered with a plastic drop cloth. I was hoping to find Cameron's notebooks and read about this cruise to nowhere he'd been on. Someone's game of solitaire was still spread on the twin bed. A skeleton's-skull bong stared at me from the top of the dresser. Inside the drawers I found a box of Müeslix, a dozen or so past issues of *Smithsonian* magazine, a Bic lighter, and overdue library books: Sartre, Arendt, and Heidegger. "I should return these," I told Carlos. He nodded. Cameron had written a poem with magnetic word tiles on the side of his microwave: *Saint Blown Apart, please help me to put all the pieces back together.*

The story goes that Cameron had let the two junkie thieves who lived upstairs store their loot in his room in exchange for a nostril's worth of crank. That night, the thieves had robbed an antique store on Main and had gotten away with a crate of Nazi paraphernalia and a pair of medieval-style war clubs. According to the thief with the ARBEIT MACHT FREI button pinned to his Iron Maiden T-shirt, Everything in the room was copacetic as the three of them enjoyed their chicken and Southern Comfort, but then Cameron began talking philosophy or whatever you call it, talking about how time is matter and bullshit like that, talking to them like they were in preschool, and he wouldn't shut up and said he could feel the effects of the future, and so the thief with the swastika armband and the *Simpson's* T-shirt picked up the three-foot war club, the one with the iron bands and the pointed studs, stood behind Cameron, took a batter's stance, lined up Cameron's head, winked at Iron Maiden, swung, crushed my brother's skull, and delivered him to nothingness.

The universe may be tenderly indifferent to our fate, but we shouldn't be. We *are* our brothers' keepers. There is right, and there is wrong. There are consequences to our actions or inactions. Disregard can be an act of violence. I may not have been vigilant enough to save my brother from himself. I was hoping I might save the Hallidays from the disinterest and haste of the legal system.

Brantley Halliday loved his Skull Candle skateboard and worshipped Tony Hawk. His brother Briely's friends called Briely "Dr. Everquest" or just "Doc." Their sister, Brianna, was crazy about the colors pink and purple and wore a pink tulle tutu and purple ballet slippers to preschool every day. Her best friend was a boy with long brown hair and blue eyes named Ocean. At every costume party she'd put on a pair of silky wings and become an angel or a butterfly or a swan. I had decided to find out what I could about the victims, so I spoke with neighbors and with the children's teachers. To take the sticky matter of confidentiality off the table, I told them all I was working with the Eden Police Department, which was not a complete lie. The EPD had neither the time for nor the interest in gathering irrelevant information about a closed case. I was trying to imagine the first two acts of the tragedy and needed the provocative details. The boys attended Jaco Pastorius Elementary School. Their sister went to Guardian Angels Catholic Preschool.

Brantley was described as happy, active, personable, popular, and was well thought of by his teachers. He especially loved reading and social studies. He liked studying maps and once wrote a poem about Dodo Preston, the man who assigned every country its map color. Brantley was independent and confident. His science teacher, Anne Beachy, told me that, of course, all of that brilliance and enthusiasm can wane in the blink of an eye; all that effervescence can fizzle and flatten—she snapped her fingers—just like that when they get to middle school. Ms. Beachy wore a personal air purifier around her neck like a pendant—a Germ Guardian. When I have them, she told me, the children are still precious, and I don't want to let them go. Some of them are crushed in middle school. Others are inflated beyond their worth. You can smell the cruelty in the air. We seem unable to do anything to stop the despondency, self-destruction, and venom. The children are so much stronger than we are. They vanquish us with their insouciance.

Several girls in the class had crushes on Brantley and were now inconsolable and in counseling. A neighbor, Mr. Matisse, showed me a photo on his iPhone of Brantley on his skateboard doing a flip kick. He was wearing board shorts, a black T-shirt, and a beanie that said MYSTERY on it. He had painted *Into the Wild* on the board.

He had dimples and bushy red hair. He listened to Mozart to put himself to sleep, his friend Fausto told me.

Briely was obsessed, you could say, with online role-playing games. All his best friends were medieval warriors and elf-princesses whom he'd never met in person. He played piano and clarinet but didn't like to practice. He seemed to be more at ease when he was someone else, like Virdo, a horned night elf druid, his avatar in *World of Warcraft*. This worried his guidance counselor, Gentry Ledee. Gentry told me over stale coffee in the faculty lounge that Briely was a kid who might have had a hard time of it later—his need for constant stimulation might have led him astray. Maybe his life would have been difficult, he said, but so what? Who said life was supposed to be easy? What's the point of ease? We're not here to enjoy ourselves, are we, Mr. Melville? I told him I didn't know why we were here. I told him I didn't even think *why* mattered. I don't know why I said that, and I was relieved he ignored me. He talked about how for the kids in private schools, the dicey and sketchy ones, how all of their tribulations would be lifted, and life for them would be all bread and chocolate. But with our kids . . . He pressed his lips, flared his nostrils, and shook his head. I asked him if he'd had a hard time of it when he was younger. He folded his arms across his chest and leaned back in his chair. He nodded and said, That's why I can relate to them. He remembered that Briely wore this wonderful T-shirt that read, DRUM ROLL, PLEASE!

Brianna cried a lot at preschool. If her friend Ocean was absent, she cried. If Ocean played with Tiffany or Harold, Brianna cried. She enjoyed helping the teacher, Ms. Houllebecq, with the cleaning and organizing. Brianna had won many holy cards for falling asleep most quickly during naptime. Ms. Houllebecq showed me Brianna's cubby, which she, Ms. Houllebecq, had been unable to empty. She thought of it as a memorial. Brianna had a friendship bracelet in there, several barrettes, a photo of a brindled kitten asleep on a mastiff's head. Brianna had yet to blossom, Ms. Houllebecq told me. Several mothers in the neighborhood said they thought Brianna was withdrawn. The adjectives I heard used most often to describe her were *quiet*, *timid*, *invisible*.

Krysia Halliday had worked as a physical therapist in Poland, she told her neighbors, and then in London, where one of her patients was the reggae legend King Nelson Philp. She met Chafin, she said, when he was in London on vacation and they were both standing in the queue at Ronnie Scott's for a John Zorn concert. Halliday extended his stay and they were married in Camden Town the next week. According to neighbors, the kids were Krysia's life. She was not one to chat or socialize, but she was not unsociable. She was pleasant and polite, if not enthusiastic and hospitable. She earned her real estate license, but did not seem to have used it. She took creative writing classes at FIU and joined the South Florida Writers' Network. Her short story "Mom Has Issues," about a single mom and her young son on a three-hour layover at the Atlanta airport, won third place in last year's Network Fiction Contest. Mom, Temple, meets a gentleman traveler, a salesman, on his way to Birmingham from Flint, who calls himself Dickie Chapdelaine. He buys Temple another mojito at Houlihan's. She says it's only nine in the morning. He says, It's ten o'clock somewhere, and they laugh. The boy, Kody, says, "*Dickie*, that's a bad name." You can find the story on the network's website.

"Mom Has Issues" may not have been Krysia's only work of fiction. One of her friends from the neighborhood, Geraldine Barry, heard that I'd been asking questions about the deceased Mrs. Halliday and her family, got my business card from Dahlia Salazar, and called to say she'd like to talk. We met at Honey's on Main for coffee. Geraldine had close-cropped blond hair and apple-green eyes. She was slender and wore no makeup. She had on an Obama T-shirt, jeans, and red espadrilles. She shook my hand and sat. She ordered hot water and ignored the waitress's raised eyebrow. She said, "Don't look now, but isn't that guy at the counter what's-his-face from the Monkees?" I told her it was. He lives at the beach and eats here all the time. "If I weren't a married woman . . ." she said.

When the hot water arrived in a little silver pot, Geraldine pulled a silky tea bag out of her leather clutch. "Nepal First Flush," she said.

I said, "You knew Krysia?"

Geraldine put her elbows on the table, rested her face on her fists, and told me about the conversation she'd had with Krysia two weeks ago over drinks at Davy Byrne's Pub. "I was telling her about my long line of loser boyfriends before I met my husband: the OCD psychologist; the married, it turns out, neurosurgeon; the philandering semiotics professor; the ex-seminarian with commitment issues; blah blah blah. I could have gone on. My life was a country-and-western ballad for a long while. And then I noticed that she was crying when she ought to have been amused, and I asked her what was going on." Geraldine lifted the tea bag out of her cup and squeezed it against her spoon. She took a sip of tea. She said, "Krysia blew her nose with a napkin and said, 'Gerry, you just don't realize how much we talk about our pasts until you have no past to talk about.' Isn't that a strange thing to say?"

"Maybe hers is a past she'd rather forget."

Geraldine didn't think so. "I said, 'Krysia, your childhood in Poland. You've told me all about it.' She told me she had to leave her past behind because of her husband, and she hated him for that. She said she'd start to make friends, but couldn't because she was afraid the truth would leak out. I said, 'How can the truth hurt you, hon?' And she put her face in her hands and sobbed. What do you make of that?"

"Did she have an accent?"

"Yes, but not very thick. Dese and dose, dis and dat. Dropping the articles. But she lost it a bit when she drank. And then she avoided me after that. Didn't return my calls or my texts, didn't answer the door when I knocked, didn't come to Zumba class."

The once and future Monkee thanked his waitress and headed for the door. He smiled and nodded at Geraldine when he passed our table. "He's the cute one," she said, and she watched him out the restaurant window until he turned the corner on Avila. "He was my favorite."

I asked her what she made of Krysia's comments. Obviously something bothered her, or she wouldn't have called me. "Krysia told me her real name was Temple Luxe."

"Sounds like a name you make up."

"I never warmed up to her husband. He was aloof, smug, indifferent. Riding a high horse. People who don't need people bother me. Do they bother you?"

"They worry me." I took out my memo pad and pen.

"Temple Luxe," Geraldine said.

Temple has issues, I thought.

9

Venise called at four A.M. to tell me that Oliver had suffered a flare-up of his gout and I'd have to drive her to Memorial for her colonoscopy. Once Django saw my eyes open, and once he got over the alarm of the telephone's chirp, he figured it was playtime. He pounced on my toes and dug under the covers. He put his paw on my cheek and nibbled my nose. I showed him where his stuffed mouse was under the other pillow. He wrestled the mouse, held it with his front claws, and kicked at it with his furious back legs. I lay there falling in and out of sleep and dreaming that I'm onstage and I try to walk and my legs melt and I fall and find myself sitting up, waste-deep in a puddle of flesh. This anxiety was summoned by the fact that I had a light rehearsal later in the day and a dress rehearsal on Thursday. We'd open Friday for our weekend run. I ran my lines while I showered and made coffee.

I poured a go-cup of coffee for me and a thermosful for Red. Outside on the walk I could see the mucus trails left by the garden slugs. A mangrove crab had fallen asleep halfway up the house. The smell of coffee woke Red, but he didn't open his eyes.

I said, "How you doing, Red?

"Everything is everything, amigo." He wiped at the drool on his cheek.

"I'm off."

"Hasta luego." He rolled over in his sleeping bag.

Venise pushed the seat back as far as it would go. She wore her pink chenille robe, silky blue pajamas, orange Crocs, and she held on to a Publix sack in which she carried the floral muumuu that she'd wear home from the hospital later and a purple plushy goose for good luck. She couldn't buckle her seat belt, so we had to listen to the chime of the reminder bell as we drove. She shut her eyes, and I asked her if she was feeling okay. She said she was visualizing a polyp-free colon, thank you very much. She told me she hadn't slept a wink, what with drinking the vile diuretic and evacuating her bowels every twenty minutes. So she watched a program on one of the science channels called *The Half-Ton Dad* about a guy who weighed over a thousand pounds. He couldn't even move his arms—just his hands. He could wiggle his fingers and turn his head a little bit. In one day he ate what the normal person eats in two weeks. I said, Who's feeding him? She said, The firemen had to knock out a wall in his house to get him to the hospital, and not in an ambulance, either, in a flatbed wrecker.

We saw a car in flames in the breakdown lane on 95. A man I hoped was the driver sat atop the Jersey barrier talking on his cell phone. I dropped Venise at the front door of the hospital and told her I'd be back at noon to fetch her.

On the way to the office for my appointment with Wayne, I stopped at Starbucks for a coffee and a chance to read B. H. Fairchild's "Body and Soul" for the hundredth time. I had half an hour to myself. Trevor Navarro sat at his usual table with his makeup mirror, cosmetic case, and box of tissues in front of him. He was applying his auxiliary beauty, midnight-blue eye shadow. He waved to me with his fingertips. I said, Trevor, can I buy you a tea? He said, Black. Shaken. Iced. Venti. Trevor had spiked his orange hair with gel and wore a yellow halter top with jeans and a pair of sleek black leather slingbacks.

I brought Trevor his tea and carried my coffee to a table by the window. I managed to lose myself in the poem until I heard a familiar woman's voice say, You don't have to speak to me in that tone of voice, and a man respond, This is no-bullshit zone, baby! I left the ball players joking about the fat catcher's sex life and looked up to see my client and housekeeper Cerise and her Russian. He slapped the table. Cerise said, Vladimir, please.

Vladimir's short brown hair was shaved at the sides so he had no sideburns. He held an unlit cigarette between his pudgy fingers—four little pelmenis, they looked like. Perhaps he sensed I was spying on them. He looked up at me with these glacial blue eyes, and my own eyes darted to my book, not by choice, but by instinct. When I looked back, I met Cerise's gaze. She flinched when she saw me like she'd been struck. She folded her napkin into a tight square, lowered her brow, then looked over at me and then at Vladimir. I closed my book and stood. I carried my cup to the trash. I got to the door just as they did. I smiled and held the door open for them. That's when I noticed the hypertrophic scar on the Russian's neck that ran from ear to ear. Yikes! Vlad the impaled. Vlad the slashed.

Something consequential had happened in Wayne's life, but I couldn't yet tell what it was. He slumped on the couch, leaned his head back, and stared at the ceiling like he was looking for answers. He held his keys in his hand. He shut his eyes and squinched up his face. I asked him what was going on. He told me he was disgusted with himself.

"Why is that?"

He rubbed his eyes, kept them covered with his hand. "There's a lot of weird shit on the Internet," he said. "Tons of porn." He looked at me, stuffed his keys into his pocket, and sat up. "You start off with tits and ass, but pretty soon that's not enough. You get desensitized to the normal porn. You have to keep going after the harder stuff and the harder-than-that stuff."

"How far do you go?"

"You know you've arrived when your brain lights up. I see a little bondage, some teeth marks, and mine lights up like the Fourth of July."

"And this disgusts you?"

"First I jerk off, and then I'm disgusted."

"Does this make you ashamed?" I brushed a piece of nonexistent lint off my knee.

He said, "Is this making you uncomfortable?"

I told him it wasn't.

"Because you seem uncomfortable." He told me that he often felt his iMac knew his weaknesses and was in control of his life.

I said, "Then shut if off."

He said, "It won't let me."

I said, "Are you listening to yourself?"

"What I mean is, is that the computer is my connection to the world. It's not just about porn for me. It's how I stay in touch with people."

"Chat rooms?"

"And instant messaging. Facebook."

"But you don't know these people you're chatting with. All thirteen-year-old girls looking for love on the Internet are forty-five-year-old cops."

"You're out of your element here."

"Are you completely honest about who you are with these chatmates?"

"The *you* online is the *you* you want to be. The *you* you can be. The better *you*. The kinder, smarter, sweeter *you*. There's nothing wrong with that. You're rehearsing to be that person." Then he smiled and shook his head. "*Chatmates?*"

"Sitting alone in a room is not sociable, Wayne. It's antisocial."

"It's no different than a phone call, than writing a letter."

"When is the last time you had a date? Not a virtual date, a real date, with a flesh-and-blood woman?"

"As a matter of fact, I have a houseguest right now."

"Someone you met online?"

"Someone from the neighborhood."

"What's her name?"

He smiled. "I have to have some secrets."

"What's she like?"

"She's quiet. I like that. I hate all that jabbering. She spends a lot of her time in the bathroom. You know how women are."

"Is it serious?"

"It's serious, but we both of us know it's temporary."

"And that's okay?"

"It is what it is."

Wayne met his current houseguest around midnight on Christmas Eve at the 7-Eleven a few blocks from his house, about the time that I was trying to erase the images of the five ruined Halliday faces from my mind. He asked the clerk, Khalid, for a Heath bar. Khalid didn't know what he was taking about. Heat bar? Like Miami Heat bar? The girl sucking on a Slurpee knew: chocolate and toffee. Khalid said, If you don't see it, we don't have it. Wayne thought Khalid was being narrow and solipsistic, but didn't say so. He told them both that he was only eating foods that began with *H*. *H* for health. His Christmas resolution. Have a Hershey, Khalid said. Have some Hot Cheetos. The girl said, What do you eat for breakfast? Huevos, Wayne said. And Hawaiian pizza for lunch. Muy healthy, she said.

In the parking lot, a couple of kids with droopy denim cargo shorts, wife-beater shirts, and Yankee ball caps, little kids who should have been at home dreaming of sugar plums and reindeer, blew up a strip of M-80s. Khalid rapped on the window and motioned for them to leave or he'd call the cops. He held his thumb to his ear and his pinky to his lips. One of the pair lit a thunder bomb and hurled it at the window. When it went off, a woman outside at the pay phone dropped her cigarette and held her heart. The kids ran off laughing and holding up their sagging shorts. Khalid shook his head and said he blamed the parents. Wayne asked the girl if he could buy her a real drink. She said he could. He bought two cans of Heineken, put them on the counter, winked at Khalid, and said they were both for him. He told the girl they should walk over to Etling Park and sit on the bleachers. Deal, she said. He asked her what her name was.

I brought our conversation back around to Wayne's self-loathing. He said there were images he saw that were so vile that not long ago he would have turned away from them. In fact, any normal human being ought to be repulsed by them. But he did not turn away. He stared at them. And they stared back.

"And how does that feel?" I said.

"There's pleasure and then remorse. Guilt. And then I think I don't recognize myself—I'm not someone who could enjoy this sick, sadistic shit."

I asked him if he ever worried about getting caught. He told me he didn't download images and didn't share them. Nothing he did was illegal. Caught looking? That's not a crime.

"But you're alarmed at your behavior?"

"Yes."

"And you want to stop this acceleration into . . . dangerous—"

"You could say *depraved.*"

"Territory?"

"I do."

"So. Let's try turning off your computer for one week."

He shrugged. "I have a closet full of magazines with the nastiest photos you've ever seen."

"All I'm saying is that pornography is your drug. And the computer is an efficient drug-delivery system."

"I'm addicted to porn, maybe." He folded his hands on his knees and then cracked his knuckles. "All right, no *maybe* about it. I'd like to be able to look at slutty pictures without jerking off, but I can't. I have urges. We all do. We can't stop. We're human. But as long as I'm in my room alone, listening to loungecore and slamming the ham, I'm not hurting anyone."

"It sounds to me like you're hurt by your behavior."

"But I'm not addicted to the computer. I'm on the computer because I enjoy it. Some people spend all their time at the movies or on the golf course, and you wouldn't call them addicted, would you? You spend all your spare time reading, from the looks of it. Are you addicted to literature? Should you put your books away for a week?"

"From the looks of what?"

"I know about you." Wayne took a memo pad out of his shirt pocket, wet his thumb, and flipped through a few pages. He read me my Social Security number. He knew that my middle name was Vytautas and that my brother had been murdered and that his killers were serving life sentences in Raiford. He knew my credit rating, and I didn't. He knew my bank account information, as sad as it was. He knew my date of birth, my driver's license number, and the number of my cell phone. I told him the number was unlisted. He smiled and said it had been until I called Hunan Wok and ordered Mongolian beef, extra spicy, and egg drop soup. He knew my debit card number, the expiration date, and the security code. No, he did not know the PIN, but didn't think it would take him very long to find it. "Shakespeare's birthday?" he said. "Girlfriend's phone number?"

Wayne knew that I had been sued by a severely delusional ex-client, a woman who claimed in court documents that I was a fraud and that the emotional trauma she had suffered on my couch had rendered her permanently unfit for gainful employment, robbing her of a lifetime's income, when, in fact, I had gotten her her job back with the collection agency from which she had been fired and where she lied for a living, making harassing phone calls eight hours a day, a woman who had sued her first attorney when he had told her she did not have a legal leg to stand on. Wayne knew that I had won the frivolous lawsuit, but not until after two years of legal maneuvering by her shrewd and perky new attorney, who was dancing to the tick of the billable clock.

"It goes to show you," Wayne said. "No matter how creepy and fucked up you are, you can always find a lawyer who is even creepier, more fucked up, greedier, carnivorous, and untouchable. Am I right?"

He told me what books I had ordered online. He told me the Modern Library edition of Proust was in the mail. "Expect delivery on Friday." He knew that I had driven to Orlando twice in the last year and that I regularly drove the Dolphin Expressway on my way home from Books & Books in Coral Gables. He knew my passport number and where I had traveled. He knew what I had bought at Publix and at Quicker Liquors. He said, "You seem to think you can live on cognac, cashews, and chocolate." He said, "Do you feel violated?"

I said, "How do you know all this?"

"Like I told you. I don't just play games and look at porn on the Internet."

"I'll have to change everything."

"Don't bother." He tore the pages out of his memo pad and handed them to me. "A bit of advice," he said. "Use cash. It'll afford you what little privacy you have left. For the time being anyway. Pretty soon every product you buy will be embedded with a microchip so that retailers and cops can track you down wherever you go. They'll have sensors in every airport, train station, and bus terminal, at every border crossing. They'll put sensors in the walls of your house that'll inventory your possessions and monitor your habits—culinary, medical, sexual, and whatever. All in the name of commerce and quiescence."

I said, "How long did it take you to get this information?"

"It took some digging."

I stared at the pages. "I can't believe this." I was thinking I should probably empty my bank account before someone else did it for me. Put the money in the mattress.

He said, "The age of privacy is over. You can't walk into a store, can't pump gas; you can't enter a public building without being on camera. Every damn traffic light in this town has a camera mounted on it. Google's got a photo of your house online for everyone to see. They put microchips in pets these days so if Fido goes missing, you can track him down. They'll be doing that to children pretty soon. You can bet on it. You'll always know where little Amber is. No more alerts."

"And on that note," I said, "I believe our time is up."

We scheduled Wayne's next appointment. We walked to the

door. I asked him if he wanted to meet at the DeSoto Street house. I was being funny. He said we couldn't. "It's occupied."

"Did the Parkers move back in?"

"Just long enough to spruce up, shampoo the carpet, touch up the paint. They're renting it out."

"They don't own it."

"They're resourceful people."

"How do you know this?"

"I answered their ad on Craigslist. I went and had a look around. Dave's a short, pudgy guy with a wandering eye. Deb's a brunette at the moment. Plump as a blowfish. They had the power and water back on and a house full of rented faux-leather and mica furniture and glass tabletops. They wanted $1,500 a month, all-inclusive. I told them they were dreaming. I could still smell the dogs."

We said goodbye and then he turned and said, "They want you to think you're being watched all the time so that you'll be good, or at least you'll be discreet."

I considered asking Wayne to do a little research for me but knew that would be inappropriate in so many ways. I called Oliver and asked him if he'd be willing to find out some information for me on a couple of people."

"My pleasure. I have nothing but time."

I gave him the names *Jack Malacoda* and *Chafin Halliday*.

I called Carlos to tell him my car had been towed out of my own parking space.

He said, "How do you know it wasn't stolen?"

"It *was* stolen. The tow-truck driver laid on his horn till I came out the door, and then he waved goodbye as he drove off."

"I'll be right there."

"I'm sick of that dickwad Shanks, and I'm calling someone."

"This will not happen again. I promise."

"I have to be at Memorial in an hour."

On our drive to the impoundment lot, I told Carlos about the carcass in the car the last time. I said, "I don't know why your department puts up with that asshole."

"That asshole is the secretary of the union."

"And?"

"He makes all of the off-duty assignments for the department. You can double your annual salary with those assignments. Triple it. No one wants to rattle his cage."

Carlos wasn't buying my theory that a left-handed Halliday—if indeed he was left-handed—could not, or would not, have fired a pistol with his right hand. But why wouldn't he have used his dominant hand? I said. We stopped at a red light. I looked up at the camera. Carlos honked the horn and waved to an older gentleman sitting with a coffee at a sidewalk table in front of the Falafel House. The man smiled and waved, and then went back to texting on his cell phone.

Carlos said, "That's Stavros Kanaracus. He owns the falafel place. He's responsible for three murders that I know of."

"So why is he sitting there?"

"He never pulls the trigger. He always has an alibi. He employs very expensive lawyers."

Stavros looked to me like a genial grandfather who'd gotten the bad idea to have his thinning hair dyed maroon and laminated to his head.

I told Carlos about the bloody carpet in the Parkers' house.

"So you broke into the house?"

"The door was open."

"Did you wear gloves?"

"No."

"Wipe down your prints?"

"I left in a hurry."

"So if there had been a crime committed, you'd be the prime suspect." He told me that no therapist had ever solved a crime.

I said I wasn't trying to solve it, but I wanted him to.

Carlos told me they found the body of the girl who went missing ten days ago, the eighteen-year-old. Kelly Kershaw.

"Where did they find her?"

"At the recycling plant on Mahogany. Workers found her in the waste. We figure her body was dropped in a Dumpster and then picked up by a truck. Looks like the killer had started to chop up the body, but quit trying. Big gashes here and here." Carlos pointed to his neck and shoulder. He asked me if I'd take a look at her room with him in the morning. Rooming house over by Banyan Circle. He said, "Even a bad cop can save your life."

I asked Carlos if it was customary for a pair of uniformed EPD officers to oversee the transfer of merchandise in a public lot from one semitrailer to another. He said, What are you talking about? I explained what I'd seen. No, that's not typical, he said.

As we drove past St. Jerome's Church, Carlos hit the brakes, squealed into the parking lot, and stopped. He pointed across the lawn. "Is that a goddamn dead mule?"

Indeed it was. There beneath a live oak lay the bloated remains of a recently expired mule that had apparently been giving children "pony" rides at yesterday's parish carnival.

"What the hell?" Carlos said.

"It would seem we're in a Southern novel," I said.

Carlos called the monsignor and then animal control, and we were on our way. I waited by the squad car while Carlos fetched my keys and cleared up any misunderstandings. I got a call from Oliver telling me to get to Memorial ASAP because Venise was apparently causing quite a ruckus. There was a new bumper sticker on the back window of my car: ARE WE HAVING FUN YET?

I could hear Venise wailing as I neared the recovery room. I was met by a nurse who told me that Venise was claiming that she'd been sexually assaulted by her gastroenterologist during the colonoscopy. Just before Venise went under, she screamed that she was being digitally violated, and why wasn't anyone doing anything to stop it. The nurse told me that Venise was still hysterical and could I please calm her down. The sedative did not seem to be working.

I held Venise's hand and told her everything would be fine now, and I was here to take her home. She wept and trembled and let out this halting kind of adenoidal moan, interrupted every few seconds by snorts and blubbery gasps, and I wanted to tell her to stop it because she didn't sound human. She caught her breath and yelled, "He sexually assaulted me!"

I said, "Venise, you know what a colonoscopy is, right?"

When the doctor stopped by, Venise wanted me to call the police. The doctor said to her, "I'm sorry if you think I was inappropriate, dear, but I have to do certain things." He handed me a color photograph of Venise's now-excised polyp.

I apologized. "Must be the medication talking."

He said, "She would have been dead in two years."

We stopped at La Sazon on the way to Venise's, and she bought ceviche de mariscos and anticuchos de corazón. She was beyond starving, she said. We found Oliver on the La-Z-Boy, his ankles wrapped in ice bags. Venise sat at the table and ate with the plastic utensils we'd gotten at the restaurant. She drank her Diet Rite cola from the two-liter bottle. She told Oliver she'd been through hell. He asked her if she was going to report the incident. She said it wouldn't do any good. The lawyers are all in the pockets of the doctors. Plus she was on many medications, including Zoloft, and everyone would just assume that she was demented. Plus the legal fees would drain their bank account. I said I'd have to be going. Had a rehearsal to get to. Plus she'd have to take time off from work. So long, I said. Plus it would expose her to shame in the community.

After a quick rehearsal spent on blocking and ironing out a few rough spots, I drove home. I saw that Red had put his name on my mailbox. He had written *P. Soileau* on an index card and affixed it with clear shipping tape. I asked him what the *P* stood for, and he told me *Pableaux*, and he spelled it for me. He pointed at the gray and glowing briquettes in the hibachi and asked me to join him for supper. Hot dogs. Fabulous, I said. I'll bring the beer. And bring some diced onions if you have any, he said. I told him to give me fifteen minutes.

At some point during the day, poor little Django slipped into the bathtub and hadn't been able to crawl his way out. He was elated to be lifted up and kissed on his silky head. He was even happier to get at the food in his bowl. I had eight hang-up calls on my voice mail, a call from Bay wanting to meet for coffee, and a message to call Almost Home. Which I would do mañana.

I carried lawn chairs out to Red's campsite and apologized for not having done so already. Red told me that he'd seen a cop snooping around the house. Dude parked out front, made some phone calls, all the time looking at the door and the windows. He drove away. Came back. Sat for a while. I'm wondering what's an Eden cop doing in Melancholy.

"He didn't see you?"

"Wasn't looking for me. By the way, this is one bad cop. Kevin Shanks."

"You know Shanks?"

"Everyone on the street knows Shanks."

"I had a run-in with him recently."

"I've seen him tie a plastic bag over a boy's head while he interrogated the kid on the street. I've seen him pummel a sleeping homeless guy with his nightstick in Heron Lake Park. He extorts money from dealers, escorts drugs through the county, steals from trucks and trains."

"Can you prove this?"

"I don't have to."

"You say everyone knows about him?"

"Common knowledge."

"You think the cops know?"

Red smiled and tucked the hot dogs into their rolls. He handed me my paper plate and apologized for the bright yellow mustard in the little foil packets. "I'm on a tight budget."

We opened our beers and sat. Red said, "The Eden cops have a well-deserved reputation for impropriety, incompetence, and mayhem." We held up our beers and drank to those who protect and serve. He said, "This friend of yours, O'Brien, what do you know about him?"

"Good man. A pal."

Red nodded and held up his hot dog. "Uncured beef. The best."

I Googled *Temple Luxe Writer* and found out that she'd published a number of stories over the years. In 1999, the earliest publication I could find, Temple's story "Unfinished Sympathy," which I was unable to access online, was published in something called *The Little Apple* in Requiem, Massachusetts. The contributors' notes had her living in Toronto, Canada, with her cats, Gretsky and Minouche. She named Margaret Atwood and Mavis Gallant as influences. In 2003, according to the notes in *Huntress*, Temple was living with her husband in Providence, Rhode Island. Her publication in *The Little Apple* was noted, and her story here was called "Thinkers to Lovers to Chance." It began, "For the past fifteen years, Minrose Applewhite has been living in Cranston with her boyfriend, Lonnie Monroe, a carpenter, handyman, and fiddle player with the country band Coastal Cousins. All of the carpenters in Cranston are, as it happens, also fiddle players, and all of them, the men anyway, and several of the lesbians, are adamantly single, but at the same time living with strong women who have an emptiness in their lives." I tried to link to the complete story, but the link had rotted. Error 404.

By 2009 at the latest, Temple Luxe was living in Norman, Oklahoma, with her husband and three kids, which made me think this Temple could not have been our Krysia Halliday, whom we knew from school records had been living in Everglades County since at least 2006. The story was dedicated to *My sweetheart Charlie.* She was certainly, however, the same Temple Luxe who had, according to the note in the *Glass Mountains Review*, also published stories in "*Tupelo Honey*, *The Troubadour*, *Bois d'Arc Fence Post*, *Four-wheel Drive*, and other journals." The story here, titled "Famous Lost Words," was also about Minrose Applewhite, now living in St. Augustine, Florida, and working as an emergency ward nurse at the community hospital. Her married boyfriend, Maverick Frye III, a personal injury attorney, who has promised and promised to leave his wife, Camille, but hasn't yet, wants Minrose to meet him tonight for dinner at the Outback, and because it's the Outback and not Sergio's, let's say, or Restaurant Tricherie, she knows this is the kiss-off, so she says, Yes, Maverick, yes, but stands him up. Trials and tribulations ensue. The weeping and the gnashing of teeth. Unhappily ever after.

There were several Luxe Temples online and a Temple Luxe interior design firm, a Temple Luxe yacht builder, an Irish Thoroughbred named Temple Luxe who had eleven races, one third-place finish, and zero pounds earned, one Sir Ulick Temple Luxe, sixteenth Baronet of Menlough, who died in 1963, and one Temple

Luxe living in the United States, but whose age and location eliminated her from having once been our Krysia.

So what did I know and what did I think? Krysia Halliday may once have been named Temple Luxe; Krysia wrote stories, as did the peripatetic author named Temple Luxe, who may have lived in Toronto and Rhode Island and Oklahoma or may have just said she had. I also knew that I knew not a thing about Krysia Halliday except what Carlos, the neighbors, and Geraldine had told me. Nothing about her online. I was reasonably sure that Krysia had been Temple, and that she had some reason to abandon her identity and her self and to begin again. But I did not know why or how. And her past, perhaps, had come calling on Christmas Eve.

10

I sat with Bay at a sidewalk table at Lovin' Spoonful on the Boardwalk. The beach was crowded with University of Texas fans here for the big bowl game. A man in a burnt-orange Speedo and a straw cowboy hat walked by with a python around his neck. Bay told me he was moving Marlena into one of the new condos at Dixie and Eden. They'd so overbuilt down here that he got the sublet for a song. I once asked Bay if he ever used his magic talents at the poker table. He told me, Why play a game if you don't play by the rules? What would be the point?

I said, "How did you do last night?"

"I was down four hundred till the last hand. I'm against this donkey across from me who's wearing a photographer's vest with no shirt and these Carol Channing sunglasses. I bet small, trying to suck him in. He shoved, representing a straight. He chewed on his finger and then leaned away from the table. I was sure he was bluffing. I called. We showed. He wasn't bluffing. He had the straight, but I paired on the river to make a full house. I finished up two thousand."

"Lucky you."

"I made the most common mistake you can make at the table. I underestimated my opponent."

"And got away with it."

"I won't the next time."

I told him about my continued misgivings concerning the Halliday killings and about the blood on the carpet in the Parkers' house. I told him about my run-ins with Shanks. He told me to back up to Halliday. Bay said, "You never saw dead bodies at that house."

"I saw photographs. I saw blood, I saw an officer collecting forensic evidence. I saw enough to know that there had been violence committed in that house."

"Maybe there were five bodies. But maybe they were not the Hallidays. You don't know the Hallidays."

"I spoke with the neighbors and the kids' teachers."

"Chafin Halliday's face was obliterated, right?"

"You sound like a conspiracy theorist."

"Consider it a thought experiment. Try to imagine all the people and conditions and events that might account for what you saw in that house."

I told him when I went to police headquarters to file a complaint against Shanks, they told me they didn't have citizen compliment/complaint forms. I told them which drawer they were in, and I pointed past the cop's shoulder. He asked for my driver's license, and when I reached into my pocket, he yelled that I was going for a weapon. I froze. And then he laughed, said I could get dead that way. I finally got the form and slid it under the glass, and the cop, clacking away on a typewriter, said to me, "I'll file this." I said, "I'm sure you will, Officer Toney," and I took the tape recorder out of my pocket and played back a bit of our conversation.

Bay reached over and squeezed my forearm. "I'm going to tell you a story, and I need you to listen."

"Listening."

"You're sitting at home with your buddy the librarian. Maybe you've got Mahler on the CD player, and you're talking about movies. How much you like Truffaut and Fellini. It's a warm, breezy day in March. You've got a dependable, juicy Malbec on the table and a plate of savory Brie with those black olive crackers. In two hours you're going to meet your pal Bay for dinner and drinks at La Playa. Suddenly your door is busted open, and ten SWAT-team cops come blasting into your house with rifles aimed at your faces and screaming for the two of you motherfuckers to get on the floor.

"Your librarian friend has a big mouth and asks what the hell is going on. He gets knocked on the back of his head with the butt of an MP5. You drop to the floor. Your buddy holds his bleeding head in his hands. Someone slaps him in the face and then punches him in the jaw. Then his legs are swept out from under him, and he falls, maybe smacks his head against the kitchen table. Maybe passes out. Then he gets a kick to the stomach. He probably needs medical attention, but he's not going to get any.

"You can feel the muzzle of a Glock against your temple. All you can think of is that you must be dreaming. You try to wake up. You hear yourself say, 'Is this some kind of joke?' 'No joke, pussy.' Someone kicks you in the back of your head. Maybe someone else Tasers you for resisting arrest. Maybe they set the dogs on you. The two of you are under arrest for drug trafficking. You're the worst kind of scum—preying on kids in the neighborhood. A cop walks into your bedroom and walks out a minute later holding two bricks of cocaine. He tells his unit, 'Looks like we struck pay dirt.'

"You're booked, you're jailed, your faces are plastered all over the news. You lose your clients; your buddy's suspended from the library; your careers are over, and you didn't do a damn thing. You hire a very expensive attorney until you realize you can't afford her. You hire an affordable attorney. You bail out. No one looks you in the eye. The guy you rent your office from lets you know that he's doubling the rent. Your friends treat you kindly, but they seem distant, don't they? They're wondering—because they know that innocent people in America have nothing to worry about. The cops have enough to do without framing a couple of middle-class, middle-aged white guys. The cops are offering you a plea bargain: plead guilty to lesser charges, and you'll only serve ten years. And your affordable lawyer is urging you to take the deal. They found the shit in your closet, man! The very best you can hope for now is to spend your life savings and hope that you walk—you'll never live down the suspicion even if you're exonerated. Once you're accused, you'll always be guilty."

I said, "That's a pretty unlikely scenario."

"I'm just saying: don't underestimate your opponent."

"Carlos has my back."

"Does he? What time is it?"

I checked my wrist. The watch was gone. I looked at Bay. He held it up for me. So today's theme was, *In search of lost time*. "When did you do that?"

He said, "The key to the con is not that the con man has your trust; the key is that he convinces you that *he* trusts *you*."

Carlos told me I should not have filed my official complaint about Shanks. "Nothing good can come of this, Coyote. You should have spoken to me."

"I did."

The motor scooter parked outside Kelly's rooming house had dozens of variously colored plastic dinosaurs glued to its frame. The rooming house, Carlos told me, had been a ten-room hotel, the Alhambra, back in the thirties and forties. The building had relinquished its barrel-tiled roof in favor of shingles, but did retain its Spanish flavor, although the stucco had been painted lavender a long time ago. One handwritten sign in the old lobby read NO SPITTING! and another, LET US KNOW ABOUT BED BUGS! I saw black mold growing high on the wall where the ceiling had leaked. I heard TV noises from Room #1: an exaggerated burp and then canned laughter. We walked upstairs to the second of three floors and to Kelly's room, #6, at the back of the building. Carlos undid the police tape, and we stepped inside.

Carlos hit the light, stepped around the plastic laundry basket, walked over to the window, and opened it. I sneezed. The twin-sized mattress and box spring were on the floor and pushed back against a dingy white wall. The bedspread was a red and green floral pattern on quilted polyester and was just the kind of egregiously unnerving monstrosity you would strip from your bed at the No-Tell Motel, stuff into a closet, and never touch or look at again. I inhaled some Nasonex.

The ceiling light fixture was a bowl of frosted glass with three identical bow-tie-wearing kittens smiling down at you. One of the two bulbs was burned out. There was no chair, no stepstool in the room to stand on to replace the bulb. There was no bathroom door, just a wooden beaded curtain with a strand of beads missing. Someone walked across the floor upstairs and then dragged a piece of furniture from one end of the room to the other. We heard the muffled sounds of talk radio from the adjoining room. Carlos told me the guy next door, Nellie Kemp, was hooked up to oxygen and didn't get out much anymore. Had all his meals delivered. The room was pretty much his world. Sat and listened to the radio. I thought about Kelly, on her bed in the middle of the night, listening to the whispers of these muffled voices.

There was no closet, but there was, on one side of the bed, a chrome rack for hanging clothes that looked like the frame of a small children's swing set. On the other side of the bed was a narrow, three-drawer wood and wicker nightstand. On top of the stand was a compact microwave oven, and on top of the oven, a small table lamp with a torn lampshade. Kelly had done what she could to make these cramped quarters a home. She may have felt that she did not deserve to take up much space in the world. On a pine-board shelf above the bed, Kelly had a boom box; a deck of playing cards; two laminated library books, *For Girls Only: What You Need to Know About How Guys Think* and *Just as Long as We're Together*, not due back for another week; a thirty-two-ounce Big Gulp cup; and an Il Divo CD. I cut the deck of cards. The four of hearts. Did Kelly have four people in her life, I wondered, who loved her? Whom she loved? I asked Carlos if he'd contacted the next of kin. He told me they hadn't yet been able to locate any family.

There was a framed photograph of Kelly on the shelf, the only photograph, apparently, that she had. She's about a year old, and she's in the arms of a woman I presume to be her mother. Little KK—I'll bet they called her that—has her thumb in her mouth and a hand in her wispy hair. Who took the picture? I asked Carlos what he knew about Kelly.

She was born in Belle Glade, her mother's only child. Mom was addicted to meth. She'd gone missing and was probably dead. Dad went to the Palm Beach County jail when Kelly was three and died there of AIDS when she was ten. She pretty much grew up on her own. She went to high school but did not seem to have graduated. Somehow she drifted here to Everglades County. "My guess," Carlos said, "is she arrived on a bus with some boy. Or some man. Folks in the building say she was very pleasant but very shy. Never had any visitors. She'd been working the lunch shift at Arby's for about five weeks. Her boss said she was a bit of a daydreamer but learned her responsibilities quickly. She'd be hard to replace."

I opened the top drawer of the nightstand. Kelly's underwear, with the exception of a single red lace thong, was conventional and threadbare. In the middle drawer she kept a blue enamel dish, a red plastic cereal bowl, a can opener, plastic utensils, and two cans of cream of mushroom soup. There was a goldfish bowl in the bottom drawer, and in the bowl an opened box of goldfish food flakes, some blue gravel, and a plaster medieval castle. Two polo shirts hung on the clothes rack, one an employee's shirt from Publix, the other from Burger King. There were two pairs of black chinos and a pair of khaki shorts.

The bathroom sink was unsurprisingly pitted and the shower stall barely wide enough to turn around in. Kelly used Ivory soap, Prell shampoo, Pantene conditioner, Crest toothpaste, and Nivea skin cream. Her green Oral B toothbrush was in need of replacement. She'd taped a magazine photo of Brad Pitt and Angelina Jolie to the wall beside the medicine cabinet. There was not much in the way of medicine in the cabinet—a small plastic jar of aspirin, a tube of Neosporin, and a stick of Blistex. The cabinet had a slot like a piggy bank's where you were instructed to drop your used razor blades.

Carlos told me to have a look in the small, unplugged refrigerator in the corner by the window. He said, "We tossed the food already. Junk."

Kelly kept her Hello Kitty diary in the fridge. In case of fire, I figured. Carlos said, "Why don't you take it home and read it."

I opened the book at random and read the entry for November 16:

> *Today at the Arb a customer who was talking on his cell phone when he ordered his Bacon & Bleu Roastburger and his Onion Petals and his Sierra Mist told me that I was underambitious and throwing my life away and then he told whoever he was*

talking to You pay peanuts and you get monkeys and he laughed and I was upset and ran to the ladies' and cried until Querida came in and said Calvin needed me he was having a conniption fit trying to keep up with the orders and I said we're at Arby's it's never crowded.

Kelly's handwriting was upright, slender, and slight. Each letter stood unattached.

"What kind of animal . . . ?" Carlos shook his head. "Who are we looking for?"

"Someone, I'd say, in his mid- to late twenties. A loner. Ill at ease with women his own age. So he seeks out younger girls. He has a kind of brash charm that would appeal to a girl not used to attention and flattery."

"Like Kelly."

"What was the cause of death?"

"Strangulation. The cutting, the gore, and the sex were posthumous."

"I don't think it's just sexual. I'm not sure the guy understands death as anything other than spectacle and the imposition of his will."

"You're not saying he's insane?"

"If he's also responsible for the other missing girl, then we may have a man who thinks he's found his calling."

Patience worked at Jaunts & Junkets Travel on Mangrove. I stopped in to ask her if she could suggest a very cold destination where I might see the northern lights, maybe at the end of the month or in early February. Patience said it was so weird—she had just been thinking of me. She turned her memo pad around and slid it across her desk to me so I could see where she had written,

Call Wylie. I wondered if she had had the diamond in her nose at Christmas, and I just missed it. It was adorable.

"And now I don't have to," she said.

"Call me about what?"

"My friend Dermid Reardon would like to see you. Professionally, I mean."

"Tell him to come to the office Monday morning at ten. I'll be free." I handed her my card.

"How about Norway?" she said.

"Something on this continent?"

"Fairbanks," she said. She woke up her computer and typed. "Stay there three nights and your chances of seeing the lights are eighty percent."

"Make it five nights. I just want an idea of the cost."

"Average high February temperature is eleven degrees."

"Sounds great."

"Let me look for flights and accommodations and get back to you. One adult?"

"Two."

"Good for you."

I stood and shook Patience's hand goodbye. "May I ask if your friend Dermid is in a wheelchair?"

"Not yet."

I drove to the Aventura Mall, went to the Apple store, and got myself an iPhone. One of the geniuses in blue T-shirts got me up and running, showed me how to use the camera and video, asked me if I thought I'd need an app for calculating my blood alcohol level. It's called iAlcohol and the Russians made it and they know everything about public drunkenness, so you know it's good. I passed. What about a sleep machine—drift off to the sound of crickets?

• • •

We had a decent house on opening night at the Eden Playhouse. I guessed seventy-five people or so. We were up against the big bowl game and Eden's Festival du Québec. I peeked out from backstage and saw Red, wearing a tennis visor, backpack on his lap, chatting with Zack Dolan, the *Journal-Gazette*'s theater critic. Hiroshi paced the green room threatening to have a migraine. His partner, James, held his hand and told him to empty his mind and let the clumsy fire arise, whatever that means. James was wearing a QUEER AND PRESENT DANGER T-shirt, pleated harem pants, and leather slip-ons with peaked heels and turned-up toes. Phoebe and Kai came backstage and presented me with a bouquet of roses. I thanked them, James thanked them, and he rushed off with the flowers to find an appropriate vase. Kai told me to break a leg and insisted that I join them for dinner after the show. I tried to back out, but he wouldn't hear of it. He'd made reservations at Ferme for ten-thirty.

Kai said that he never ate anything that had had a mother. We were dining by flickering candlelight on the sidewalk. I'd finished my braised lamb shank, Phoebe her coq au vin, and Kai his crêpe Christina. Kai had offered his culinary observation just out of the blue, and I was inexcusably pleased that he would never get to taste fois gras in his life. Phoebe said, "Let's not get started, sweetie." No fois gras, no pork bellies, no escargot, no caviar, no Belon oysters, no sea urchin roe, no crawfish, no stone crabs at Joe's.

Kai told me how much he enjoyed all three plays, how distinctly American he thought they were, and how impressed he was with my performances, which was kind of him to say. The waiter took our dessert orders. Kai and Phoebe decided they'd split a crème brûlée. I said I'd drink my dessert and ordered a cognac. Phoebe rubbed Kai's neck and stared at me while she did. Kai said the guy who played T-Bone's friend Euly could use a spinal adjustment. I heard what sounded like a car backfiring. Kai said, "Holy shit!" The blast was followed by the shattering of glass. I turned and saw a shirtless man in a Panama hat firing a pistol into a closed-down fitness center. Shot after shot. Flash after flash. Kai said, "He's trying to kill the StairMaster." Why weren't we crouched behind our table or running away? A man eating at the next table shook his head and went back to his meal. The waitstaff from the restaurant joined us on the sidewalk, and some of them took photographs with their cell phones. We heard sirens. I saw Kanaracus, the Falafel King, his jacket draped over his shoulders, standing on the corner, watching the show. When the shooter was out of bullets, he dropped his pistol, put his hands behind his head, and knelt on the sidewalk. A squad car squealed to a stop, and a cop got out brandishing his own pistol, which he aimed at the kneeler's head. One of the waiters said, "Thank god for the police." The cop slammed the shooter's face into the asphalt.

When the excitement died down, our waiter, Fletcher, arrived with dessert and three spoons. He said, "No charge for the entertainment!" and bowed. I had a feeling all waiters and waitresses were adopting table names. How many *Crispins*, *Fletchers*, and *Rhiannons* can there be? And all of them in food services?

Kai bent over the dessert, closed his eyes, and inhaled. He said, "Has Phoebe told you that we're thinking about moving?"

"She hasn't."

Phoebe tasted her crème brûlée.

Kai said, "Time for a change."

"Out to Banyan?"

"Arizona."

I looked at Phoebe, who looked at Kai. Kai smiled and patted Phoebe's arm. "I've been offered a position with a notable healing institute in Sedona."

"You'd leave paradise for the desert? You know what that dry air does to your skin?"

Kai said, "When I moved here you could sit down in the middle of Neptune Drive and not have to move for hours."

I said, "Nosebleeds, flyaway hair—"

"There used to be trees full of roseate spoonbills in Eden Lake Park. Now everything's paved from Homestead to Jupiter."

"When?"

"Well, I've got to clear the decks here, of course, but I'd like to see us out there by the start of summer. Right, sweetheart?"

Phoebe wiped her mouth with a napkin.

"Phoebe," I said, "are you excited?"

"I really can't get my head around the idea yet."

I was up early after a fitful sleep, interrupted by the same annoying dream over and over again, in which I'm onstage and dumbstruck. I can't remember my line, and the audience is shuffling their feet and murmuring to one another, and Hiroshi has fainted in a tidy heap, and the actors are furious, and I can see my fifth-grade nun, Sister Cerritus, in the front row, and she's smiling and nodding her head and fingering her gigantic rosary beads, and I know the line is something about ducks, about clearing the ducks, but I can't remember it for the life of me.

I put Django in the steel bowl on the kitchen scale. He'd doubled in size to five ounces, but he was still all adorable eyes and extravagant ears. I knew I'd regret this decision one day, but I put Django on the kitchen table where he could watch me surf the Web for all I could learn about Sedona, Arizona. He opened his mouth but no meow came out. That's how grateful he was. He sat on the keyboard and then pressed *command*. I put his bowl on the table, and the food kept him busy while I worked. I don't know why

I thought I had any control over Phoebe's life or why I thought she would always be close by. Sedona had once been called Red Rock. There are 11,220 residents, many metaphysical shops, and several spiritual vortices.

I found an old linen postcard of the Alhambra on eBay. The hotel looked prim and respectable. The grass was trimmed and monochromatically green, the sky a powdery blue. There were two red tulip chairs set on the lawn beneath an inflorescent coconut palm. An American flag rippled in a light breeze from the flagpole. I entered my bid.

I put Django on the floor, poured a cup of coffee, and went out to get the paper to see what Zack Dolan had to say about the show. Red looked up from the paper when he heard the screen door slam and said, "Congratulations, Olivier!" I handed him his coffee and sat in the extra chair.

Red told me, "Dolan called the evening 'professional, thoughtful, provocative.' He cites the 'spunky production and the solid, energetic cast.'" Red smoothed the paper and cleared his throat. "'Wylie Melville does most of the heavy lifting as Davy in *A Man Walks into a Marriage*, a play I found entirely satisfying and at times exhilarating.'" Red looked up from the paper and smiled. "Bravo!"

"Well, that makes my week." Red handed me the paper and I read the whole review.

Red said, "Euly shouldn't slouch like he does."

I said, "He's feeling the weight of the world on his shoulders."

11

Cerise let herself in the house and dropped her keys in the empty Our Lady of Lourdes holy water font on the wall by the door. I poured her a coffee with cream and three sugars. I introduced her to Django. She asked me how a little cat like him could get up on such a tall table. I lifted Django and took the napkin out of his mouth. I put him on the floor and rolled his little spongy soccer ball across the room. He bounded after it and slid into the wall. Cerise and I sat. She apologized for Vladimir's loutish behavior at Starbucks. He'd been upset ever since his friend shot his wife and himself.

"The lawyer?" I said.

"You know Kouzmanoff?"

"I read about him. Were he and Vladimir pals?"

"Vladimir did some work for Kouzmanoff."

"What kind of work?"

"He doesn't talk to me about his work."

"And how have you been?"

Cerise told me that she'd been restless and confused lately, more so than usual. I wondered out loud if her meds might need some readjustment.

She said, "Sometimes my tongue feels like a worm in my mouth."

I said, "You need to tell them that at the clinic, Cerise."

"I will."

"Promise me."

"My faith is all I have, Mr. Wylie." She told me that Ellery had refused to see her.

I said, "He's grieving. Maybe he needs to be alone for a bit. He'll come around. He's been through hell."

"Do you know what that does to a mother?"

My car wouldn't start. I turned the key, and click! Nothing. I flipped the hood release, got out of the car, and opened the hood. I didn't know what I was looking at except that I knew the big cube with the cables clamped to it was the battery. It looked fine. I shook it a little. I got back in the car and turned the key. Nope! I counted to fifteen and asked Saint Jude for some assistance. I pumped the gas pedal and tried it again. I seemed to remember my dad doing that when I was a kid. Nothing. Could it be the choke? Is there a choke in here somewhere? Click! Red leaned in the window and said, "Your battery's dead."

"I'll call Triple A."

"There's an AutoMen right up on Main. We'll take the battery out—" Red could see my eyes glaze over. "How did you ever live this long?" He shook his head. "*I'll* take it out. We'll bring it to AutoMen, get a new one, pop it in, and you're good to go."

"How?"

"You've got tools, right?"

"Let's look in the garage."

Red said, "Everything under the hood of this Scion is ten millimeters—a beautiful design. All I need is one ten-millimeter wrench." And I had one. Who knew? Red took out the battery, aired up the tires on my bike, put the battery in the basket, and sent me on my way. "Give the man this baby; he'll hand you the correct replacement. I'll be right here finishing my coffee."

When I got back, Red took the battery and gave me back the seven-year warranty. "You're going to lose this, aren't you?"

"Probably."

He dropped the battery onto its seat. "These cars today come with maintenance-free batteries, and yours was, what, three years old? So I'm thinking, unless you left the lights on, and I saw that you didn't, then someone may have deliberately drained your battery."

"The car's always locked. They wouldn't be able to release the hood."

"Unless they had a code cutter." Red explained how keys could be made.

"Who has code cutters?"

"Car thieves and cops." He attached the cables to the battery and tightened the nuts. "Car thieves don't drain batteries."

"I can understand why," I said. "If you need the bike, it's yours."

"Thanks, but I like walking. Maybe in an emergency."

"The garage door is always open."

"Start locking it."

Dermid Reardon wore a blue linen suit and a white silk shirt, open at the collar. He told me he was an architect who designed retail spaces for stores in malls and also for some freestanding independent bookstores. He was originally from Boston. He was wearing thin argyle socks and sleek brown loafers. Dermid sat rather stiffly on the couch and adjusted his elegant designer glasses. He said, "All my life I've known that I was supposed to have one leg."

"Supposed to?"

"Some people look in the mirror and see a thinner person. I look in the mirror and see a man with no right leg."

"And the real you is the man in the mirror?"

"Reversed." Dermid rubbed his forehead and pressed his lips. "I want my left leg removed above the knee."

"And are you hoping to understand that desire, that obsession?"

"I *do* understand it. I don't expect you to rid me of my desire. I want you to listen." Dermid took a long, deep breath, filled his cheeks, and blew it out. "I want you to help me remove the leg. Think of this as radical plastic surgery. Limb reduction."

"If you don't mind my asking, Dermid, why would you want to disable yourself?"

He sat forward, rubbed his hands together, and that's when I noticed the lopped pinky finger on the left hand. "I'll be whole without the extra limb." He told me he rehearsed being an amputee at home by binding his leg behind him. "Every morning," he said, "I wake up in the wrong body, and it's agonizing."

"Your leg is perfectly healthy?"

"Perfectly redundant." He asked me if I was a religious man.

I said, "I believe in the saints but not in God."

He quoted Mark: "'And if thy foot offend thee, cut it off: it is better for thee to halt into life, than having two feet to be cast into hell, into the fire that never shall be quenched.'"

Dermid told me that for years he thought he must be insane and did so right up until he met Patience, who helped him see that he was not abnormal. He was simply trapped in the wrong body. And now he wanted the palliative surgery that would make the correction. He told me he could do the surgery himself, but there were so many obvious risks involved. “But I will,” he said, “if I have to. I want peace. I want this compulsion exorcised. I want to wake up in the morning and smile.”

What Dermid wanted from me was to listen to him tell his story, and if I was convinced of his desperate need, his life-threatening requisite, and convinced that he suffered from Amputee Identity Disorder, then I would refer him to a surgeon who would perform, he hoped, the transfigurative operation.

I said I would listen. I asked him to be open as well—maybe the story would lead us to a different resolution. He said he would.

“Your finger,” I said.

“Building up the courage.”

It can prove difficult to reason with desire.

I was driving to Arby’s when Bay called on my cell phone to tell me a BOLO had been posted for me on the police union’s Web page. My name was there, and so were my address, my date of birth, height, weight, eye and hair color, my driver’s license number, the year, make, and model of my car, my tag number, and my unflattering driver’s license photo. Bay read me what else it said. “This man will be getting you on tape and will try to set you up and aggravate you so you will make a mistake.”

“Public enemy number one.”

“This isn’t funny, Wylie. They’re going to war with you. You don’t want that. As far as they’re concerned, you’re a criminal.”

“Maybe I should get a lawyer.”

“Get one who’ll take a bullet for you.”

Bay told me that his ex-partner, Ed, the guy who’d stiffed him in the Ecstasy deal, was dead. His naked body was found in a field swaddled in Saran Wrap, head to toe, except for a small hole for his dick to peek through.

I said, "What the fuck!"

"Apparently a bondage session gone bad. On purpose, I'd guess."

At Arby's I parked beside a Colorusso Landscaping Company step van whose logo was an abundance of plump and colorful fruits and vegetables tumbling from a wicker basket, and beneath this cornucopia, the words WEED 'EM AND REAP! Querida had modified her red Arby's polo shirt so that it showed off her attractive midriff. She had a tattoo of a hummingbird feeding at the unfurled flower of her navel. She took my order without looking at me. I took my Santa Fe salad and Diet Pepsi to a booth and opened Kelly's diary. On November 3, Kelly wrote, *Today I thought about Bobby Carrigan (we called him Carrots) who was my boyfriend in seventh and half of eightht ~~eighth~~ grade, remember? I wonder where he is right now and what is he doing? I tried to look him up on the computer at the library but there are too many Bobby Bob Robbie Rob Robert Carrigans in the country and none of them live in Belle Glade.*

In an entry written only a week before she was abducted, Kelly wrote, *I have met someone. Very cute but you might not think so. I do! He has a job and a house he rents and he bought me a Snickers, which I am saving, at the 7-eleven. He told me his name is Dutch. How cool is that?* And two days later: *I washed my hair & set it. I wore the shorts and painted my nails Strawberry Margarita. I waited outside the 7-eleven. He must like me else why the Snickers?* I made a note to let Carlos know about Dutch, but realized Carlos must have read the diary before he gave it to me. But just in case. *I invited Querida to come here after work to see my place & just gab or she could totally sleep over if she wanted to but she was busy with her boyfriend Hector who is a player & so not good for her. I went to the ~~launder laun-dro-mat~~ laundramat.*

I could see the Laundromat, Tiny Bubbles, from my seat at

Arby's. Several years ago I was walking home one night, and I saw a movie crew filming a scene in Tiny Bubbles with Demi Moore, who was playing a stripper, I think. Phoebe and I were once in the Margaret Truman Laundromat in Key West drying our sleeping bags when a young woman who had been staring at us over her paperback novel said, "You two look so beautiful together."

The longest entry was dated October 9:

> *I was on the bus to New River & I was staring at the ladybug crawling along the woman's poufy hair in front of me & we were past the airport & I caught something out of the corner of my eye & it was the clown that had scared me when I was 5 at the fair in Pahokee & so I turned to look but it was just a guy in a red wool hat working at the car wash. But I couldn't get the nasty clown out of my head. I was holding Mom's hand in the midway & she was smoking a Pall Mall (Pell Mell was how she said it) & we're standing in mud & my hand is sticky from the funnel cake & the clown bends down & squeezes my nose & it honks & the lights of the ferris wheel look like a halo behind his enormous head & his teeth are yellow & his breath stank of fish & I cried & wanted to go home & the clown slapped my mom's butt when he walked away honking & Mom smiled before she shook me quiet.*

I was sitting in the doctor's office with my father at the Gulfstream Beach Geriatric Clinic, and I was trying to imagine what my life would have been like if Phoebe and I had not split up way back when, if we had married and settled down together. I realized that this quixotic exercise was not unlike watching a chop-socky on the big screen or reading a cozy—a simple diversion from the current unpleasantness in the doctor's office and the general aggravations of my life. Dr. Hamburger helped Dad down from his desk and led him over to the examining table. He said, "I need your cooperation, Myles. Myles! Look at my eyes, Myles, and listen to my words." Dad peeked over Dr. Hamburger's shoulder and winked at me. Dr. Hamburger said, "Who's the President of the United States?"

Dad said, "I can see his face, but I can't remember his name."

Dr. Hamburger asked Dad to take off his shirt—easier said than done. Before I knew what I was doing, I was counting things. Dr. Hamburger had seventeen promotional ballpoint pens advertising prescription drugs in an Australian Pines Golf Club coffee mug. There were three silk philodendrons on a windowsill and thirty-six books on the bookshelf. I don't know why I count. To keep myself from thinking, maybe. There were two photographs of grandsons in soccer uniforms on the desk. I once counted the number of different cheeses in the refrigerated case at Central Market in Austin. There were 486. I was in Texas to deliver a paper called "Coming to Know What We Know" at a therapists' conference, but I got the dates wrong and scheduled my flight home two days after the conference ended. I was the only therapist left at the Days Inn, and I felt abandoned. I bought a bus pass and toured the city.

Dr. Hamburger was trying to unknot Dad's T-shirt from around Dad's neck. I intervened. The doctor sat in his Posture Tech office chair, leaned back, cast me a glance, raised his articulate brow, and lifted his upper eyelids. Lid-lifters tend to be a tad melodramatic. I took Dad's prescription slips. Dad put the doctor's Lexapro calculator into his pocket. Dr. Hamburger handed Dad a plastic cup and told him to pee into it. "You know the drill, Myles." Dad unzipped his fly. I stood and took his arm. I walked him to the hall and pointed to the toilet. Carlos called on my cell. He said he'd seen the BOLO and was working to get it taken down. "I told you not to fuck around. Didn't I?"

"You act like this is my fault."

"We found the other missing girl's remains."

"Where?"

"In the mangroves by the barge canal. Cut up and stuffed in a plastic tub."

"Similarities?"

"Too decomposed for me to know just now. We've got a head and a torso."

"Have you checked the 7-Eleven near the Circle?"

"I did. The night clerk told me he saw Kelly with a guy at the store. I asked him to describe the guy, and he said, 'White.' I said, 'Anything else?' He said, 'Blond hair, black shirt, khaki chinos, white, this tall.' I say, 'What kind of guy was he?' 'Asshole guy,' he says. I say I want to see the security videos. He says the camera hasn't been working. 'Why?' 'Sunspots,' he says. And then he says his boss, Mr. Goodgame, is too cheap to fix the camera."

"I've got to go. I'm with Myles."

"How is he?"

"He's not himself."

I told Dr. Hamburger that Dad had stolen his calculator.

"I've got a dozen more."

"That's not the point."

"I'll be right back." He got up to check on how things were going with Dad.

I looked at the dusty philodendron simulacra and felt a wave of despair. What's the use? I thought. What's the difference? Why the effort? There are no miracles. Dad will not recover. There is nothing to be done. There was no deliverance for Cameron when he sold everything I owned and stole meds from old ladies on oxygen because the brief rush of inhaling Spiriva was better than nothing at all. There was nothing to be done for him when he'd declare his sobriety as he was failing yet another drug test, and he'd cry and tell me he'd get better despite my mistrust of him, and when he was clean, I would regret I ever betrayed him with cynicism and a lack of faith. Cam did not survive his hunger. Mom did not survive her guilt. Dad will not survive his dementia.

I stood and shook my arms and my legs and drew a long, slow breath, and held it. I decided that Dad needed a break from his routine, or I from mine, and he would stay with me tonight. I called Almost Home and told them where he'd be. The receptionist seemed unduly pleased.

Red had an easel set up beside the cooler, and he was sitting down, painting a watercolor of my house, only he made the pale house orangey. I introduced him to Dad. Red talked about opacity and hue. Dad sat in Red's other lawn chair and shut his eyes. Red told me that a green apple contains every wavelength except green, and I took his word for it. He said that the little black smudge in the window was Django. Phoebe arrived unexpectedly, parked behind my car, and joined us on the lawn. At first Dad didn't recognize her. It had been twenty or so years since he'd last seen her. But then he smiled, shook his finger at her, and recited a verse:

Now Phoebe may
by night or day
enjoy her book along the way.
Electric light
dispels the night
Upon the Road of Anthracite.

Phoebe looked at me. "We need to talk."

I could tell she was angry by the set of her jaw, which jutted out a bit in what she must have considered a gesture of casual indifference or chilly condescension. The jaw and the lifted brow suggested, however, a rather vehement indignation. Red said he'd entertain Dad while we went in the house for our chat. "Use your inside voices," he said.

We sat at the kitchen table. I said, "*You're* angry at *me* because *you're* moving away?"

"You knew the end was coming. You have to move on."

Django walked across the kitchen with one of my socks in his mouth trailing between his legs.

Phoebe said, "You've got a date tomorrow with Heather Price at the King's Arms Pub."

"I'm not going."

"She'll meet you on the patio at eight. Here's her photo. She's a teacher, no kids. She's into classic rock, Caribbean cruises, and the Food Channel."

"Do you love Kai?"

She nodded. She brought her fist to her mouth and said, "I do."

12

Oliver called and said he had the information I had requested on "Mal" and "Hal." He was dying for kefta, so we met at the Falafel House. I ordered tabbouleh. There were four small tables with blue tablecloths. A boom box behind the counter played Algerian raï. The only other diner inside wore a black nylon tracksuit, the jacket unzippered to his protruding stomach. He sucked on a kalamata olive and spoke very loudly in Russian on his cell phone while he scratched—make that *massaged*—his balls. Some of what Oliver told me about Malacoda I already knew—the bogus nonprofits, the GOP fund-raising, the Beltway connections, the lobbying, the casino boats, of course, and the dubious philanthropies. I learned that he owned a popular D.C. restaurant, Dante's, where he exchanged food for favors.

Oliver opened his manila folder and slid several photographs of Malacoda toward me. The Russian said, "Khorosho, khorosho." The cook turned up the music. There were pictures of Malacoda in silky T-shirts, in polo shirts, in dark suits and blue shirts with white collars, and in one photo he wears an improbable black, double-breasted, belted raincoat with epaulettes and an awkward black fedora. Not only was he never smiling, he seemed to have swallowed his lips.

Oliver said, "Little Jack was born with a silver spoon up his ass. Daddy owned a very prosperous luxury car dealership. Jack went to Oberlin undergrad and on to Georgetown Law. He was a wrestler in college, president of the Young Republicans, glee club, debate team, fraternity, all that Jimmy Stewart sort of thing. He's the kind of guy who'd cross the street to be unpleasant to you."

Oliver finished his kefta. He reached across the table and helped himself to my tabbouleh.

I said, "How did you burn yourself?" He had a nasty wound just above his wrist.

"On the stove. I wanted to see how the shea butter worked on wounds."

"You did this on purpose?"

"In the name of science. You should have seen what it looked like yesterday." He took another forkful from my plate. "Jack Malacoda lobbied for several dozen Indian tribes who got casinos and for a few that did not because he took their millions and sold them out."

I pushed my plate across to Oliver. "I'm stuffed." I noticed for the first time that Stavros Kanaracus was in the corner, sitting at a table for one and fiddling with his cell phone—reading his e-mail or taking our picture, you couldn't tell.

"He's got a partner in the boat business."

"Park McArthur."

"That's him. Jack sent Park an e-mail about his Indian clients calling them chimps and morons."

"You tapped his e-mail? You're good."

"I'm no Romanian teenager, but I know my way around the Internet."

"Did Malacoda work for the Tequestas?"

"Briefly."

"So you know, of course, that Halliday sold the boats to Malacoda and McArthur."

"And I know they reneged on the payments, claiming Halliday misrepresented the actual value of the business."

"Really?"

"I know what you're thinking—that Malacoda put Halliday on ice—"

"Halliday on ice?"

"The cops don't think so. Doesn't make sense. He didn't need to."

"Did you come across someone named Pino?"

"Some old dude's staring at us."

"I know."

"Want me to tell him to stop?"

"You don't want to do that. He owns the place."

"He's being rude." Oliver turned toward Stavros. "What are you looking at?"

Stavros smiled.

I touched Oliver's wrist, leaned toward him, and whispered, "He's a bad man."

"So am I."

"No, you're not," I said. "Pino?"

"Pino Basilio."

"What about him?"

"Halliday's associate. Not much on him. He maybe had an interest in the boats and the restaurant. I'll keep looking."

The Russian walked to the doorway and stood there staring at a man talking to his reflection in the window of the antiques shop across the street. The Russian picked at his teeth with a key and sucked up what he'd dislodged. The man across the street waved his arms in disgust and walked away from his reflection. Oliver told me that the local attorney who handled the boat transaction was a fellow named Mickey Pfeiffer. I knew the name from somewhere. Maybe the papers. "Mickey Pfeiffer," I said.

"Pfeiffer, Kline, and Lukeman. Downtown New River."

I paid our bill. I swung by the house to check on Django. I found him sleeping in the bathroom sink. Red was off somewhere. I called Patience and asked her what she knew about Sedona. She told me it was about her favorite place in the universe. Red rock canyons, serenity, hummingbirds, wildflowers, healers, and visionaries under every stone. I told her to put the Alaska tickets on hold for now.

She said, "You know, Wylie, we don't all crave to be symmetrical."

"What are you talking about?"

"Dermid. Matching body parts."

"I can't talk to you about Dermid."

"Living with amputation is easier than living with the obsession that demands it."

That afternoon I had three straight hours of marriage counseling that began with Wes and Ellen Hillistrom. Wes was a professor of finance at Everglades College and liked me to call him "Doctor." When I asked Ellen a question, he answered for her, and so I'd ask her again. Wes thought that Xanax was the solution to Ellen's current marital discontent. Xanax would grant her the serenity to accept what she could not change.

Mr. Finn Wallace owned a lucrative chain of electronic stores where you probably bought your wide-screen TV. He could afford his expensive prescription drug habit. This was the Wallaces' first session. Linda said she wanted her old husband back. Finn said he was happy with his addiction, if that's what you want to call it, and with his assortment of hangers-on. His pals all had culinary nicknames: Sloppy Joe, Captain Crunch, Hoppin' John, Big Mac. Like that. "I won't lie to you," he said. "I want to live until I die—balls to the wall." I asked him why he was here. He said, "For Linda. Her happiness is the second most important thing in my life." When I asked him what he wanted out of counseling, he said he wanted Linda to let him have a mistress. When I asked Linda, she said she didn't want him to die.

Bill and Dottie Aubuchon walked in holding hands and smiling, so I assumed they'd done their homework and dealt with Bill's recent infidelity. He'd been seeing Ellen Hillistrom since the two of them met in my waiting room a month ago. I wasn't sure if Ellen knew that I knew, and, of course, I couldn't say anything that would violate confidentiality. Dottie said that Bill had apologized, and she had accepted the apology, and they were ready to move on. "I know that every husband cheats," she said. When I told her that wasn't true, Bill flashed his brows and rolled his eyes at her like, Isn't he a card?

Bay and I were sitting in the grandstand at Tropical Racetrack catching the last three races. I'd bet three long shots to show. I looked up to see Crooked Letter drifting serenely around the far turn eight lengths behind the pack.

I told Bay that in every dream I'd had the night before someone or other in the dream mentioned a guy named Willard Daggett, so when I got up in the morning I Googled Willard. He goes by the name "Tuck" and doesn't look anything like I expected him to. He wore a black cowboy hat in all the pictures. Had a bristly mustache and bifocals. "What do you think this means, Bay?"

"Maybe he works for Malacoda."

"You think I'm obsessed with Malacoda?"

Oxygen Man ran fourth in the eighth, but had me going until he faded in the stretch. Bay ripped up his tickets. I said of Malacoda, "How much money does a person need?"

"It's not about money."

"It's about . . . ?"

"Power. Money's just how you keep score."

"And a conscience would be a serious inconvenience for him."

"He probably enjoys watching people suffer as much as he does making them suffer."

When I mentioned Mickey Pfeiffer, Bay brightened and sat up. "I knew that clown when he was chasing ambulances and running commercials on *News at Noon*."

The horses paraded out of the paddock. My horse, Shambles, was a gorgeous but skittish gray mare. Bay said he once played a house game with Mickey and Mickey's cigar-chomping amigos and lost. "They were so bad I couldn't figure out what the hell they were thinking. Then I realized I was the mark, and the boys were in cahoots. I bade them adieu."

"How much did they take you for?"

"I left with a Rolex Tudor and a Hermès Cape Cod, so I figure it was a wash."

"They didn't come after you?"

Bay smiled. "I bet you know this Pfeiffer. He's a wheel on the local charity circuit—splashy philanthropist, Republican fundraiser—the governor was best man at Pfeiffer's most recent wedding."

And then I remembered: I had met him briefly, shaken his hand. He hosted a fund-raising event for the Everglades Arts Commission at his home, and I was there on behalf of the theater. "I've been to his house."

"What did you think?"

"It was like an upscale eighteenth-century Venetian bordello."

"Where the priests go on their Saturday nights."

"He had his initials monogrammed on the cuff of his shirt, MVP." Pfeiffer lived on the Intracoastal, owned a fleet of luxury cars and an eighty-five-foot yacht docked behind the house.

Bay said, "He has his own police force—off-duty Eden and New River cops and ESO deputies. Uses them as guards and as investigators."

Shambles stumbled out of the gate, and my dream of a new iPad was over. By the time the horses crossed the finish line, Bay and I were the only people sitting in the grandstand.

I said, "Investigators for what?"

Bay told me that Pfeiffer made his first millions settling sexual harassment lawsuits. He figured that any guy with ten million bucks would be willing to spend two million to keep a mistress quiet. And three million if that mistress was sixteen. Mickey got half. And he was often the guy who introduced the young lady to the happily married big shot. And if the big shot wouldn't play ball, Mickey took him up to his office and ran the video of the big shot fucking his mistress. He'd say, We can end this right now, or I can depose your wife. Do you think she'll enjoy the movie?"

"And justice is served."

"Or he's had his cops hack a computer, bug a phone, make a video, go through the garbage."

We headed to the clubhouse. Bay said that Pfeiffer owned Knives & Forks, a popular restaurant on Las Brisas where the wealthy and careless meet the blond and enhanced and where many a shady political deal had gone down. "I have to make one stop," Bay said. "I just won the trifecta, my friend!"

I turned to look at the tote board. Bay had won $1,345.

"Dinner's on me," he said.

"I wish I could," I said, "but I'm meeting someone."

• • •

Heather seemed surprised when I shook her hand and introduced myself. I sat down and ordered a vodka martini for me and another Long Island iced tea for her. "So," I said, "we meet at last."

She pulled her head back and half smiled, like, what was I talking about? A man at the adjacent picnic table adjusted his tracheostomy tube and smoked his cigarette.

"What do you teach?" I said.

She flipped a strand of hair over her ear. "You don't look anything like your photo," she said.

"I know. I'm much taller and not so flat."

Heather taught third grade at Dan Marino Elementary in Progresso. She wore an orange madras jumper over a white short-sleeve jersey. She said, "I Googled you."

"On our first date?"

"There's a photo of you with orange hair."

I told her I had been in a play at the time, that I played an aging novelist with writers' block who has a crush on a pretty young fan. He figures her amorous attentions might rejuvenate his prose. But he knows she would never fall for a guy with gray hair. "Do you enjoy the theater?"

"I've never been."

Our drinks arrived. Heather finished the last of her first drink and handed the glass to our waitress, who had an intricate tattoo of a muscular snake coiled around her calf.

"You like that?" Heather said. "The tattoo?"

"It's striking, isn't it?"

"Why aren't you on Facebook? Do you have something to hide?"

"It never occurred to me."

Heather stirred her drink. "You look pretty hot."

"Why, thank you."

"No, I mean you're sweating a lot."

I wiped my forehead and neck with a napkin.

"You're not married, are you?"

"No."

"Of course, you wouldn't be the first guy to lie about that."

I found out that Heather owned a time-share at Disney World, that she, at thirty-seven, was already looking forward to retirement, when her real life would begin. Her dream was to own a Hallmark franchise, a card and gift store in a heavily trafficked mall. She said she collected pandas, and jiggled her dangly panda earring for me, and said that some days she'd just sit at home all day and watch like fourteen episodes of *CSI: Miami.*

I said, "Where do you live, Heather?"

She smiled. "Not on the first date."

When I got home, I checked my e-mail. Phoebe had pasted Heather's e-mail to my account:

> *Sorry, Riley, I guess I'm looking for someone younger and, I don't know, peppier, funnier. Thanks for the drinks and good luck on your search for a soul mate.*

To bolster my flagging spirits, I suppose, Phoebe attached a thatsamore link to another woman in the area looking for romance. The profile indicated that she loved "to live life to the heights, making the most of every day" and that she spoke English with a charming accent, was fluent in Bulgarian, had some Russian and Polish. She was looking for a polite and interesting man "to hang up with." She finished by saying that while she was by no means a "religious fantastic," she would "like more a guy" who follows in the footsteps of the Lord. "And while we all sin, I just want one who makes the effort to not. I would like to live a pure life, get married, and then get to the freaky." And there was Marlena's photo.

13

I asked Red if he'd ever given any thought to marriage. He peeked at me over the top of his newspaper and said, "Yeah. I have so much to offer a woman." He folded the paper and placed it on the grass by his chair. He freshened our coffees from the carafe he'd liberated from IHOP. We were dining al fresco, sitting at a card table he'd rescued from the Melancholy Library Dumpster and revived with wood-grain contact paper. Scrambled eggs, bacon, and grits.

"Bay's girlfriend needs a green card."

"Then he should marry her."

"It's not in his constitution."

"You should marry her."

"He'll give the willing groom ten thousand dollars."

"I can't use the money."

"And a condo."

"Condos come with fees and commandos."

"I told him I'd ask."

Red told me that his first marriage was tepid, aimless, and mercifully brief. The second was prosperous and pleasurable, and he'd still be married to Barbara Ann if only he hadn't started snorting coke. He told me he'd been the CFO of an IT start-up, owned a four-bedroom home in a gated community in Houston and a vacation cottage on Lake Livingston. He drove a Lexus and a Tahoe fish-and-ski boat. He squandered it all, squandered it quickly, and found himself among the lost and foundering.

"You're okay now."

"Detox, rehab, halfway house, twelve-step meetings. I have a second chance. Peace of mind. A happy ending."

"Are you afraid that drinking will send you back to the life?"

"No, but I'm afraid money will."

I was sitting alone on the couch in my office distracting myself with an L. Manning Vines novel, *No Regrets, Quixote*, and trying very hard not to imagine myself encased in Saran Wrap like Bay's ex-partner. Things looked desperate for the four starving Alaska gold miners trapped in their tiny cabin at the mercy of a raging blizzard. Forget your waterboard; just bring out the box of Stretch-Tite, and I'll tell you whatever truth you want me to tell you—right now. My shoulders and neck tensed; my heartbeat accelerated. Just then a propitious knock at my door delivered me from my diabolical imagination. I closed the book.

The stranger entered without waiting for my response. I said, "Please, have a seat."

He said, "I understand you want to speak to me."

I said, "Who are you?"

"Pino Basilio." He sat across the coffee table from me in my therapist's chair. "So talk to me," he said.

Pino wore a black linen sport jacket, a starched white shirt, open at the collar, jeans, black tasseled loafers, and no socks. His hair was white, his eyebrows black. Luis must have given him my card. I told him about my marginal involvement in the Halliday murders. I explained my misgivings as to the official cause of death. "I know you were his partner—"

"You don't know anything."

"And I was hoping you could shed some light on the tragedy."

"Why?"

"I'm trying to understand it."

"There's nothing to understand." Pino sat with his hands folded in his lap. He looked around the office.

"But nothing about the killings makes sense," I said.

He sat forward. "Why do you think anything has to make sense? Nothing makes sense. That's a given, a starting point. Only children think otherwise."

When I begged to differ, Pino brought a finger to his lips and shushed me. "Forget about this," he said.

"Do you think he was suicidal?"

Pino shrugged.

"Did he seem despondent at all?"

"That is none of your business, my friend. Stick to what you know. You're not a cop."

"No, I'm not. I'm just bothered."

"See a shrink."

"I don't think this was murder-suicide, but I don't know why someone would kill the entire family."

"Because they could?"

"Take innocent lives for no reason?"

"Sometimes the pleasure's in the taking."

I may have raised a dubious eyebrow.

"Yes, Mr. Melville, there is malice in the world. In your world, you can hold on to the illusion that you're in some kind of control, that you know the rules. Only thing is, your world doesn't exist. As long as you stay put, no one will give a shit, and you'll be fine. But you get involved in what does not concern you, you will be dealt with."

I wanted to be dauntless and say, Why, that sounds like a threat, Mr. Basilio, but I was afraid to.

"I represent the interests of the federal government in this matter, and I'm advising you not to get mired in this swamp."

Frank Sinatra sang "Sentimental Journey." Pino reached inside his suit jacket and retrieved his phone. He checked the display, punched a button, and returned the phone to his pocket. He stood. "Stick to what you know." He held out his hand. I stood and we shook.

He squeezed my hand until I asked him to stop. I remembered what Bay had once told me—never let a stranger take your hand. Pino could have crushed the bones, but he smiled and released my hand. He patted my face. He pointed at my novel with his chin. He said, "All the miners die." He walked to the door. He turned back to me. "That's the only real ending, isn't it?" He gave me a casual salute. "Adiós, mi amigo. Todos nos morimos."

I was meeting Bay for blinis and caviar at Baikal. I'd called him earlier to report on my unsettling encounter with Pino. He told me he wasn't having such a splendid day, either. He'd fill me in over lunch. I sat at a red light on Main. My phone rang—Georgia, who hadn't talked to me in a year and only ever called to extol the pleasures and virtues of her perfectly exciting and delightful life. I didn't answer. I called Phoebe's cell, and she didn't answer. I watched a disheveled man and a leashed pit bull cross the street. The dog carried a stuffed toy bunny in his mouth, and the man's T-shirt read, HI! I'M YOUR MOM'S NEW BOYFRIEND.

Bay was already sitting at a shaded sidewalk table. He told me that he'd found out that morning that Marlena had a husband in Romania, one Ion Marcu, who was serving time in Jilava Prison for jewel theft. He wouldn't be getting out anytime soon. Marlena couldn't divorce Marcu from the States, but if she left, she couldn't come back. And there was the visa problem as well. Bay said, "I have to do something, but what can I do?"

"If you're not going to marry her, what's the problem?"

"Trying to help her out of a jam. She doesn't want to be married to Marcu. She'd prefer an American husband."

I said, "Where is she now?"

"I sent her to the day spa at the Silver Palace."

Our food arrived. We raised our glasses and drank our shots of Russian Standard. Pretty soon we were talking about trust, and Bay was sour on the whole idea. I told him about Marlena's thatsamore profile. He said he knew about it, but that it seemed unimportant in light of the new revelation. "She's an enterprising girl."

"She's not who she said she is on the site, is she?"

"You can't trust anyone, Wylie, not even me."

"I trust you."

"You shouldn't."

"I have to."

"Don't say I didn't warn you."

"You're just upset that Marlena lied to you."

"Some people will use trust as a weapon. Malacoda would. The Lehman Brothers people. They cultivate your trust. They win your confidence. They arrange for your reliance on them. And they've got you right where they can fuck you."

"I don't want to live in a world without trust."

"Then you'll be conned and betrayed."

"That's the price I'll pay."

Bay moved his plate to the side, took a deck of cards from his pocket, and fanned them faceup across the table. He told me to cut the deck, and I did. He said they teach sociopathy in business schools. No right or wrong. Just the bottom line. It's all that matters. He told me to pick a card, look at it, remember it, slip it back into the deck. Eight of spades. And then he went off on a rant about Ayn Rand and her cretinous drivel. He said Alan Greenspan was a felonious sociopath. Bay said sociopaths have the advantage—they know they're right. Decent people always have misgivings. He never touched the deck. The check arrived. I said I had it, took out my wallet, and there was the eight of spades folded around my credit card.

"How the hell did you do that?"

He said, "The closer you get, the more you're being fooled." He reshuffled the cards, spread them faceup. He said, "Don't pick one; just think of a card. Just picture it."

I did, the ten of hearts. He put the deck away. He said, "The harder you try to figure out an illusion, the easier you are to fool."

I said, "We've done this one—Lincoln's collar."

"We have? Never mind, then."

I said goodbye. When I got to my car, I got a call from Bay. He told me to open the glove box. I did and there was the ten of hearts. I asked him again how he'd done it.

"There can only be one answer—the card was already in your car."

"Then how did you get me to pick that card?"

"That's the magic."

I watched a slide show on Mickey Pfeiffer's Web page, Pfeifferlife, to remind myself what he looked like. He was stocky and looked to have a low and dense center of gravity, like he'd be impossible to knock off his feet. He was mid-fiftyish, I'd guess, with a thin brown crew cut and tiny blue eyes closely set in a beefy face. His ubiquitous smile was all business—forceful and fluorescent. There were dozens of photos of Mickey with this or that professional athlete and with an assortment of South Beach celebrities. Mickey and his lovely wife with the governor; Mickey in a cowboy hat at the Republican National Convention; Mickey shaking hands with the Israeli ambassador. Mickey had a taste for snug vests, ostentatious watches, and expensive cigars.

Knives & Forks was spacious and sleek, with white tables, a gleaming white-tiled floor, white leather chairs and bench seats. There were several tall clear glass vases of elegant white calla lilies on the glass and granite back bar. I was led to my table by the hostess, Sinead, who urged me to enjoy my meal. I asked her where she was from. "The accent," I said. "British?" She told me she was a Saint. "I'm from Saint Helena. In the South Atlantic."

"You're the first Saint I've ever met."

I told Thatcher, my waiter (*Thatcher?*), that I'd like an Innis & Gunn, and I watched the muster of young professionals relaxing after work at the bar. Many of the gentlemen wore bespoke suits, their starched shirts opened two buttons at the collar. Others, the single guys who had gone home after work to freshen up, wore these graphic Ed Hardy T-shirts—lots of geishas and skulls. The ladies, for the most part, had straight, shoulder-length hair, wore silk and satin sheath dresses, and drank blue martinis. The men leaned toward the women—all the better to hear them—and the women's earnest smiles revealed spectacular dental work.

Thatcher returned with my beer and enthusiastically recommended the evening's entrée special, the pan-roasted Niman Ranch leg of lamb. "It rocks," he said, and he kissed the tips of his fingers. *Mwah!* When I ordered an iceberg wedge and the crispy pork bellies, I could see that I'd lost his respect. He didn't even bother to say, Excellent choice. He didn't bother to write the order down. I handed him the menu and asked him if he'd seen Mickey

Pfeiffer this evening. He pointed with the menu to an empty and secluded corner booth. "That's Mr. Pfeiffer's table."

The lights dimmed just a bit, and I heard Charlie Parker playing "Ornithology" on the sound system. I noticed a handsome couple at a table about fifteen feet away. She had pushed her salad dish away and sat with her elbows on the table and her head in her hands. He said something, and when she did not respond, he leaned back in his chair, crossed his legs, and stared at the ceiling. He tapped a finger on the table like he was saying, Sign here, and here, initial here, sign, sign, initial, and sign. He had that five o'clock shadow the fashion models affect in *New Yorker* ads. His short blond hair was combed forward and rose to a quiff like the Gerber baby's. He looked like a Cal or a Kim. I could see that he was not being forthright with her. She looked hurt and confused.

When I want to know what a person's thinking or feeling, I mimic, as discreetly as I can, his facial expressions, his gestures, mannerisms, his posture, his general behavior. If you mirror a person's behavior, you'll see that you become infected with her emotions, and you'll be better able to imagine her thoughts.

Cal leaned toward the woman and spoke, his arms spread, his palms up. He was asking her, begging her, to please be reasonable, please. She sat with her arms folded across her chest, taking rapid, shallow breaths and staring at her impenetrable future in the unblemished white linen tablecloth. I leaned in to my table, spread my arms, palms up. I looked over and saw Cal shaking his head deliberately, telling her she must have known it would end like this. Cal's been seeing Brigid here on the side for eighteen months. Mondays and Thursdays after work and the occasional weekend indulgence up at Chalet Suzanne or tucked away at his friend Gordon's cottage on Big Pine Key. She knew he was married, of course, unhappily so, he had claimed. "My wife and I have an understanding." A year and a half wasted on this sorry son of a bitch. Has one word he's ever spoken been truthful?

I looked over and saw that she had a tissue squeezed in her hand and her shoulders were trembling. Cal had sprinkled a mound of salt on the table and was trying to balance the shaker on its edge in the pile. Thatcher brought my salad, said, "Bon appetite!" and slipped away without asking if I'd like another beer. When I looked back, Cal had actually bared his teeth and was now pointing a finger in Brigid's face, and I knew that she had threatened a phone call to the wife. Cal dropped a couple of bills on the table, stood, and walked away. He did not even give Brigid the dignity of appearing to walk out on him. Brigid stifled her tears. I hoped she'd gather her things and go home, and I worried that she might end up at the bar batting her eyelashes at the fellow in the Tommy Bahama aloha shirt.

And then I saw Mickey Pfeiffer himself, standing by the hostess station, talking on his cell phone. Blazing smile. Expansive voice. He held his forehead with a thumb and finger as he listened. His pink linen shirt was untucked, rolled at the sleeves, unbuttoned at the collar. He wore white trousers, blue loafers, and a braided leather necklace. The lenses of his red-framed glasses were softly tinted. Every so often, as he talked, Mickey rose up on his toes. He signaled Thatcher to fetch him a drink at the bar and deliver it to his table.

By the time I finished my meal—really quite wonderful—I had decided to introduce myself to Mickey, remind him of the fund-raiser we'd mutually attended, say something in lavish praise of his prodigious philanthropy, and see what happened. Maybe he'd ask me to join him for a drink, and maybe I'd still be there later when Jack Malacoda and his dreary entourage arrived. But before Thatcher returned my bill, I saw Kevin Shanks, out of uniform, stroll into the restaurant with the elegant Mandy Pfeiffer,

Mickey's radiant wife. She sat with Mickey, gave him a peck on the cheek. Shanks gave a casual salute, a quick bow, and made his way to the bar.

I called Carlos. I told him where I was and whom I was looking at. Carlos told me this was Kevin's extra-duty assignment—Pfeiffer's bodyguard and security chief.

"There's a lot you don't tell me, Carlos."

"There's a lot you don't need to know."

"Friends don't let friends wander in the dark."

"Get the leg of lamb."

Brigid had slipped away while I was preoccupied. I signed my check. Knives & Forks had added an 18 percent tip, thus screwing Thatcher out of the 2 percent more I would have given him, which was fine with me. I stopped to ask Sinead if she'd seen a woman in a black dress leave in the last few minutes.

"Linda?"

"Linda?"

"She came with Kim Swain, but he left in a huff a while ago."

"She'd been crying."

"She's a big girl."

I looked at the bar and didn't see Tommy Bahama. "Did she leave alone?"

"Would you like her phone number?"

Red had left a Post-it on my door telling me he'd be at a fortieth birthday party for Nikki S. over at the NA house on Lantana. Django let me tickle his belly for a few seconds before he looked reassuringly into my eyes and bit me. When I asked him if he knew who might have unrolled the paper towels, he blasted off for the bedroom. I remembered the call from Georgia. I poured myself some cognac, put on Mendelssohn's *Songs Without Words*, slumped into the couch, and listened to Georgia's distressing message. Her husband, Tripp, had apparently fallen off the ship, was lost at sea, and was presumed dead. "Wylie, what am I going to do?" He'd gotten up at dawn like he always did, went off for his stroll around the deck, and vanished. She and the boys were now in Martinique dealing with forensic bureaucrats and criminal investigators. I called but found that her voice mail was full.

So I was lying awake in bed later, trying to imagine exactly what you would have to do to fall over a railing on the promenade deck and plunge fifty or so feet into the water. Django was asleep and wheezing serenely on my neck. I thought of Brueghel's Icarus splashing, unnoticed, into the sea and of Auden's poem about the old masters and how they were never wrong about suffering, and how Tripp's drowning would have happened while the officer steering the ship whistled a melody that his father had taught him and watched a frigate bird hover over the bow and while the cook fired the grill in the galley and while someone else was brushing his teeth or was slipping out of bed, trying not to wake the baby, and while, on the sundeck, a Catholic priest reading his breviary, watching the sunrise, thought he heard a forsaken cry and listened, shrugged, checked his watch, and walked to the dining room.

I gave myself ten more minutes, and if I wasn't asleep, I'd get up and read. Django slid off my neck and onto the mattress, but didn't wake up. I saw the ten of hearts, on the ceiling, I thought, but my eyes were closed, and that's when I realized that Bay had figured out what had happened at the Halliday house, why none of the neighbors saw anyone enter or leave the place—the killers were already in the house.

14

I bounced Django's Ping-Pong balls across the living room until, at last, spent from the chase, he surrendered, curled up on the terrazzo floor, stared up at me, closed his eyes, and made me disappear. I sipped my coffee and for no reason at all thought about Red, and realized I had no idea where he bathed or carried out his other ablutionary and expurgatory affairs. The phone rang and Django stretched himself into a bow. Dad told me that he had once seen an eight-millimeter movie after the war that featured a zaftig brunette with bobbed hair having intercourse with various dogs, one of which, he was sure, was a blue heeler. He said he would like for me to purchase that film for him, if I wouldn't mind. I'll also need a screen and a projector, he said. I asked him if he was out of his mind, which I shouldn't have.

On my way to the car I asked Red, "Where do you, you know, where—"

"The outdoor showers on the Boardwalk and the public restroom."

"That works for you?"

"Just fine."

"Well, in an emergency—"

"Wouldn't think of it."

I drove to the Barnes & Noble at Maplewood Plaza to pick up a novel that Inez thought I would like. *An Air of Baffled Silence* was ninety-two-year-old Pilar Lamb's first book. I read the opening sentence, "You don't lie unless the truth is dangerous," and I bought the book. I thought I'd sit and consider what I knew about the Halliday killings. Jake Karbowski, local gadfly, had set up his office, as usual, in a corner of the café. He'd commandeered the only large table, as usual, and set up shop beneath the mural of famous coffee-drinking authors. He had his laptop, his printer, his phone, and his engraved nameplate on the table. Jake is a conspiracy theorist, attends every city and county commission meeting, and posts a cranky blog, *Everything's Jake*. I bought him a coffee and pulled a chair up to his table.

Jake said, "I'm gonna take out the Goldman Sachs assholes." He put a finger to his temple and depressed his thumb.

"No, you're not."

"And the AIG, BP—all the fucking thieves."

"That's crazy talk, Jake."

"If this were China, you know what would happen? They'd frog-march those cocksuckers out to the middle of a soccer stadium and shoot the motherfuckers in the back of the head."

"Calm yourself; you'll have a stroke."

"They steal us blind; they bankrupt their companies, and they get bonuses!"

"You'd only get the first one shot, and you'd be arrested."

He smiled. "I misspoke. I'm going to *have* them taken out. I'll be sitting right here at my desk, sipping a nonfat vanilla latte." His phone boinged. "I have to take this," he said.

I stood.

He told me, "This conversation never happened." He turned his back on the room, looked up at Franz Kafka, and said, "Talk to me."

I took an empty table by the window and noticed that I had a voice mail from Georgia. The cops aren't buying her story. She and the boys are being held in Martinique for questioning, and their ship has sailed. The cops, for some reason, suspect that Tripp may have arranged his own disappearance and that she may have known about the plan. Can you imagine that? They're calling me an accessory, she said. Do I look like an accessory? A pearl necklace is an accessory. I called back but got no answer. Mailbox full.

Someone had left a printout of a Craigslist personals ad on my table after folding it into an airplane. I smoothed it out and read:

> My name is Karma. My lips drip as hunneycome. My mouth is smoother than virgin olive oil. I been divorced & am curintly involved with someone, but would like out of it. Could you be my way out? I have 3 kids: I aborted one when I was 14. One I lost to DCFS, and one that live off and on with me and the daddy when he is outta jail. I am curintly dancing at a gentlemen's club, but my dream job would be to cut and style hair at the mall. I have cheated on all the sorry men in my life before but would like to change this. Would you like to be my first faithefull relationship? Please write.

If Karma's ad were to appear on a college board exam, you might be asked the following questions:

1. Karma's opening remarks echo, one might even say "parody," what great masterpiece of literature?
    a. *Tom Jones*
    b. *Beloved*
    c. *Song of Songs*
    d. *Hiawatha*

2. How many children did Karma actually have?
    a. 3
    b. 6
    c. 2
    d. Insufficient evidence to ascertain

An older couple in matching tropical-themed cabana outfits were now talking to Jake, asking him about local restaurants and scenic attractions. They'd assumed he was the café's concierge, I suppose. *You don't lie unless the truth is dangerous.* Was Inez sending me a message? Surely not. What did she even know about the Hallidays and Shanks and Malacoda? I opened the novel to a random page and read the first complete sentence: "While her husband was dying on the floor of a florist shop, Nan James was at home getting herself ready for their big night out—dinner at Creola's and dancing at the Ballroom of Romance." Brueghel and Auden all over again. I thought I should probably read the book as soon as I could. I don't believe in the efficacy of magical thinking, but what I do like about this kind of pre-logical, associative thinking I was engaged in is that it will lead you to places you would never have gone on your own. And who doesn't love a surprise? And, anyway, who said that logic was thinking? It's only one kind, and a dull one, at that. I do believe in coincidences because they happen, but they don't happen for any meaningful reason. Events coincide because we notice. The synchronicity is in our heads. And then I looked up from the book and into the café walked someone I recognized but couldn't place, and she was walking toward me. She smiled and took a seat across from me. "You never called," she said.

"Make yourself comfortable, Ms. Curry."

She folded her hands together on her purse and smiled brightly. "Why do you dislike me, Wylie Melville?"

"Just a gut reaction."

"I grow on people."

"So does fungus."

"Ouch."

"Sorry." I asked her how her book on the Halliday case was going. She told me she'd moved on to a juicier story. Sex, drugs, and corruption. She asked me if I'd heard of Mandy Proia. I hadn't.

"Mandy Proia doing business as the Melancholy Intimate Dance Academy."

I still had no idea, so Perdita explained that when Mandy's obtuse and well-lubricated husband, Arnie, found out after only ten years in business that the only dance Mandy did was the supine samba, he threatened to kill her. Said so in front of witnesses at Gino's Deli, and then he clubbed her with a hard salami, appropriately enough, and had to be restrained by Gino's sons.

"So did he kill her?"

"He vanished. Three months ago. Without a trace. Until last Friday when a meat-cutter at Señor Carne found a human leg in the freezer—still in its cotton Dockers pant leg and wearing a tube sock and a penny loafer. This morning the medical examiner's report identified that leg as having belonged to one Arnold Proia. And I think the tube sock tells you all you need to know about the late, lamented one."

Perdita's source told her that Mandy's dance card had been signed by some of the county's most illustrious and influential citizens. Judges, politicians, cops, lawyers, and so on.

"And you believed this guy?"

"I saw the list."

"How did you manage that?"

"A brilliantly executed blow job."

"Please!"

"There's nothing some horn dogs won't surrender for oral sex. It amazes me. It amazes all of us girls, actually."

"I assume that no arrests have been made."

Perdita said that she was told by the police chief himself that there was no proof that a crime had been committed. "I told him he had to be kidding. He said, 'Where's the rest of him?' I said, 'You think he might be out there hopping around?'"

"They're covering it up?"

"Protecting someone."

"Can you prove it?"

"It's like physics, Wylie. You don't have to prove it—not yet—to know it's true."

I thought, Let me assume for the moment that Chafin Halliday murdered his wife and his three children and then turned the pistol on himself. That was Carlos's conclusion, the official version of events. People snap, after all. Hadn't Ivan Kouzmanoff—whom I suddenly realized may have known Halliday—hadn't he killed his ten-year-old daughter, his wife of twelve years, and his very successful and prosperous self? Unthinkable, and yet every man has his reasons. Yes. If Halliday's our killer, then the killer was, indeed, already in the house as Bay's legerdemain suggested he would be. Let me assume that scenario and ask, Why would he slaughter his own family? Or if you prefer, *execute* his family. He must not have been enraged, to act with such collected deliberation. There was method to this madness. And maybe that was the answer—

madness, insanity. I didn't know. What I did know was that someone had removed all photographic evidence, save the stolid Olan Mills family portrait and the evangelical wanted poster of the boys, from the house. Would someone about to die bother? And I was also certain that someone other than Halliday composed and typed that suicide note on a typewriter that Halliday did not seem to have owned. And I knew that the EPD had Halliday's computer in storage and off-limits even though it might contain illuminating and incriminating data. Carlos assured me that there was nothing of forensic interest on the hard drive, but Carlos himself did not examine the hard drive. I would love for Oliver to take a crack at it. What I knew convinced me that Halliday did not kill his family.

And then it dawned on me why Halliday had no photos or videos of himself in his house or on his phone or, I would bet, on his computer. He was planning to vanish. He would also have destroyed his credit cards, probably, and tried to erase or trash his computer's hard drive. But why would he have needed to disappear?

The late Ivan Kouzmanoff, Esquire, whose intermittent employee, Vladimir Drygiin, was my client and housekeeper's live-in mushina, worked for the illustrious Mickey Pfeiffer, CEO of South Florida's largest and splashiest law firm and counsel to Jack Malacoda, a vainglorious lobbyist with the same interest in tribal gaming as Kouzmanoff, who, Malacoda, that is, with his Mafia-connected business partner Park McArthur, purchased Gold Coast Cruise Lines from Chafin Halliday and perhaps his furtive and pragmatic associate Pino Basilio with Pfeiffer's able guidance; Pfeiffer, who employed eager law enforcement officers as his personal security and investigative force, hired Shanks, a cop with a nasty reputation on the street, who, if Red was to be believed, and he was, wanted more than anything to be a made man in the mob, and who moonlighted for Caserta Wholesale Foods—did the guy ever sleep?—a Siciliani Family operation that, I would learn, catered Gold Coast Cruise Lines, then and now, hired Shanks as a personal bodyguard for his wife—Shanks, the first cop at the scene after (or before) the Halliday murders, maker of threatening phone calls, who answered, it seemed, to only one man, the thug, as Carlos called him, Clete Meatyard.

Were things that rotten in Everglades County? Well, let's see. Five elected officials had been indicted in the past year for fraud, extortion, bribery, money laundering, and conspiracy to commit wire fraud. Six cops had gone to jail for assault (on camera), extortion, fraud (on camera), coercing sex from illegal immigrants, groping female suspects at traffic stops, distributing Oxycodone, and grand theft (a tractor). A half dozen other public officials had been arrested and faced charges. A town manager was busted for stealing $500,000 from town coffers. One county commissioner made the mistake of accepting a doggie bag stuffed with cash from an undercover FBI agent.

Nothing happens in Everglades County, a Democratic stronghold, by the way, without some unctuous bootlicker getting his or her payoff. These slopsuckers will accept anything, doesn't have to be a feed bag full of greenbacks. Golf carts, hot tubs, blacktop for the driveway, tickets to a Dolphins game, bottles of single-malt, rental cars, a little landscaping in the front yard, a cruise to Nassau, dinner at a supper club, country club memberships, swimming pool resurfacing, iPod nanos, gift certificates for an Asian massage, in-kind campaign contributions, of course, window tinting, carpet cleaning, lap dances, reserved parking spaces, use of the corporate jet, shoes, workout equipment, anything except a check. The idea of doing business with honesty and integrity is laughable, apparently.

My phone played "Help Me, Rhonda." Venise. I told her I'd pick her and Oliver up at six. That should give us plenty of time to get there. We were attending a benefit fund-raiser for a friend of Hiroshi's whose daughter had some rare form of cancer. It was being held at the estate of Dr. Jordan Jordan in the Isles of Las Brisas. That's right, two first names, three spectacular children, four plastic surgery clinics, one flawless wife, six vintage automobiles. We'd be meeting Bay there. Dr. Jordan had once hired Bay to teach him how to win at the poker table.

"Make it five-thirty," Venise said.

"It doesn't start until seven."

"I'll need time to inspect the items in the silent auction."

"Quarter of six." I asked her if she'd talked to Dad this morning. "And did he say anything about movies?"

"Well, he thinks he's Lionel Barrymore."

Venise decided to bid on the dinner for two at Yardbird but wouldn't go any higher than a hundred bucks. She was very much enjoying the hors d'oeuvres and spotting the occasional ex-professional athlete.

Bay said I should forget about my obsession with Halliday. "Someone you don't know has decided that the case is closed, and that's it."

"Who?"

"Some wheel in one of the gangs."

"What gangs?"

"The police brotherhood, let's call it. The Police Benevolent Association. The Mafia. The Russians. All of the above."

Venise announced that she was going for more food. Bay brought me across the courtyard and introduced me to the DA, Ken Millard. "You two should meet," he said and then excused himself. He had to get to work.

"Bay tells me you don't care much for Mickey Pfeiffer," I said.

"For ten years he chased ambulances out of a tiny office in a

Colahatchee strip mall. And then in five years he has the biggest law firm in South Florida." Millard stirred his old-fashioned. "And so on."

We walked to a small, unoccupied table by the pool and sat. "Pfeiffer needed an expert at getting government contracts, so he hired ex–Sheriff Jacques as a consultant."

"He's out of jail?"

"As of Monday. Unbeknownst to Pfeiffer, Sheriff Jacques will be working both sides of the street."

"Interesting."

"Of course, I can't trust Jacques. But neither can Pfeiffer."

I told him I thought Pfeiffer might be involved somehow, maybe just tangentially, with the Halliday killings. I connected some dots for him, Halliday to Pino to Malacoda, the boats, the casino, and even Kouzmanoff. I explained why murder-suicide seemed preposterous.

He handed me his card. "Give me a call."

We heard gasps and muffled screams and saw people rushing toward the patio. And then I heard my sister yell, "Don't touch me! Don't look at me! Don't come near me!" Oliver made his way through the circle of guests and bent over his wife. He held out his hand. Venise said, "Get away from me!"

I excused myself. "Family emergency."

From what I could tell, Venise had tripped and tumbled down the three steps and landed facedown on the concrete. She still held a sweet bun in one hand. She rolled to her side with some effort, but refused to stand. She told Oliver once again to leave her alone, and he did. He walked to the abandoned buffet table and began to fill his plate. People shrugged, whispered, and backed away from the spectacle. I sat beside her. I said, "Venise, let me help you up."

"Don't look at me!"

She had an angry knot over her left eye and scrapes on her

wrist and forearm. She told me to cover her head with my sport coat, and I did. I waited. I patted Venise's shoulder, told her everything would be all right. She mumbled, gurgled, moaned, and whined for another ten minutes or so, and then got up and bit into the sweet roll.

I took a call from Inez. Had I seen Carlos? No. He had told her he was meeting me for dinner. I said I hoped I hadn't stood him up. Inez said she was worried about him; he was working too hard. He couldn't relax. I told her to call me later if she wanted to send out a search party. I hung up and called Carlos, got his voice mail, apologized if I screwed up, and asked him to call me back.

After I dropped Venise and Oliver at home, I drove to Leo's and spotted Carlos's Camry in the back parking lot. I found a space and headed for the back entrance when I heard, "Where the fuck do you think you're going?" and then got slammed on the back of the head so hard that I felt immediately nauseated. My assailant grabbed me by the back of the collar and turned me around. He was not holding the tire iron I assumed he had hit me with. His head was as smooth and round as a muskmelon, and he was otherwise built like a cast-iron furnace. I said, "What the fuck, man!"

He stepped on my foot. "Get the fuck out of here."

"You assaulted me."

"Call the cops."

"I will."

"Did you hear what I said?"

"Get off my foot and I'll leave."

He did. By now the buzzing in my head had subsided a bit, but my nose was bleeding. I walked to the car but couldn't find my keys. Maybe I should just keep walking. I patted my pockets and found my iPhone. I figured I'd speed-dial Carlos and let him ride to the rescue, and that's when two cops walked out of the bar and asked Muskmelon what the trouble was. I, rather imprudently, decided to tape the proceedings and opened the video app. I found the keys, but dropped them. One of the cops said he recognized me, and I knew that wouldn't be good. The other cop said something about going Disney on my ass. Muskmelon laughed and said I'd attacked him; I was like a wild man, probably high on angel dust. We'll probably have to Taser him. The second cop saw what I was up to. "We got us a filmmaker." That's when they rushed me. Muskmelon grabbed the phone and stomped it flat. The cop who knew me asked what hand I used to jack off with. Then he grabbed my hand and bit through my baby finger to the bone.

15

Carlos drove me to the hospital, but he wasn't happy about it. Caught him in the middle of a cribbage game. He brought along his drink in a go-cup. He told me if I'd been looking for trouble I'd come to the right place. I said I'd been looking for him. I had rolled-up wads of tissue stuffed up my nostrils to stanch the bleeding. He said, Let tonight be a lesson to you.

Carlos got me attended to immediately. I held a cold compress to my fortuitously unbroken nose while a nurse cleaned my wounded finger. Carlos told him that I'd been mauled by a Rottweiler. The nurse didn't look up when he said, These are human teeth marks. Two stitches, one tetanus shot, and one painkiller later, we were out the sliding doors. On the ride back to retrieve my car, I asked Carlos about Halliday's computer, said I wanted to examine it. He said I didn't have that authority and anyway the computer had gone missing. I said, How do you lose a computer? He said he needed Kelly's diary back before it, too, went missing. I'd forgotten I still had it.

I told him that Inez had called looking for him, which was why I'd been at the bar in the first place. He said she was getting ready to leave him again—he could read all the signs.

"You were supposed to meet me for dinner."

"My excuse to get out of the house. I didn't want to give her the chance to tell me she was leaving, and this time for good."

"I'm sorry to hear it," I said. "If there's anything I can do . . ." I sounded like an idiot right there, didn't I? "That sounded disingenuous, Carlos. Sorry. Let me try it again." I cleared my throat—a fatuous gesture, I realized. Jesus. "If I can be of any help." Nope. The same hollow sentiment as earlier. I must have been feeling the effects of the painkiller. I said, "You're a good man, Carlos."

"Are you sure you should be operating heavy machinery?"

"I feel spectacular, actually. I could drive with my eyes closed."

"That's what I'm worried about." He pulled alongside my car. "Here you go, Coyote. Be safe."

"You guys owe me a phone."

"Don't push it."

Red had set up an umbrella canopy over his campsite. He was dead asleep when I got home. Django was waiting by the door. I picked him up and rubbed his belly. When I tried to put him down, he wrapped his four legs around my wrist and gnawed at my thumb. I walked to the kitchen with him upside down and busy like that. When I laid my hand on the counter, he let go and lay on his back with his legs in the air and his baby claws exposed, ready for more funny business. I set the little goon down by his empty bowl. He looked at the bowl, up at me, back at the bowl. I fed him some of the ocean whitefish in sauce that he loved. I brewed some coffee, took a quick shower, careful to keep the throbbing finger dry. I got the diary out of my desk drawer. I put a shot of Paddy's in the coffee, sat at the table, slipped the diary out of its Ziploc bag. I opened to an undated entry about two-thirds of the way through the book. Kelly had written a list:

LONELINESS IS NOT:

- a blank face in an empty window
- a solitary figure way out there at the end of the pier
- anyone curled in the ~~fatal~~ fetal position
- it is not a white fucking horse galloping through the fog
- a girl with a bandaged ankle crying into her knee
- the bus is pulling out of the station and you're standing there in the parking lot
- a choice

I opened my wallet and took out the note I'd found at the DeSoto Street house. *Love what you've done with the house.* Kelly's handwriting on Wayne's note. I checked the time. Eleven-fifteen. I didn't want to believe that what I was thinking could be true. I felt faint. I put my face in my hands, closed my eyes, breathed slowly and deeply, and tried to picture Wayne sitting there in my office for all these weeks. How had I missed the blood on his hands? I tapped my pocket and remembered I no longer had a cell phone. I called Carlos from the home phone and left a message for him to meet me at Wayne's, and I gave him the address.

The gravel driveway was empty and the lights were out at Wayne's house, a squat and charmless box on a scrubby lot with a spindly princess palm growing against the screened-in front porch. I walked around the carport to the back of the house. No lights there, either. I tapped on the cracked and duct-taped window on the back door and waited. I tried the doorknob. Locked. I looked under the doormat and saw a rusted key. It fit the lock. I stepped away from the door and looked around. What the hell was I doing? A rat ran along the telephone line above the cyclone fence. A Weber grill stood beneath a satellite dish that was mounted on the eaves. A green and black softball bat leaned against the house. The label on the barrel read WORTH MAYHEM, and I'm not making that up. I went back out front to look at the carport. The trash bin lid was weighted down with a large brain coral to keep out the raccoons. Beside the bin was a white plastic chair and on the floor a small wooden crate with garden tools, a boom box, and a machete. I tried the front door. Rang the bell. Walked to the back of the house and let myself in. Where was Carlos? I felt along the wall for a light switch. Where was Wayne? I put on the backyard light, and that was sufficient for me to see the living room.

Wayne's laptop was opened on his computer desk. I depressed the space bar and woke it up, and there was Wayne's Facebook page. He had 374 friends. One of those friends, one Daisy L, had posted a quote from Mitch Hedberg: *The Dufresnes are in someone's trunk right now with duct tape over their mouths. And they're hungry . . . you can eat when you find the Dufresnes.* Wayne's profile picture was a little blond Dutch boy in a blue cap, blue overalls, and wooden shoes, sitting on a plank beside a bucket of paint, holding a brush, and painting the air above his head.

Across the room, a ragged sofa faced a TV sitting on a coffee table. On the far wall an unfinished wooden bookcase was devoid of books, but did support piles of magazines and rows of DVDs, a few computer keyboards and what looked like old hard drives. I shut the back door and cut the yard light. I peeked into Wayne's spare and dismal bedroom—an unmade mattress on the floor, an iPad on the pillow, on the wall above the bed a photograph of a woman wearing only bacon panties. The other bedroom was used for storage—a bicycle, a treadmill draped with jackets, unopened cartons, a rolled-up rug. I walked into the tiny kitchen and opened the fridge. Five cans of beer, one of them opened; a two-liter bottle of Coke Zero; a plastic bag of moldy citrus; a jar of barbecue sauce; a bowl of hard-boiled eggs; and an opened box of baking soda. The cabinets above the counter were empty. Whatever dinnerware Wayne owned was apparently in the sink. On the counter were a white toaster, a compact microwave, and a Teflon-coated electric griddle. Beneath the counter I found a carbo cabinet full of cookies and Pringles and Cheetos and Twinkies, and most of the Little Debbie snack food family.

A heavy-duty orange extension cord ran from a three-prong outlet in the kitchen to the bathroom and I followed it. Nothing was presently attached to the business end of the cord. There were several long gouges on the insides of the bathtub and what appeared to be blood smeared on the faucet and spout. The walls above the tub were splattered with blood. I turned out the lights and let myself out onto the dark front porch, took a seat in the corner, and waited for Wayne to come home or for Carlos to come to the rescue.

I must have dozed off. I was startled by headlights, and then I heard a scratchy woman's voice. "Today salvation has come to this house."

Wayne said, "It's a rental, but we won't be here all that long." He opened the screen door and let the woman inside. He stood beside her, put his key in the front-door lock, and froze. "It seems we've had an unexpected visitor."

Out of the darkness I said, "Wayne, we need to talk."

The woman gasped, brought her hands to her mouth, and cowered, understandably, against Wayne, who said, "The doctor makes a house call." He opened the door and invited me in. We stood in the lighted kitchen. Sable leaned against the sink. She folded her arms and unfolded them. She tapped her hands against her thighs. She put her hands behind her back and leaned against them.

Wayne introduced me to Sable and told me that she'd saved his life. He stood beside her and put his arm around her shoulder. He inquired about my finger. I told him I had been bitten by a pit bull. Wayne whispered in Sable's ear, and they giggled. Sable's brown hair was highlighted with blond streaks. She wore jeans, blue sneakers, and a red JESUS IS MY BFF T-shirt. Her eyes were slightly swollen like she'd been crying. Wayne explained how Sable had led him to Jesus Christ, and now he was washed in the blood of the Lamb. They each professed their undying love for Jesus and for each other. Wayne smiled at Sable and kissed the hand he now held in his.

Sable said, "Dutch is my soul mate."

"I thought this would never ever happen," Wayne said.

I said, "You haven't asked me what I'm doing here."

Wayne said, "And now that I have a purpose in life, I won't be coming back to therapy. My problems weren't in my head after all, but in my soul."

I asked Sable if she was okay.

Wayne said, "We're getting married."

"Otherwise no sex," Sable said.

Wayne thanked me for all I'd done for him. I told him I didn't think we were finished. I asked Sable if she would mind if Wayne and I had a few minutes in private, but Wayne said they'd made a pact never to be more than three feet from each other.

I said, "Wayne, do you have anything you want to tell me?"

"Like what?"

"Your fantasies, perhaps. 'Weird,' you called them once."

"So you *were* listening."

"You wouldn't talk about them."

"That part of my life is over."

Sable said, "Except a man be born again, he cannot see the kingdom of God."

I said, "Did you know a girl named Kelly?"

Wayne stared at me. And then he seemed to deflate.

I said, "I'm here because you wanted me to know the truth."

Sable lifted her arms over her head and mumbled in tongues.

I said, "You wanted to get it off your chest."

"*It?*"

"What you did to that girl."

Wayne said, "Shut the fuck up, Sable!" Then he hugged her, rocked her, kissed her hair. "I'm sorry."

We heard a car door slam outside.

"You could have done something to stop all this," Wayne said to me. "You did nothing. You were useless."

I watched Carlos and Wayne in a tiny, shadowless interview room through the two-way mirror. Wayne declined his right to have an attorney present. He hated lawyers. Slimeballs, he said. While Wayne was telling his story, EPD officers searched his house. They impounded his computer as evidence, along with his DVDs, his CDs, his crate of pornographic magazines. If Wayne hesitated in answering a question, Carlos clicked the push-button on his ballpoint pen, and when he did, Wayne looked up and spoke.

"I don't know what it is. I can't see things clearly sometimes. Everything gets fuzzy, so I just stare straight ahead. And all the sounds I hear are tinny. When I listen, I can't tell where one word ends and the next begins—it's like everyone's talking Mexican."

Carlos said, "What do you have written on the palm of your hand?"

"My mother's phone number. In Illinois."

"Would you like for us to contact her?"

"This'll kill her." Wayne tapped his foot a mile a minute. He folded his arms across his chest. Carlos clicked his pen. Wayne smiled. "Why don't you go ahead and call her." He held up the palm of his hand, and Carlos wrote down the number.

"Her name's Diane Stalmok. She remarried some dishwasher at the Chicken Shack after my old man dropped dead on the crapper." He spelled *Stalmok*. He said, "She'll tell you what a nice, quiet boy I am, how I could never have done what you say I've done. She's a clueless twat."

Officers found the decomposing remains of a human leg in Wayne's trash barrel. They called the hazmat team. They switched off the blinking lights on Wayne's little synthetic Christmas tree.

"That Kelly was too trustworthy. If it hadn't been me, it would have ended up being someone else. She was a murder waiting to happen. Her own worst enemy, you could say."

The officers found a video of two laughing assailants torturing a disabled man with their carpentry tools. They found a movie called *Cannibal Holocaust*.

"I hit her with a twelve-inch cast-iron frying pan. A lot." Wayne demonstrated how he brought down the pan on Kelly's head again and again. "She kept asking me to stop. She kept telling me she was sorry. I said, 'What are you sorry for? You didn't do anything. I should be the sorry one.'"

Wayne closed his eyes. "I wish I could take it all back." He ran his hands over his face. "I've always been shy, you know? That's the source of my troubles right there. I've got no personality. I am expressionless, silent. I'm withdrawn so far into myself that I've vanished. I wish I could be human. But on the Internet you can be who you want to be, not who you are. I'm liked on Facebook. I'm followed on Twitter. I have a blog."

Here's Wayne's blog post on the day he kidnapped, raped, murdered, and mutilated Kelly Kershaw:

> I told Ed Heeb at work that I was the poster child for unrealized potential, but that it didn't bother me. He said, "If you leave it unrealized, it remains potential, and that way you can keep

> on thinking that you might have been a contender. Very clever, Dutch!" But he's an assclown, which is why I call him Special Ed. So now I'm eating supper and writing about it. LOL! Had a snack earlier but I can't seem to fill myself up. Now I've got a toasted peanut butter and banana sandwich, a bag of Cheez Doodles, and a can of Bud Light. Life is good!

The officers found two retractable dog leashes hung on the kitchen doorknob, but no evidence of a dog.

"I strangled Kelly after she blacked out, just like I strangled the other one."

"Vera."

"That was her name?"

"Vera Chapman. Fourteen."

"She lied to me."

"About?"

"Told me her name was Annie and she was sixteen. Little shit." Wayne smiled.

Carlos clicked his pen.

Wayne said, "Funny how on TV they said she'd been abducted by two guys in a black car."

"Funny?"

"Was just me and my hammer."

Carlos tapped his pen on his notepad. He leaned toward Wayne. "Why?"

"Did I kill?"

"Yes."

"I don't have any reasons."

"I have a hard time believing that."

"And that's *my* problem?"

"Why these two girls?"

"The first was just random. Kelly was the chosen one."

"And why did you choose her?"

"She made it easy. She made herself available. She offered herself to me as a sacrifice, you could say."

"Have you killed others?"

"I know what I've done here. I'm not making excuses. I don't behave like this normally. There's nothing you can do but put me away. Snuff me out. I didn't kill anyone else, but I can't promise that I won't. There's a beast inside here I can't control. Am I responsible for who I am? I was made like this. I didn't choose to be a monster. Sometimes I disgust myself. But I want you to know that I am capable of goodness, too."

"I'll make a note."

"There were other girls. I could have eliminated them, but I said, 'Dutch, leave them be,' and I saved their lives if you think about it."

"What were your intentions with Sable Chestnut?"

"Honorable."

Carlos clicked the pen.

"Going to do the right thing and marry the girl." He smiled. "Till death do us part."

Carlos said, "Now we're going to go through both murders step by step. You're going to tell me exactly what went on with the girls."

Wayne confessed to murdering, butchering, marinating, grilling, and serving cuts of Vera to Myka Flores and two other cashiers at Publix. He told his guests they were eating wild boar—that's why it tasted gamy.

"I must have hit her just right," he said. She never woke up. He strapped Vera in the front seat of his compact car with the seat belt and rested her head on his shoulder as he drove the few blocks home. He parked the car in his backyard and carried her into the house. "As soon as I hit her I wished I could have taken it back."

He opened her up in the bathtub. "I should have checked her for a pulse first, but I suppose she was beyond feeling by then." He gutted the corpse, let it bleed out, and iced it down before he went off to Home Depot. He had planned the same fate for Kelly, he said, but after raping, beating, and strangling her, he said he lost heart, figured she had suffered enough. "It took me maybe fifteen or twenty minutes to get her completely dead."

So why had Wayne come to therapy for those several weeks when he had, it seemed, no intention of ever dealing with the sadistic compulsion that drove him to savagery? What signs had I missed? He claimed to have had a trauma-free, if not exactly blissful, childhood. Loved Mom, respected Dad, made a few friends, wept when his pets died. Maybe that was all a lie, but then why seek therapy for a fictitious self? He told me he'd been picked on by older boys, but claimed he never harbored any revenge fantasies. He was a man who liked to be in control. Anger was a loss of control. Was anger the beast inside he talked about earlier? Orgasm put an end to the chaos of sex and rage and restored order?

After the interview, on my way to the parking lot, I saw Clete Meatyard leaning against the door to my car, hands in his pockets, cigar in his mouth, and I knew I was in for some unpleasantness. I asked if he'd mind stepping aside so I could open my door. He held out his hand. "Clete Meatyard."

"Wylie Melville," I said. "But I assume you know that."

"Did you just tell me to fuck myself?"

I said, "What's the matter with you?"

"Why don't you tell me what's wrong with me."

"I wouldn't know where to begin." I don't know why I said that, why I felt I had to provoke him. I stepped back, and he smiled.

"You've had a little accident, I see."

I held up my bandaged finger. "And I'll be reporting it."

"I have some, what-do-you-call, 'avuncular' advice. I'm worried about you."

I unlocked the door and opened it. Clete slammed it shut. "Don't be rude. Listen to your uncle."

I crossed my arms. "I'm listening."

"All your life you've been living in a world of light. I'm worried that you're about to step into the dark."

"That's it?"

"Well, the advice part is stay put where you can see who's coming after you."

"Thanks."

"People like you have no idea."

"People like me?"

"Like you."

"What am I like?"

"Clueless." He smiled and chucked my cheek.

The DA's mahogany desk was piled with neatly stacked and overstuffed manila file folders. Millard and I sat on two worn leather chairs. Millard gripped the armrests and called my attention to his twenty-gallon fish tank. He told me that watching the fish relaxed him. We stared at the fish quietly for several seconds. He pointed out an electric blue hap, his particular favorite, nibbling on a plant, an Amazon sword, Millard told me. He had a small fridge, a microwave, and a coffeemaker on a glass table by the window. I pictured him here at night, in the comfy chair, feet up on the ottoman, which was now covered in magazines (*Oxford American*, *Lapham's Quarterly*) and files, reading through depositions or whatever it is that lawyers read. In one of those desk drawers, I figured, was a bottle of single-malt scotch and two highball glasses. I asked him if the young girl in the photo on the coffee table was his daughter. It was, but the picture had been taken ten years ago. Millard told me his daughter and he hadn't spoken in eight years—ever since the divorce. He had a grandson he'd never met. Theo.

He told me what I already knew about the Halliday case—that it was closed—and said he could find no compelling reason to ask that it be reopened, not solely based on my hunch, at any rate. He crossed his legs and adjusted his tie. He said not every crime in Everglades County could be traced to bad cops and Mickey Pfeiffer. I told him about Halliday's computer in storage at EPD. He made a note and said he'd look into it. I told him about last night's assault. He said it would be hard to prove—my word against theirs. He said he'd suggest an Internal Affairs investigation to the chief, but couldn't promise anything.

Millard looked out the window at the New River skyline and told me that we were living in the most corrupt county in the state, maybe in the country. Everyone's hands were dirty. The thieves kept getting reelected. There was no will here among the citizens to change anything. We could have good schools if schools were important to us. We could have honest and responsible government. He told me that sometimes he just wants to toss in the towel and walk away. "We are watching the decline and fall of the American Empire," he said. "Some days I'm not even sure it's worth saving."

"I caught you at a bad time."

He laughed. "I try to do my job."

Millard was happy that Wayne had confessed and saved his office a bundle of money in legal fees. He said that what Wayne had done, ghastly as it was, was an aberration. What people like Mickey Pfeiffer and Jack Malacoda did was a way of life.

He said, "Let me ask you a professional question. When you have someone come into your office and tell you he's got everything he ever dreamed of having, but he feels empty, what do you say?"

"I might ask him if there's something he wants but doesn't have."

Millard sat forward, put his elbows on his knees, and folded his hands. "He wants another life."

"I'd tell him it's never too late to be the person he wants to be."

"No, seriously."

"I'd say you can have anything, but you can't have everything. You have to drop the cookie to get your hand out of the jar."

"I have these dreams," he said. "I have a son, and the son is me when I'm seven or eight. And the son has no respect for the man he will become. He won't do his homework because what's the point? When I ask him a question, he shakes his head and walks away. When I try to explain myself, he pretends to play a little violin."

I left a message on Mrs. Stalmok's answering machine. I explained who I was and said I'd be happy to speak with her if she had any questions about Wayne. I used to think the worst thing that could happen in a person's life was the loss of a child, but now I thought that even worse must be to have that lost child take the life of another child.

Mrs. Stalmok called. She told me how talented her boy had been—could swim like a fish, could have made junior lifeguard, but couldn't be bothered. He could sing like an angel, but quit the church choir. When he was seven Wayne built a radio that worked. He had squandered his many gifts. He was never much interested in what he was good at. But he was not a cruel child and was never unruly or troublesome. "He grew more and more, I don't know, blurry," she said, "like he was losing his edges, his definition. I don't know how else to explain it. Like he was fading away."

I asked her if she would be okay. No, she would not, she said. Ever. I said, "You have your husband, your faith." She said, "We were strict, but not harsh. We spoiled him a bit, the way an only child is spoiled. You have no idea how much this hurts, how empty and fragile I feel." And then she told me she almost didn't go to the state fair that year. She was supposed to work the weekend at the DQ, and if she had, those babies would still be alive, but at the last minute her boyfriend, the shift manager, arranged to get her hours filled, and off they drove to Springfield. In Springfield, at the Mansion View Motel, after a Loverboy concert, Wayne was conceived.

16

At the end of Bay's dock, a five-foot-long absinthe-green iguana was languidly chewing magenta hibiscus flowers from a straw basket that Bay had set out. I sat in a lawn chair on Bay's patio. He came out with two martinis on a tray and set them on an oak side table. He handed me a black sports watch with a busy black dial face, a half dozen control buttons on the shoulder, and a compass bezel, said he took it off Shanks at the casino bar.

I said, "Do you think . . . ?"

The doorbell chimed, and Bay went in to answer the door, saying over his shoulder, "Someone has a story to tell you."

The someone was Open Mike. His aftershave arrived before he did. When I asked about the fragrance, he told me it was called Drakkar Noir and said he could get me a case. I said, Thanks for the offer, but no. He said, Gratis. Free for nothing. He clapped his hands clean and held them up. My pleasure. He sat in the third chair, and that's when he spotted the iguana.

"What the fuck is that?"

"Godzilla," Bay said.

"We got nothing like this in Gulfstream. Does it bite?"

"Razor-sharp teeth."

The iguana was now up on his forelegs, fanning his dewlap. His scales looked like beads of jade. Open Mike took off his Mets cap and placed it over his knee. Bay nodded. Open Mike cleared his throat and began.

He had this friend, he said, not family, but close, like a brother, someone he could trust to tell him the God's honest truth and nothing but. The friend was an occasional business partner of Kevin Shanks. The friend was what they call an "eraser"—he made things go away. "You know what I'm saying?" So when Shanks found himself the victim of an extortion attempt, he called this associate.

Bay said, "So Shanks had some criminal activity he did not want exposed to the public."

"Alleged activity."

"Not simply some embarrassing behavior."

"Correct."

"Go on."

"How do I put this?" Open Mike pressed his palms together and brought his hands to his lips. "This woman, Miss X, let's call her, claimed that Shanks sexually assaulted her in the parking lot of Leo's, and furthermore claimed to have a witness to said assault. She told Shanks she wanted fifty large or else. Shanks had been in hot water previously and could not afford another legal kerfuffle. But he was not going to pay the bitch a penny. The principle of the thing."

Bay filled me in. Four years earlier, Shanks had been picking up his son at Bambiland Day Care in Ocean View when he told another little boy to stop running around like a berserker, and the kid said no, and Shanks told the kid to address him as "sir," and the kid gave him the finger, and Shanks slapped the kid and broke his jaw. All that in front of a teacher, his own terrified kid, and several other parents. At the trial, the judge said that Officer Shanks had led an exemplary life of service for twenty-some years with the exception of this brief error in judgment, and since he was off-duty, though uniformed, he had not violated the public trust.

Open Mike said that when Miss X was not paid, she filed a complaint with EPD and told Shanks she now wanted $75,000, and the meter was running. Open Mike looked at me and nodded. "Nobody likes a shakedown. Am I right?" She also told Shanks her next move would be to hire an attorney and to speak to the press. Internal Affairs, so Open Mike was told, let Shanks know about the complaint, and he decided to put an end to this harassment. Arrangements were made. The friend was on standby at home when he got the call from Shanks, who was circling Miss X's home in Golden Hills. Shanks told the eraser that his target was sitting there on her front porch with a drink in her hand. "Do it now," Shanks said.

I said, "Why are you telling us all this?"

Bay said, "Michael owes me quite a bit of money, and this information will lower his vig."

"Maybe he's lying."

"Aren't you supposed to be able to tell?"

"I ain't lying," Open Mike said. "On my mother's grave. And my friend has no reason to lie."

Bay told me he'd checked the records on the cell phones and verified the calls. It's so easy even the cops could do it.

"My friend, however, had a what-do-you-call-it, a dilemma. His wife had not yet returned from Target, and he couldn't very well leave his one-year-old baby home alone. He's that kind of father." Open Mike lifted his eyebrows and nodded. "He kept looking out the blinds, pacing the kitchen, jiggling the fussy baby in his arms. Then Shanks called and wanted to know what was the delay.

Anyway, my friend strapped the baby into her car seat, plugged a pacifier in her yap, and off he went. He pulled up right in front of the woman's house. Shanks, who was parked down the block out of sight, couldn't believe this. This isn't how this shit usually goes down. So he calls again and says, 'Is that a baby I'm hearing?' My friend saw the woman on the porch. Good-looking, he told me, legs up to here. She stood and put her hand on the doorknob. My friend picked up the baby to quiet her down. That was a good move, it turns out, 'cause Miss X immediately lets down her guard, smiles, and comes down the walk toward them. My friend shifted the baby to his left arm, reached behind him, and drew the gun from his belt and shot Miss X in the face. And off he goes."

"Jesus Christ," I said.

Open Mike held up his finger and continued. "Shanks handled the investigation, planted some pot and a throwdown, and made the whole thing look like a drug deal gone bad." Open Mike looked at Bay. "Are we square?"

"For now."

I said, "He took the baby?"

Open Mike shrugged. "You gotta do what you gotta do." He excused himself and stood. He was off to Tropical Racetrack. He looked at Bay and pointed to me. "Tell him the rules."

Bay said, "You can't tell your buddy Carlos, any cop, where you heard this."

"But I can say what I heard?"

"Why would you start that snowball rolling down the hill?"

I said, "Do you suppose Halliday filed a complaint, too?"

"I don't know, but you did."

The first person I saw at Almost Home was Avalon's resolute mom, Gabriela, who told me that Junior Torres had returned to his senses and come back home. She's in love all over again, she said, and little Avalon is over the moon. Junior doesn't have a job yet, but he's looking almost every day.

I knocked. Dad said to come in if I was beautiful. I came in anyway. I was delivering his dry cleaning from Mar-Flo—a brown plaid sport coat and a pair of brown flannel slacks. Tonight was Prom Night at Almost Home. A few dozen students from South Everglades High were coming to dance with the seniors. I hung the garments on the back of the closet door and joined Dad at the table. He crumbled some oyster crackers into his Lipton tea. He'd already buttered his brick of shredded wheat and now he poured the kettled hot water over it. He said, "I'm planning on getting me some tonight."

"Some what?"

"I forget what you call it." He put the kettle back on the stove. He said, "What you get when you're with your best gal in the backseat of her mother's Chevy out at Lost Lake."

When I turned back, Dad held a pistol in his hand, the barrel pressed against his temple. He looked at me and smiled.

"Put it down, Dad. What the hell are you doing?" I tried to exude an aura of tranquillity. I did not want him getting jumpy all of a sudden. I held my breath and then held out my hand. I said, "Give me the gun, okay?" He pulled the trigger. I shut my eyes. I heard a snap, not the explosion I was expecting. I opened my eyes. He pointed the cap pistol at my heart and fired. I leaned back against the stove. "You son of a bitch."

He laughed. "I ain't had such dadburned fun since the mule kicked me in the head." He was being Myles Stone, a character he'd based on Gabby Hayes. Long before he was married and I was born, before the shoe company job, Dad had a brief season of celebrity as a sidekick to Tex Comstock on early TV at WBZ in Boston. Myles was Tex's grizzle-pated partner until Tex decided he wanted the limelight to himself. The gun was a prop Dad used on the show. Every time he fired a warning shot over the heads of the nasty varmints, a rubber chicken fell from the sky.

I said, "That wasn't funny."

"If I wanted to kill myself, I wouldn't wait for you to show up." He crunched his shredded wheat.

I told Sinead I was here to meet District Attorney Millard. She picked up a menu, smiled, and asked me to follow her. I reminded her that we had met the other night.

"I meet so many people."

"You told me you were from Saint Helena."

"And you believed me?"

"I did."

"That's sweet."

"You're not?"

I saw Linda, the woman scorned by Kim Swain, at the bar, shaking her hair, stirring her drink, sitting in the middle of a cluster of standing Ed Hardys.

I sat. Millard raised an eyebrow, lowered his eyelids. He had a secret, I could see, and he was eager to tell me all about whatever it was. He'd ordered us the fois gras appetizer; he hoped I didn't mind. I said, "What's going on?"

He took a half dozen photos from his shirt pocket and handed them to me. They had been taken at Mickey's three-day wedding reception at Mar-a-Lago. There was Mickey and the governor; Mickey and the Donald; Mickey, his bride, and the famous stuttering country singer; Mickey and the Miami Heat backcourt; Mickey and a four-star general; Mickey and Malacoda.

The redoubtable Thatcher arrived with our appetizer. I ordered an Innis & Gunn. Millard checked his watch. "We have a surprise party planned for Mr. Pfeiffer." He turned to the bar. One of the popinjays nodded and returned his attention to Linda. Linda looked our way, smiled, and winked. Millard nodded.

I said, "You know Linda?"

"Lacey."

"Lacey?" I looked at Sinead, who was chatting up a gray-haired gentleman in a navy blue linen suit, probably telling him about her home in Antigua. Does anyone tell the truth anymore? "What's Lacey's story?"

"We had a little fling some time ago."

"Is she a cop?"

"She likes lawyers."

"She likes them married, I'm guessing."

"She likes their money."

I told him I heard the Internal Affairs has been known to leak the news of complaints and investigations. He said it's always a crapshoot with IA. He told me that Mickey owned homes in Florida—two in New River, one in Tallahassee—in Manhattan, Maine, Morocco, and one on Grand Cayman. "What better occupation for a criminal than the law?"

Thatcher arrived with my beer. Millard said, "The law is useful. That's why Mickey is a lawyer. He knows the rules of the game." He cut into his fois gras. "The law does not serve justice. The law serves those who know it and understand it." He told me that the Indian tribe and the developer had settled their dispute. The Calusa burial ground would be preserved.

"Justice," I said.

"And a casino will be built over and around it." Millard checked his watch. He told me about Mickey's selling court settlements, about his forging court orders. He told me that Mickey's law partner was murdered by his CFO's ex-husband."

"You can't make this stuff up."

"We're here to bust him. He's expected momentarily."

"How did he think he could get away with this?"

"I expect he'll sing like a canary."

"Maybe we'll learn about Halliday."

Millard excused himself and put in a call to the sheriff. "What's the delay?" He listened and then ended the call.

"What is it?"

"He's putting in a call to your friend Shanks, who was escorting Mickey here."

When the sheriff had called back and Millard had listened and hung up, he folded his napkin, shook his head, and looked toward the bar. One of the Ed Hardys smiled. "He's gone."

"Where?"

"Vanished."

17

Aldore LaFlamme, a competitive bass fisherman, with a second-place trophy in the Palatka Citrus Slam to prove it, whose sixteen-foot Diamondback airboat cost him considerably more than his modular home, was out in the Everglades just east of the Miccosukee Reservation near dawn, poaching alligators out of season. He'd already snagged and dispatched an eleven-foot bull with a bangstick when he spotted what he thought might be an engorged Burmese python in the sawgrass and shone his searchlight on it and saw a naked human body. He poked at it with his gaff and found it to be headless, handless, bloated, and blue. To Aldore's credit, he got right on the radio and reported what he'd found to the authorities.

While he waited for the ESO to arrive, he noosed his gator around its forelegs and eased him off the deck and into the water. This way maybe the cops wouldn't notice. Of course, they'd have to be blind, what with the tail afloat like it was. He examined the male human body and the damage inflicted. He got out his Shakespeare rod and spinner bait and began fishing. He thought about the story he'd tell his pals later that night at Betty's Starlight Lounge and about how he'd tell it. He'd mention the stillness in the air, the ripe smell of the swamp, and the ratchety call of a snail kite. He'd describe the slices carved into the victim's shoulders, forearms, and wrists, how the butchering had to have been done with a machete. He'd pause right there to give them all a solemn moment to consider the swift tarnished steel blade, the gush and splash of blood, the damp, fatty business oozing out from the parted skin, the thud of the bone below, resisting. You're bound to think, he would say, that drugs were involved, but ask yourself, would a cartel's bagmen bother with a disposal twenty minutes out into the Everglades? Think about it. Those jamokes are anonymous and untouchable. No, the guys that clipped this swamp hog did not want the victim ID'd because one of those missing fingers would point right to them. Aldore's theory, which he would expound upon after buying the sparse house a round, was that a betrayal of friendship was involved here. That betrayal might have taken many forms: marital infidelity, financial shenanigans, judicial testimony, slander—you name it. The kind of savagery Aldore had seen chilling evidence of required a fury that only intimacy dishonored could incite. Remember, you're losing someone dear and close to you, close enough to have stabbed you in the back. Aldore felt a nibble on the line and then nothing. Damn tilapia, he thought. He wondered if he'd be on the *News at Noon*, and he listened for the whoop of the approaching News 10 chopper.

The deputies released Aldore after getting his statement and information. He asked them if he should stick close to town. One of the deputies said, Where else would you go? Aldore said, To be available for questioning, I mean. We know where to find you, the deputy said. They confiscated his alligator and delivered it to a butcher they knew in Colahatchee. Then they delivered the mutilated corpse to Everglades General Hospital. The next day, the deputies got a call from the butcher.

"Guess what I found in the gator's belly?"

"A pair of hands?"

"A BlackBerry."

"For real?"

"He swallowed it recently, so it's likely the owner was present at the scene of the dumping."

"We'll pick it up with the meat."

"I hit redial, and the fellow who answered said, 'I told you never to call here, douche bag,' and hung up."

"Rude."

On the drive out to Fat Willie's Fish Camp to sell the alligator meat, the deputies read through the contact list on the phone and recognized some of the names: lawyers, cops, and criminals. They learned that the phone belonged to Pancho Phinn, which turned out to be a phony name. An interesting name, but a fabrication nonetheless, a lie.

Dad and I had just sat down in our booth with our early-bird dinners at Svensen's Buffeteria when Carlos called with some news. A couple of kids looking for a secluded spot along the barge canal to shoot their heroin had discovered Mickey Pfeiffer's severed head in a sealed Tupperware bowl. Mickey had taken a machete to the face before, during, or after the decapitation. The head matched the body found in the Everglades, of course. By then the 'Glades in west Everglades County had been burning out of control for two days, so it's fortunate that they found the body when they did. Of course, if you have the head, that's really all you need.

I watched Dad scoop a mound of sweet-and-sour brisket into a plastic Ziploc bag. I put on my incredulous face and shrugged, like, What-the-hell-are-you-doing? Carlos said there was no lack of suspects. Mickey had stolen money from the mob, from the Russians, from an Israeli defense organization, from the school board, from the Hadassah, from a host of banking CEOs, and from thousands of small investors. The thing about running a Ponzi scheme is if you're not going to go to jail, you have to keep at it. And then Carlos told me that Kevin Shanks had been missing in action for a week.

I dropped some Optivar into my stinging eyes. Dad returned from his second pass at the buffet, this time with coconut fried chicken tenders and broccoli florets. My swiss steak was not "braised to tender perfection" as advertised. Not even close. I should have gotten seafood, but the salmon patties looked forlorn, and you would need a circular saw to cut through the immiserated parmesan-crusted mystery fish. Why did we come here? I said, "Dad, it's all you can eat, not all you can take."

He said, "It's expected. We all do it. It's the cost of doing business in Seniorville."

"How are you going to get it out of the restaurant?"

"Big pockets."

I bit into my savorless chess pie. Dad told me that he had put his pistol back in the trunk with his hat and his boots. I hadn't asked about it.

"Dad, do you know where we are right now?"

"Melancholy, baby."

"We're at Svensen's Buffeteria."

"I went to high school with a guy named Buff Ateria."

The Everglades fire was now so intense that in places where the grass had burned out, the ground was now on fire, all that dry and decayed organic matter going up in flames. You could write your name or your sweetheart's name in the layer of ash on the plastic café tables on the patio outside the Wayside. Bay and I decided to sit inside where we could breathe. The bartender, Helen Foley—her dad, Doody, owned the place—brought us our drafts and woke up Dusty Boswell, who was napping at the next table, his head up against the wall beneath last year's Marlins schedule. Dusty had the word NO tattooed on his right eyelid, the word HOPE, on the left. Helen said, Let's go, Dusty. This ain't the Sleep-It-Off Motel. Dusty opened his right eye and nodded. He smacked his lips, wiped his mouth, opened the left eye, and tried to focus on Helen. He looked over at the two of us and shook his head. He stood and patted his trouser pockets. He was unzipped. Dusty took a deep and revitalizing breath and shuffled off to the door, running a hand through his tousled hair. He stared out at the parking lot, held the doorjamb with two hands, and stepped off into the night.

Bay told me that he'd learned that Marlena was more addicted to painkillers than he had realized. That burn she'd gotten on her arm at the Universe was intentional and self-inflicted. Her practice was to cut or burn herself and then head off to several of Everglades County's three hundred pain clinics for prescriptive analgesia. She'd gone through the bottle of sleeping pills and the bottle of Percocets in his medicine cabinet before he noticed. He'd gotten Marlena into a residential rehab program, but he wasn't sure if she'd stay. He'd gone to a couple of group meetings with Marlena at Discovery House and was not encouraged by what he'd witnessed.

Most of the guys in the group were dressed like hip-hop singers—white and Latin guys with unlaced high-top athletic shoes and droopy, baggy denim shorts that reached to just above their ankles. They favored wife-beaters and gold chains and wore their Yankees caps like Rootie Kazootie, with the visors off to the side.

When the women weren't sitting on their hands or biting their nails, they were clasping their knees like they were about to stand and bolt for the door.

As a group, the addicts seemed chastened but smug and were all adept at saying what they knew the counselors wanted them to say. Or maybe I'm just being cynical, Bay said. There were thirty or so addicts at the meeting, many there with a parent, a sibling, or a spouse. The addicts knew how badly their families wanted them to heal themselves and knew how easily such hunger could be sated. Someone would say, "Now that I'm an adult, I've put away my childish things," and humbled heads would nod. Someone else would lean forward and stare at his folded hands and say, "The difference this time is that I know I have to surrender my life to a higher power." Blame was always on the table. Parents and spouses were asked if they understood how their own behaviors were enabling little Joey's addiction, as if they were somehow responsible for their addict's self-destruction, self-absorption, and baffling unconcern for others.

When one of the dads asked for clarification on that point, he was told that his letting his daughter stay at home rather than on the street had made it easier for her to be a junkie. The dad said, "So I should let her fend for herself?" The impassioned counselor, an ex-addict himself, said yes, he should. The dad stood up and said, "Fine, give me back my twelve grand, motherfucker," and then he turned to his daughter and told her to get her ass out on the street.

Bay said, "What's scary is how readily they've surrendered their free will and how pleased they are to hear that relapse is a part of recovery."

Just then the Statue of Liberty walked into the bar, shook the ash from his drape and gown, brushed a mantle of white ash from his shoulders, and stomped his feet.

Bay said, "And then at the end of the session we all pray for serenity, but only the addicts know where to find it."

The Statue of Liberty put his plastic torch on the bar and ordered a Jack and Coke. Helen said, Jack and Pepsi okay? I recognized him as the Statue who stands out on Main waving to passing motorists, trying to drum up business for the income tax preparation service in the strip mall behind him. I heard Helen ask him if he'd had a rough day, and I thought any day you have to dress up as an inanimate object has to be rough. I heard him say that it might only be a costume, but it stood for something nonetheless. The Statue took off his foam headpiece and set it next to the torch. He told Helen that he was being paid under the counter.

She said, "*Under the table*, you mean."

"Say again."

"Money under the table; drugs over the counter."

"Bottom dollar: I don't have to declare it."

Bay said, "Are you listening to a word I say?"

"Sorry, eavesdropping."

"I said maybe your dad is beyond your ability to help."

"He's not."

"Maybe you're doing more harm than god . . . good."

"Why are you saying that?"

"I thought you might want to hear it."

Bay told me he'd won a couple of hundred at the poker table the previous night, but should have won a lot more. The casino was packed with tourists and the picking was easy. One guy, Bay said, wore a neck pillow the whole night, so he could nap when he mucked his hand, Bay guessed.

Bay said that the big winner was an attractive, middle-aged LPN named Claire, who favored turquoise and silver jewelry and drank great quantities of Mountain Dew. While they played, Claire told the table about the last job she'd found on Craigslist.

She was hired to diaper a man who had multiple sclerosis. She was paid six hundred bucks a week, cash, to go to his house at nine A.M. and seven P.M. to clean, powder, and swaddle-in-cotton Mr. Buzzy Meltzer's bum. So imagine her surprise when she found out at an LPN website that the healthy Mr. Meltzer was a chronic abuser of nursing services who had been busted wearing Dr. Dentons and sucking on a pacifier at an S&M hospitality room at the Ambassador Hotel. Claire told the cardplayers what she did next. She showed up for her usual seven P.M. visit, removed the soiled diapers, and slammed Buzzy's own cell phone up his filthy ass and then dialed his number and left a message.

"Did you believe her story?"

"I enjoyed it."

I smelled patchouli and found myself carried away—back to the Halliday house on the night of the killings, in the boys' room where I had first caught the scent. I could find no incense cones or sticks, no bowl or holder, no evident source of the fragrance. I smelled it again when I was speaking with Carlos in the living room.

I looked up and saw the newcomer wearing patchouli walk toward the bar. He wore a very white T-shirt, pressed jeans, and black loafers. His gelled brown hair was receding, stylishly short, and flipped into a Kewpie-doll curl up front. He had a gold loop in the ear I could see and stored his cell phone in a holster on his belt. He sat at the bar, took a plug of chewing gum out of his mouth, wrapped it in a cocktail napkin, and dropped it in an ashtray. He ordered what looked to be whiskey and soda. I thought about the other smells in the Halliday house—the pine resin from the Christmas tree, the redolence of baked cookies from the kitchen, the lavender in the bathroom coming from a plug-in air freshener. Brianna's room smelled bleachy and clean, like freshly laundered linen. Only the patchouli seemed imported.

I said, "I thought Carlos had no reason to lie to me about the absence of photographs in the house. So I didn't bother looking very hard."

"Why would he have wanted you there if you wouldn't have access to everything?"

"I should have been more diligent."

Bay held up a finger. "Don't look now, but our friend at the bar is watching us in the mirror. Excuse me a moment." Bay walked to the bar and stood between the Statue of Liberty and Kewpie. He ordered our drinks and said something to Helen about the arrest this morning of the undocumented Honduran farmworkers picked up in the Redlands. Kewpie turned his head like he might have something to add but then went back to staring at his straw. The Statue of Liberty said without a shred of irony that the illegals should all be sent back to where they come from. Bay paid Helen for the drinks.

Bay sat down; the Statue of Liberty sneezed three times; Kewpie walked to the men's room. Bay said, "Hold the fort," and got up and headed for the men's room. He bumped into the returning Kewpie on his way, apologized, squeezed past him, and went on down the hall.

My phone vibrated and I saw Bay's name. He told me to keep talking into the phone after he hung up and to make like I was losing the call and get up and sidle my way toward the door. He'd meet me outside in two minutes.

He hung up. I pretended I was speaking to my new psychiatrist, Dr. Conrad Wondolowski, who didn't exist. "What is it I'd like to work on? Well, let's start with my self-esteem, shall we? In short supply. Guilt; depression; commitment, or lack thereof; shame; regret; paranoia; aimlessness; meaninglessness; dullness; delusions; claustrophobia; fear of dying too soon; fear of living too long. You're breaking up, Doctor. Hold on." I walked to the center of the bar. "That's better. Where were we? Did I mention guilt? Anger. Anxiety. Fear of failure, fear of success, fear of intimacy, fear of nonchalance." I looked over at Kewpie, who was now being regaled by the Statue of Liberty. "I've only got the one bar right now." I stepped to the door. "There we go. Can you hear me? Okay. My life is in turmoil. We could start there. That should keep us busy." I stepped out of the bar. "No, that's Friday the thirteenth, and I don't plan to go out of the house. Can we meet on Thursday?" I saw that Dusty had made it as far as the mailbox. He was staring up into the night sky.

A cab pulled up in front, the back window opened, and Bay waved me over. "Let's go!"

I got in and off we went. I said, "Why are we in a cab when my car's at the bar?"

"Our nosy friend back there is a cop."

"Are you sure?"

"I had the opportunity to examine his wallet."

"You stole a cop's wallet."

"I borrowed it."

Our driver turned on the wipers and cleaned the ash from the windshield.

Bay said, "Detective Ernest Kind."

I said, "I bet he's neither."

"EPD. He's thirty-four, five-eight, one-forty, hazel eyes. He is not an organ donor. He shops at Winn-Dixie, flies Delta, has just one more hot dog to buy at Wiener Takes All before he gets a free one. He left home today with eighty dollars in cash and a Kimono micro-thin large condom. He may be in the market for a house in Palmetto according to the address scribbled on the back of an L. D. Nash Realty business card. *Everything I Touch Turns to Sold*!"

"Why would he be spying on us?"

"I suspect he was told to catch you at something illegal, like drinking and driving. Followed you from your office. As soon as you got behind the wheel, he'd phone it in, finish his unpalatable drink, and then cruise by Bartram and Main where Officer Barleycorn would be giving you a sobriety test, which you fail, and you spend the night in jail and the next several weeks in court. And you lose your license, et cetera."

Bay checked his watch and said, "Right about now Detective Kind is wondering where you are—he knows where I am—and so he peeks outside, sees you've vanished, and wonders if he's been hoodwinked, and runs back in to settle with Helen, which is when he realizes his wallet is gone, so he backtracks to the head and finds the wallet but not me. He opens the wallet and counts the money. It's all there but he already knows he's reporting it stolen in the morning at the station. He runs out of the bar. Dusty will tell him, sure, he's seen two guys matching that description running like mad, and he'll say, They went that-a-way! And he'll point toward the IHOP, the way I paid him to, and Detective Kind will drive a few blocks west until he stops and calls his overseer and reports his failure.

A metal tree frog, about six inches long and bright yellow, adorned with painted hibiscus flowers, was attached to the back of the driver's seat and seemed to be climbing to the cabbie's permit. Our driver was Cajuste Marcelin, and he was speaking with a friend on his Bluetooth. "De kriminèl isit la nan taksi mwen!"

I reassured Cajuste that we were not criminals. We went to Bay's house. We ordered jerked pork and oxtail from Irie Isle, ate at the dining room table while Charlie Haden played on the sound system. Bay wondered what had caused this latest escalation of harassment, if that's what it was. What had I done to piss off whoever-it-was? Could I think of anything? I couldn't. And where the hell was Kevin Shanks? Bay noticed that his Howard Finster angel was gone from its spot on the bookcase. Marlena must have taken it. It was unlikely a pawnshop would be interested in outsider art, but a collector or a gallery might be. Goddammit! Bay wondered if this meant she had left rehab and let herself in or if she'd taken it weeks ago, and he just hadn't noticed. I told him to take an inventory.

We talked about the late Mickey Pfeiffer, of course. The story was all over the news. What those last few minutes of his life must have been like. Christ! The Feds had taken over the investigation of the Ponzi scheme and the murder/kidnap. I didn't want to think that the people after me were the people after Mickey. Bay said he thought Mickey was a simple man despite his audacious opulence. He wanted what we all want: respect, attention, affection, security, and control. He figured the surest way to get all that was to buy it. And the surest way to get the money to buy it was to steal it. And all that wealth brought out the child in Mickey, and the child liked cars and watches and ladies and friends in high places and boats and gaudy clothes.

While I cleaned up, Bay went to his utility closet and got out two flashlights and a box of latex gloves. I said, We're not playing doctor, are we?

"We're going to the Hallidays'."

We parked a block away from the house, slipped our flashlights into our pockets, and snapped on our latex gloves. By then it was just past eleven. The Halliday house was already on the market. This would be a tough sell. You'd need to bury a few statues of Saint Joseph in this front lawn. An L. D. Nash Realty sign was affixed to a vinyl yard post out front, as were three deflated open-house balloons. There was a photo of L.D. himself on the sign looking confident and honorable. We turned the corner and walked around back and saw that someone had staked a makeshift cross into the lawn and left a bouquet of now-desiccated cut flowers. Something was different about the yard, but I wasn't sure what it was. Something missing. When I saw the dying lantana, I remembered the Everglades Home Security sign. I told Bay about the sign and said it was curious that I'd seen no evidence of security systems on Christmas Eve. He said some people just put out those signs. Bay fiddled with the back door and opened it. I told him that breaking and entering would earn me more than a night in jail. He said, "Are you sure that sign was really there?" and, of course, I now was not.

Some previous intruder had spray-painted an Old Testament quote on the wall: *Woe to them that devise iniquity and work evil upon their beds.* The house had been meticulously scrubbed. There was not a pine needle left in the den, not a trace of the slaughter anywhere. The house smelled of Lysol and citrus floor wax. The drawers had all been emptied, the medicine cabinets removed from the walls and left on bathroom floors. Light fixtures and wall plates had been removed. The toilets had been unseated. The only carpet in the house, in the master bedroom, had been untacked, lifted, and hauled away. The stove was gone and so was the water heater in the garage. The intruder needed appliances?

I said, "How do you sneak a water heater out of a house?"

Bay said, "You don't sneak. You act with impunity. If anyone sees you, you say you were installing a new water heater, and that's what they'll remember."

I said, "We're not going to learn anything new here."

Bay dropped me at the Wayside, and I got in my car and headed home. I hoped Django's bowl wasn't empty. I decided to stop at Walgreens for surgical masks and Visine. I figured Red would need to move inside until the fires died out. I drove toward the glow in the western sky and then turned south on Main. The car behind me flashed its brights and then bumped me when I slowed.

I thought the guy must be drunk, and I should just pull over and let him pass. And then he bumped me again, a little harder this time. So I stopped, got out of the car, raised my arms like, What the hell are you doing? As I walked toward the car, a dark green Ford, the driver kept backing away, keeping about twenty feet between us. When I stopped, he stopped; when I approached, he retreated. And then I got nervous about my car, back there in the middle of the road, running, door open and lights on, so I hurried back, hopped in, and drove on, the Ford once again on my ass. And that's all I could remember that made any sense until I woke up the next morning in a semiprivate room at Memorial Hospital with an Eden cop and Venise at my bedside. Apparently I drove another two blocks on Main and was driving through the intersection at Oleander Road when a stolen white Escalade blew through the red light and T-boned my car dead-on. The driver got out of the car and ran, and no one stopped him. He got into a car in the IHOP parking lot and drove away. For some reason the cop at my bedside kept calling it an accident.

None of my bones was broken. I wasn't hurt, thanks to the airbag, but everything felt loosened. Carlos came by with a book from Inez, said he couldn't stay. *The End of the Affair.* I asked Carlos if he knew Officer Kind. He did, but Kind didn't work undercover. He drove a bike on the Boardwalk—a cushy detail. I asked him if he thought someone was trying to kill me. He told me not to be so melodramatic. I asked him who bit my finger and broke my phone. That's been handled, he said. Have they been arrested? I said. He said, I've got to go.

Venise assured me that Red was taking care of Django and was sleeping in the Florida room. The papers were saying this was already the worst fire season in history. There was no chance of getting the fires under control. They'd have to consume themselves. Alligator Alley would remain closed until that time.

Bay picked me up in a gold Studebaker Lark Wagonaire that he'd won in a card game. It was mine as long as I needed it. It had a sliding roof above the rear cargo compartment. The Pope could stand in the back and wave while I drove to PetSmart.

I said, "The crash. What do you think?"

"I think you need to find out why it happened."

18

It smelled like the house was on fire. I had all the windows closed and the ceiling fans on. Red stood at the stove scrambling eggs, wearing a surgical mask and dark glasses. Django was asleep in a potted bromeliad. I told him he was a bad boy. He yawned and rolled on his back. I turned on the radio news and learned that several homes out on 27 had been destroyed by flames. People in west Everglades County were reporting pythons in their yards and alligators on their streets. What we needed was a prolonged soaking rain in the Everglades, but the rainy season was still months away. A shift in the wind to the west would offer some relief, but that seemed unlikely anytime soon. In the meantime, we were to stay indoors if possible. Hospitals were full. The Red Cross was setting up emergency shelters; the fires were creeping closer to heavily populated areas. People with respiratory problems were urged to evacuate.

Red lifted his mask and said, "This is what happens when you divert most of the water from the Everglades so the wealthy can float their boats in Palm Beach." He stirred the eggs and lifted the mask again. "This is what happens when you let engineers run the show."

I felt sore and stiff and tried to stretch out my back. I started coughing and couldn't stop until I drank a glass of water. A lot of folks were taking the county's Emergency Management's advice and were heading out of harm's way. Traffic to the Keys was backed up from Islamorada to Cutler Ridge. The turnpike and interstate north were gridlocked. The Highway Patrol estimated a three-hour drive time from New River to Palm Beach. The phone rang. Django hopped down from the plant and clawed his way up my pant leg and onto the table. I answered the call. A crisis at Almost Home. Dad had pulled a gun on Mr. Jake Machinist and threatened to fire a bullet through his eye. No, I'm not making the name up, Mr. Melville. Mr. Machinist is . . . was . . . a prominent attorney before his recent series of strokes. He's been rushed to Memorial with an apparent heart attack. The police were interviewing my father as we spoke. I said I'd be right there.

Django was at my plate licking my eggs. I told Red to stay inside. He said he'd regrout the bathroom tiles. I said that wouldn't be necessary. He lifted his eyebrow and looked over the top of his sunglasses. On the way to Almost Home I listened to a voice mail from Georgia: "A miracle has happened, Wylie. Tripp is alive, praise Jesus! He was found wandering disoriented, weak, and starving in a little seaside village in Barbados. The last thing he remembers before being saved is these two menacing black men heading his way on the deck. The boys have flown back to the States to be with their grandmother. You remember Carolina, don't you?" Yes, I did. The unforgettable Carolina, who spent her days shoplifting at Walmart and her nights in front of the TV watching *Perry Mason* reruns.

When I arrived at Almost Home, the cops told me that Myles was incoherent. Yes, they knew the pistol was a prop, but that didn't change anything. Officer Troupes said, "Your dad keeps saying he's got a lot of ham in him. He's not Jewish, I take it."

I said, "He's doing Lionel Barrymore."

"Who?"

Officer Troupes said, "We've Baker-Acted your old man. He'll be held for seventy-two hours in the psych unit at Everglades General, and if all goes well, and if Mr. Machinist survives and doesn't press charges, you can have him back."

Officer Bradley stated the obvious. "Your father's certainly not competent to stand trial."

They allowed me five minutes with Dad. I asked him what he thought he was doing. He laughed and said he'd made Machinist piss his pants. He pulled a gun on him because Machinist was the man they sent to kill him. Who sent him? The drug lords.

"You've done it now, you know. They're throwing you out of here."

I later learned that Attorney Machinist had represented unscrupulous mortgage lenders who were being sued by the home buyers they defrauded, and maybe I shouldn't have, but I did, in fact, feel just a little pleased at this manifestation of instant karma. Shame on me, of course. I sent a breathtaking floral arrangement and sincere apologies to Mr. Machinist, Esquire. I wished him a swift and complete recovery.

DA Millard arranged for me to meet with Wayne for thirty minutes at the county jail. I sat at the metal table in the middle of the ten-by-twelve-foot room listening to the hum of fluorescent lights above my head and wondering who was watching me shift uncomfortably in my chair. The room was four cinder-block walls painted a glossy, but sallow, green. The green metal door had a small window of reinforced glass. I assumed the room was bugged and that whatever we said would be recorded. The squashed body of a cockroach was stuck to the wall a foot from the ceiling where someone at some time must have dispatched it with the heel of a shoe. Some wag had drawn a circle with a Magic Marker around the roach and written, *Gregor S.*

Wayne was led into the room by an ESO guard with tiny blue eyes and a cast on his left wrist. Wayne's head was shaved, and his left cheekbone was swollen and bruised. He wore an orange jumpsuit, white socks, and plastic sandals. He sat and held up his hands. The guard unlocked and removed the handcuffs and told me to buzz him when we were finished. He pressed the white button by the door to illustrate and stepped outside.

I told Wayne that I'd spoken to his mom. He said if I spoke to her again to tell her not to come see him and not to attend what would be a very brief trial. He'd plead guilty, and he expected to receive the death penalty. That would be the only justice, wouldn't it? He touched his mouth with the tips of his fingers, brushed his hand along the side of his head, grabbed his nose between his thumb and index finger, and wiped his face on his sleeve. He said, "So why have you come?"

"I want to know why you killed those two girls."

Wayne tried to gather a yawn in his hand. "I don't know why." He pumped his right leg.

"Or you don't *want* to know why?"

"I did it because I could."

"You could rob a bank, but you didn't."

"Money doesn't interest me." He stopped pumping his leg, folded his hands between his thighs, and began swinging his knees together and apart over and over.

I said, "Do you think about those girls?"

"I think they aren't suffering anymore."

"What did it feel like to kill them?"

"You want an honest answer?"

"What kind of question is that?"

"I found it disappointing." He stood and stretched. He walked to the wall and leaned back against it. He put his hands behind his back and stared at his feet. "At first it was kind of a rush. I guess the thrill was that I was doing something new and powerful. And then it just felt like work. I resented having to finish the job, and that just made me angry. I wanted to be alone with a bowl of cereal and my computer." He shut his eyes. "It's hard to kill someone who doesn't want to die."

He walked behind me and stood. "I remember being in school—Ronald Reagan Middle School—in the cafeteria, sitting alone, watching other kids smile and talk to each other, and I looked at my miserable uncut bologna-oleo-yellow-mustard-white bread sandwich and my carton of warm milk, and I hated my life so much I squeezed the sandwich into a ball until the bread began oozing out between my fingers." He walked to his chair and sat.

I said, "You sound more sad than angry."

He looked at me for the first time. "Don't tell me how I feel. I'm sick of people telling me how I feel. You can't know what's going on in here." He pointed to his head and then his heart. He told me what a fraud I was. And then he stared at me and waited. "Go ahead," he said, "tell me I'm angry and ask me if I want to go with that." When I didn't respond, he said, "We're finished here."

I stood by the door and pushed the buzzer. I waited. I pushed it again. Wayne said, "The guards are fucking with you."

Phoebe had gotten me an appointment with Kai to work on my aching and stiff back. He told me to throw away the Flexeril I'd been prescribed. No one ever got better by treating the symptoms, he said. The body will heal itself once the insults have been removed. Kai had set up a temporary office in the back room of the house. Phoebe was in the kitchen when I arrived, packing dinnerware into cartons. She blew me a polite kiss, said Kai was in back waiting for me. I asked her when they were leaving. Soon, she said.

Kai had me lie on my stomach on the adjusting table. He bent my left leg at the knee and raised it. He touched my lower back. He did the same with my right leg, touched my lower back again, and whistled. "We need to loosen the muscles here. The trauma has contracted them into a steel knot." He made a fist. I moved to a massage table and lay on my back as rollers in the cushioned bed slowly moved along my spine. Kai told me to alternate ice and moist heat, to take an Advil every six hours. He said I'd need to come back to see him. He asked me how many chiropractors it took to screw in a lightbulb. I didn't know. He said, Just one, but it takes ten visits.

Dad remained under observation at Everglades General for eight days, the extra time being necessary, doctors said, to build up his strength and to treat a bronchial infection. By the time I fetched him and brought him home with me, a lot had changed:

- Wayne Vanderhyde was dead, murdered by inmates—allegedly—at the jail, stabbed with a soup spoon whose handle had been filed to a point, stabbed fifty-one times, stabbed in the eyes, in the throat, in the ears, and elsewhere. How a prisoner on suicide watch could somehow manage to get himself killed is a mystery, the sheriff admitted, but the ESO had promised a swift and thorough investigation.
- Georgia and her husband were suing the cruise line for criminal negligence. I learned about this on the local news as Tripp told his harrowing story to a credulous

Channel 7 reporter. Only a miracle saved my life, he said. It was not his time to go. Tripp clasped Georgia's hand and said that God must have a plan for him. I also found out that Tripp's given name was Bynum. Bynum Fleming "Tripp" Morris. And that his lawyer was Ron Ellis, who had worked for Mickey Pfeiffer.

- An ESO deputy shot and killed his ex-wife, a thirty-year-old waitress at Eggstasy. About a half hour before Cricket Dorval was murdered, ESO had been warned by Cricket's sister-in-law that Elton Dorval had an assault rifle and was driving to Lake Ellie to kill his ex. Sheriff Hayes told his dispatcher not to issue a BOLO to other law enforcement agencies, saying he would take care of the situation himself. "I thought I could get the quickest response by making personal contact," he told the press. He could not.
- Phoebe had gone ahead to Sedona to get their new house in order. No bon voyage dinner at Kurosawa, no goodbye drink at the Universe, no e-mail farewell, no phone call, no heartfelt letter, no nothing. I decided to believe that saying goodbye would have been too painful for her.
- Two of our more bellicose senior citizens, strangers who, improbably, shared the same name—Irving Ross—(I wouldn't lie to you) got into an altercation while standing in the ticket line outside the Regal Maplewood Plaza Cineplex. Unpleasantries were exchanged, voices were raised, and embarrassed wives were shushed. Jostle led to shove led to push led to punch. The recipient of the roundhouse right to the jaw fell and struck his head on the concrete. He died on the way to the hospital. The living Irving Ross was arrested for manslaughter.

- Dermid Reardon, worried that I would somehow talk him out of his voluntary amputation, found a more sympathetic therapist, a psychiatrist who, in turn, set him up with an accommodating orthopedic surgeon, and the operation had been scheduled. Patience told me that it's easier to live with no legs than with the overwhelming obsessive desire to have them gone. I said, He's having them both removed? One at a time, she said. She also said she had seen my profile on thats amore.com and wanted to know why I had never asked her out. I said, I have all my parts. She said, I'm sure you're missing something. So we made a date.
- Early on Sunday morning, two groups of refugees were found on beaches in South Florida. A dozen Cubans reached the shore near Matheson Hammock and were taken to the Krome Detention Center, where they were processed and released to their relatives and welcomed to America. The thirty-six Haitians who landed on Melancholy Beach were also taken to Krome, where they would be detained until their imminent deportation.
- *Django* the Intrepid caught his first anole in the house and pranced across the living room with the slender fellow in his mouth. He set his trophy on the floor, placed his paw on the anole's tail, and glanced around the room to see if any admiring eyes were watching. When the tail detached itself and writhed on the floor like a beached eel, Django leaped straight up in the air. While he wrestled the frenetic tail into submission, the bobbed anole dashed away. *Red* moved his belongings into the Florida room and began painting interior landscapes. He had found himself a volunteer job caring for sick and injured animals at the Wildlife Care Center.

> *Sable* delivered a sermon at the Holiness Church of the Saved but Struggling on the subject of "The Body Is a Temple of the Soul." *Bay* and I went searching for Marlena, who had gone AWOL from rehab. We checked the motels along Main and Dixie, the bars, the strip joints, and the greasy spoons. We showed the working girls a photo of Marlena, but no one had seen her. We checked the homeless shelter, the weeds along the railroad tracks, and the sea grape thickets along the beach. Every morning Bay got up and sat in front of his iMac and scrolled through the arrest records in Miami-Dade, Monroe, Everglades, and Palm Beach Counties. And then he read through the obits in the *Herald* and the *Journal-Gazette.*

And some things remained the same. The fires had not abated; the winds had not shifted; the tourists had not returned. Some folks had taken to wearing military surplus gas masks, so it looked like a fifties sci-fi movie out there on the streets. Everyone anonymous and insective. And you half expected some colossal, monstrous A bomb-mutated creature to rise up out of the sea beyond the reef, terrify the few innocent sunbathers on the beach, and flatten our Eden. Kevin Shanks was still among the missing.

Dad was quiet on the drive home. He sat with his surgical mask on, coughing once in a while, and staring straight ahead. I saw the same bicyclist we'd seen on Christmas morning, the guy in the Santa hat. Hatless now, he'd somehow attached a beach umbrella to the bike's frame, and now he pedaled in the shade.

I settled Dad into my bedroom, showed him where his clothes were and his toiletries. He sat on the bed, bounced a bit, nodded his approval. Not wanting to miss a trick, Django climbed up the bedspread and onto the bed. He bounded over to Dad's hand and bit it.

"He's playing," I said.

"Who's he?"

"Django."

"Where will you sleep?"

"On the couch."

I reintroduced Dad to Red, who was leaving for work. I asked Dad what he wanted for lunch. He said, Canadian peas. I said, How about eggs? He told me he liked his eggs "easy on the over and out." After lunch he said he'd take his pills with a Bloody Mary. I told him we were going to see how life without meds would feel. Maybe it's all the drugs screwing you up. I made the Bloody Mary. He drank two sips and went to the bedroom for a nap.

I had a three o'clock with Vladimir, so I drove Dad to Venise and Oliver's. On the way, he told me that Geronimo slept on his chest and scratched his throat.

"Django."

He asked me how the hit man was doing.

"Machinist?"

"The guy who pissed his pants."

"He's back at Almost Home. It wasn't a heart attack after all. You're not a killer."

"Your uncle Guy used to drive a red and white Studebaker Silver Hawk. He loved that car. Kept blankets over the seats to keep them spotless. Only took the blankets off when he had a date, which was every Saturday night with Baby, his Swedish girlfriend. We thought he was making her up for the longest time. They usually went to the drive-in, he told us, but one Saturday night he got all dressed up, so I followed him in my Dodge all the way to the Scandinavian Club. Sure enough, inside there was Guy and Baby, his blond beauty and a head taller than him. When he was with Baby, Guy looked like the cat that swallowed the canary. Happy as a vulture on a slop wagon."

Before I got to my office, Venise called. She said, “He’s not the same person.”

I said, “He’s confused.”

“I’m not taking care of someone I don’t know.”

“Give him time. He’ll adjust. I’ll be back at five to get him.”

“Who’s Fernando?”

“I don’t know.”

“He keeps saying someone named Fernando bit him.”

Vladimir shook my hand and dropped into the chair. He sat with his hands folded on his lap. I did not stare at his neck. I did and I did not want to hear the story of that scar. He wore a starched blue oxford shirt, black slacks, black socks, and black shoes—clothes you wore if you didn’t want to be seen. He began by quoting Pushkin:

> Я жил похоронить моего желания,
> и посмотреть мои мечты разъедать ржавчиной;
> Теперь все, что осталось бесплодны пожары,
> которые горят мои пустое сердце в пыль.

Which he translated as:

> *I’ve lived to entomb my desires,*
> *And see my dreams corrupt with rust;*
> *Now all that’s left are futile fires*
> *That sear my barren heart to dust.*

And then he wrote it down for me. He touched his heart. “Pushkin speaks for all Russian people.”

I said, “Tell me what’s going on.”

He shook his head and leaned back. "The money in this machine is over."

"I don't understand."

"Is metaphor."

"Help me out."

"Like ATM with no more cash."

"You're spent?"

He nodded.

Vladimir told me that he was depressed for the first time in his life and had been now for some weeks. He had assumed this cloud would lift, but it had not. He'd been sad before, of course: when his father, Sergei, died (banquet/fishbone); when Zenit lost to Spartak Moscow in the Premiership semifinals; when he remembered his childhood friends and their games of cowboys and Indians in Kirov Park. Sadness seemed almost quaint to him now—a tug at the heart; a whiff of regret; a brief, sweet taste of nostalgia, and then a shrug back to composure.

Depression felt like a crushing weight that left him feeling sluggish, dull, and apathetic. Yes, Kouzmanoff's death had something to do with this. It was like losing a brother. Vladimir said he was staring into the abyss and was angry because he felt helpless to do anything about it. I asked him what he saw in that abyss, and he said himself.

"You have done something. You've taken a step. Today is the day you began to take back your life."

"I haven't been able to work."

"Do you enjoy your work?"

"You know I work for some bad guys."

"Why do you?"

"Is family."

"What do you do at work?"

"I see that all the bad guys play well with each other."

Vladimir crossed his legs, untied his shoe, and retied it. Recrossed his legs and did the other shoe. I asked him what was on his mind right now.

"My dream from last night." He uncrossed his legs and sat back on the couch. "Was with a large, headless woman. She was naked and had pale, pinkish skin, smooth and hairless like a baby. She was relaxing on a gray sofa. Each of her breasts was the head of a pig." He looked at me.

I said, "What do you think it means?"

"The pigs were smiling at me."

I asked him if he thought about his future.

"Never. It will come whether I think about it or not."

I asked him what he admired about people, and he told me a strong will, physical strength, and silence. I explained that it might be difficult to change his thoughts and feelings, but that it would be easier to change his behavior, and when behavior changes, the thoughts and feelings will follow.

He quoted Lyndon Johnson. "If you have them by the balls, their hearts and minds will follow." He smiled.

"Yes, that's the idea. You feel better for that smile, don't you?"

"I suppose."

"So what is it you enjoy doing?"

"Eating blinis and shooting pistols."

"Well, why not take Cerise out for blinis at Baikal and then off to Point & Shoot for target practice."

He nodded. "Blinis calm me down; pistols pick me up."

I told him he should maybe keep a notebook and write down what's going on when he feels blue and when he feels like himself, when he's content. Maybe that way he can understand the causes of his depression and avoid them. He told me never to write anything down, ever. When he was leaving I asked him about his throat. He smiled. "You should have seen the other guy."

19

Every therapist has a therapist. Mine is Thalassa Xenakis. I talk with her when I need some reassembly, when I feel lost in dark woods and all that. Stress I can handle. Stress is what martinis are for. And there I generally follow my father's advice: martinis are like breasts, one is not enough and three are too many. This is not a rule I'd share with Thalassa, necessarily.

Thalassa is semiretired. She sees me and a few other clients of long standing, does not accept insurance, credit cards, excessive whining, or personal checks. She rents out her big house on the Intracoastal to snowbirds in winter and South Americans in summer, and she lives in her own backyard, in a 356-square-foot bungalow she built by herself in eight months. She's got a small kitchen, a full bath, a loft with a queen-sized futon mattress, a cozy living room where she meets her clients, and a lovely, intimate front porch.

We sat on the two brown leather chairs, a rattan tray between us on which Thalassa had set two tumblers of fresh lemonade.

On the wall across from us hung a large beaded Haitian voodoo flag depicting a siren with a red fish in one hand, a white trumpet in the other. When I walked in Thalassa was reading the poems of Alan Dugan, and she read me the opening line of a poem she liked. "*What's the balm / for a dying life, / dope, drink, or Christ, / is there one?*" And then she said, "Talk to me, Wylie." We'd been on a first-name basis since my first session at her old office on Gumbo Limbo, years ago, around the time of Cameron's death, when I introduced myself and called her Dr. Xenakis. She said, "Call me Thalassa, Melville."

I put down my lemonade and said, "I'm finding it hard to focus lately."

"Why?"

"Myles is deteriorating. Venise is even more hysterical. I'm obsessed with a murder case. My friend Carlos is avoiding me. Phoebe's moving away. I'm not doing my job as well as I should. All the distraction." I watched Thalassa's scribbled angelfish glide through the salt water in the aquarium.

"What do you need?"

"I don't know that I need anything. I'll survive. I'll muddle along."

Thalassa looked at the ceiling. "I'm hearing a lot of words, but no substance."

"I guess what I want is, I don't know, more control, maybe."

"You guess?"

"I do."

"Can you control your father's health?"

"No."

"Can you control Phoebe's leaving?"

"Only if I can change the past. I keep thinking that soon I'll be in Dad's place, but there'll be no dutiful child there to look after me."

"Your abandonment issues."

"And somebody is trying to kill me."

Thalassa pressed her hands together as if in prayer and brought her fingertips to her lips. "You think someone is trying to kill you?" She raised her left eyebrow and nodded at my still-bandaged pinky. "One finger at a time?"

"I'm serious." I explained what had been going on. "I'm not making this up." I told her, yes, I had called the police, but the police, you see, were the problem.

"How do you feel right now?"

I stared at the angelfish as they carved their way through the water, swerving along the glass, rising to the surface, diving to the gravel, picking up pebbles, and spitting them out.

"I swear to God, Wylie, I'll kill those fish if you don't stop staring at them. I asked you how you felt."

I was even a poor analysand. "I'm confused."

"Confusion's not a feeling. Confusion's in your head. What's in here?" She brought both fists to her gut. "Where are your metaphors, Wylie?"

Thalassa is fond of quoting Paul Valéry, saying that that which resembles nothing does not exist. I could have told her that I felt like her fish, swimming all day and going nowhere, but I didn't want to further imperil the fish. So I closed my eyes to see what was there, and I saw myself as an exploding diagram with all my body parts at a distance from my body. Every muscle, bone, and organ was there on display and clearly labeled, but nothing was working. I told Thalassa I felt like the exploded man.

"Now we're getting somewhere." She smiled.

By the end of our session, we had concluded that:

- Perhaps I should spend my money on a bodyguard and not a therapist.

- Everything that we love vanishes (my abandonment issues).
- We cannot live without love.
- A vacation was in order—time to rest and recreate; and since I "could not" (me) or "would not" (Thalassa) leave my father in Venise's care, he would have to tag along.
- I should do a cost-benefit analysis of my stubborn pursuit of equivocal justice.
- Guilt is the gravity weighing me down.
- I could sure use some buoyancy in my life (Django, Red, Bay, Patience—it's a start).
- Guilt reflects my inflated sense of self-importance ("At least consider the possibility, Wylie").

When Thalassa's alarm went off, she stepped into the kitchen with our empty tumblers and returned with a chilled bottle of Pedro Romero amontillado and two sherry glasses. She poured; we toasted the end of the Everglades fires. She said, "You mentioned changing the past."

"I did?"

"I've been thinking about this exact thing, about retrocausality. Can the present affect the past? Can the future affect the present?" She put down her glass. "If we imagine the future we want for ourselves and that imagined future causes us to strive to attain it—"

"But it's not the actual future."

"If we get what we imagined, it certainly is."

I sipped the sherry and stared at the hardwood floor, trying to see my future in the grain. All I saw was myself at the end of a very long hallway, an open door ahead of me, and a dark room beyond the door.

"If you revise your memories," Thalassa said, "you change the past, and your clarified past will change your present. You remember what you've been trying so hard to forget—that awful time you left your lover, and you realize now that your leaving was hurtful, but not malicious, was not motivated by contempt or by gloom; you left to save your life, yes? You were terrified of waking up in thirty years and saying, I relinquished my dreams for this humdrum routine with this pleasant and contented person. And now you can unburden yourself of that grief and guilt and breathe again."

I told her about nonlocality in the quantum world, a subject I'd gotten interested in when I played Ridley in Tom Stoppard's *Hapgood*. I said, "If one particle can instantaneously affect another, even from the other side of the galaxy, if this can happen, then anything, time travel, anything at all, is possible. And then what happens to our stories? To narrative coherence? How do we help our clients shape their life stories?"

Thalassa said we'd still have stories with beginnings, middles, and ends, but maybe not in that order. We'd have plots, cause and effect, but maybe the effect precedes the cause. You'd be able to read a story backward or from the middle back to the start and ahead to the end at the same time. I'm not saying a thing to Inez.

20

Bay called and said he was happy to hear my adenoidal voice. He told me he'd heard from Open Mike, who'd heard from a reliable but anonymous source that I was dead.

"I'm not. Here, I'll give you to Venise, who can verify."

"There's a body in your front yard."

"No, there isn't."

"I'm telling you."

"I'm on my way." I hung up, excused myself, called Carlos, and told him what I'd just learned. He told me to meet him at the house. Melancholy is out of Carlos's jurisdiction, but he knew about every deputy with the ESO.

Red did not see who it was coming up behind him. It was dusk, and he was cleaning up after trimming the bougainvilleas. His forearms were cut up despite the long-sleeved shirt I'd given him to wear that morning. He was listening to the radio when whoever it was walked up behind him and fired a bullet into the back of his head. Red was dead before he fell into the pile of thorny branches he was carrying. The shooter may have used a pistol suppressor. No one in the neighborhood heard a shot. Red lay there on what passes for a lawn for several hours before he was discovered by Jem Rowan, who was out walking his Airedale, Duncan. About the time the killing happened, I'd been at the playhouse auditioning for a role in a new play, *Lobotomobile*, which is about the real-life doctor who popularized the ten-minute transorbital lobotomy in the States in the forties and fifties. I was trying out for the part of one of the patients, a Mr. Felix Fortune, who was trying to confront the doctor, wanted to express his outrage and his shame, but couldn't find the words. It's a play about the arrogance of certainty, and God knows there's a lot of that going around.

We stood outside my house, Bay and I, behind the crime scene tape, waiting for Carlos to finish his consultation with the lead detective on the case. Perdita Curry, wearing a teal jumpsuit and gold slingbacks, leaned against a squad car and whispered into the ear of a uniformed officer. She saw me, smiled, and waved. "This just keeps getting better and better," she yelled.

Bay said, "She needs to get off of her knees and onto her meds."

Carlos asked me if Red had any enemies.

"Not that I know of."

"Who would want to kill him?"

"Maybe they thought he was me."

"That's unlikely."

"Someone ran me down last week, remember?"

"We're working on that."

"Maybe he came back to finish the job."

Bay said, "If they're after you and find out they botched the job again, they'll be back."

I said, "Thank God for police protection."

Carlos gave me a look. He said, "Don't stay here tonight."

"My cat."

Carlos pointed to the pet carrier in the driveway. I walked over. Django was looking out the mesh window. I pressed my finger on his nose.

We went to Bay's and set Django loose, and he went right for the terrarium and meowed at Grendel the bearded dragon. I called Venise and Oliver to say they'd have to watch Dad tonight, which was fine because he was already asleep at the kitchen table. I told Venise about Red. She said, "Who's he?"

We sat on the dock and drank and talked about Red and what we thought might be the motive for the killing.

1. The killing was a senseless and random act of violence, some gangbanger's initiation into the Melancholy Kings, maybe.
2. Red may have made an enemy back in his derelict life, someone he may not have even known about. You can't leave the past behind, Bay said.
3. The killer thought Red was me. This was, I had to agree, a possibility, but wasn't one I could reasonably consider. It was like your brain trying to conceive of its terminal unconsciousness.

Bay said, "You should be afraid."

"I am."

He plucked a stirrer out of the air and stirred his blue ruin, Sapphire and Schweppes. "How's Myles?"

"He hardly eats. He's pissed off a lot. He told Wolf Blitzer that Obama was never a liberal to start with. The only thing he cares about is not pissing off the rich."

"You should bring Carlos with you when you go to your office tomorrow."

That's when I realized I had no clean clothes for work. Bay said we should get them. Technically, the yard's the crime scene, not the house. We drank and drove.

I looked at Red's gray camp pad and his tattered sleeping bag laid out on the tile floor of the Florida room, and at the bouquet of paintbrushes arranged in a cobalt-blue Fiestaware coffee mug on a footstool by the door. I'll just leave everything where it is for now, I thought, in here and out at Camp Soileau. A half dozen of Red's watercolors of the beach and the pier were clothespinned to a length of twine he'd strung across the room. I expected to feel, or I assumed I would feel, outrage at this moment, or some other violent emotion, but all I felt was surrender, and I was disappointed in myself. Red had salvaged his broken life, had left the gloom and squalor of Act I behind, and just as he was redefining himself as a painter and a humanitarian, some cold-blooded asshole killed him.

Bay asked me why I had my thermostat set to seventy-two. I said I kept it at eighty when I bothered to turn it on. It's freezing in here, Bay said. Maybe Dad had turned it down this morning. I played the voice mail on my landline while I packed a few things in a Publix grocery sack: Hang up; hang up; hang up with whispered aside, which neither Bay nor I could decipher; Jack Roberts of Citizens wanting to speak with me regarding my flood and windstorm insurance policies. And then some guy affecting a soothing, high-pitched NPR radio voice: *Took care of your little vagrant problem for you. No thanks necessary. Let's just say you owe me one, and I plan to collect.*

Bay said, "You really need to take a vacation, get out of town for a while. Until they nab whoever did this."

"I'd have to reschedule appointments, take care of Dad, the cat. I'll have to think about this."

"Don't think too slowly."

I grabbed a bag of cat food and a box of Cat-Sip, a clean bowl, and a little red catnip mouse. I looked around the kitchen, and something in my field of vision seemed different, but I didn't know what it was, so I stopped and stared. Something—but what?—was out of place. The junk drawer was open an inch or so, I noticed. I opened it fully. The box of blue-tip matches was there, and so were the chopsticks, the Kirin beer bottle opener, and the take-out menus from the local restaurants, but not snug in their rubber band and no longer in alphabetical order. The door to the microwave was ajar, not something I would do, and Red never used the microwave. Every item on the counter had been moved, it looked like, and then put back, but not quite correctly. I said, "Someone's been here."

"The cops were inside getting your cat and the carrier."

"And snooping around, maybe."

"Make sure your valuables are here."

I got my computer, my extra set of keys, got my locked metal safe of important papers out of the freezer. We turned off all the lights except the one over the stove. Bay opened several drawers in the bedroom an inch, crumpled a dollar bill, and tossed it on the bedroom floor. He slipped pieces of paper between cabinet doors and the molding.

Django went to bed with Bay. I couldn't sleep and was too distracted to read more than the same paragraph of a Georges Simenon novel over and over again. So I grabbed a glass and a bottle of Hennessy and went out back to sit on the dock. I felt more relaxed, but every few minutes I looked around and pricked up my ears. What I heard was the occasional airborne mullet slapping the water and the plangent squawking of a night heron. The light was on in the living room of the house directly across the canal. I could see a young couple having an animated conversation. The sliding glass doors were uncurtained and screened. I thought about my intruder and wondered if I was, in fact, meant to understand that I had had an uninvited visitor. Or maybe he just didn't care enough to cover up his home invasion, as they called it on Channel 7. Back in the day when Cam would steal my car, he'd return it to the driveway with the gas tank empty, with cigarette butts and roaches in the ashtray, with condoms and Ziploc bags of twigs and seeds on the floor. And then he'd vociferously deny that he'd been anywhere near my car. That must have been a chapter in *The Scumbag's Manual*: pitch a royal fit if you get caught, scream till you're blue in the face, act like a persecuted innocent, and later forgive your mark for his unwarranted, unseemly, and vicious attack. You're a compassionate man, after all.

I heard the man in the living room yell something about the woman's enjoying Brazilian cock, and I knew he was not talking about barnyard fowl by the way he was standing over her and jabbing his finger at her face. I walked to the end of the dock. He was screaming now, and he grabbed her by the throat and lifted her out of her chair. I figured I could swim across the canal, but I knew that wouldn't happen as soon as I imagined swimming into a barracuda or a severed head. The woman was crying. The dog chained to a pole in the yard began barking and lunging for the house. I yelled out, "Are you okay, ma'am?"

He said, "She's fine!"

I said, "I wasn't talking to you."

He said, "She's my wife," meaning, I guess, My punching bag.

I said, "Ma'am, are you okay?"

He said, "Fuck off, ass monkey!"

The dog howled and ran in circles around the pole, his leash getting shorter and shorter.

She said, "I'm fine, really."

He said, "You heard her."

I said, "I'm calling the cops."

He said, "You do and she'll regret it."

She said, "Please, please, don't call the police. Ever."

And then the light went out and they vanished. I went back into the house.

In the morning I called Carlos and told him about the threatening message I'd received. I lied so he wouldn't know I'd gone home and told him I used my new cell phone to retrieve messages, which I didn't even know for sure was possible, but he bought it. He told me they'd located Red's family in Texas and that one of the brothers was already on his way to claim the body and collect Red's possessions. But he wouldn't be able to get the body until after the autopsy, which wouldn't take place today because the medical examiner was going to be tied up in court all day. His son, Dr. Junior, had been busted on racketeering charges and for trafficking in Oxycodone and conspiring to traffic. He made $150,000 a day off his seven pain clinics. I hoped they'd put him away for the duration plus one, but I already knew he'd get a slap on the wrist.

Bill Aubuchon and Ellen Hillistrom told me that they were head over heels in love. In seventh heaven, Bill said. Tickled pink, Ellen said. Euphoric. But they were also still married to others. I said, Why are you here if you're so happy? They both agreed that things on the home fronts were not going very smoothly. Can you imagine why? I said. You only have so much time and emotional capital, Bill explained. I'm tapped out. He took Ellen's hand. Of course we understand, Ellen said. We're not children. Life is complicated. They told me that they both intended to continue couple's counseling with their respective spouses. You're asking me to lie, I said. They seemed taken aback. I told them I would not collude with them in their fraud. It's time to choose, I said. They were downcast. Wow, Ellen said, we didn't expect this from you, Mr. Talking-Will-Make-It-All-Better. They stood. Bill said, We don't expect to be charged for this. You will be, I said.

There was a brief article about Red's murder in the *Journal-Gazette*, which mentioned, incorrectly, that he was homeless. I read that Sable and five other dancers had been busted in a raid at the Taste. Seventeen cops were in on the operation. I picked up Dad at Venise and Oliver's. Venise told me Dad wouldn't eat his soup. He loves soup. Back home the crime scene tape was down. I put Dad to bed. Bay came by with Django and a new toy, a little stuffed Olivia the Pig. Only Bay told me Django called her YaYa. You're as bad as I am, I said. Patience came by with Chinese. Django walked around with YaYa in his mouth, put her down, sat, and waited for her to flee, and when she didn't, he swatted her and pounced. The phlegmatic YaYa remained composed.

Patience told us that she believed you could judge a Chinese restaurant by the quality of the typos on its menu. And she had ordered accordingly tonight from Five Chinese Brothers. We were dining on *steamed dumpings*, *wanton soup*, and *spicy Human beef.* I also noticed an admission on the menu that the fried scallops were *imitation*. I shuddered to think . . .

Bay wondered if maybe it was Kevin Shanks who shot Red.

I said, "Shanks might be dead, for all we know."

"What better alibi?"

And then we were talking about cops in general and the EPD in particular. "The job attracts the best if not always the brightest," Bay said. "And it also attracts the scum of the earth." He cited the arrest yesterday of three cops in three separate cases, one for meth trafficking, one for coercing a woman to have sex with him while on duty, and one for kneeing a handcuffed and handicapped woman in the face and breaking her nose and then not listing her injuries on his arrest report. This guy was last year's "Officer of the Year" in the state of Florida. And the official spin was that the department was getting rid of the few bad apples. The cops were all on administrative leave and the one busted on meth charges was already living in his mother's house with an ankle bracelet pending an earlier arrest. He had the PBA fighting to see that his lost wages were restored and the officer was suing the county for a pension, claiming to be suffering from post-traumatic stress disorder. Bay, obviously, did not subscribe to the bad apple theory. "Even the best of men, exposed to the culture of corruption in the police departments and witness to the considerable spoils of crime, will inevitably succumb to temptation, knowing that no one will rat them out because a rat is toast in law enforcement."

Patience said, "They do put their lives on the line every day doing what we're unwilling or unable to do. That means something."

Bay said, "But it doesn't mean they've earned the right to do whatever the hell they want—because who's going to stop them?"

Dad walked out of the bedroom naked and told us he couldn't find his diapers. His skin seemed to be glowing like a radium face on an old clock. I led him to the bathroom, opened the cabinet, and showed him again where we kept the Depends. When I got back to the table, Patience was telling Bay that as bad as things could get with cops, she wouldn't want to live here without them. Bay agreed, but said we might try raising the qualifying bar a little. "If cops had to graduate from college, we might all be a little safer." And then he told us to open our fortune cookies.

Mine said: *You will be taking a long journey.*

Bay's: *Presto! Change-o!*

And Patience's: *With love and patience, nothing is impossible.*

Patience, Dad, and I were having breakfast at Mother's on the beach when Cerise called and asked me when I had bought the gun, and did I think it was a good idea to stash it in the linen closet where she would find it between bath towels and have a heart attack. I told her I didn't own a gun. She said, I'm looking at it. It's got a snub nose, a silver barrel, and a black butt. She didn't blame me one bit for getting one after what happened to Mr. Red, but didn't my father have some issues with firearms? I told Cerise to put the gun in my desk drawer. She told me she wasn't touching it. Patience tried coaxing Dad into eating his grits, at least. He was having none of it. I'm getting out of the eating business, he said.

I dropped Dad at Venise and Oliver's. I called Bay and told him about the gun. He was sitting at a poker table. Someone beside him went all in. He told me, "Get rid of it now. Get it out of your possession. Put gloves on, drop it in a Ziploc bag, and get rid of it."

"Where do I lose it?"

"Not anywhere near your house."

I did as Bay instructed and then got lucky in that it was bulk pickup day, so I put some of Red's outdoor stuff in a pile by the street, the flamingo, the hibachi, and whatnot. I stuffed the gun into a torn pillow, put the pillow under the camp chair, and watched the pile get tossed into the rubbish truck and crushed. Bay had told me not to say a word to Carlos. When I asked why, he said no one but the cops could have planted the gun in the house.

When I arrived at Venise's, Oliver and Dad were playing checkers at the coffee table in the living room, and Oliver was cheating so that Dad could win. The TV was on and a hammerhead shark was circling a diver in a shark cage. The diver was teasing the shark with bloody meat. Venise finished washing her hair at the kitchen sink and wrapped her head in a Miami Heat beach towel.

I said, "Did you shave your eyebrows?"

"How do they look? Or not look?"

This was a beauty option that would take some time to get used to. "Good," I said.

She was wearing a black V-neck tank top and black stretch

Capri pants, which she called performance wear. She said, "Dad says you're taking him to see the northern lights."

"I plan to take him as soon as he's feeling better."

"He's never going to feel better."

Dad yelled, "King me!"

The phone rang. Venise said, "It's for you."

"How do you know?"

"And anyway you are too taking him."

I answered when I saw Patience's work number on caller ID. "Hi," she said. "I'm glad you're there. I got the tickets for Fairbanks leaving Friday, nonrefundable, return next Friday. I think it's great you're taking your dad."

"What's going on?"

"Bay didn't tell you?"

"Tell me what?"

"He bought you and Myles first-class round-trip tickets to Alaska."

"He had no right."

"I'll work on the lodging and get back to you."

"I can't go."

"It's a done deal. Someone's trying to kill you, remember."

Good point. "I'll have to clear my calendar."

"You're a big boy. You can handle it. You've got two and a half days."

And so on Friday, Patience drove Dad and me to the airport. And off we flew. But before we did, I got two surprise visits at the house.

W*ednesday afternoon:* Dad was at Venise and Oliver's. Carlos arrived at the house in the company of two uniformed ESO deputies and a warrant to search the place for the weapon used in Red's murder. I said, "What the fuck, Carlos?"

"They gave me a courtesy call on this one. I'm here to see they follow the letter of the law."

"I don't own a gun."

"Didn't say it was yours."

He sounded like a robot and looked like shit and I told him so. He thanked me. I said I hadn't seen Inez in a while and I had a book for her, William Trevor's *Love and Summer*.

He told me Inez was staying with her sister Igdalia in Orlando. "Igdalia has Lou Gehrig's."

"Yikes. I'm sorry."

They didn't find a gun, not even in the linen closet. I said, "Did you expect to?" The uniforms assumed wide stances and folded their thick hands at their crotches.

"I hope you put everything back where you found it." I told Carlos we should get a drink soon.

He said, "This weekend. You don't have any plans, do you?"

"No plans."

Thursday morning: Red's brother Blaise and Blaise's wife, Euliss, showed up unannounced with a rented minivan, which Blaise backed up onto the lawn. I had a feeling folks back in Texas called him Tiny. He was armoire-sized, with wispy gray hair tied back in a ponytail and a scraggly gray beard. He wore the uniform of the geriatric biker: jeans and a black T-shirt, leather bifold chain wallet, garrison belt with a Harley-Davidson buckle. Dad, who was sitting on the couch talking to his imaginary friend Pudgie Gage, told Blaise he was a big galoot.

If Euliss was sixteen, I'd be surprised. She was short and slight. Her blond hair was banged and bobbed and may have been a wig.

I couldn't quite tell. She was blue-eyed, freckled, and gap-toothed. She wouldn't sit down, didn't want coffee or water or juice, and didn't like Django in particular or cats in general. They're satanic, she told me without a hint of irony. Calico cats are the worst. And, of course, the impetuously sociable Django kept pursuing the child bride as she backed away from him. Dad said, "He's a biter, that Alejandro." I asked Euliss how she was enjoying her visit to Florida so far. She asked me to take Django away, please. I explained that this was his house and that if she had a problem, perhaps she'd prefer to wait outside where there were no cats. She closed her eyes, mouthed a prayer, and tried to levitate. Dad said, "Come sit by me and Pudgie, little darlin'."

Blaise didn't want help, didn't want me touching his brother's stuff, any of it. I told him how sorry I was about Red's death.

Blaise said, "He fell in with the wrong folks."

"When?"

"I'd say recently."

I asked him to tell me about his brother. He declined. When finally he had carried everything to the minivan, he looked around the Florida room and noticed a framed watercolor over the bookcase. "What's this?"

"He gave it to me."

Blaise took the painting and said, "What else are you stealing?"

I didn't mention the bulk trash or the painting of the house in my bedroom. I walked them to the car. Blaise said, "God bless."

I said, "It was a pleasure to have you stop by."

21

The van from the Aurora Lodge was there to meet us at the airport. We had stayed the night in Anchorage and caught a quick flight to Fairbanks on Saturday morning. We landed at eleven; the sun was low in the sky, our shadows long on the sidewalk, and the temperature a brisk seven below. We were wearing the thermal vests I'd bought at Bass Pro Shop in Melancholy before we left. Bay had come with me and spent most of his time at the electronics department. He tried on my vest for size, said this was something you'd want to keep on 24/7 up there. Gayla Wise Beesting, our driver, helped us into our hooded down jackets. I'd ordered them from a local Fairbanks outfitter, the Prospector, online and had them delivered to the lodge. Gayla got our bulky selves belted into our seats and then covered us with quilted comforters. Dad was quiet, drowsy, but smiling. Gayla told us she hailed from Rockford, Illinois, had studied medical coding and billing at Rockford Career College, followed a boyfriend to Alaska so he could work on the pipeline, but the boyfriend then followed an Inuit woman home, and the two of them, Ty and Paj, married and had three kids, 1-2-3, just like that—cutest paipiiraqs you've ever seen. Gayla and the ex are still pals. She's like part of the family, Auntie Gee. After the breakup, she dated casually and took a class in Web design at the university, which was where she met the widower Clement Beesting. That was thirteen years ago. They married and now owned the lodge. She said, Once you come north, you never go back. She stopped at Guvara's Liquors and Fine Wines so I could stock up for our week in town.

We had a suite with a north-facing picture window. I put Dad in for a nap. He'd sleep in the double bed in the bedroom, and I'd be sleeping on the pull-out sofa in the living room. We had a gas fireplace, two comfy chairs matching the sofa, a desk with a swivel chair, a small fridge, a two-burner stove, a microwave with complimentary popcorn, and a counter with three bar stools. The walls were exposed logs. Such a cozy place to just settle in, kick back, and read like crazy. We had a TV and a Wi-Fi hookup. I turned on my laptop and read an e-mail from Patience assuring me that Django was his old young self. She attached a photo of him curled asleep in a salad bowl. I looked up the Fairbanks phone numbers I thought I might need if anything happened to Dad—nearest hospital, doctor, pharmacy.

I made myself a drink and unpacked the rest of the arctic wear I'd ordered from the Prospector: the Polarmax thermal tights and tops, the cold-weather socks, the watch caps, the down bib overalls, the lace-up boots, the balaclavas, and the wool scarves. I checked in on Dad and asked him if he wanted lunch or anything. He said he wanted to sleep. I took my drink and went down to the lobby, where a fire was blazing in the stone fireplace and music was playing on the Bose: a CD of the Alaska Orphan Band playing the songs of John Denver. Gayla had set out a plate of oatmeal cookies and a decanter of brandy, bless her heart. I found a copy of John

Straley's *The Curious Eat Themselves* and sat down in a leather chair by the fire to read. I hadn't read long when I fell asleep, sedated by the warmth of the fire and the spirits. I dreamed that my neighbor Larry Marinelli, who doesn't read much because he works all the time—he's a painting contractor—had an essay he wrote, "What We Talk about When I'm at a Party with My Friends," in *Enzyme*, a slick literary journal out of Vancouver. I woke myself up with my own snoring and wiped the drool from my chin. I went up to the room and found Dad rummaging through the cabinets for a can of navy beans. "I know I put them away," he said. We had pizza delivered from College Town Pizza. We sat on the sofa and waited for the light show to begin. I saw a figure in the parking lot, a man, I presumed, wearing a bright yellow and black jacket, overalls, and hat to match, and a scarf pulled up to his eyes. He was looking up into our window. I waved. He turned and walked to the stand of spruce trees.

Dad said, "The end is near," and he smiled.

"Don't be melodramatic."

"I didn't want to go out this way, but it's okay. It'll have to be."

"How did you want to go?"

"With everyone else." He stared at the slice of reindeer sausage pizza in his hand.

In a while I saw, or thought I saw, a faint greenish and shimmering light at the horizon. I put out the lights. I shook Dad, who had dozed off. "Dad, look, this is it." But he was having none of it. He pushed my hand away and said, "Here comes Bruce Lee, coming over the top."

In the morning Gayla drove the two of us out to Paws for Adventure, where we took a one-hour ride in a dogsled. The cold was murderous, the windchill factor at thirty below, and the ride bumpier than I'd expected. Dad kept his scarf wrapped around his eyes, the only exposed part of him, for most of the trip. Was I insane, subjecting a sick man to this idiotic excursion? Back at the lodge, I ordered us lunch and had it delivered to our suite. Dad ate a bite of his halibut sandwich and took a few sips of his cream of mushroom soup. After his nap, Dad vomited the lunch into the bathtub and asked for a martini. After I cleaned the tub, I made us two. We sat on the sofa, Dad with an afghan around his shoulders. He wiggled his toes, sipped his drink, and said, "This is the life," and we raised our glasses and drank. I got out my laptop and opened to a family slide show and clicked through the scanned photos for Dad. He couldn't tell the difference between Cam and me, but then most people could not. He did say this about Cam: "There are many ways to lose a child, and death isn't the worst one." He told me that the fellow in the New Year's party photo, the guy on all fours being ridden by my aunt Louise, the guy I didn't recognize, was his cousin Hercules. "His real name was Howard, but we always called him Herc. Herc Fontaine." Herc was a motorcycle cop back in Massachusetts, retired now. And he was quite the lounge singer, Dad said. Sang all the standards, all your greats: Sinatra, Bennett, Dino, Billy Eckstine, Mel Tormé. Billed himself as "Herc Fontaine, the Cop with a Beat" or sometimes as "The Blue Velvet Fog." I showed Dad a picture of Archie Lambert and me at a family Fourth of July picnic. Archie's making horns on my head and squeezing his dick.

"The kid was an asshole like his old man," he said.

I told Dad that Archie was a school principal somewhere.

"Not anymore. One day he started smelling like a pancake at school, making all the little ones hungry. Then he got really tired like the flu and then he began to forget. They took him to the hospital. He got the maple syrup urine disease and had to retire."

"You're making this up."

"As God is my witness!"

Dad recognized Mom, of course. "Wasn't she a beauty?" But

he couldn't remember the pet name that he called her. "Not *Num-nums*, but something like that. It wasn't the word; it was the way I said it."

Dad told me about the beatings he took from his dad, from the nuns and priests, from the bullies Lavigne and Mulhearn, and all of it with a smile. No hard feelings. He insisted on the happiness of his childhood. Yes, he'd been expelled from St. Stephen's, but he deserved it. But he couldn't remember the last dozen years with any clarity. "After your mother died, I kind of lost interest." He held out his empty glass. "Hit me!"

"Cognac this time?"

"That'll work."

"And then we'll head out to see the lights."

At seven, we bundled up, filled a thermos with coffee from the lobby, and went out to see the aurora borealis. The few other guests had, apparently, decided to watch from the cozy warmth and darkness of their rooms. We walked through the parking lot and along a plowed pathway to a small amphitheater beyond the spruce trees and took our seats on a stone bench. The trees were mantled in creamy snow. And all at once a pink and smoky light rose from behind a distant mountain. I tapped Dad's shoulder and pointed. He nodded and gave me a mittened thumbs-up. And then a sheer and undulating curtain of green dropped from the sky above us. Dad looked up and said something, but I couldn't make it out, so I smiled, nodded, and imagined he'd said, What a great place this is, this earth. A shimmering violet ribbon appeared below the green, and the snow around us turned rosy. And then these yellow bands of light began to charge across the sky driven by magnetic winds. Dad tapped my arm and motioned for me to take off my hat, lean close, and listen. He said, "Hunbuns."

"What?"

"The pet name."

• • •

While we thawed out by the fireplace in our room, I tried to imagine how anyone could have survived in this bleak and frigid place before electric lights and central heat. In this darkness, exposed to the unforgiving elements, not to mention the predatory wildlife. In cold like this your body can't help itself. It shakes and trembles and shivers involuntarily. Your only desire is to get warm. Warmth is joy and salvation. And the best way to do that would be to wrap yourself in grizzly bear pelts and slip inside an igloo and cover yourself with sled dogs and drift off into a never-ending sleep.

Dad's hands were still icy. I rubbed them in mine. We tried running cold water over them. I put them under my armpits. "Those lights," he said, "they were something. This trip was a crackerjack idea."

I made coffee so that Dad could warm his hands around the mug. We cut the lights and sat in the dark looking out at the incandescent sky.

I asked him what he wanted to do tomorrow. He shrugged. I told him about the antique auto museum and the ice museum. I said we could go to the movies. Whatever we ended up doing, we'd take cabs—we'd had enough of the cold. And we had, I realized, several more long, dark days ahead of us. "So what do you think?"

"Whatever you want to do."

Well, I didn't want to have that circular conversation, so I said, "Let's play it by ear."

I'd brought my small digital recorder with me. We could sit and talk. A little drink, a little chat, another drink. In vino veritas. He could tell me his story. I could coax it out of him. "Why do you think Mom surrendered to her past? Why did she give up the fight?"

He'd probably say, Her pain became unbearable. The injustice was intolerable. That monster Dushanski alive, dandling his grandchildren on his knee and smiling for family photographs. But what he really said was, "So what do you make of me?"

"What?"

"How was I as a father? What grade would you give me?"

"You get an A."

"Bullshit."

"All right. You were on shaky ground for a while there, but you mellowed as you aged."

"I resented the hell out of you when Cam died. So did your mother. Cam had a gift."

"For self-destruction. You were relieved when he died. 'Thank god it's over,' you said."

"I was heartbroken. I was never able to help him. Cam, he got the smarts, the genius, and the charm. You got the stability, the even disposition, and the sincerity."

Swirling ribbons of white light spiraled up and away from the mountain, and a great arc of blue light stretched across the sky.

Dad said, "We should get going."

"Where?"

"Home. See that crazy cat, Renaldo."

"We're in Alaska."

"Are you sure?"

I recounted our last few days for him and he nodded. Then he said, "Did Donny Bullens just leave?"

"I don't know who you're talking about, but no one left. We're here alone."

"He was a funny son of a bitch. Any asshole can be funny when he's drunk. Donny was funny always."

I felt like I should call the airline and try to get us on an earlier flight out. ASAP. The nasty business back home seemed like a fairy tale. Bad guys don't kill people like me. Dad saw the lights. Mission accomplished. But then I reminded myself that this was a chance, maybe a last chance, to talk with Dad while he still knew who I was—most of the time.

He said, "I shit my pants."

"Let's get you cleaned up."

I got him to the bathroom. I turned on the heater, stripped him down, wiped him clean, drew a very hot bath, and helped him ease into the tub. "This'll really warm you up. Just sit here awhile till you're toasty, and then give me a shout. I shut the door to keep the steam and the warmth inside. I got online and saw that it had been in the mid-eighties at home. It made no sense calling Patience in the middle of her night.

I turned down Dad's bedcovers, figuring the hot bath would soothe and temper him, get him so relaxed he'd sleep like a newborn. I set out his flannel pajamas and a pair of woolen socks. I have to read myself to sleep, even if it's for five minutes, have to ease my way to dreamland. Dad, on the other hand, was blessed with the gift of immediate slumber. His head hit the pillow, and he was gone.

I poured Dad two fingers of cognac in case he wanted a nightcap and set the glass on the bedside table. I called to him to get a move on—"You don't want to turn into a prune"—something he'd always said to me. As kids, we'd all take our Saturday baths in the same water—to save money, I imagine. And it was great to be first and to luxuriate in the silky and steamy water. And it was hell to be third. I suppose it was five or ten minutes later that the silence became alarming. Oh, shit! I opened the bathroom door and saw Dad lying there in the tub, the water to his chin, his eyes shut, his head resting on the back of the tub. I knelt by him and said his name. I shook his shoulder, shook it harder, and yelled his name. I ran to the phone and called 911 and then Gayla, who said she'd be right up. I drained the tub, felt for a pulse, but couldn't find one, but I assumed I didn't know what I was doing. I thought I should probably do CPR, but I wasn't sure I knew how. Gayla did. We lifted Dad out of the tub and set him on a blanket. Gayla got to work, told me to fetch Clement and have him warm the car. When I left with Dad in the ambulance, Gayla said she'd meet me at the hospital.

Dad was pronounced dead of a heart attack at ten-fifteen. Gayla said she would handle any arrangements. I told her I wanted Dad cremated. She brought me back to the lodge, where I got my laptop, sat by the fire in the lobby, and e-mailed Patience, Phoebe, and Bay with the doleful news. And then I called Venise, who said, "Do you have any idea what time it is?" I said I didn't and told her about Dad. She screamed, "You killed my father, you bastard." I hung up and shut off the phone.

Clement came over to express his condolences. I thanked him and asked him to sit. I told him it was very sad, but not unexpected. Clement tugged at his suspenders and told me that Dad was the third guest of the lodge to die during his stay. The first was a semi-famous rock singer from Boston who had checked in with a girlfriend. On their second night, he overdosed on pills and alcohol up in his room. "I never say which room," Clement said. The cuffs of Clement's long johns extended beyond the cuffs of his brown corduroys. The other unfortunate was a young man from Seattle, a grad student in philosophy, a very personable fellow, who one day put on a pair of snowshoes right out there by the amphitheater and started walking across the snowfields toward the mountains. They found his body during the spring thaw. Clement asked me if I was a man of faith.

"I'm not, I'm afraid."

"Would you mind if I kept you and your father in my prayers?"

"I would like that."

"He lives on, your father. That's what I believe."

"I wish I believed it."

He smiled. "You don't have to." Clement leaned forward and turned to face me. "Death is like walking into a new room. The door closes behind you, and you hear the snick of the lock engaging. And then someone turns on the lights, and for a second it's so bright you can't see, and then you realize you have been living in the dark all this time. Once you were blind. There's so much around us here that we don't see, that we cannot see." He clapped his chest with his hands. "This husk," he said, "this body, is a mere vessel for the soul, and when the vessel breaks, the soul is released, and it shines in paradise like the lights here in our sky."

"That must be comforting."

"It's exhilarating, this heavenly life."

I woke up, sort of, feeling drugged, slumped in my leather chair, covered by a crocheted afghan, in front of the spent fire. I didn't know where I was or who I was or what day or year it was. Something about Dad's dying—how his fingertips were all puckered. What was that about? When I saw the man in the yellow and black ski suit sitting so conveniently in the chair beside mine, I realized that, in fact, I was still dreaming. There was a lamp somewhere behind me, enough light so I could almost make out the man's face, and he looked like Carlos, which should not come as a surprise. So I was back, I figured, in my bed in Melancholy, lucidly dreaming about this chilly lobby and about some unclear and disturbing events because I was anxious about the impending trip to Alaska, about everything that might go wrong. And it appeared that I had killed my father earlier in the dream, and so the man who looked like my friend the cop had come to arrest me, but he was being cute about it.

The man whispered, "It's about time you woke up."

I said, "You look like a friend of mine."

He put a finger over his lips for me to speak quietly. "Sorry to hear about Myles."

"Oh, he's not really dead."

"Coyote, it's me, Carlos." He snapped his fingers. "Are you okay?"

I whispered, "Carlos, what the fuck?" but it was a stage whisper, and Carlos gestured for me to tone it down a bit.

"Yes, it's me," he said.

I sat up and looked around. I could smell smoke. The moose head mounted over the fireplace was a convincing detail. "What are you doing here?"

"I'm not here."

"That's what I thought."

"I'm in Florida, and I can prove it."

"I believe you."

I shut my eyes, and he was still there; in fact, his face had more definition than a moment ago.

He said he was here to save my life.

I watched myself and waited to see what I'd say. At first I didn't say anything. And then I said, "But you're not here."

He said, "Open your eyes when you talk to me. It's creepy."

I opened them.

He said, "Our friend Vladimir is here, somewhere, in Fairbanks."

"Have you seen him?"

"No, and he hasn't seen you, or you would be dead."

"That's absurd."

"He's a torpedo and he's been dispatched to find you and . . . prishit', as they say in Sunny Isles."

Either he was speaking gibberish or I wasn't dreaming, because I didn't know those terms.

"Why?"

"His employers think you know too much."

"I don't know anything."

"You don't know what you know."

"So you followed me here?"

"When I see Vladimir, I'm going to kill him."

I told myself to wake up.

"One of the ways we keep order is to dispose of the disorderly."

"I can't believe you're saying this."

"It's not like I want to kill him. I have to kill him."

"Noble corruption, is that what you call it?"

The man who might have been Carlos reached over and tapped my knee. "Listen to me." He leaned in and told me I needed to protect myself. "Tomorrow," he said, "we buy you a handgun and get you some shooting lessons. This way, at least you can look formidable for a few seconds, long enough, maybe, to save your life."

By then I was willing to believe that the conversation, as ridiculous as it was, might be happening. "I don't want a gun."

"Trust me," he said. "You need a gun. I can't be everywhere all at once." He stood, told me to get some rest, you're going to need it. He said he'd call me in the morning.

I just sat there, closed my eyes, wondered if I should get off my ass and walk upstairs to our suite, thereby proving, one way or the other, if this was a dream or not. I felt a frigid breeze, turned, and saw the front door closing.

Venise called at three in the morning. I couldn't sleep anyway. She asked me what she was supposed to do with our father's cremains when they arrived. I told her to put them on the mantel or scatter them in the ocean. She told me if I hadn't dragged Dad to Alaska he'd still be alive, and I couldn't argue. She told me she was going to have to quit her job. Her gastroenterologist and his team of butchers were intent on harvesting her organs.

I said, "Why?"

She said, "Commerce in human organs is big business. Read the papers."

"Well, they won't want your stomach, Venise."

"You think this is a joke?" And then she screamed at me, and I asked her if I could talk to Oliver. She put him on.

I said, "What's going on?"

He said, "It's all she has right now, Wylie. Don't take it away from her."

I always had to share Dad with Venise and Cameron, and I hated that I did because I needed him more than they did, or I imagined I did, which amounts to the same thing, but couldn't get Dad to see that, and I couldn't compete with Cam's charm and exuberance or with Nisie's (we called Venise Nisie when she was young) effusive and adamant amiability. There are all these photos in the family album of me watching Dad holding one of my siblings and me looking alarmed with a brittle and provisional smile. I was never ignored or neglected, but I did feel overlooked now and then, and I was confused. I couldn't figure out how to get what I needed without becoming someone else.

Some of my childhood memories of Dad are of his absence. He wasn't there at my elementary school graduation. He wasn't at the hospital when I broke my left wrist falling off my bike. My mother drove me to Memorial's emergency ward, walked me through the intake, and handed me a quarter to catch the bus back home. Dad didn't teach me to drive, to balance a checkbook, to repair an appliance, or to speak up for myself. But, of course, he had his own life and had to navigate a difficult marriage while raising the three of us as a married single parent, and my resentment was unfair and unwarranted. Georgia used to say that Dad knew how to push my buttons because he installed them.

Dad tried to teach me to swim by carrying me out until the water was over my head and throwing me in. I learned to sink. He taught me not to be afraid of a pitched baseball by making me stand still and then bouncing the pitches off my ribs and arms. One night I was sitting on the front porch when a car pulled up, the back door opened, my father got out, the door closed, the car pulled away. Dad wore a Panama hat and a discomposed expression. He looked at me, took a deep breath, tried to put his hands in his pockets, worked to arrange his droll mug into a smile but failed, and then suddenly dropped to his knees as if in prayer, and from his knees, he fell forward onto his face. It was as if he had unfolded. And I thought it was the funniest thing I had ever seen, and I laughed like crazy until I ran over to him and saw that he was out cold, that his nose was emphatically broken, and he was bleeding from his mouth.

When we buried my mother, Dad decided to wear the blue suit he had been married in. It was now a bit large. Venise hemmed the slacks and pinned back the cuffs of his sleeves. She found pocket litter in the jacket and gave it to me. A matchbook from the Patio Pit in Melancholy, "Barbecued Delicacies of All Kinds." A shopping list in Biruté's tremorous script:

Rice Crispe	foot massager
mixnut	~~2 chip beef~~
9 eggs	crab toasties
pads	knox gelatin
rinso blue	

At the cemetery he tried to console Venise and me, who were in no need of consolation, who had long ago given up trying to know Birutė, trying to earn her respect and affection or at least her attention, and who realized that she had never left that forest near Telšiai, and who could blame her? Dad was having none of our sympathy. He was, he insisted, the most fortunate fellow who ever lived. "Birutė was a great beauty," he said. "She could have had any man she wanted. She was my sweetheart, my one and only, the light of my life."

One night not too many years ago, but before Dad's dissolution was evident, we sat up at my house after slurping down dozens of oysters and several bowls of cheese grits. We were sprawled on the couch with our legs on the coffee table, drinking Irish whiskey and talking. Satchel, my old pal, was asleep in Dad's lap with a paw over his eyes. For some reason we started talking about phrases you never wanted to hear or read, like when the doctor looks at a mole on your face and says, "I don't like the looks of that." We got a pen and an envelope and made a list. I've saved it:

- I've met someone.
- Family meeting.
- You'd better sit down.
- You have the right to remain silent.
- We have to talk.
- I do.
- I did.
- Greetings.
- Some assembly required.
- Attention passengers on Miami Flight 431.
- Have you accepted Jesus Christ as your personal Lord and Savior?
- I wouldn't lie to you.
- I've got your back.
- Would you mind shaving my back?

- I know a guy.
- I have your biopsy results.
- Trust me.
- Stop me if you've heard this before.
- Can I be totally honest with you?
- There's no easy way to say this.
- Would anyone like to share his or her feelings?
- Can I have a word with you in private?
- Can I have a word with you in the shower?
- You've been served.
- Do as I say and no one gets hurt.
- I'm not sure how else to say this.
- Because I'm your father.

22

I met Carlos at Great Northern Coffee Roasters, where he had a coupon for a free coffee from his motel. I asked him where he was staying. He said it was better that I didn't know. I was about to say that didn't make any sense when he nodded to an empty table in the back and said we should sit there. He took the chair facing the window and the entrance. I picked up our coffees and told him I thought he'd been a dream last night. He looked over my shoulder toward the window. I said he was making me paranoid. It was Monday morning, and he told me he'd already been to seven o'clock Mass at Immaculate Conception. When he took off his cap, I saw that he'd dyed his hair blond—though it looked more tangeriney—and clipped it short. He took out his wallet and showed me his Florida driver's license. His name was Paul M. Kunkel, and he was an organ donor. I said, "Who's she?" meaning the woman in the photograph beside the license.

"That's Mrs. Kunkel. Alberta."

"Quite a catch."

He said he wanted to see Vladimir before Vladimir saw him. I said no one's out for a stroll in this weather. He reminded me that Vladimir was Russian and that ice was in his blood. And then he said that this Carlos O'Brien I spoke of was actually—but not really—scuba diving in Key Largo.

I said, "How do you make your living, Paul?"

"CPA."

"I could use a new career myself. I used to be an observant guy, or at least I thought I was. But now I seem to miss everything."

"You could play second base for the Marlins."

"Dad always said I was too gullible for the job."

"May his soul rest in peace."

"When your dad dies, you're next."

"My old man, God bless his Irish soul, is ninety-two and claims he's still banging all the widows at Century Village."

We raised our mugs and toasted Barney O'Brien, the randy old goat.

A woman carried a coffee and a plastic take-out box of salad to a table and sat. She took off her jacket and loosened her scarf. She took the plastic lid off the box, opened her foil packet of salad dressing, and squeezed it over the salad. Lucinda Williams was singing about a sweet old world over the sound system. The woman resnapped the lid to the box and began to shake the box. And she kept shaking it for a minute, at least, and I was seized with a terrible urge to rush across the room and snatch the goddamn box away from her and maybe dump the salad in her lap. I hate annoying and ridiculous rituals like this and like the smokers who slap the new pack of cigarettes against the heel of their hand a couple of dozen times, thinking they're somehow packing the tobacco so it burns slower. Finally, she stopped. She folded her hands, closed her eyes, and prayed over the food. And then she ate, stabbing her food and then masticating it so slowly and deliberately that I knew she was counting her chews. And then a large, contented breath before the next bite. Carlos bought two more coffees to go, and we bundled up and went. We were driving to North Pole to buy me a weapon. I insisted I didn't want one and wouldn't fire one. If I was seriously in danger, then I should leave. "That won't stop them," he said. "Get the gun; it'll make me feel better."

Carlos had rented himself a burly black GMC Yukon, built like a mobile brick shithouse, and he was still having trouble keeping it steady against a perilous crosswind. The stark beauty of the landscape east of Fairbanks contrasted sharply with the agonizing ugliness of the indigenous architecture. Each structure we passed stood as hideous and bleak as its distant neighbor. It hurt to look at the warehouses and homes and imagine the lives going on behind those walls. I'm sure I was seeing the barren and hostile world through the gloomy lens of my father's death, but even that did not explain the despair I felt. I understood I was subtropically biased, but still, I wanted to carry these huddled and hermetic folks away and set them on a beach in Florida, under a coconut palm, with drinks in hand. Resurrection!

I asked Carlos where the name *Paul Kunkel* came from. He told me that Paul was a guy he shot dead in an armed robbery when he was a rookie. Carlos got himself a commendation and a promotion. "So he's always been kind of a lucky charm." We passed what may once have been a home or a restaurant or an auto parts store with a mansard roof. Half the front was brick, half wooden siding with peeling red paint. All the windows were boarded with plywood—an emblem of some failed dream.

I said, "How old was Paul Kunkel?"

"Sixteen. Seventeen."

"You couldn't just wing him?"

"He'd just killed the convenience store clerk, a single mom with two kids."

"Jesus."

"You aim for the center of mass, not a wing. That's your first lesson in marksmanship."

In North Pole there were, not surprisingly, streets named St. Nicholas, Kris Kringle, and Santa Claus. There were Donner, Blitzen, and Mistletoe Drives. A sign at the town limits welcomed us to a place where the spirit of Christmas lives year-round. We drove by Santa's house and by the largest Santa in the world. We stopped for a bracer at the Refinery Lounge because nothing goes together like drinking and shooting, unless it's drinking and driving. Carlos kept the car locked but running while we went inside and ordered Irish coffees. The bartender, Tiffany, told Carlos he looked familiar. He said, "I'd remember you," and stuck out his hand. "Paul Kunkel."

She said, "You don't look like a Paul." She told us we should stop by on Friday for karaoke. Carlos said, "Maybe you and I could sing a duet." She said it was hard getting a sitter on Friday nights. Her boy Connor was six.

We said goodbye and left. We drove a mile or so and turned off on a single-lane gravel road, which we followed for a quarter of a mile to a modular home that doubled as a gun shop, Alaska Under Arms. It was, Carlos said, a family-owned business, meaning no sales tax. Carlos suggested a Taurus PT 738, .38-caliber, and who was I to argue? Made in Miami! He also bought two hundred rounds of Remington bullets, earplugs, and a belt-ride holster. The owner, Jed Broadbent, who smelled like he'd last bathed in tepid curdled milk, took out a tube of K-Y from his shirt pocket and smeared the jelly over his face. He swore by the product as a skin moisturizer and offered us the tube to try. In the car, Carlos handed me the gun and a box of bullets. "You're a big boy now, Coyote."

"Don't I need a license to carry this?"

Carlos smiled and told me to read the instruction manual. I told him I didn't read instructions. It was a serious character flaw. He insisted. I opened the manual, said I wouldn't be caring for or maintaining the gun, so I could skip those pages, as well as those about disassembly and reassembly. I read him this line: *The product is not intended for use by criminals.* He told me to read the operating instructions, and I did: removing the magazine, inserting bullets into the cartridges, inserting a cartridge into the chamber.

We pulled off the highway and parked in the lot of a derelict filling station. We walked out into a field of snow. Carlos pointed ahead about twenty yards to a fence post, took out his service revolver, and fired. He hit the post on his second shot. He loaded the magazine into "your gun," two words I thought I'd never hear in relation to me. I took off my mittens and put in my earplugs. Carlos had me make a gun with my index finger and thumb and fitted the Taurus into the web below my thumb and told me to grip it firmly. He adjusted my stance, feet shoulder-width apart, left foot forward, told me to straighten my elbow. I lined up the rear site with the front with the fence post and then focused on the front site. He told me to consider wind and adrenaline. "Think of someone you'd like to dispose of."

I saw Cam's drug dealer, even though I didn't know what he or she looked like. I saw him as a physician in a white smock. I squeezed the trigger, followed through, hit the snow about thirty feet beyond the fence post. Carlos told me to breathe in and fire on exhale. Another wide shot. He told me to set up, get ready, and to close my eyes before firing. Closer. He said we'd stay till I hit the target three times in a row. It took under an hour. Maybe I'm a natural. Back in the big rig, Carlos told me not to put my hands near my mouth. Gunfire residue can be toxic. And then he said, "Never point a gun at anything you are not willing to destroy." I thought about Dad and how he would soon be just ashes in a cardboard box in the hold of a plane on his way to Florida. An undertaker standing behind me once in line at the Melancholy post office told me that fat people burn faster than thin people. I took out my phone to check for messages. It wasn't responding. The cold, I figured. Wouldn't turn on. Carlos wondered if Vladimir was tracking me through the phone. I said, "The Russian mob has tech support?"

Carlos didn't think I was funny. He took the phone, lowered his window, and tossed the phone to a snowdrift.

"Carlos, what the hell?"

He bought me a prepaid throwaway phone when we got back to Fairbanks. He told me to lie low, and he'd be in touch. I went to the suite and packed Dad's clothes in our two large suitcases. I'd drop them off at Goodwill, or better yet, give them to Clement. I thought about my cell phone playing "Coyote" out there in a snowdrift and my voice telling the caller I couldn't come to the phone right now. I went to the lobby and asked Gayla if any new guests had checked in. No one. Good. I thanked her for all she'd done.

Carlos called to tell me he'd spotted Vladimir downtown near Great Northern Coffee Roasters. He told me to grab two glasses of brandy and come out to the car; he was parked by the front entrance. I did. He told me that Vladimir had been on foot, so Carlos had parked and followed him. But he lost Vladimir when Vladimir went into a hardware store and never came out. Not out the front, at any rate. Vladimir was wearing a red down jacket and matching ski pants and yellow boots. He was hard to miss. Carlos told me to be vigilant inside the lodge and stay put. Stay away from windows, keep the lights dim. I told him I was leaving. I can't live like this. He said there were no seats on any flights out until Friday. He'd checked. I didn't believe it, so we got online. I said we should drive to Nome. He told me you can't drive to Nome and to keep the pistol holstered at all times. My sweater would cover it. He said he'd meet me at eight at the amphitheater. I borrowed the computer a moment and checked my e-mail. Patience said that Bay was worried about me, so I wrote to Bay that it was okay. Dad's death was merciful, really; he'd been in pain and hadn't been himself. But thanks for your concern. What I didn't know then, of course, was that Bay was not worried about my handling the loss of my dad. He was worried that my life was in danger, and he had already boarded a flight from Miami to Fairbanks, dropped out of a poker tournament at the Silver Palace to do it, but then got a game going on the plane with his seatmate in first class, a marketing director for some dot-com, and Bay wound up winning a little more than the price of this ticket before he changed planes in Seattle.

Carlos said we could watch the lights for a bit and then catch something to eat at this restaurant he stumbled on that featured authentic Japanese, Chinese, Thai, Mexican, Italian, and American cuisine. He told me to meet him at six at the amphitheater.

Back in the suite, I packed all my stuff into a carry-on, just to be ready. I put the loaded gun on the kitchen counter, made myself a martini, and thought how preposterous my situation was. I went down to the lobby without the gun. I felt ridiculous with it on and concealed. Gayla was on the couch, reading a self-help book. She held the cover up for me to see—something about silencing your inner critic. She said, "I'm always trying to become a better person."

"Having any success?"

"Clement thinks I hung the moon, but I know better." She confessed that she had hundreds of self-help books, all in their bedroom, floor-to-ceiling bookcases. "If you want to borrow—"

"How long have you had this . . . this fondness for self-help?"

"Ever since I can remember." She told me about her *When Am I Going to Be Happy?* books, her *Achieving Your Full Potential* books, the *How to Please Your Partner* books, the books on healing the heart, on wealth, on dysfunction and codependency, on queen bees and wannabees, and one called *The Elder Wisdom Circle Guide for a Meaningful Life*.

"Do you ever read fiction?"

"I know I should, shouldn't I?"

"I didn't mean that as a criticism."

She told me she would like to master her communication skills. When I told her that she was engaging and lucid, she told me that it's possible for a person to be *too* outgoing. And then she scolded herself for not asking about how I was handling my terrible loss.

"I'm sad, but relieved. You don't think that's callous of me, do you?"

"It's the most natural thing in the world." She got up and poked the fire, set a log on the grate. She told me that when her father died suddenly, she was twelve, and she was knocked for a loop, let me tell you. Her mom took to her bed and to the bottle and so the care of her three younger sisters was then Gayla's responsibility. She sat and wiped her hands on her jeans. "I grew up fast and resentful."

Her dad had been at work walking across a field when a sinkhole opened and swallowed him. All that remained on the surface was his silver hard hat, which the company gave the family along with its thanks and a plaque.

"Your mom still alive?"

"She lives with my baby sister Twyla."

"The other sisters?"

"Kayla and Layla live in the house we grew up in. We don't speak." Gayla bit her lip. "They have no use for me."

"I'm so sorry, but it's their loss."

"People never forgive you for the good you do them." Gayla shut her eyes and seemed to be talking to herself or praying. She opened her eyes and smiled. She said she'd just counted her blessings and realized what a fortunate person she was. She told me she and Clement wouldn't be back till very late. They were going out for a romantic dinner at Levelle's Bistro and then to his and hers massages as recommended by one of her relationship-rescue workbooks. And since I was the only midweek guest, I'd have the run of the place. What fun!

If Vladimir had been spying on me, he would be expecting to see a man in a green jacket and black pants. So I unpacked Dad's brown jacket and his orange cap. I covered my head and face with a balaclava, holstered the gun, felt like a fool, put on the jacket, zipped it up, put on the cap, pulled up the hood, tied it under my chin, and then thought to check my e-mail before leaving. An e-mail from Bay marked urgent and *for your eyes only!!!* I took off the hood, the cap, and the balaclava and opened his attached file. This was what had happened. On the day Dad and I left for Alaska, Bay was off to the poker tables at the Silver Palace and was dressing as a sports fanatic, the kind of guy who plays fantasy football and is used to losing money, expects to, and does his wardrobe shopping at Sports Authority. He wore a silky black Heat jersey, matching baggy basketball shorts, and black high tops. He put on a gold chain with a crucifix. Something he'd touch on occasion at the table when he wanted the others to think he was holding pocket rockets. He opened his watch drawer and pulled out the clunky sports watch he'd retrieved from Kevin Shanks and buckled it on. He pressed a couple of the seven or so buttons on the side of the face and a red light blinked on and off. He pressed the button and the light blinked again and went out. Bay got online and looked up the make and model of the watch and learned that it was a very expensive audio/video recorder as well as a rather ordinary timepiece. He bought a duplicate from a spy store online so he'd have the necessary cables and software and had it shipped overnight. He sent the attachment from the business center at SeaTac Airport, but I didn't know that yet, and didn't know, either, that he had been planning to wait till he arrived to show me and then changed his mind.

In the e-mail itself, Bay reiterated his warning not to show this to anyone and the reason why would become obvious. He wrote that what I wanted to see began at thirty-four seconds and ended at twenty-three minutes. I didn't have time to watch it now. It was 6:05, and Carlos was probably at the amphitheater waiting. But I got it started as I re-donned my Arctic protection. The first thing you see in the video is Kevin Shanks's craggy face looking right into the camera. He smiles and says, "Sweet!" And then apparently he buckles the watch to his wrist, and we see a Christmas tree and the familiar Halliday Christmas gifts, and then the screen goes black, but we hear a woman's voice say, "We weren't supposed to leave until after Christmas. This is total bullshit." My cell phone rang. I clicked it on and said, "Be right there," and hung up. I switched off the e-mail and shut down the computer. Wow. Bay was right. I'd want to watch this straight through with a drink in my hand. I went outside and headed to the amphitheater, but not before looking around very carefully. For a few seconds I'd forgotten all about Vladimir. If I could just talk to him, I was sure we could put an end to this foolishness. Shanks had been there when Krysia was alive. I'd told Carlos that Shanks was a psycho. Wouldn't believe me.

I thought I'd disguise my walk, so I took these tiny, uncertain steps like an old and feeble man, but it would have taken me a half hour to reach the amphitheater, so I opted for jaunty and took long strides as I swung my arms, and I felt suddenly and strangely Scandinavian, somehow. The lights were spectacular undulating sheets of green and red. I thought I heard a crunch on the snow, or maybe

I just had a premonition. At any rate I turned toward the lodge and saw, I was sure of it, a figure, dressed in what might have been red, duck behind a spruce. I took off a mitten and put my hand on the butt of my gun. I was trembling. Where the hell was Carlos? Six-fifteen already. He'd just called. I needed to make myself a smaller target, so I knelt in front of the stone bench and peeked over the top. I yelled, "Vladimir! It's me, Wylie," which I immediately realized was the wrong thing to do—so much for my clever masquerade. He stepped out from behind the tree and walked toward me down the shoveled path until he was about fifty feet away. He took out his gun. I pleaded with him to stop and think. And then we both heard someone hurrying our way—Carlos, thank God. Vladimir turned and fired at the figure. I didn't hear a gunshot, but I saw a burst of green from the barrel, and I aimed for the center mass and fired. He dropped to the snow.

Carlos came running with his hands raised and screaming his name so I wouldn't shoot him. He knelt beside the body and felt for a pulse. "He's dead." The bullet had torn a ragged hole in Vladimir's down parka near the heart. Blood seeped like black ink onto the silky fabric. Poor Cerise, I thought. Fuck! Carlos told me to get what I needed from the suite and meet him back here in ten minutes.

"Aren't we going to call the cops?"

"Are you insane? You just killed an unarmed man."

"I saw the gun."

"You saw a glove," he said. "This glove." And he held it up.

"I saw it fire."

"You thought you did. You panicked. It happens. Now go."

When I got to our suite I didn't know what I needed. I heard what sounded like a gunshot and I jumped. I put on my vest, my own jacket, grabbed the cognac, and left a note at the desk for Gayla and Clement saying I might be very late. Not to worry. I got back to the scene. Carlos had wrapped Vladimir's body in what looked like a body bag. "I improvised," he said. We carried the body to the SUV. Carlos went back and removed the bloody snow in a bucket that we set in the backseat.

"Where are we going?"

"Get in." Carlos pulled onto the Richardson Highway and drove east toward North Pole. We were towing a Ski-Doo on a trailer, and in the Ski-Doo, wrapped in plastic and swaddled in blankets, was Vladimir with a bullet hole through his heart.

I said, "The only way to make things right is to come clean, tell the truth, and whatever happens, happens."

"That may be how to make yourself feel better or noble or whatever, but it makes nothing right. And this is not about right or wrong. We're way past right or wrong." He asked to see my phone. I handed it to him. He lowered the window and tossed the phone out. "You wouldn't have had any service anyway."

We drove on, heading for Delta Junction, ninety miles south. I felt terrible remorse. I didn't know what I would tell Cerise, and then I thought, Tell Cerise? Am I crazy? But what if she knew he'd come to Alaska—on a hunting trip, he would have told her—while I was also here? Alaska's a big state, Cerise. I didn't run into him. I'd killed someone, but it didn't seem possible that I had. I said, "I could go to prison for this, Carlos."

"You're not going to prison." Carlos pulled over, got the snow out of the backseat, and tossed the bucket over the mounds of plowed snow.

So we were fleeing the scene of a crime, which was wrong in every way, but I didn't know what else to do. I tried to imagine my life back home in a year when all of this was a dim memory. Does murder ever dim? I wanted to sleep. I rested my head against the window and shut my eyes. I wanted to wake up and see that this nightmare had been just a dream. I reminded myself that this wasn't actually a murder. There was no premeditation. So how would I explain the handgun purchase and the shooting lesson? I'd just tell the truth, was all. And the truth would set me free? Probably not.

We were barreling down the highway near Salcha, and Carlos had the radio on to the college station, and Bon Iver were singing about "Skinny Love." And then, out of nowhere, our car was bathed in red and blue light, and in my half slumber I thought maybe the aurora had descended to earth, but it was, of course, a state trooper on our tail. It took Carlos a while to stop safely. He told me not to utter a word, to keep my hands where the officer could see them, and to take a deep breath. I put my hands on the dashboard.

Carlos said, "Don't get antsy. We don't want this turning ugly." He was extremely polite and deferential, and when he was asked to provide his license and registration, he must have flashed some kind of police ID because that was the end of our hassle. The trooper told Carlos to drive more prudently. The roads, he said, were treacherous already, and it wouldn't be unusual to round a bend and see a dumbfounded moose standing in the middle of the highway hypnotized by your headlights. He tipped his hat and walked back to his cruiser. He stopped at the Ski-Doo and apprized its contents. Carlos slipped his hand into his pocket and yelled to him that we were on our way to Kenai.

"You have a pleasant trip," the trooper said. "You can put your hands down now, sir," he yelled to me.

Carlos laughed. "You done good, Kimo Sabe." He checked the rearview mirror. "You know how lucky we were, don't you?"

I felt something in my jacket pocket, but I couldn't touch it. Something hard and about the size of a business card. Carlos was paying close attention to the sideview mirror and to the speedometer. I figured, no, it must be in the vest pocket. And I was right, an inside vest pocket that I hadn't taken note of before. I took out what turned out to be a Spark Nano GPS. I read the Post-it note attached: *Keep in pocket. Tell no one. Bay.*

"What's that?" Carlos said.

"Myles's iPod thingie. No headphones."

Carlos pulled off the highway and drove a hundred yards down a narrow snow-packed gravel road. He cut the lights and took his foot off the brakes. We waited until we saw the trooper drive past on the highway. "Cops are some devious bastards," Carlos said. "He'll be waiting for us at Delta Junction." Carlos smiled, and backed us down the road, trailer and all.

Twenty minutes later, back on the highway, we could see there'd been an accident up ahead at the bottom of a winding hill, and as we slowed down we saw that it was our trooper, who'd gone off the road and into a ditch. The car was a wreck, but the trooper seemed okay. He stood in the middle of the road, flagging us down. From the skid marks, it looked like he had hit his brakes and swerved, lost control, then skidded several hundred feet while spinning in a big circle, coming to rest against a tree facing back the way he'd come. Carlos lowered the window.

The trooper waved us to the side of the road and yelled for us to pull over. Carlos nodded, waved, shut the window, put on his directional, told me to put my head between my knees, and drifted down the hill, tapping on his brakes, and I thought, Oh, shit, the cop knows! But what does he know? He doesn't have to know much for us to be in big trouble. And then Carlos hit the accelerator and we took off.

I said, "What are you doing?"

"It's better that we don't stop. Do I have to explain why?"

About five miles north of Big Delta, we took a left off the highway onto a small road leading to Quartz Lake.

"The trooper got your license tag number."

"Paul Kunkel is in big trouble."

23

I split a length of firewood with a whetted hatchet and slid the piece into the wood-burning stove. Carlos and I had commandeered ice hut D10, the farthest of the fishing huts from shore on Quartz Lake and the only one now occupied. When we arrived, Carlos shot off the combination lock just like they do in the movies. While I got the fire going, Carlos slid the now-frozen corpse off the Ski-Doo and laid it on a seven-foot pulk. He backed the Ski-Doo off the trailer, hooked the pulk to the Ski-Doo, and drove another seventy-five yards out toward the center of the lake. He left the pulk and drove back. He moved the SUV to hut D8, the nearest hut to ours, so that any late-arriving sportsmen would think it was taken.

We sat on camp stools by the stove and warmed our feet, which only made them hurt more. Carlos kept jutting his tongue and running it along his lips. That sort of thing sometimes indicates that you've been caught doing something naughty, but he hadn't been caught, had he? I told him what we were doing was wrong. He told me to stop whining. We had no choice.

"You're a cop. Cops'll listen to you."

"I'm not here, remember?"

"You've got an alibi. Is that what you mean? Well, good for you."

He took a swig of cognac and passed me the bottle. He said, "Let me explain something to you. You're in a world now where nothing you value is of any importance. Tolerance? Compassion? Civility? Kindness?" He shook his head. "Meaningless."

"So what matters?"

"Survival. And I am the only person who can save you right now." He stood and put on his gloves. "It was your life or his life. You did the right thing."

The plan was to sink Vladimir's body in the lake. Sometime in the spring the body, or a part of the body, might surface, the body of an unknown man who would seem to have died of a self-inflicted gunshot wound. "People go apeshit all the time up here," Carlos said. "The Inuit call it pibloktoq. People run naked into the snow, screaming their heads off, eating their own shit, and hallucinating like mad."

"How do you know all this?"

"Give me your gun. They'll find the weapon in question when they send down divers. Suicide. Case closed."

"I don't know how I'll live with myself."

"Time will put it all into perspective. You shot a cold-blooded assassin, a man who was out to kill you. You'll be able to look Cerise in the eye and tell her you're sorry for her loss."

I didn't think so. I didn't think I'd ever feel happy again.

Carlos told me to sit tight. He grabbed the power auger he'd packed along with the body, the auger extension, one of our two lanterns, and went out to drill through what he figured to be three feet of ice. He didn't want to drill more comfortably through one of the fishing holes in the hut because he worried that the corpsicle, as he was calling it, might bob up through the hole when the next fisherman drilled, and anyway, the drilling area was too narrow.

My nose hairs were frozen; my ears stung; I couldn't move my face. The crushing pain in my hands was wretched and exhausting. I wanted to stand and move around, get the circulation going, but I couldn't. I knew alcohol would only make everything worse, but I took another sip of cognac and warmed my throat for a moment. I nodded off or I didn't and dreamed or imagined I was in Florida on the beach asleep and dreaming about being in an ice hut on a frozen lake in Alaska and knowing that the dream was a lie, even as I dreamed it, and when the sound of the auger stopped, I woke up. I stood, lifted the canvas from the window, and looked out on Carlos bathed in the heavenly green light and saw him slide the pulk to the hole, lift the body, and try to wedge it into the water. Not even close. And then he tried it feet first—a breech delivery. Still no go. He unrolled the blankets and removed the improvised body bag from the corpse. I watched the several black garbage bags swirl up, float away, and then drop to the ice and get blown toward the distant shore. Vladimir, parka-less but wearing the balaclava, still would not fit. Carlos shook his head. I thought I should get out there and help, take the skimmer, at least, and keep the hole free of ice. But I didn't want any part of it.

Carlos rode the Ski-Doo back to the ice hut to warm up. He said he needed to widen the hole about five inches. I told him how depressed I was, how frightened. He said about ten to fifteen more minutes should do it. "I'll drop him in; we'll wait for the ice to refreeze in the hole—not solid, just enough—an hour ought to do it." I asked him how he knew so much about the cold.

"In the Army. I was stationed at Fort Wainwright in Fairbanks. I spent two years up here. I fished this lake—all the lakes around here."

"You were in the Army?"

When we had driven the SUV out onto the ice earlier on the way to the hut, Carlos had told me to take off my seat belt and crack the window. I thought he was joking. He insisted. If we go through a hole in the ice, you don't want to be fooling with a seat belt. You got about forty seconds to surface and fifteen minutes to get out before hypothermia puts you to sleep. Open windows are easier to break, and electrical windows won't operate in water.

When I asked him now about Inez and the kids, he told me she'd moved out, gone with the boys to her sister's, filed for divorce. She told him, "You're married to that job, so you can just fuck that job."

"She's pissed."

"We'll never be divorced in the eyes of God."

He told me we wouldn't be here in the morning to see it, and we hadn't drilled a fishing hole inside, but if we had, then just when the sun peeked over the horizon, and we were sitting here in the dark shack, we might see the sunlight shining up at us from the hole. The sunlight penetrates the ice and gets inside however it can.

I said, "Can you believe how much our lives have changed since Christmas?" I shut the door of the unsteady stove with my foot. And then I told him my theory about the Halliday killings, how I thought the killers were in the house before the family got home. No one saw them leave because they didn't leave. They called in the crime. The killers were the cops. Shanks, Sully, and whoever else. And they were inside long enough to stage the scene and sanitize the place. And that cop from the Wayside, Kind, I thought he was in on it too.

Carlos's eyes locked on mine, not with interest or curiosity, but with something more visceral that I would have guessed to be fury, except I knew him too well for that. Clearly, however, he was upset. He had a right to be, I supposed.

He said, "You think there was a conspiracy of cops to commit murder?"

"Maybe."

"A death squad?"

"It makes more sense to me than anything else."

"You're starting to piss me off a little."

"Sorry."

"You forgot I was there?"

"I didn't forget."

"How can you look me in the eye and say this crazy shit?" Carlos went back outside to finish his grisly business. I sat and looked at the inch of cognac left in the bottle and thought about how much colder it was going to seem when that was gone. And then I took a drink. I wondered if Vladimir ever took my advice and wrote things down in a notebook, and if he had, would it now be evidence? Would Cerise, having found it, already know what his Alaskan hunting trip was all about? I heard the auger start up and hoped the hard labor would help Carlos work off some of his irritation with me. I didn't want him staring bullets at me again. And with that thought and its attendant image, I remembered something that Carlos said earlier that now seemed curious. He had said that I would be able to look Cerise in the eye and express my condolences for Vladimir's disappearance. But I had never told Carlos that Cerise lived with Vladimir or even knew him. But maybe the cops had Vladimir under routine surveillance, given his line of work. That must have been it, of course.

I picked up the skimmer and walked outside and headed for Carlos, whose back was to me. I wondered if it was conceivable that Carlos would cover up a murder to protect cops. He was covering up a murder now, sort of. A killing. To protect a friend. I tapped him on the shoulder and he jumped. I held up the skimmer, and he shook his head. I looked at the corpse and saw the entry wound in his chest and a bullet hole in the middle of his forehead. His balaclava was stained with blood. I pulled it off, and when I did, the mystery of Kevin Shanks's whereabouts was solved. I looked at Carlos. We both knew I hadn't shot twice. And I hadn't shot Vladimir. I said, "What's going on?"

He said we should go back to the hut where we could talk. We sat on our camp stools, and I asked Carlos to take off his ski mask so I could see his face. He did, and I did the same. I took off my mittens and rubbed my itchy head. Carlos's blond hair stood out in spikes. He put his gloves on the stove to warm. Then he said he had a request as well, and he took a set of handcuffs out of his coat pocket and asked me to hold out my right wrist. I laughed. I wasn't sure why—things had gone past funny a while ago. I refused. He took the gun—my gun—from his other pocket and held it to my forehead.

"You're not going to shoot me, Carlos."

"I'm not?"

"Put the gun away. Please."

And then he hit me on the side of the head with the gun, and my brain exploded with a searing and lacerating pain. When I grabbed my head, he slid the cuff over my wrist, locked it, and then cuffed the wrist to the leg of the stove. My eye was already swelling shut; I was bleeding and I felt nauseated.

He apologized and said, "Promise me that you'll take everything I tell you to the grave." And he laughed. "I was not present when it all went down, but, yes, the Hallidays were dispatched."

"By cops."

"They were caught, you might say, in an unfortunate cross fire. Plans gone awry." He shook his head. "A shame."

"What did Halliday do that was so bad you all murdered his family?"

"It was something he was about to do."

"So you know the future? Are you insane? What the fuck happened to you?"

"And, of course, I had your destitute friend dispatched."

"Why?"

"For the halibut."

"Making jokes? You set me up with the hidden gun?"

"And you got lucky and found it." Carlos wiped his runny nose with the sleeve of his jacket and then picked up the hatchet I'd been using to chop the firewood. "And you knew enough to dispose of it. Give you credit for that." He chopped at the ice where the wooden floor ended and the ice began, picked up a chunk, and handed it to me. "Put that on your face there. You're going to need stitches." He clapped a hand on his knee. "Time's a-wasting." He stood. "I just want you to know that I don't enjoy any of this."

"Save it for the priest."

"That's the beauty of the Catholic Church, isn't it? I have been forgiven all my sins."

"By whom?"

"By the only one who matters."

"Why do you do it?"

"You get locked in. You make a decision when you're young—to do a man a favor, to accept a token of gratitude—and that contract becomes the bedrock of your life. Everything you ever do from that moment on is like predestined. Still, I've got no regrets, Coyote." Carlos raised the gun, pointed it at me, and fired a bullet past my head. "Loud, isn't it?"

I was crying. I begged him to stop for the love of God.

"I always wonder if you hear that blast when you're really shot."

"Carlos!"

"I told you to back off a while ago."

"What have I done?"

"If you dive into the shark tank and get shredded by the sharks, that's not the sharks' fault. That's what they do."

"What are you talking about?"

"You dove into the tank, my friend."

"You invited me to the crime scene."

"And then I dismissed you, but you wouldn't go away."

"So you're a machine. You do whatever you're told to do."

"Our work is closely scrutinized, and failure is unacceptable. You don't expect a man, Halliday, any man, to sacrifice his family to save his own skin."

Carlos heard what I heard—the sound of an approaching vehicle. He opened the door. We saw the flashing lights of a state police cruiser slowly headed our way, maybe summoned by the last gunshot. Carlos turned to me. "Don't wander off."

"What happens to me?"

"If I die, maybe you live." He headed out for the hole and the Ski-Doo, leaving the door open.

I knew the stove wasn't bolted down. I rocked it with my shoulder. Burned my jacket, but I didn't feel the heat, it was so thick. The police SUV headed for the hut and stopped. The trooper stepped out of the vehicle, holding his pistol with two hands and pointing it at the ice about five yards in front of himself. Where was Carlos? I yelled for help, said I was in the ice hut, which I then realized might sound like a ploy to the trooper, an invitation to an ambush. I yelled that I was alone and couldn't come out like he was asking me to because I was handcuffed to a stove. You have to believe me, I yelled. He approached, gun raised. I begged him not to shoot. He crouched, pointed the gun inside, and swept it across the room. He told me to put my hands on my head. I put on the one I could and reminded him about the other. I said, "Thank god."

He said, "You're under arrest."

"For what?"

"From the looks of the body on the ice, I'd say murder. And from the looks of your face, I'd say he put up a good fight."

"I killed him and then cuffed myself to the stove?"

“People do funny things.”

I tried to explain, realized it would be quite a long story. He said I’d have plenty of time to tell it all. This was not the trooper from the traffic stop and accident, but he knew about us, apparently. Just what he knew he wasn’t saying. “Where’s your partner?”

I said the man who was trying to kill me was out there.

As the trooper walked back to his vehicle to call for backup, I heard a shot and then a thud, and saw the trooper collapse to the ice. I rocked the stove more desperately than before and was able at last to topple it off its stone pad, and when it fell to its side, I was able to free my hand. I tucked the loose half of the still-attached handcuff into the sleeve of my jacket. The broken flue stayed in one piece and was somehow still attached to the roof. I stood and looked out the window and saw Carlos kneeling behind the Ski-Doo. The trooper got himself up on one knee and fired at Carlos. Carlos fired back.

The trooper told Carlos to put down his weapon, to lie on the ice, and to lock his hands on top of his head. The trooper got to his feet, steadied himself, and stepped toward the vehicle. Carlos shot him again. The trooper dropped to the ice and seemed to be out, except that his right leg was twitching. Carlos walked up to the trooper, put the gun to the back of the trooper’s head, and pulled the trigger, but either the gun was jammed or he was out of bullets. Carlos put the gun in his pocket and walked to the hole. This was my chance to run for it. Carlos lifted the corpse of Kevin Shanks and slid it into the water. Apparently he’d widened the hole just enough. When he turned, he saw, and I saw, the trooper lumbering toward him, gun raised. Carlos looked almost amused. The trooper fired wildly and then fired again and hit Carlos in the foot. Carlos screamed and fell. He yelled, “Look what you’ve done!” He stood and limped a couple of steps, grabbed the auger, and started it up.

The hut was filling with smoke. I crawled outside and got out of sight behind the hut. Maybe Carlos would think I had died of asphyxiation and leave me alone. If I could make it to the SUV without being seen or shot, I could call for help on the radio. If Carlos saw me, however, even if he couldn't get to me just then, he'd hunt me down. I knew the keys were in the ignition of the Ski-Doo. I could run, but I would never make it to the shore and the pine forest.

The trooper shot at Carlos. Carlos walked toward the trooper, dragging his right foot. He held the auger up in front of him and drilled it into the trooper's gut, tearing into the jacket. You could hear the blades quit turning for just a second, while the motor continued to run, and then reengage. Carlos pushed the trooper off his feet with the auger. He landed on his back, screaming. The trooper reached for the auger's blades, which seemed to grow like some spiral flower out of his stomach, but the blades sliced through his hands. Carlos leveraged his body against the handle and the engine housing and drove the rotating blades through the body and into the ice in a spray of blood, cloth, and viscera. He reversed the auger and drew it out of the body, shut it off, dropped it, picked up the trooper's gun, and fired a shot at the hut.

Then he lay back and moaned, and I ran to the SUV, but it was locked. I dashed back to the hut, covered my face, crawled inside, and retrieved the hatchet. I had to hope Carlos had passed out from the pain or the shock from the loss of blood. Then I could take the Ski-Doo and flee. But then what?

Instead, Carlos got up and dragged the corpse by the legs over to the hole in the ice. When he began sliding the body into the hole, I saw my only chance of getting out alive. I walked up behind him as quickly and quietly as I could, and when he leaned over the hole to push the head under the ice, I shoved him in the butt with my foot, and he went shoulder-first into the hole, but not all the way in. His right arm had grabbed the edge of the hole and his right leg was still on the ice. I stomped his hand and his broken foot, which I could see was a soup of gristle just above the ankle. I brandished the hatchet. He thrashed in the water, struggling to get out, and I let him have it. I hit him square on the head with the hatchet, with the blunt, not the blade side, because for some reason I couldn't bring myself to split his head open. He slipped into the water rather quietly, and I fell to my knees, spent. Before I could stand, Carlos's arm shot out of the water, and he grabbed the handcuff that had come loose from my jacket sleeve. It was locked so he couldn't get his hand in, but he had a firm grip on the loop and tugged—trying to pull me in or himself out. His other hand gripped the lip of the ice. I got the hatchet in my left hand and chopped his hand with the hatchet and pinned it below the knuckles to the ice. He let go of the cuffs, got his elbow on the ice, and pulled his head above the water. I ran to the Ski-Doo, started it up, and drove toward Carlos and over the hole in the ice and parked. I heard Carlos call my name in the few inches of air he had above the ice. I heard him punch at the underside of the Ski-Doo. I heard him scream.

I didn't know what would happen now, but I knew I had to move. I headed toward the hut where Carlos had parked the Yukon. It, too, was locked, and the keys were now under the ice with Carlos. I hoped that, after the initial feeling of his lungs being torn and the burning in his windpipe, Carlos slipped into a feeling of calmness and tranquillity. I knew that the shock of the frigid water would shut down his heart in minutes. I headed for the parking lot. From there I could find the road and then the highway. And from there, who knew? I started walking backward into the wind, and I saw the hut ablaze, the exhaust fumes in the lights of the police cruiser, the headlight of the Ski-Doo pointing off onto the ice, and above us all, the sheets of green lights in the shimmering sky.

When I turned back to get my bearings, I saw headlights coming down the road, and I thought, So this is the way my world ends. I'll just make it easy for them, easy for me—so I stumbled for the headlights. At least I'd be warm.

And when I finally got warm, when I thawed out and quit shaking uncontrollably, when I no longer felt the stabbing pain in my hands and feet, when I'd had a cup of hot coffee, then I'd tell my handlers the story of all the recent nasty business, and I'd tell it properly, with sufficient backstory, with eloquent and convincing detail, with the kind of keen psychological insight you'd expect from a guy with robust mirror neurons. I'd utilize all the appropriate and seductive narrative techniques so that, as improbable as it all might sound, they would have to believe me. My only salvation, then, would be to tell a compelling and credible story.

I might preface the story by saying that life does not always make sense, but a story does. And courtroom testimony must. And that's what we're after, are we not, gentlemen? Sense equals truth. They'll ask me to begin. They'll turn on their video recording equipment. I'll speak right up. I'll tell them how it came to be that a mild-mannered therapist from Melancholy, Florida, was able to survive a bloody vendetta that he did not understand at all, and survive that carnage on the frozen lake, and how he—I—had nothing to do with the deaths of the three police officers, not really. And here I'll explain that Paul Kunkel was not a CPA, was not, in fact, a Paul Kunkel, was a Detective Sergeant Carlos O'Brien, an insidious member of the Eden, Florida, police department, as was the naked and heretofore unidentified victim, who was at first purposefully misidentified as a terrifying Russian assassin, like someone out of a Dostoyevsky novel, but who was, in fact, one Officer Kevin Shanks, a steroid- and citizen-abusing rogue cop, like someone out of a Charles Willeford novel. One of my auditors will make a note of the names in his memo pad, and I'll caution myself about the further use of incendiary modifiers like *insidious*. Let the actions speak for themselves. I will not, for example, use the phrase *death squad* in the interrogation room or the word *police* as an adjective. I'll explain how it all started on Christmas Eve, although the seeds of the chaos were sewn much earlier, and leave it at that. In life we always want to know what happened in the past in order to understand the present, but in stories we don't need to know. We trust the storyteller, who does know. I will earn their trust. I will appear to digress but I will not digress. I'll watch their eyes and their postures and gauge their involvement and proceed accordingly. Once I have set the plot in motion, I'll follow the chain of surprising and inevitable events that resulted in the horrible deaths of three men. Along the way I'll mention the fourth death—my father's—because it is thematically resonant, revelatory, and tangentially but significantly related. I'll explain—no, I'll illustrate how Carlos fired the kill shot with my gun (actually, there's no reason to include ownership) into Kevin Shanks's forehead, how he savagely murdered the state trooper, and how, wounded and perhaps in shock, he . . . And perhaps here I would lie a bit to tell the truth, the truth of the story being the point, not the facts of the events.

As the approaching car drove onto the ice and toward me, I raised my arms in relief and in blessed surrender. The car slowed, the headlights blinding me, and stopped. The driver's window lowered; I shaded my eyes; Bay said, "Looks like I got here just in time. Get in."

I ran around the car and hopped in. I jacked up the heat and said, "What took you so long?"

Bay fumbled around in his knapsack, took out a lock pick, asked for my hand, and undid the handcuffs. He turned the car around. "I see you burned down the hut. Where's Carlos?"

"Carlos is no more."

Bay clapped my leg. "Good to see you."

"How did you know I was in trouble?"

"I didn't until I learned that Carlos was on his way to Alaska with a friend."

"But the GPS."

"A precaution. I snuck it into your vest when I tried it on at your house. Lucky you."

"Carlos set me up."

"Yes, he did."

"I killed Shanks for him—"

"And he had you under his thumb."

We drove to the Richardson Highway and headed south toward Paxson.

I said, "What time is it?"

"Four A.M."

"I can't feel my fingers."

He told me we had a flight out the next afternoon, not this afternoon, from Anchorage. I told him all my stuff was back in Fairbanks. "All taken care of," he said. "Your carry-on's in the trunk with your computer. I checked you out of the lodge and left a note in your handwriting for your hosts." He said he'd gotten the e-mail about Myles, of course, and was so sorry. I told him everything that had happened since the shooting at the lodge. I said we needed to call someone. I said I'd gotten his e-mail but hadn't seen but a minute of the video. And I thought, Christ, if I'd taken the computer with me, it'd still be locked up in the Yukon, and I'd be screwed.

He said, "They're all dead out there, right? Okay, then, let the dead bury the dead."

"But the trooper was killed."

"And won't come back to life."

"The family will want to know what happened."

"They can make up their own story."

Fifteen minutes later, we saw several police vehicles, lights flashing, speeding north. A minute later an ambulance followed. Bay slowed the car and pulled to the shoulder. He told me to roll down my window and toss the cuffs as far as I could. I did.

We were met with a roadblock in Big Delta. Bay told me to put the hood over my bloody face and pretend to sleep and not to wake up. The trooper asked to see our drivers' licenses. Bay explained how I was sleeping one off, and reached into my jacket pocket, after he'd asked the trooper if that was all right, and pulled out a wallet that hadn't been there.

The trooper said, "Where are you and Mr. Clockedile headed?"

Clockedile?

"Northway and then on to Juneau."

The trooper ran his flashlight through the car or at least past my eyes. "Could you open your trunk, sir?"

I heard some shuffling of bags and then the closing of the trunk. The trooper told Bay that he'd been to Florida one time. South Beach. "Not for me," he said.

"It's an acquired taste," Bay said.

"A lot of salacious behavior going on."

"Well, it's surely not God's country."

"Amen."

I heard the hissing of air brakes behind us. The trooper said, "You have a safe trip, Mr. Tremblay."

Bay told me that Inez had filed charges against Carlos for domestic abuse and Carlos had been on paid administrative leave beginning the day I left.

"I thought she moved out."

"She tried to."

We stopped for gas in Delta Junction, bought coffees and stale cake doughnuts. I asked Bay what would have happened if the trooper had run the licenses. Bay said we were covered. He did business with the same folks Carlos did. At the fork in the road, Bay slowed, checked his rearview, and took the highway to Anchorage.

I said, "What's my first name?"

"Lincoln."

"Lincoln Clockedile."

"Got a ring to it." He held out his hand. "Luc Tremblay. Pleased to meet you." He told me to get some sleep. We'd make Anchorage around noon; we'd dump the car, find a place to stay, get a fabulous meal, watch the video, and get a disturbing night's sleep.

24

We didn't wait until after our fabulous meal to play the video file from the purloined black sports watch. I suspected this would be horrific. Worse than you can imagine, Bay said. Better, then, on an empty stomach. We sat in Bay's room at the Hilton looking out in the dim light at the low clouds over Cook Inlet. Bay told me he'd sent the video file to DA Millard, to the federal marshals, to the FBI, and to the local newspapers and TV stations. He'd keep the watch for now. He was wearing it. He'd answer their e-mails when we got back to Florida. When I asked why the marshals, he said I'd see why shortly. He opened the file.

We heard a man's voice tell Krysia that there's been a change of plans; everyone is leaving tonight. She says, Pino didn't say anything about a change of plans. The time on the video read 6:37 P.M. I figured she must be referring to our Pino, Pino Basilio of the crushing handshake. Krysia says she'll wait for the marshals. The man says there's been a leak, and your lives are in danger. Krysia excuses herself, says she has cookies in the oven, and Shanks asks her what kind and follows her into the kitchen. We see the black and white floor, the opened oven door, and hear Krysia say they need a few more minutes. Another male voice addresses the children, whom we now can see from shoulders to shins standing in the kitchen doorway. The voice says, Why don't you kids go play in your room. And Brantley, it sounds like, says, Why don't you make us? And another adult male voice says, Smart-ass. Krysia tells the children to go put on their pajamas and watch TV in the den, please and thank you. A uniformed officer's face appears briefly and Bay hit pause. I told Bay that was Sully. Bay hit play. Krysia blows her nose off camera. The man who spoke to the children earlier now tells the others in an exaggerated whisper that we're wasting time here. This is not a fucking tea party, he says. Sullivan wants to know the time, and we see Shanks's face again. And then Shanks must rest his face in his hand, and the camera shoots the empty kitchen door space. When Krysia walks by we see her, and it goes quiet for a moment. Sully says, Put that away. And then Shanks lays his hands on what we see is the dining room table, and we get a clear but sideways look at Officer Kind and another guy who is not in uniform. This guy, in a blue polo shirt, is rolling his eyes and tapping his foot like a madman. Kind has his hand on the guy's arm, calming him. You can hear the TV blasting in the background, and then someone must close a door, and the racket is muffled.

Bay paused the video. He pointed to the skinny little agitated man on-screen. "That's Chris Bolzano, Internal Affairs, EPD. He's got something on everyone in the department, but he's a crack addict, as is his wife, and so his ethical bar has been lowered."

"How do you know that?"

"Our paths have crossed. He was placed in IA by Meatyard as an informant. No more secrets, no more surprises. And, of course, you recognize our friend from the Wayside."

Bay resumed the video. Krysia stands by the table. Sully says, Not too many people get a second go at the Witness Protection Program. Krysia says, Shouldn't you boys be home with your families on this of all nights? Shanks says, Crime doesn't take a holiday, I'm afraid. Sully asks where they're relocating the family this time, and she answers that even if she knew, she couldn't tell him. You get to start all over, Sully says, get to be whoever you want to be. What an opportunity. Shanks says he'd like a do-over himself, and Kind asks him who he'd like to be the next time. We're looking at Krysia's face a moment, and then the camera sweeps across the room, and Shanks says he'd really like to own a nightclub, a classy one, says he'd call it Dino Martini's. He says, All that free booze and whatnot, all those desperate, sexy women. Kind asks Krysia what she'd like to be, and she says, Alone with my children, and she tells them all it's time to leave, but nobody leaves, and we see the ceiling and a bit of the ceiling fan. Sully tells Krysia they just need to talk with Chafin a minute and they'll be off, and he asks her to call her husband, please. She says she's been instructed not to call him under any circumstances. Sully says the circumstances are extenuating. I've explained that your lives are in danger, have I not? Bolzano slams his fist on the table and says, Call the fucking number! Sully says, That's enough. The screen goes dark. Shanks may have his hand under the table. And then the oven's alarm goes off, and Krysia hurries to the kitchen. And then her cell phone rings, and she says, What the hell is going on and where the hell are you? And then there are some seconds of erratic camera movement and the scraping of chairs and the shuffling of feet, and then we're in the kitchen looking at the measuring spoons on the wall. And then Shanks, who must have grabbed the phone from Krysia, tells Halliday he has ten minutes to get his ass home or else. And then there's the noise of the TV, and Kind says, I'll take care of it.

Or else you'll regret it, Shanks says. And then we see Krysia being restrained by Sully. And then all hell breaks loose.

Bay and I reconstructed what must have happened that gruesome Christmas Eve based on the evidence presented in the frenzy of unfocused and dizzying visuals and on what we heard in the muddied garble of shrill and blustering voices and in the turmoil of clamorous noises. We used our imaginations to fill in, or to fire across, the narrative gaps.

- The man whom Pino Basilio sometimes called Charlie became Chafin Halliday when he testified against the Ianotti crime family in Rhode Island.
- Halliday was set to testify before a federal grand jury about the racketeering and collusion between local law enforcement officials, the Mafia, the Russians, a handful of elected municipal office holders, and the late Mickey Pfeiffer's merry band of jurisprudent thieves.
- Pino was the U.S. marshal assigned to Halliday's case.
- Pino had arranged for another relocation and for new identities for the Hallidays.
- As was customary, WITSEC officials notified local authorities, in this case our sheriff and the chief of the EPD, as to the whereabouts of Chafin Halliday upon relocation so that local law enforcement might keep an eye out for any suspicious behavior and also to ensure that the betrayed terriers were not coming after the rat.
- One week earlier, Officer Kind had investigated a possible burglary at La Mélange and confiscated Chafin Halliday's Colt Woodsman "as evidence."

- Officer Kind had given the confiscated Colt handgun to Officer Bolzano.
- Officer Bolzano had loaded a magazine into the Colt before he holstered it earlier that Christmas Eve.
- The police officers in question arrived at the Halliday house in an unmarked vehicle.
- Bolzano took a black leather driving glove out of his pocket, slipped it over his right hand, and tucked the glove up the webs of his fingers. Halliday, we know, was not at home, but where was he? Was he with Pino? Did Pino realize that word of Halliday's testimony had leaked to the very people under scrutiny? We thought that the answers were: At a secret location. No. Yes.
- The contents of the Halliday home, modest and austere as they were, had been packed and carried off to a government warehouse in Hialeah.

The Slaughter of the Innocents. Apparently when Shanks presented Halliday with the ultimatum—come home or else—Halliday refused. Shanks walked out of the kitchen and lowered his voice on the phone. He asked Halliday if he was willing to accept the responsibility for what would happen to his wife and children. Sully released Krysia, who screamed at him. I couldn't make out what she said, but Bay heard her call him a mackeral-snapping nancy boy. Sully took the phone from Shanks and tried to reason with him. He said, Yes, it does seem to come down to that: your life or the lives of your family. Bolzano told Krysia to shut her pie hole. Krysia bent down over the opened oven door and appeared on-screen when she did. She mumbled something to Bolzano, some back-sass or other. Bay thought she told him to kiss her Polish ass. That was followed by a surprisingly dull, almost perfunctory blast, and Krysia fell onto the opened oven door dead. That was followed by a confusion of visual images, as Shanks was unable to still himself. He called Bolzano a motherfucking moron. Sully said, Aw, fuck-it-all! Bolzano said the bitch had it coming. Kind picked up a pile of linen napkins and left the room. Sully asked Halliday if he had just heard the gunshot. That was your wife. Your wife. You heard me. In ten minutes, we'll shoot one of your children. And then in ten minutes more, another. Just tell us where you are, and we'll send the welcome wagon. Shanks said, We really don't have much choice now, do we?

Shanks stood in the den. The gifts were unopened. The children were elsewhere and being quiet, or being quieted, evidently unaware of the gunshot. We saw the pistol in Bolzano's gloved hand, his index finger on the barrel. He said he remembered one Christmas when he was seven or eight, and he woke up and there was nothing. No gifts, no tree, no breakfast, no heat in the apartment, no lights, no parents. Not a fucking thing. And these little shits live like royalty. Shanks said, You just killed their mother. Oh, yeah, Bolzano said, end of fairy tale. And then the younger boy, blindfolded, was led into the den by Kind, who told the boy to sit. Briely had been told he would be allowed to open one gift, and one gift only. He asked where his mother was and was told she'd run to the mall for some last-minute shopping. Someone turned up the volume on the TV. That kid who wants a Red Ryder BB gun was screaming, Oh, fudge! Kind asked the boy if he was ready. Briely smiled and held out his arms and Bolzano shot him. Sully told Chafin, You just killed your son. And then Sully told the others that Chafin hung up. And Kind said, What kind of a father . . . ? The other two blindfolded children were brought out to the den. Their mouths and wrists had been duct-taped. Bolzano shot them.

Shanks said, What's our story, Sully? Kind said, Drug bust. Sully asked Bolzano for the weapon. Then he said, Murder-suicide.

Shanks said, Where's our suicide? Sully put the pistol on Bolzano's chin and fired. Sully told Shanks to make it look right and told Kind to type up a suicide note on the typewriter in the office and then dispose of the typewriter. Kind wanted to know what to say. Sully told him to use his imagination. What would you write if you had killed your own family?

Good riddance.

And if you were going to kill yourself?

Shouldn't I know their names, at least?

Sully spelled the names for him, told him their ages, then called Meatyard while Shanks opened the gifts, looking for something else he liked, maybe. And then Sully called in the crime. We're at the scene, he said. Send backup. Quietly.

Bay and I had come back to the hotel after an aimless and silent walk in the late-afternoon dusk and plopped down in a booth in the stifling Bruin sports bar. I felt like I had the flu. My throat was dry and swollen. I was achy and congested. My limbs were leaden. I wanted to put my head on the table and fall into a dreamless sleep, but my nerves were crackling and my bruised and swollen cheekbone throbbed. A dozen muted TVs were tuned to cable news or Jerry Springer. We ordered smoked caribou nachos and beer. Every business you enter in Alaska is arid and hot. I wanted to strip down to my T-shirt. If only I could have lifted my arms. I closed my eyes. In his magician's voice, Bay said, You are getting sleepy . . .

On our walk, we had watched a dark sedan fail to negotiate a left-hand turn and slowly drive across two lanes of sparse traffic, over a snow pile, onto the sidewalk, and into an empty bus shelter, all without making a sound. The driver opened the door and fell to the ground. Then he got up and walked away.

On the Springer TVs a man wielding a chair over his head was being reasoned with by several burly men in black T-shirts while the audience stood and cheered. And then he was being tackled. On the news TVs military troops were firing on people assembled in a plaza in some Middle Eastern country.

Bay said, "There was never a mystery to solve."

I said, "If I lived here, I would kill myself."

"But there's still the mystery of Halliday's whereabouts."

I thought about going home and painting all the rooms white, putting in a skylight, building a patio and a greenhouse.

Bay said, "Now that Halliday's no longer dead, perhaps he'll testify."

"I'd love to see Malacoda and company implicated in all of this."

"Someone must have tipped off the cops."

"Pino?"

"Likely."

"I hope he's looking over his shoulder."

Our beers arrived. We thanked Godfrey, who told us our nachos would just be a minute. I thought about the three bodies in Quartz Lake and how they must have been discovered by now and how the hunt for the perpetrator, the cop killer, must be already under way. We'd seen nothing on the news about it. I said, "They're looking for whoever drove that Ski-Doo over the hole in the ice."

"They'll be looking for Paul A. Kunkel, whose rental SUV and Ski-Doo they are." He reminded me I hadn't killed anyone, and I was happy to believe that. Godfrey arrived with the nachos and we devoured them. More beer. More nachos.

"Can you believe Carlos?" I thought about Myles, whom I would never see again, but I was certain I would always feel his presence. And not in a prison cell, I hoped. I'd rather be in Alaska than in prison.

• • •

Christopher Michael Bolzano entered the Peace Corps after graduating with honors from Bridgewater (Mass.) State College as a sociology major. He was stationed in Uzbekistan, where he helped construct irrigation systems in remote villages and cultivated root vegetables for sale at markets. It was here he met his future wife, Lily Preston from Maryland, at the English language puppet show in Bukhara. After a grand wedding at the Sheraton Inner Harbor in Baltimore, the newlyweds vacationed on the Eastern Shore and then settled here in Everglades County. Lily worked as an ER nurse at Memorial Hospital and Chris as a social worker with the Florida Department of Children and Families. Eventually, Chris realized that he was not changing the world as he had hoped, was not even making a significant difference in any of his clients' lives, was not making any child's burden more tolerable, was not the bearer of hope that he had supposed, and he quit the underpaid, ineffectual, and powerless life of a social worker and became a cop, where he could do more good.

So he began his new life, and that life began to include a host of pharmaceutical drugs that he had confiscated from dealers in the hood. Chris and Lily moved from Xanax and Vicodin to Adderall and Oxycodone to crack and meth in relatively short order. After Chris was suspended from the department for the third time, he was punished with an assignment to Internal Affairs. Lily lost her job at the hospital when she was caught pilfering patients' meds and replacing them with Wal-Zyr and vitamins. Several times over the holidays, Lily had thought to report her husband missing, but that would have meant people and questions, and she was not up for the emotional turmoil sure to ensue. The son of a bitch was probably spending the holidays, or the rest of his life, with one of his skanky girlfriends.

• • •

Francis Xavier "Sully" Sullivan departed Saint Joseph's Seminary in Yonkers after two years of prayer and study to become a police officer, leaving his mother in tears, her express lane to heaven now blocked; his father elated; and his uncle Tim Cooney, a New York City cop, proud. When he was a boy, Francis told anyone who asked that he wanted to be a cowboy priest when he grew up, riding the range in his Roman collar on his palomino, Archangel, bringing the sacraments to cowpokes and buckaroos around the campfires and bunkhouses. He joined the Eden Police Department in 1986 and had maintained a sterling reputation as a no-nonsense, straight-shooting, stand-up guy. He never married, but he did have a longtime steady girlfriend, Mary Ellen Twombly. They drank together every free night he had at the bar at Moynihan's on Main. Francis liked his Canadian Mist (Misty and water), while Mary Ellen preferred rum and Diet Coke. Mary Ellen's forbearing husband, Davy, sat at the other end of the bar drinking Bud Light, watching the TV, smoking, shooting the breeze with the bartender Scotty Bain. When Davy's colon cancer finally took him out a year ago, Francis and Mary Ellen's relationship began to lose its steam and purpose. What had once been a reliable and uncloudy future had now become a shadowy maze. Francis began to do most of his drinking at Leo's. Mary Ellen adopted a feral cat and bought herself a flat-screen TV. On the evening that Channel 10 aired portions of the video of the murders, she called Francis to have him tell her it wasn't true, that it was as fake as that man-on-the-moon video. While the phone rang, Francis knelt by his bed beneath a picture of the Sacred Heart, with a rosary wrapped in his hand, and shot himself through the temple.

• • •

Ernest Abel Kind joined the Eden Police Department because, as he confided, without a hint of irony, to a reporter for the *Beachcomber*, Gals, he said, love a man in uniform. Any uniform, he said, projects a sense of security, panache, competence, and a certain "journey say quad," to quote from the article. He grew up as an Army brat, the only legitimate child of Corporal Gerald Kind, his philandering old man. His mother, Maureen, lost herself in Harlequin romances, reading four a day most days, smoking cigarettes, and growing morbidly obese. When Ernest reached sixteen, and the family was stationed in Schweinfurt, Germany, he and his dad went hunting for women together, "trolling for Brunhildes," they called it. Ernest had a GED, earned an associate's degree from Everglades College and a BS in criminal justice from Florida Tech online. He drove a metallic gray Hummer, owned a Sea-Doo jet ski, a Kawasaki motorcycle, and a Scrambler ATV. Weekends he enjoyed boar hunting in the Big Cypress. He took an annual holiday to Thailand to sample the local Asian cuisine, as he put it. Easy to get lost in Thailand. No one would ever find you.

Kevin Alan Shanks played defensive end on the Tequesta High School football team, was president of the Choral Society, and was chosen king of the senior prom. His mom, Emunah, was a local politician, a Gulfstream city commissioner, who favored large floral hats and capacious handbags. His dad, Thomas, better known as Roadkill, died when, high on psychedelics, he tried to stop a southbound freight train with an outstretched hand at the Cypress Avenue crossing. A witness, his pal Warren Stamp, said that just before Roadkill was launched by the locomotive, he glowed a bright orange like something you might see in a blast furnace. After high school, Kevin joined the Navy, hoping to become a SEAL, but washed out in training. He did learn how to take orders, sacrifice for the team, and shoot the wing off a mosquito at a hundred yards. Back home, he worked as a bouncer in South Beach until the opportunity with the EPD knocked. He'd had two brief marriages, the second to an escort who told him on their first assignation that she was ready to settle down. She was not. His son, Jude, had refused to speak with his father for some years now. Kevin, as you know, vanished early in the year. After he did, police found video files on his computer showing him, in his bedroom, raping a series of women he had drugged with Rohypnol. He followed the rapes with glasses of celebratory champagne.

25

I hadn't slept well on the red-eye despite my sleep mask, my earplugs, and my Ambien. Every time I nodded off, I dreamed that my hands were on fire. I was agitated and apprehensive as we taxied to our gate at the New River airport. Bay was fooling with his iPhone, seemingly oblivious to our potential peril. Would the press be swarming the concourse wanting to speak with the man responsible for the release of the appalling and incriminating video file? Worse, would the cops be waiting with arrest warrants? But no one we could see was even vaguely interested in the two of us. Bay reminded me that we were not on this flight. Clockedile and Tremblay were.

We walked out of Terminal 3 and into the resplendent sunlight and the spectacular humidity. I love to feel the air wash over me when I walk. I could feel all my thirsty pores open and my puckered and brittle cells rehydrate and pop back into shape. Bay asked me for Lincoln Clockedile's IDs. I handed them to him and they vanished. We hopped into a cab. I borrowed Bay's iPhone and saw a photo on the screen of two arms outstretched and each hand a blazing torch. Bay flashed his brow and smiled. I called Patience and told her I was home. Bay had the cabbie drop me at my place. I'd almost forgotten about the Studebaker there in the driveway. Inside the house I found a case of Drakkar Noir cologne, actually a knockoff cologne called Our Impression of Drakkar Noir, that Cerise must have brought inside on cleaning day. She'd also left me a note on the counter beside the pile of mail. She said how sad she was to hear about Mr. Myles's passing. She said that she and Vladimir were going to be married on the beach at sunrise on Easter morning and would I perform the ceremony, something that my notary-public status allowed me to do. I opened the window to air out the house and brewed some coffee. I put the laundry in the washer. I poured myself a cup of coffee and sat on the couch with the mail. Bills addressed to Dad from Almost Home—into the circular file. A book from Inez—*Skylark* by Dezsö Kosztolányi—that had made her weep. But everything made her weep these days, she wrote. She mentioned the breakup with Carlos, her hopelessness, and the relief that was its gift. The letter from the New Orleans law firm of Foley, Ticholi, Terhune & Pickens said that I was being sued for art theft by Red's brother Blaise. Into the circular file. (A childish response I would come to regret.)

I switched on the TV to see if there might be some news on the fallout from the Halliday video file. I put a shot of brandy in the coffee. I asked myself if that was a good idea, drinking at 11:14 in the morning. I answered it was indeed. Bay called and said let's meet for supper at the Universe. I clicked through and erased voice mails until I heard Georgia's voice. She said she'd tried texting me but got answered by a stranger who wanted to know who she was. *I thought it was you goofing around. The guy—Cyril Something—said he'd found the phone and it changed his life.* Georgia said her lawyers expect to win the suit, but it might take years and they are considering a settlement. In the meantime the family is staying in the law firm's condo on Grand Cayman. She knew it would show up on the lawyer's bill, but it sure was fun, except that Tripp had horrible nightmares and was being treated for post-traumatic stress disorder.

Eden Interim Police Chief Mia Kafka stood before a lectern and addressed a roomful of journalists. She promised a quick and thorough investigation into the murders and the conspiracy to murder, a thorough housecleaning of the department and its apparent culture of cronyism. She dismissed the call for a civilian review board to oversee police operations. She talked about a few bad apples, et cetera. Clete Meatyard stood behind her, hands folded over his belly, nodding his bulky head, perspiring heavily.

Chief Kafka took a question from someone who sounded like Perdita Curry and then repeated the question. "Do we know the whereabouts of Mr. Chafin Halliday? No, we do not." She scratched her nose. "There is speculation that he may have fled the country under cover of his new identity." The chief listened to a follow-up question and tugged at her ear. "We are not at liberty to divulge that information." She told the press that the EPD was optimistic that Halliday would, indeed, testify before the grand jury. I switched off the TV and called Venise. Oliver told me she was still grieving.

"Can you put her on?"

"I can't."

"Why?"

"You're dead to her."

"Come on, Oliver."

"She needs this rage to see her through the hard time. Sorry, Wylie." He hung up.

Patience knocked once and walked in with Django sitting on her head and his cat carrier over her shoulder.

"My two favorite cats," I said. I reached for Django and kissed Patience on the forehead and the nose. Django gnawed on my finger.

"He never bites me," Patience said.

"I don't believe it."

She put her finger on Django's mouth. He licked it while he watched me.

"Great to see you," I said, and put Django on the floor. He ran into his carrier and wrestled with his toys. I made us two Bloody Marys, and we sat together on the couch. I told Patience I wanted to disappear, go someplace where I would never be found.

"Can I come?"

"Of course."

"How would we live?"

"We'd be rich."

"By whom do you not want to be found?"

"Everyone."

"What happened up there?" she said, meaning Alaska. Yes, she really wanted to know. So I told her. "Holy shit."

We filled Django's cat bowl and lined up his toys on the arm of the couch. We went out for oysters and beer at Slappy's Wonderland on the beach before Patience had to go back to work. We sat at the bar, ordered two dozen oysters, hold the saltines, and a pitcher of Sam Adams. I mixed up the cocktail sauce, horseradish, Crystal, and sriracha. Patience dipped her baby finger in, tasted, and tapped in more Crystal. She stared at me and shook her head. "All of that was true?" she said. I nodded. Our shucker, Elwood—it said so on his Slappy's ball cap—had sharpened his oyster knife to a point so it worked more quickly. He wore a latex glove on his left hand, not neoprene or steel mesh. We ate as he shucked. I asked him if he'd ever stabbed himself.

"Not often," he said. "Maybe once or twice a week. I've had

about fourteen stitches over the years. Usually, though, it's just a scratch."

When Elwood took off a torn glove, we noticed his hand was wrapped in duct tape. "Redneck Band-Aid," he said. He told us when he does get a cut that bleeds, he pours bleach on the wound—stings like a sumbitch—dries the hand, and rewraps it with duct tape. "You can't take a chance with filter feeders."

Bay and I were at the Universe, drinking martinis, sharing a bowl of steamed mussels, and trying to piece together the story of Chafin Halliday's Christmas Eve. We knew that the official version of events was dead wrong, and deliberately so. People who had seen Halliday that evening had already come forward and spoken to the press when they realized they had been ignored by the police. Bay's partly imagined scenario was closer to the facts and proved to be remarkably accurate:

On Christmas Eve, Chafin Halliday, who had already assumed his new identity as Steven (with a *v*) Snowhite of Greeley, Colorado, was late getting home to Krysia and the kids because, on a lark, he'd stopped at an unfamiliar liquor store to make his first purchase with Snowhite's shiny new Visa card, and he ran into the loquacious Tyler Lopate, a food broker, with whom he had an appointment at La Mélange on the twenty-eighth, and whom, Chafin knew, he would never see again. Tyler was all excited about this new organic farm in the Redlands, heirloom tomatoes to die for! And then he insisted on bringing Chafin out to his car to show him the Rösle food mill he'd gotten his partner, Lawrence. Chafin called home to tell Krysia (he'd have to get used to calling her Leah soon) he was on his way, heard Shanks's voice, and that's when he realized that things had gone hellishly wrong.

Bay washed his fingers with a moist towelette and called my

attention to Stavros Kanaracus in a blue jumpsuit and herringbone fedora, standing across the street from the Universe, speaking with a young boy, maybe his grandson. Stavros put a cigarette in his mouth and his hands in his pockets. The boy produced a lighter. Stavros bent toward the boy, and the boy lit the cigarette. Stavros inhaled and blew the smoke out the side of his mouth. He picked a bit of tobacco off his tongue. He looked over to us and smiled. When the boy shrugged at something Stavros said, Stavros slapped him soundly on the back of his head.

Our waitress, Flor, from Montevideo, brought our martinis. Bay plucked a rose out of thin air and handed it to her.

She said, "Que es esto, señor?"

"Una flor para una Flor."

We toasted the Oriental Republic of Uruguay, and then Bay summarized what we knew or what we might assume to be true about the Halliday case: Chafin was alive; Chafin's life was in peril; those he would testify against were on his trail; he had not stopped acting badly when he became Chafin Halliday, and he had been threatened with arrest and incarceration once again, or he would not have agreed to testify in the corruption investigation; he had no choice on Christmas Eve, he could not have saved his family; he would have vengeance on his mind, which he could achieve in one or two ways; he could forget the vengeance and vanish, but disappearing was hard to pull off anymore, especially without the government's help; Pino's job had been to protect the identity and person of Chafin Halliday and Halliday's family; instead, he betrayed Halliday and sacrificed the family; an Eden Police Department death squad, if that's not too melodramatic, had been dispatched to do the dirty work. Who sent them? And where did all of this leave us?

I told Bay that sure, maybe I could learn to live with what had happened in Alaska, that maybe one day in like thirty years I'd stop worrying that at any minute an Alaska state trooper would be knocking at my door. Maybe I could do that, but I did not want to also live at home in Melancholy with all the uncertainty and the veiled threats. I wanted all the bad guys to be in the jails, not running them. I said, "We need to find Halliday before Pino does."

"We can do that."

"And they can't?"

"We know where to look."

"We do?"

Bay pointed his chin to his left. "We're being surveilled."

I looked and saw Meatyard and Pino, speak of the devil, sitting together at a table, pretending not to be spying on us. They were both on their phones. Calling in reinforcements? I said, "I suppose they know who sent the video."

"They have a good idea. That's Basilio, am I right?"

"So he told me. You know him?"

"I've seen the face."

"Do you suppose those two clowns dispatched Carlos to Alaska?" Kanaracus was gone, but the grandson was there, leaning against a gumbo-limbo, smoking a cigarette, and staring at us. The guitarist outside the adjacent tapas place played "Bamboleo" for the al fresco diners.

Bay said, "We should say hello to our friends."

"Are you insane?"

"It's the polite thing to do." Bay summoned Flor and told her he was buying drinks for the two gentlemen at the curbside table. He said, "We should pay our respects."

"Are you trying to start something?"

When their drinks arrived, and Flor pointed our way, Meatyard and Pino put down their phones and looked at us, and Bay raised his glass and smiled. After we had finished our drinks, and after Bay asked Flor if she'd like to be his date for an Easter wedding, and after Flor blushed and said she'd think about it, and after he asked her to save our table, we'd be back, and after I asked Bay if he'd been invited to Cerise's wedding, Bay and I walked over to the curbside table. Bay said, "Good evening, gentlemen."

Meatyard rubbed his forehead. "We're conducting some private business here, if you don't mind."

"No need to thank us for the drinks."

"Beat it!"

Bay introduced himself to Pino. "You look familiar. Have we met?"

Pino slid his chair back. "You heard the man."

Bay said, "Your phone's going to ring." And it did. Actually, it whistled. How the hell did Bay do that? He told Pino, "You should answer it. Could be important."

Pino said, "Hello." He kept his eyes on Bay. "Who is this?" Pino pressed his lips, listened, and hung up and put the phone on the table next to Meatyard's.

Bay said, "Wrong number?"

Pino stared at Meatyard. Meatyard shifted his gaze to Bay. Bay said, "Does anyone else here smell roses?"

In fact we did, and so did the folks at adjoining tables, who turned our way. Bay seemed theatrically puzzled at this curiosity until he sniffed his iPhone and smiled. He placed the phone on the white tablecloth between the two other identical phones. We all watched as carmine roses bloomed on Bay's screen and then faded and withered to brown. We saw petals drop, and then the screen went black and the fragrance was gone. Bay had Pino and Meatyard's attention, and that of several other diners, who had gathered around the table and were applauding. Stavros's grandson drifted over. He said, "How did you do that?"

Bay said, "I didn't. You did." He looked at Pino and Meatyard. "May I, gentlemen?" And now they were onstage themselves and under scrutiny. Bay put the three phones beside one another, passed his hand over the phones, and the phones' screens lit up, theirs with the usual app icons and Bay's with an image of a gold EPD badge. He said, "We all trust our eyes to see what's in front of us." He shuffled the phones as he would cups in a shell game. "But it's not the eyes that see. It's the brain. Eyes are just the pinholes where the light gets in."

He ended his shuffle with the badge back in the middle where it began. "To really see, you have to pay attention. Is everyone paying attention?" They were. Stavros's grandson was capturing the performance on his own iPhone. Bay took my elbow and moved me over a step, so the grandson would have a clearer shot. Bay flipped the phones over, screens down, and asked Meatyard to find the badge. Meatyard tapped his finger on the middle phone. The onlookers agreed. Bay turned it over: icons. He turned the others over: the same.

"All vision," he said, "is an illusion." He passed his hands over the phones, and the letters *ill* appeared, white letters on the first blue screen, the letters *us* on the second, and the letters *ion* on the last. The screens went black and then the middle screen shimmered and displayed an EPD badge. Bay touched the screen with his thumb and index finger and seemed to lift the badge out of the phone, and what had been an image of a police badge became a real—whatever that means—badge, appropriately tarnished. Bay held it up, and our small audience applauded. The men at the table did not. "When your gaze stops on a stationary object, the visual neurons in your brain are suppressed, and the image . . ."—he looked at the badge, and we looked where he looked—"vanishes!" And it did. The badge was suddenly back on the middle screen and fading away.

He arranged the phones vertically and pointed to each screen in turn. On the bottom screen in a video, waves lapped on the shore of a deserted beach; on the middle screen, gentle swells on a blue-green sea, and on top, the sun setting—or rising—into—or out of—the ocean. Bay said, "You can see what's not even there." Our audience drew closer to the table. "Three-dimensional depth cannot, of course, exist in two dimensions, and yet you see it. The sun is way off on the horizon, far, far away from the sandy beach. And the screens went black in order from bottom to top. "You can fail to see what's right in front of your eyes." Bay took *my* wallet from *his* pocket and held it up. "Who saw me lift my friend's wallet?" No one had. He turned to Stavros's possible grandson and asked him to play back the video recording. "Start where I asked Wylie here to step aside." We watched the replay as Bay, in plain sight, not only touched my elbow but drew my wallet from my pocket and slid it into his own. He handed me my wallet. I put it in my pocket. Then he took a modest bow.

He rearranged the phones horizontally and pointed to each screen, and the *No Evil* monkeys appeared: *See*, *Hear*, and *Speak.* "If we see no evil, and we hear no evil, and we speak no evil, then perhaps we can believe there is no evil, and we can go right on with our happy lives." He passed his hands over the phones, and the monkeys became the smiling faces of the Halliday children. I recognized them and so did Meatyard and Pino. "But evil does exist," Bay said, and the faces faded to black, and then we heard what might have been gunshots. Pop! Pop! Pop! Pino grabbed his phone. "Show's over," he said.

Back at our table, Bay said, "The son of a bitch took my phone."

I said, "Your phone's right here."

"The other two were also mine. I've got their phones right here, but I didn't get the chance to switch them back." He took them out of his pocket and put them on the table.

"Anything interesting on them?"

"They're locked."

"Use your magic."

Bay handed the phones to Flor along with a twenty-dollar bill and asked her to wait till we were gone and then return the phones to our friends. "Tell them they can also keep the substitutes. And tell the slender gentleman to check his e-mail."

When we were out of sight, Bay showed me the JPEG he'd attached to his e-mail—a still photo of Pino taken from the murder video. He had been at the house, as his face reflected in a mirror at a confusing moment attested. I confessed I hadn't noticed him in the video. Bay said he hadn't, either, the first few times he'd seen it.

I said, "Should we be worried about those two?"

There was, it turned out, no longer any reason to fret about a fractious Clete Meatyard. The emphatically lifeless goon was found the following morning, naked, hung by his trussed ankles, and run twenty feet up the flagpole at the Melancholy Public Library. He'd been sloppily disemboweled, cut open from groin to gullet with the nine-inch stainless steel game shears found in the slop of organs at the base of the flagpole, some of which had been nibbled at by some razor-toothed nocturnal critter or other. Meatyard's neck had been cleanly sliced and vehemently carved, his head was nearly severed, and he had pretty much bled out by the time Muriel Spence, reference librarian, arrived for work. Muriel was aghast, but unruffled. She took out her smartphone and snapped a picture of the eviscerated and exsanguinated union president and sent it off to her BFF, Perdita Curry, and then she called the police. Perdita posted the gruesome image—with a warning—on her blog, *Curry On*, along with a brief interview with Muriel. When Perdita asked Muriel what had gone through her mind when faced with that horrifying sight, Muriel said, "The Parrot Sketch."

Perdita got her fifteen minutes of fame. Over the next few days she appeared on all of the local noon and six and eleven o'clock news reports talking about the shocking death of a public servant. Out at Betty's Starlight Lounge, Aldore LaFlamme, gator poacher, may have nursed a Dark & Stormy and wondered what this unappealing gal talking to that beautiful Sofia Niente had that he did not. He, too, had a story to tell, a story to make the hairs on the back of your neck stand up, and they wouldn't let him tell it to the world. Sometimes his life just seemed to turn to shit while he was doing nothing but having a drink, minding his own beeswax.

So:

- Chafin Halliday was still in the area and was set on revenge.
- Pino Basilio was likely his next target. And he, Pino's.
- Chafin had nothing to lose. Pino, everything.
- Bay had a hunch where Chafin might be staying, but did we want to find him, given the menacing circumstances?
- Chafin was something much more than a serial snitch. He was a certified badass malefactor.

In fact, and in time, and in installments, we would listen to and read the story of how Chafin Halliday found himself without friend or family, without a negotiable identity, and without protection.

Chafin Stuart Halliday was born Charles Anthony Houde in Providence, Rhode Island. His father, Remy, was a butcher, his mother, Nina, née Cinelli, a seamstress. He selected the name Halliday when he entered the Witness Protection Program (WITSEC). Charles (aka Chuckie, Chick, Carlo, Chaz, and Charlie Machine) dropped out of high school and began working for Coin-O-Matic Distributors. His official duties included servicing vending machines and jukeboxes and seeing that there were ample Sinatra, Damone, and Bennett 45s in every bar from Central Falls to Cranston. His unofficial, but more crucial, duty was to collect payment on the fees levied on businesses by his boss, Mr. Ianotti. Tributes, you could call them.

An eager beaver, a self-starter, a team player, Charles worked his way up to bagman in the Ianotti crime family, transporting family cash between Providence and Boston, and eventually earned a promotion to enforcer. When he was arrested for the murder of Eamon Delaney in Dorchester, Charles expected Junior Ianotti, who had taken over the business operations while his father was in prison, to bail him out and take care of the legal defense. Junior did not. "I don't know what I ever did to him. I must have been slandered," Chafin told FBI investigators. "There's a lot of backbiting that goes on in my line of work." Charles admitted to three murders—jerkoffs from the Winter Hill Gang, no big loss—and was suspected to have carried out several others. He and his recently married wife, Temple Luxe Houde, were put in WITSEC along with Charles's parents and a favorite aunt. The parents refused, saying they were not moving off Atwells Avenue after fifty years. "We have our infrastructure in place," Remy told his son. "We can't start over. You know how hard it is to find a mechanic you can trust?" One Sunday morning Remy started the Buick to drive to Mass at Our Lady of Mount Carmel, and the car exploded, killing him and his wife.

Charles had met Temple in an airport bar in Newark. He was on his way to meet a girlfriend in Myrtle Beach, where he owned a condo on the Strand. He told Temple he was in industrial sales and was on his way to a trade show in Birmingham. He bought her a prickly pear margarita and one drink led to another and one thing to another. He changed his flight to hers, upgraded them both to first class, and they flew off to Rochester, where he wooed her for three weeks at the Americana Hotel before they drove to Niagara Falls and married, her second, his first. It was not until after the whirlwind courtship and elopement that Charles told Temple what he really did for a living, and she told him about Roger LeMoyne, to whom she was technically still married. At least in Canada and in the eyes of God.

When she was seventeen, Temple married LeMoyne, an eighteen-year-old dropout and drywaller from Port Perry, Ontario, who had black hair, blue eyes, broad shoulders, and a strange and wonderful ass. He liked to fish and drink and screw, but he did not like to work or bathe or take his time. He'd come home from the Comet Pond with a lunch cooler full of gutted perch, open a Molson, and expect Temple to fry up the fish in cornmeal, but not before they did the dirty deed, as he called it, on the raunchy sofa in the den with the TV blasting away and all the lights on. Temple grew sick and tired of washing fish scales off her privates when he was finished with her, tired of his wheezing and snoring, his insults, his graceless manner, his rotting teeth, his loutish behavior in public, tired of his sloth and complacency, tired of his rank smell and his drunken rages. She hated the way he chewed his food with his mouth open, how his jaw cracked when he chewed, how he picked his teeth at the table. When he held her off the floor by her throat one evening and threatened to beat the shit out of her if she so much as talked to the faggot clerk at Testor's Market again, she settled herself with a glass of wine, went to the closet, grabbed the claw hammer, and struck the sleeping LeMoyne three times in the forehead. His hands went to his face after the first blow, but then he didn't move. She thought she should leave before she killed him, if she hadn't, or he killed her. She packed a few clothes, cut the phone cord, broke his Shakespeare rod over her knee, took the keys, his wallet, and the F-150, and drove out of her old life and into her new.

The tale of Temple and LeMoyne was sent as an attachment in an e-mail to Geraldine Barry by Krysia when she knew she was about to vanish once again, but sent to Geraldine's seldom-used AOL account, and Geraldine didn't read it until weeks after Krysia sent it. When Geraldine read it, she forwarded it to me. Krysia's subject line read, *Somebody has to tell the truth sometime.* This was the opening, and the only, chapter, perhaps, of Krysia's memoir. Or her novel.

So Temple and Charles would get their names changed. The name changes would be legal, they were assured, but would be sealed. At first Temple told Charles this was fucked up and she would not be going. But when she was advised as to the possible fatal consequences of her decision, she agreed and then actually threw herself into her new self. She had always wanted to be Polish (Chopin, Pope John Paul, kapusta), but she had to settle for Polish-American if she wanted a bona fide birth certificate. She could tell people she was from Gdańsk, but the certificate would read "Dudley, Massachusetts."

Charles's testimony had put some New England crime family bosses away on murder, fraud, and racketeering charges. He became Chafin Halliday in Everglades County, Florida. He would have preferred New York or Chicago or Philly, which was exactly why he wound up here. They got the house, a monthly stipend, and the documentation they needed to start over. Chafin had some discreet and effective facial plastic surgery. He was given a job as security guard for Wackenhut riding the Tri-Rail between Miami and West Palm. He had a healthy Swiss bank account the Feds knew nothing about and used the money to buy the restaurant and later the boats. It was a wonderful life for a while until the lucrative cash business attracted the attention of the mob. Two pasta-fed gentlemen in leather jackets showed up at his restaurant very late one night. He shot them both, put their bodies in his office on board the gambling boat, and dumped their weighted bodies overboard while the gamblers reveled on deck. Now he had himself a considerable problem. If the mob found out who he really was, he'd be iced. And the Feds could not protect him if he committed a crime. He called Pino. He was ready to flip again.

Chafin had been waiting for Meatyard in Meatyard's darkened living room. He sat in an upholstered chair in a corner with a black leather doctor's bag on his lap. In the bag, a Cash Special captive bolt stunner gun, a five-and-a-half-inch boning knife, and the game shears. The house smelled of stale cigars and citrus air freshener. Earlier, Meatyard's unsuspecting and genial wife, Melody, had opened the front door for Halliday, who was standing on the doorstep in a brown uniform, balancing an awkwardly large, but empty, carton on his knee. He smiled, put down the carton, and smashed her head, just once, against the doorjamb. He then hog-tied Melody with butcher's twine, duct-taped her mouth, dragged her upstairs to the attic, and dropped her onto a bed of pink fiberglass insulation. Maybe she would be found alive; maybe she wouldn't. (She would be.)

Meatyard walked into the house, dropped his keys into a wooden bowl on a small marble-topped table in the foyer, unholstered his service revolver, and locked it in a desk drawer. He took off his jacket and holster and hung them on a clothes tree. He walked into the dining room, unbuttoning his shirt. He sorted through the mail on the table and called to his wife. He unbuckled his belt and undid the button on his trousers. He walked to the answering machine and listened to his message: a voice he didn't at first recognize, Halliday's voice, told him he was a dead man. He swore at the voice and shut off the machine. The voice said, "Don't even turn around." Meatyard may have felt the cattle gun as it touched his head just below the occipital protuberance the doctors had told him not to worry about, but that would have been the last thing he felt. The gun's fired mushroom-shaped bolt may or may not have destroyed Meatyard's entire brain, but it certainly killed him. Halliday stripped Meatyard's body and set to work with the knife. He took Meatyard's keys, started up Meatyard's Cadillac, hefted the body into the trunk, and drove to the library.

26

And then for weeks all was strangely, welcomingly, quiet on the Halliday front. Halliday himself was in hiding, we assumed, or he had left the area, which Bay and I thought unlikely. Pino, we figured, was using his vacation time to furtively track down his former charge. Bay was back at the tables at the Silver Palace. I was seeing clients, seeing Patience, and not seeing, and not speaking with, Venise and Oliver. Django was learning to walk across the Florida room on the window screens. Vladimir and Cerise, mostly Cerise, were planning their seaside wedding and the subsequent tour of Melancholy's historic sites (there are only two: the statue of Cristoffer Østergaard, the city's founder, and the Tomato Monument in Festival Park, a relic of the time when Melancholy was the tomato capital of the world, before saltwater incursion rendered farming impossible) and the reception/brunch at Sputnik on the Intracoastal. The Halliday murder investigation and the coincident departmental housecleaning at EPD plodded along like an Ayn Rand novel. Our citizens were distracted by the influx of spring breakers and snowbirds and by some juicy new scandals in the news. The principal of Veronica Lake High, Gulley Seyforth, was busted for possession of cocaine; a Catholic priest at St. Sophia's was photographed on the beach with his sweetheart, the mother, it turned out, of his two-year-old twin daughters; a school bus monitor and a cop were arrested in a child prostitution sting; and a city commissioner in Gulfstream was caught with child pornography on his City Hall computer.

Late one rainy night, Bay and I let ourselves into La Mélange, now boarded up and closed. We found evidence that Halliday had, indeed, been staying here—a cot, blankets, fast-food cartons, and dirty clothes—but had cleared out. The cops were after him—the good ones and the bad ones. The mob, the Russians, assorted bribable politicians, and unprincipled attorneys—all had a vested interest in seeing that he did not testify before any grand jury or any other investigation or inquiry. Halliday couldn't trust anyone he knew. He would need to rely on the kindness of strangers. He would be easy to trace if he used his new identity, at least for Pino. He couldn't be Halliday, or Houde, either. He'd need plenty of cash, which he might have already and was certainly resourceful enough to obtain. He knew, we knew, that he would never live to testify. How long, we wondered, until he surfaced? How long could he hold his breath?

Bill Aubuchon labored to stop his sobbing. His head was back against my office couch, his forearm thrown over his swollen eyes. He was a man seemingly at the end of his rope, and he was boring me to death. I know that bad decisions make for good stories, and I should have perked right up when he told me that he'd confessed his love for Ellen Hillistrom to his wife, Dottie, and told Dottie she should hire an attorney, or use his, and commence with the divorce proceedings, but his blubbering sentimentality and self-pity were infuriating. Dottie called her pharmacist instead and then swallowed a handful of Xanax. Bill found her unconscious in the bathtub and called 911. He was sure this "suicidal gesture" was a manipulative attempt to keep him from leaving, and, of course, he did care "enormously" for Dottie, and he did feel "monstrously" guilty, but if he failed to assert himself, then he would lose Ellen, too. He shook his head and looked at the ceiling and then at the lady in the Automat in the Hopper painting lifting her coffee cup from its saucer, and there he saw, I'm sure, Ellen, near tears, waiting for him to arrive. I took notes for my own upcoming session with Thalassa. I'd wanted to talk about Myles and Red and Carlos, my anger and my grief and my guilt and my general unease and anxiety, a hangover from the crazed business in Alaska. Bill said, "Why? Why? Why?"

"Why what?" I said.

Bill blew his nose, made a fist, and bit his bottom lip. He then took a deep breath, held it, and put his face in his hands.

I began a to-do list: plastic storage boxes, ink cartridges, vodka . . . I wanted to say, Yes, Bill, life is a lose-lose situation. I did say, "What do you want now?" No answer. "What do you want to happen?" And I waited.

He folded his hands and brought them to his mouth. He leaned back and looked me in the eyes. "I want it to be a year from now. I want this to be over. I want us all to be in a better space."

"And how will you get to that better space, Bill?"

And that's when my office door opened and Pino Basilio, looking somewhat blunted and louche in his wrinkled Mr. Anonymous suit and with his unshaven whiskers, walked in, pointed at Bill and then at the door.

I said, "What the fuck!"

Bill said, "Who's this asshole?"

Pino took a step toward Bill. I stood, but Pino shoved me back into my chair. I said, "We're in a session right now."

"The session's over." He looked at Bill. "Get off your whiny ass and get the fuck out right now."

Bill looked at me. I shrugged. He got up and said he didn't expect to be billed for the hour.

Pino moved my Sigmund Freud bobble-head doll and sat on my desk. He swung his feet and wanted to know what happened to Carlos. I said as far as I knew Carlos was scuba diving in the Keys. Pino rubbed his stubbled face, then gripped the desk with both hands and sat up straight. He said, "Don't. Fuck. With. Me. We both know that you and Carlos were in Alaska together."

I feigned bewilderment. "I went to Alaska with my father."

"You came back without him."

"He died."

"He did?"

"My father."

"The airline says you haven't used your return ticket."

"That's strange."

Pino hopped off the desk, grabbed my shirt in his fist, and leaned in to my face. I told him to get his fucking hands off me, and I was both startled and alarmed by my courage or by whatever it was that provoked my imprudent, if righteous, outburst. Pino twisted the shirt and pushed me back into the chair. I asked him why he had thrown away a decent life. He grabbed me by the throat, and that's when Bay said, "Smile for the camera, douche bag." He was standing by the door in a mantis-green suit and school-bus-yellow shirt, aiming his iPhone at us and making a movie.

Pino let go of my throat and said to Bay, "Hand me that phone."

Bay put the phone in his coat pocket. "I don't think so." He took an open deck of cards out of his pocket and fanned the cards. "I'll cut you for it."

"No, I'll take it from you." Pino stepped toward Bay, who took a single card from the deck in his right hand, lifted it over his head, and threw it at Pino. The card pierced Pino's throat just below the chin. He didn't know what had happened. He choked, grabbed for his neck, and dropped to his knees. The second card impaled his cheek and must have cut his tongue as it passed into his mouth—he began spitting up blood.

Bay said, "The next one's in your eye."

"All right, all right." Pino pulled the cards out of his flesh. "I'm bleeding here, for Christ's sakes."

"Paper cuts," Bay said.

I said, "Get out of my office."

Bay said, "You know if I can find you so easily, so can Halliday."

Pino walked past him to the door.

Bay said, "You're not going to save your ass by icing Halliday. I sent the video to your bosses at WITSEC."

Pino said, "You're a dead man."

Bay lifted another card, and Pino left. Bay threw the card. It circled the room and came back to his hand. He said, "Shit, I probably shouldn't have told him that."

Bay and I sat at the Center Bar at the Silver Palace. He nursed a diet soda. I was on my second martini. My nerves were raw and taut. I knew I could drink all day and not feel unconstrained, not go slack and sloppy. Bay tapped his phone, and I heard a swoosh. He said he'd just sent the recent video taken in my office to the WITSEC folks.

"Not to the cops?" I needed to get myself a new phone. And hold on to it.

"They have no interest."

"Where do you suppose Pino is right now?"

"Probably trying to arrange a new identity for himself before he loses all access to his contacts."

We heard a commotion and turned to see a woman, quite inebriated apparently, drive her Hoveround into the chair of a man sitting at a slot machine. When she tried to back away she ran over another man's foot and then into a slot machine. The man's wife or girlfriend threw a drink in the driver's face. The driver grabbed her cane and swung it at the woman, but missed. Security arrived, in the form of two large bald guys with goatees, who escorted the driver away, and the gamblers went back to their darling machines.

I smelled Drakkar Noir and turned to see Open Mike. He clapped me on the shoulder and said, "What do you know. What do you know."

I thanked him for the cologne.

He said, "De nada, amigo. How's it working out for you?"

"Let me buy you a drink."

"Actually, I'm here to speak to Bay about some business."

"I'll take a walk."

I took my drink and headed for a less deafening area of the casino, unsure of where that might be. By the food court, I figured. And that's where I found Vladimir the perfidious, sitting with a woman in a black satin crepe dress at a table for two outside the deli, the both of them holding hands. I stopped. "Vladimir."

He looked up. "My friend."

"What's . . . going on?" I flourished the whites of my eyes in a gesture meant to express befuddlement and disapproval. The woman had an unusually deep jugular notch, cadmium-orange hair, a gap in her front teeth, and tiny eyes with Prussian-blue irises that were perhaps slightly misaligned in a way that made you stare into them until you realized you were being rude. She wore Scrabble tile earrings, an *X* on one ear, an *O* on the other. She told me her name was Geisha, but Vladimir called her Iljana. She regarded me with amusement and impatience. She asked me if I liked tongue. I confess to feeling flustered. I blushed. She pointed to her sandwich. "It's scrumptious," she said. "Get it sliced, hot, on rye with a smear of Dijon."

Vladimir said, "Iljana works here at the casino."

She said, "I'm a slut attendant."

I said, "Excuse me?"

"The slut machines."

"Ah."

"When your machine goes off, I give you the payout; you give me the zuke."

"The what?"

"The tip."

Vladimir told me that Iljana was from Odessa in Ukraine. She understood the Russian soul. Iljana asked me, if I were an animal, what kind of animal would I be. I said I didn't know. She cocked her head and studied my face, looked me up and down. "A lemur, I think. You know lemurs?"

"Big eyes, long tail."

"Toothcombs and toilet claws." She fiddled with the *X* earring. "Now you ask me impertinent question."

I wanted to say, Are you ever just yourself? Or, Do you know that Vladimir is soon to be married? And Vladimir may have sensed the uncomfortableness that might ensue should I do so, and he asked Iljana to visit the Design Outlet across the way, pick something out she liked, and he'd meet her there shortly. She stood, grabbed her gold clutch, blew Vladimir a kiss, curtsied to me, and said, "We say in my country, 'The word *enough* does not exist for water or fire or women.'" And she left.

I said, "What are you doing, Vladimir?"

He smiled. "You know what I'm doing."

"Why are you doing it?"

That smile again. "You know why I'm doing it."

"You're putting me in an awkward position. Am I not supposed to tell Cerise, your bride, what you're up to?"

"That would wound her."

"You're cheating before you're married."

"I'm sowing the last of my wild oats." And then he changed the subject and asked me what I made of the Halliday affair.

I told him I hoped Halliday would testify and put the criminals in jail, but I didn't think he would.

"Perhaps is dead."

"He's not."

"Perhaps soon."

You see precious few stalwart and attractive young people at the casino like the stylish and carefree urban professionals you do see in the ads for the casino—no dazzling and confident high rollers in casual suits and evening dresses clapping their hands and congratulating one another for hitting the jackpot, breaking the bank, looking wholesome, hearty, and sober with their Cole Haan loafers and Fossil handbags, and flashing their brilliant white teeth. Fashion at the Silver Palace runs to off-brand tracksuits, Bermuda shorts and sandals, fanny packs, ball caps, and visors. An inordinate number of gamers have loose and persistent coughs. Bay calls a walk down an aisle of slots a symphony for catarrh. Their skin is sallow and can take on the color and texture of catfish belly, the bodies are either lumpy or wizened.

People-watching at casinos is fascinating—there's a story in front of every machine—but it, like aging, is not for the timid. I was back sitting at the bar with Bay and watching a man with a portable oxygen cylinder and a nasal cannula pull the handle with one hand and smoke a cigarette with the other. Ching! Ching!

Ching! Lucky bastard won again. I asked Bay what Open Mike needed to talk to him about, if it was any of my business. He told me Open Mike had noticed I wasn't wearing the cologne I supposedly liked so much, and he was a little hurt. "Open Mike heard from Kanaracus that there's an internecine power struggle under way in our Russian community between the Petersburg Russians and the Moscow Russians. And the former Soviet republics are picking sides. Georgia and Kyrgyzstan with Petersburg, and the Tajiks and Uzbeks with Moscow."

A thickset fellow wearing an I'M WITH SNOPES ➔ T-shirt stood at the rail across the circular bar from us. He seemed to be looking at me. He chomped on an ice cube and flipped up the shaded lenses on his eyeglasses. He *was* looking at me. Maybe he knows me, I thought. Maybe he thinks he knows me. Maybe he wants to know me. Maybe he's trying to pick a fight. I don't know why I do it, but whenever unsmiling people stare at me, I stare back, and when I do, I can feel myself becoming belligerent, like I'm ready to start something I know I can't finish. And that's what I did. Clearly the mind was not in charge at the moment. The arrow on the T-shirt pointed to a drinker at the wearer's left, a man with a Band-Aid on his cheek and another on his throat. A man in a rumpled suit. Pino Basilio, in the flesh. Pino smiled and lifted his drink. I told Bay we had a stalker. He turned and waved. He said we should pay our respects. Do we have to?

When we arrived at Pino's chair, the thickset fellow put down his drink, bowed, and left.

I said to Pino, "A friend of yours?"

"Don't know him from Adam."

"He seems to know who you are."

Bay said, "Shouldn't you be transforming your identity and burrowing underground?"

"I will when I've settled my affairs." Pino sipped his cocktail.

"You won't try anything in here."

"I'm a patient man."

Why I looked away at just that moment I can't say, other than I felt an urge to do so, and when I did, I saw him sitting at a blackjack table. How was it my eyes fell on him, of all the people in this swarm of bodies? He had on a pair of enormous sunglasses, the kind that fit over your prescription eyeglasses, the kind you wear if you're planning on flying too close to the sun. Later, after the bloodshed, if some investigator were to ask you to describe the assailant's face, all you would remember would be those glasses. You'd remember the unzipped black hoodie—although there'd be others who would call it blue. You'd remember the orange WHEATIES, BREAKFAST OF CHAMPIONS T-Shirt, the Cubs ball cap, and the hood pulled over it. You might even remember the scuffed-up desert boots, but you wouldn't remember the face.

The man tapped his losing cards and stood. He stretched his arms and yawned, and I knew immediately and with an inexplicable certainty who he was, and this epiphany ignited a peculiar sensory response in me. Suddenly the racket in the casino muted, and I could see everything with clarity, focus, and definition because my perceptual chronometer had slowed. Or maybe I just paid exceptional attention because I knew something horrendous was about to happen, and so it only seemed like time crawled. I once dreamed that the air around me had thickened like corn syrup, and I could still move and breathe by extending a little more effort; I could even climb the air, and I was not alarmed. I felt like I was sheltered in amber. That was sort of what it felt like now. I was curiously unconcerned for my safety, even as I saw the avenging angel close the distance between us.

I looked at Bay, who was listening to whatever new threat Pino was dishing out, and I tried to will him to look my way because right then I was too panicked to say anything. Surely, I thought, he must sense the urgency in the message I was drilling through the side of his head. I couldn't move, either, immobility being my usual first response to danger. Pino tapped a cigarette out of his pack. Bay snapped his fingers, and a plasma of flame shot up several inches before it settled. He lit Pino's cigarette and blew out the flame. Across the room, Vladimir and Iljana walked arm in arm toward the sports book, past an elderly couple having their photo taken with a local celebrity judge, famous for crying on TV during a custody hearing. Bay finally did look my way, and when he did, I looked at the approaching menace, and he followed my gaze, but did not, apparently, see what I saw, nor did he read the obvious alarm on my face. He turned back to the nattering Pino, and I didn't take another breath until it was over. Pino put his finger on Bay's chest. The crowd seemed to part for Chafin Halliday, now just yards away and bent on annihilation. I yelled a warning at Bay, but may not have made a sound. All I could do now was impede Halliday's progress and hope for some miraculous intercession. I saw the man with Snopes sitting on my former bar stool, talking to Open Mike.

I stepped in Halliday's path and braced myself. Pino lifted his head and blew smoke up and away from his face. Halliday shouldered past me, drew an eight-inch ice pick from his sleeve, stepped up to Pino, grabbed him by the scruff of the neck with one hand, and drove the ice pick into his throat with the other, through the larynx, and on up into the brain. No one moved. No one but Bay and I may have even noticed. Everyone at the bar had turned away quite leisurely from the disaster. Pino stared at his assailant. Bay stepped away and jostled a young woman behind him, who turned to see what oaf had upset her drink and stained her silk blouse, and she will have to live with the memory of what she saw. Halliday slipped the ice pick out of Pino's throat and plunged it into Pino's eye, and when the ice pick stopped, he gave the wooden handle a punch with the heel of his hand. And then the sound returned to me, only amplified. Someone screamed; electronic music played; another jackpot! Halliday turned and walked toward the exit, shedding his hoodie and hat and glasses as he did. Some surveillance officer, of course, had witnessed everything on a video monitor somewhere in the bowels of the casino and had notified the security officers on the floor, who met Halliday at the door and us at the bar. Halliday offered no resistance that I could see. By now a small crowd had gathered, more curious, I think, than horrified. Most people kept their seats at their beloved loose machines, and Open Mike and his friend were gone. Bay and I were asked to show our driver's licenses. We were witnesses and would be called to testify. Only that would never happen. The official report said that Halliday resisted arrest and began fighting with the officers, who were subduing him in a vigorous but appropriate manner. They twice Tasered him and later used pepper spray. Perhaps the Taser did not complete a circuit, a police spokesman said. What? At some point a patrol sergeant arrived on the scene to help out. Paramedics were called to the scene because of the violence with which Halliday resisted. While the paramedics were evaluating, Halliday's heart stopped. And the broken neck? Due to the violence of his thrashing about. That was the official version, and, as Carlos always said, "What's true is what's written down."

We stood on the beach by the fishing pier, looking out at the twilit horizon and waiting for the sun to rise on Easter morning at Cerise and Vladimir's wedding. The temperature was in the mid-sixties; the sky was cloudless; a slight breeze drifted in over the water. The Russians, Vladimir included, had arrived en masse in a convoy of Hummers, having come directly from an all-night bachelor party at Lenin's Mating Call. The men in their high-regulation haircuts, all wore enormous wristwatches and suits of muted dark colors. The women, blondes every one, and all draped in silk shawls, held their very high-heeled shoes in their bejeweled hands. Patience, Bay, and I lit the bamboo beach torches. A Russian in a linen kosovorotka stood at the shore and played a waltz to the pale and waning moon on his garmoshka. Down the beach a blind man walked with his service dog, which wore a reflective blue saddlebag. Plovers pecked their beaks in the sand and ran from the slowly advancing waves. The dog barked at them.

Cerise arrived with Ellery and Ellery's date, my old acquaintance Trevor Navarro. Trevor's blue hair was cut short and matched his blue mustache, his new blue suit, and his old blue eyes. Ellery wore a white linen suit with a pink carnation boutonniere and a pink silk pocket handkerchief. Cerise's now-red hair was cut in a chin-length bob. She wore a simple and elegant heliotrope dress and a string of pearls. She clutched a small bouquet of lavender and sage. She beamed. She held on to Vladimir's hand and leaned her head against his arm. Trevor looked to the horizon and said, "The sun, he is risen," and the ceremony began.

Vladimir, Cerise, and I were joined in the center of the assembled circle by the witnesses, Anna Andropova and Misha Gurov. I heard the raucous call of a laughing gull overhead and the faint drone of a motorized paraglider somewhere down the coast. I cleared my throat and welcomed our guests to the celebration of the marriage of Cerise Beaudry and Vladimir Drygiin. Anna presented the bride and groom with a small round loaf of bread, sprinkled with salt. She held the dish while the couple each took a bite of the bread. Misha then handed Vladimir a shot glass of vodka. Vladimir lifted his glass; someone yelled, "Gorka!" He downed the vodka and tossed the glass over his right shoulder. Vladimir recited Pushkin's "Wondrous Moment" in Russian and then in English. Cerise read a poem by St. John of the Cross about the living flame of love. I spoke about marriage being our way of reminding ourselves how essential and invigorating love is, how if love is faith, then marriage is hope, the loftier virtue; if love is blind, marriage is perception; how love is the map and marriage the journey, love, a poem, marriage, a story, and how if you tell a story right, it never ends. I smiled at Patience. And when I asked who presented this bride in marriage, Ellery did. The couple exchanged vows and rings. Ellery wept. I pronounced Vladimir and Cerise husband and wife. The guests cheered. Bay said, "That's very odd."

We followed his pointing finger down the beach and saw that the blind man had released his service dog and was now walking away from us. The dog, however, was bounding in our direction with lolling tongue and flopping ears. The garmoshka player put down his instrument and drew a pistol from under his kosovorotka, aimed it at the dog's flank, and fired. The explosion vaporized the bomb-carrying dog and sent a thirty-foot mushroom of brilliant orange flame into the sky. One of the Russians on the perimeter set off running after the blind man. The rest of us lay on the sand, holding our breaths.

I heard the droning paraglider getting closer, but I couldn't see him. I did see a fisherman at the end of the pier put down his rod, turn his visored cap around, pick up a Kalashnikov, lift the sling over his shoulder, and take aim, but before he could fire, Vladimir, who was standing right where we had left him, shot the bastard dead. I felt myself cheering at the killing. What was happening to me? The three of us, Patience, Bay, and me, got up and ran, crouching, flinching at every shot fired, stumbling, holding our arms over our precious heads, toward the cover of the sea grapes.

From our new vantage point, we could see Ellery and Trevor playing dead, lying facedown in the sand. At least, I hoped they were playing. I couldn't see Cerise anywhere. I asked Patience if she was all right, and she looked at me like I was on fire. Right, I thought. Stupid question. Sorry. She said she was too terrified to cry. I thought about my mother under the shelter of juniper bushes in the forest near Telšiai, helpless to do anything as she watched the execution of her family and friends, hopeless, because what was hope now but betrayal?

The Russian men were armed and alert and were cautiously backing away from the shore. The women, some of them screaming, some weeping, hurried away from the beach and toward the parking lot. Out on the water, a cigarette boat raced toward shore. Not cops, of course, but reinforcements, I was certain. The paraglider sailed over the beach, and the pilot, I saw, was armed. He fired and hit at least one Russian before he was hit himself. He slumped forward in his harness. The engine sputtered; the device swirled and drifted as the engine died and began a slow descent to the sea, where the engine dragged our pilot under. The last things we saw were his white legs disappearing into the blue water and the red parasail settling like a shroud over the pilot's watery grave.

The cigarette boat drove onto the shore, and the engine died, and that's when the Russians, at arms and poised to engage the reinforcements on board, looked at one another and realized that there were no reinforcements aboard, that this go-fast boat was a forty-two-foot explosive device, a ticking bomb, remote-controlled, most likely, maybe by that chopper circling at sea, and so did we realize it, and we scrambled through the sea grapes toward the beach road. The blast threw us to the ground. My ears were blocked and ringing. We got back up and made it out of the sea grapes and ran south down the beach road away from the disaster. Bay said, "Run and don't ever stop." The sea grapes and beach were to our left and in a few blocks some houses and condos on our right. No traffic on this one-lane, one-way road so early in the morning. We were gasping for air. My knees hurt, my feet hurt, my lungs burned. We passed below a man standing on his third-floor balcony holding a cup of coffee. He waved as we passed. He pointed back toward the beach. A woman out walking her Yorkie wished us a happy Easter, and a man heading for the beach with his metal detector and his headphones asked us where the fire was. Finally we were spent. Patience said she couldn't go on. We stopped. She vomited. Bay fell to the ground and lay on his back. I saw a redheaded vulture drift in the wind, letting the breeze carry him over the sea grapes to the beach, picking up speed as he went. My old exhilarated friend, I thought.

Bay said, "I think we're okay."

We heard sirens in the distance.

I said, "I need a drink."

"We should call a cab," Patience said.

The sirens were louder now. Just then an ESO squad car turned onto the beach road and headed toward us. Bay said, "Oh, fuck!" We decided we couldn't outrun the cops, so we just pretended to be three early marchers in the Easter parade. The officer drove by. We smiled at each other. But then, a few blocks away, she hit the brakes. Bay said, "We need to get out of here."

Patience said she couldn't possibly. But she could. The squad car began to back up. We walked to the corner of Aviles Street, turned, and took off. Bay tried the door of several cars. One, an older-model Lincoln Town Car, was open. We hopped in. Patience and I got down in the backseat, Bay in the front. We heard the squad car squeal its way around the corner and speed by us.

I sat up and peeked out the back window and saw the lady with the Yorkie waving, running, yelling something about her car. She seemed unwilling to come any closer than ten feet. Bay opened the passenger door and told her to hop in. She did. The little Yorkie was barking furiously. "Can you shut him up?" Bay said.

"This is my car," she said.

Bay asked her politely for the keys. I recognized her as the woman I'd often seen walking her dog in a baby stroller on the Boardwalk.

Patience leaned forward, touched the woman's shoulder, and said, "It's not what it looks like, hon."

The woman turned to look us over and said, "You all are in trouble, aren't you?"

I said, "I'm not going to lie to you . . ."

"Charlotte," she said. She held up the Yorkie. "And this is Henry."

"Charlotte," I said, "yes, we're all in trouble."

She said, "I am, too?"

Bay held up his tarnished Eden Police Department badge for her inspection. She handed him the keys. He drove the one block to Ocean Avenue and turned south. The police had closed the Cypress Avenue Bridge.

Charlotte soothed the very agitated Henry. "Oh, dear," she said. She kissed his black nose and said, "This is about Mr. Kurlansky, isn't it?"

"Go on," Bay said.

"He was not the man he said he was." Charlotte leaned her head against the window and shut her eyes. She tapped her forehead with a fist. "It happened so long ago," she said.

Bay turned right on Dixie Boulevard and drove west. Henry sat up on Charlotte's lap and whined. He sensed her agitation and may have felt distraught at being unable to relieve it.

I said, "He hurt you, didn't he?"

She nodded and took a deep breath.

"He punched you."

"How did you know?"

Patience handed Charlotte a tissue. Henry whimpered and licked Charlotte's hand. Bay caught my eye in the rearview, raised his brow, shook his head like, *What's going on?*

"Always in the stomach," I said.

"Sometimes in the back. And he would pinch me until I bruised. Here," she said, and held her breasts.

It takes a toll, Carlos had said, dealing with depravity day after day.

"I thought I was safe." Charlotte sniffled. "I thought I was far enough away."

I thought about Cerise's recitation of John of the Cross. *O delightful wound . . . in killing you changed death to life.* There is life after a death, I wanted to tell Charlotte. Here. In Melancholy.

"It was dark on that cliff," she said. "This was in Mendocino. A moonless night. We were near the edge. The surf was pounding below us. He misstepped and fell. One minute he was squeezing my shoulders, shaking me, threatening me, and the next he was gone." Charlotte put her face in her hands. Patience rubbed Charlotte's neck.

I said, "We believe you. It's okay. You're not in trouble. Bay's no deputy."

Bay flourished the badge and made it disappear.

I said, "Accidents happen. And sometimes they happen to people who deserve them."

"If you talk about it," Patience said, "maybe it will help."

Charlotte shook her head. "I can't."

I said, "How do you feel right now, Charlotte?"

"Like I'm going to explode."

I said, "Try to remember what you've been trying so hard to forget."

Charlotte turned and looked me in the eye. "He would accuse me of being with other men. He would touch me to see if I was wet."

I now felt certain that she had been waiting—waiting for too long, even if she didn't know it—to tell someone other than Henry what had happened to her, someone who would listen and not judge. And who better than strangers? Mr. Kurlansky might be gone, but Charlotte was not yet free of him.

"Sometimes, when he choked me, I just wished he'd get it over with." She patted Henry's head. "Most of the time I felt numb and stupid."

Patience said, "My man Wylie here is a therapist."

Charlotte loosened her seat belt and set her back against the door so she could see us all. She said, "You don't look like a Wylie."

"Why don't you begin with the day you met Mr. Kurlansky," I said.

"It starts before that. Way before. First you need to understand the foulness I was coming from." Charlotte shook her head and dried her eyes. "I thought he was my savior." She took a restorative breath. She cleared her throat. And as Bay drove on deep into the Everglades, and with Henry curled in her lap, Charlotte stared ahead at her past, just a foot or two in front of her face, and told us the unexpurgated story, and in the telling she was carried away, and gradually, as she spoke, and as we sighed, nodded, exclaimed, and lamented, the heaviness in her heart was lifted and she heard, as if for the first time, the story of her triumph over the misery and squalor, the treachery and cruelty to which she had been subjected and which she had survived.

Acknowledgments

I would like to thank the John Simon Guggenheim Memorial Foundation, Florida International University, and the Florida International University Faculty Senate for their kind and generous support of my work. And thanks to my colleagues who make my teaching so pleasurable and my life so rich: Lynne Barrett, James W. Hall, Campbell McGrath, Denise Duhamel, Debra Dean, Julie Wade, Maddie Blais, and Les Standiford, who gave me the opportunity to first write about Wylie Melville in *Miami Noir*. Thanks to Jamie Sutton who has steadfastly supported and promoted the Creative Writing Program here. Thanks to David Beatty, an early reader of the novel, and to Mitchell Kaplan who makes Miami a safe and exhilarating place for writers and whose bookstore, Books & Books, is every local writer's second home. As always, my greatest love and thanks to my wife, Cindy Chinelly, who makes everything possible. To our friends Bruce Harvey, Liz Kortlander, Jeremy Rowan, and Kimberly Harrison and to our invigorating weekly moveable feast. Thanks to Debra Monroe, who keeps reminding me how important this writing business really is. Thanks to another Texan, Joe Young, out there in Cheese, who helps me with his esoteric research. Without my friend and agent Richard McDonough, who has been a tireless champion from the start, I would have had no writing career. Thanks, Dick. To Dave Cole, sculptor, poet, and copy editor, who once again saved me from potential lexical embarrassment. Thanks to Jill Bialosky for whipping an unruly manuscript into shape. She always does. Thanks to Don Bullens for a lifetime of friendship, encouragement, and stories. Thanks to my friend and writing workshop co-conspirator Kim Bradley. Special thanks to my young friends who don't yet read my books, but do let me try to entertain them: Phoebe Barzo, Charlie DeMarchi, and Theodore David Harrison-Rowan. Thanks to my parents, Lefty and Doris, my sisters Cyndi and Paula, my brother Mark. And to Tristan, of course. This book is dedicated to the memory of Steve Street, Jeffrey Knapp, and Jack Roberts, friends, writers, and provocateurs, who left us too soon.